Korunah's Gift

S. Pitt

Firsthale

Author's Notes.

The fictional Meelayginnee first appear in *Trouwerner*, my series of short stories about the indigenous Tasmanians through the period 1791-1835. To escape the fate of their peers, I had some of them hide deep in the wild south-west of the island. In 2006, while I was researching that project, my father visited and we took a tourist flight from Hobart to Bathurst Harbour in what is now the Tasmanian Wilderness World Heritage Area (WHA).

The sheer scale (13,838 sq. km.), and diversity of this wilderness (some of which remains unexplored), made me think it possible that small hearth-groups of indigenous people could have survived there undiscovered into the early 21st century, especially if they took measures to avoid contact. But with the advance of high-definition satellite and infra-red technology, that now seems even more unlikely than it did then. *Korunah's Gift* is therefore set around 2004.

The use of 1080 poison (sodium monofluoroacetate), to control native browsers (wallabies, possums etc.), is not fiction. Despite being banned in Tasmanian Public Forests from 2005, 1080 is still widely chosen for pest control in agriculture and forestry. This is the poison whose effects are described in Chapter 10. Its use is legal in all Australian states.

With the exception of 'Ngali-kiri', which is my own invention, aboriginal words are from: Plomley, N.J.B., (1976). *A word-list of the Tasmanian aboriginal languages*. Published by N.J.B. Plomley in association with the Tasmanian State Government.

Korunah's Gift

Chapter 1.

Tangalenna left the cave and strode swiftly down the cliff path. The rays of the westering sun turned his hair and beard to flame; his naked figure was proud against the sandstone. He paused to glance towards the camp, tempted to eat and rest before setting off but he was unsure how to face the women, could not think of Manalewa without shuddering.

Korunah wagara: (Eagle fly:)
If he delayed, he might fail.
mana tagara. (I follow).
He entered the forest.

From where the children played, the soaring wedge-tail was no more than a black speck. The air was clear, the distant mountains sharp-edged against a sky of the pure azure peculiar to springtime in southern Tasmania. Around the horizon's rim this hue was paler, as if reflecting the encircling sea. In this crystalline light wind-stirred leaves shone silver, making fields and forest shimmer like a mirage. But the breeze was cool and bore the scents of tea-tree and high remote places where the last snows had just melted.

A kookaburra sat on a post, watching for skinks. It tilted its head and spotted the eagle, uttered a harsh warning cackle and flew to the safety of the trees. The raptor, wings fully outstretched to test the wind, glided closer, alert to everything that moved below. From over a kilometre it could discern the girl's eye-colour.

Against the background murmur of trees, insects, the growl of a distant logging truck, the children's voices were loud and shrill, interspersed with the thud of a ball being kicked. It bounced away down the sloping paddock and the five boys chased after in an unruly pack. The girl followed reluctantly, not really part of the game yet determined not to be left out.

'Ellie – yours!' The eldest boy pivoted on one foot, lofted the ball towards his sister. The pass was skilfully aimed but at the critical moment she was distracted by the eagle's shadow sliding over the grass and the ball hit her shoulder.

'Aw – loser!' As the girl, taken by surprise, staggered, they were onto her. 'Get lost: you're worse than useless!'

Ellie stared after, hands planted on hips, as the boys tussled over the ball, working their way across the rough pasture to where a line of old oil-drums served as goal. Like them she was dressed in faded jeans, tee-shirt and trainers but while her brothers were grey-eyed and blond, hair streaked to the colour of oat-straw by the sun, her hair, tied in a pony-tail which hung almost to her waist, was a deep, lustrous red. Her eyes, described as 'green' on the posters soon to be stuck on the notice-boards of every police station, school and post office on the island were, in fact, a subtle blend of hues which changed according to the light and her mood: sometimes they appeared amber, like a cat's. Her skin was pale and freckled: the hat she was supposed to be wearing marked one side of the goal at the opposite end of the improvised pitch. She was ten years old.

Irresolute, the girl pulled the head off a grass stem and twisted it between her hands, plucking the umbels as she wandered slowly towards the farm. She moved with a straight-backed hauteur intended to convey contempt for the boys and their rowdy game but when the sheds and dilapidated weatherboard house came into full view, she stopped. Although the buildings were more than two hundred metres away, the sound of raised voices came clear. Ellie could have picked out every word but the accusations and insults were so familiar she heard only the tone, took no interest in the content. A door slammed and she sighed, tossed away the stripped stalk and turned. Her thin, rather pointed face was closed and hard with resentment.

The boys, absorbed in their game, did not notice their sister trudge to the gate at the far corner of the paddock. Beyond the fence there was a narrow fire-break and then the edge of a forest which stretched unbroken into the South-West Wilderness. The hulk of an old Holden lay on its side just beyond the firebreak, the rusting metal barely discernable under seventy years' accumulation of leaf-mould and moss. Wattles had rooted through the cab, anchoring the truck like a pin stuck through a beetle. An old logging track ran past it but this penetrated only a kilometre or so into the forest before coming to a dead end against a creek.

Ellie leant on the gate and stared along the sun-dappled line of the old track. To go beyond this point was utterly forbidden. There were too many cases of children lost in Tasmanian forests for any parent to be complacent: once beyond sight of a family picnicking; a father fishing or collecting wood, many were never seen again. Some drowned in fast-flowing rivers; others simply disappeared as if the ground had opened and swallowed them. In such rough terrain it was possible for a body to lie undetected only a few metres from a walking trail or logging track.

A flock of Fairy Wrens twittered as they darted from the shelter of the tea-tree scrub into the open. The brilliance of the male's springtime plumage reflected the colour of the sky; the females swooped and teased, luring him further along the track. Ellie watched the birds absently, recalling how she and her brothers had promised never to venture beyond the gate without an adult. Kyle, the eldest and the one she was closest to despite their five year age gap, had sealed the pledge as solemnly as he knew how, licking a forefinger and drawing it swiftly across his throat: 'Blood-oath, okay?' And their father had nodded gravely.

Standing with the warm metal bar beneath her hands, the girl remembered making the same gesture though without understanding its significance, being barely four years old at the time. But instead of acknowledging her promise, their father had grinned and walked away. Even now, the memory of his indifference acted as a spur. Ellie took a final look round to make sure no-one was watching and climbed swiftly over the gate. It seemed an age since she had left the boys but as she hurried along the track she could still hear their shouts and the thud of the ball.

Where the track dipped, Ellie slowed. She was panting, more from the kind of apprehension that attends wilful disobedience than exertion. The leaf-filtered sunlight made a delicate tracery of shadows at her feet and the scents of eucalypt, decaying wood, damp humus, were heavy and intoxicating. The flock of wrens fluttered ahead as if inviting her deeper into the forest.

Where the track abutted the creek, there was a clearing. Originally meant for turning vehicles, it had become a favourite picnic place. Fine grass grew there, kept short by wallabies that came to drink and graze but bracken fronds had pushed between the charred logs in the stone-ringed fireplace.

When she saw this, Ellie stopped. Here, her parents had fought openly for the first time, screeching like white cockatoos. Ellie remembered standing in that very spot, shocked and bewildered by their savage, all-consuming, anger which took no account of the boys' silence or her tears. Kyle had comforted her on that occasion: now even he had rejected her.

'It's not fair!' She stepped into the fireplace and stamped hard. The charcoal was dry and easily crushed but the bracken was tough and springy. Ash rose in a choking cloud, dirtying her trainers and jeans. A kookaburra swooped to perch on a nearby branch. Its eye was bright and mocking as it tilted its head to watch.

'What's your problem?' Ellie stooped, picked up a pebble and flung it at the bird but the missile dropped woefully short and the kookaburra edged closer along the branch, opened its long kingfisher bill and let out a raucous chuckle.

'I'll show them!' The words seemed loud and intrusive in the forest quiet and the girl felt a strange thrill. She stepped out of the stone ring and went to the creek to drink. Emerging from a nearby spring, the water was so cold it took her breath away. It tasted of earth and moss. A few metres to the girl's left, the creek plunged down one of the deep holes local children called 'goblin caves'. It ran underground for almost a kilometre before rising again to flow down and join the Huon River.

When she had finished drinking, Ellie got slowly to her feet. She listened hard for any sign that she had been missed but there was only the rippling of the water and a hollow glooping where it dropped underground. It would be easy to go back to the farm: no-one would ever know where she'd been and she would be free of the disquiet that had gradually crept upon her, as if hidden eyes were watching. But then the whole venture would be wasted.

Close to the watering place, a square-cut length of timber spanned the creek. There was no vehicle track on the other side, merely a narrow path. Since being cut by surveyors long ago, the way had been kept clear by the feet of animals going to drink. Ellie took a deep breath, clenched both hands at her sides and walked defiantly across the beam. To climb over the gate was one thing; to cross the creek was a different level of disobedience. She dared herself to go as far as the tree marking the corner of the property. If she left something to prove what she'd done, the boys would have to believe her and then they'd be ashamed of how they had dismissed her. In any case, this was far more exciting than any footy game.

Even though it stretched only a couple of hundred paces from the crossing, Ellie had never been on this path alone. Once, when they had picnicked by the creek, her father led the children along it, cutting deep notches in the trunks of young dogwood and wattles to blaze a trail to the marker tree. This was a massive Swamp Gum, a broken-crowned widow-maker hollow with age which towered over the other trees in the vicinity. In its prime it must have stood more than ninety metres tall and there was room for the whole family to stand inside and look up to a tiny circle of sky high above. The red-brown lining of the trunk was scored with deep vertical grooves as if a trapped beast had tried to claw its way out through the top.

It was the nature of secondary forest that what was an obvious landmark seen from kilometres away could be invisible from fifty paces, so dense was the growth and so deceptive the shifting patterns of light and shade. Fallen trees, rotting, moss-draped hulks thicker than the tallest man, acted as barriers to vision and so fierce was competition for light and space that saplings had sprung in the middle of the path, forcing the animals to make diverging trails. But at last Ellie saw a smooth silver and red mass loom through the dense undergrowth and hurried towards it.

Through gaps in the leaf canopy, the soaring eagle watched her.

Having reached her goal, Ellie scrambled over the massive buttress roots to where the hollow trunk was split into a triangular opening that she could enter without having to bend. Flakes of rotten wood the colour of rust carpeted the inside: it crumbled to dust beneath her feet. Settler's home, monster's lair, bush-ranger's hide-out: the tree-cave had been all these to her and her brothers. But now the magic was gone. It was simply a half-dead tree, smelling of decay. So profound was Ellie's disappointment that she put out a hand to touch the wall as if to confirm it was the same place. The wood was soft and dry and a lump the size of her fist broke away and thudded to the floor.

It was the unexpected loudness of that sound which made Ellie aware of the silence. Inside the tree she was cut off from the noise of the creek and the air was still: not a leaf stirred. Even the ceaseless background hum of insects seemed to enhance the lack of any other sound. An irrational terror seized her. The forest seemed suddenly huge and menacing, a place where she was irrelevant. Soil, trees, mosses, ferns and fungi melded into a single looming presence whose power bore down upon her, irresistible and inexorable. It was as if the very air wanted to crush her into oblivion.

Yet though her whole body lurched to her heartbeat and her mouth was dry, Ellie hesitated. She had come for a specific purpose and was still determined. After digging in her pockets and finding a twenty cent coin and a piece of chewed gum scrunched in its wrapper, she stepped out of the tree, turned and knelt. This took a great effort of will because her fear had intensified rather than diminished but pride would not permit failure. Carefully, she buried the coin and gum, smoothed wood-dust over to cover them and traced her name over the place with a forefinger.

Had she not been so engrossed in her task, the girl might have sensed the man's approach though his bare feet were almost silent on the beaten earth of the wallaby trail. As it was, the first she knew of his presence was sudden darkness when his shadow stretched across her. For an instant she froze, the breath stilled in her throat, then whirled round, ready to flee, to run faster than she had ever run before, away from the crowding trees to the open fields and home.

But it was too late.

Tangalenna had followed eagles for days, knowing they would lead to what he sought. It was of no account to him that he might have seen different birds because Korunah was his totem, his guide through dreaming, the daemon that would claim his spirit when he died. His faith in Eagle was so intrinsic to his being, he would no more have doubted where it led than he would have questioned the actions or validity of his right hand. And, in any case, Korunah had not failed him. The girl-child was alone and small enough for him to handle unaided.

Ellie had no time to cry out. He covered her mouth and nose with one hand whilst scooping her up. His left arm was clamped around her torso, pinning her arms to her sides; her legs dangled free. She kicked and struggled with all her strength but his hold was unyielding. When she succeeded in butting her head against his chin, he squeezed her nostrils shut between his thumb and forefinger, keeping the palm of his hand hard against her mouth. Black spots danced and coalesced before her eyes and she fought with panic-stricken frenzy but his power seemed limitless. Her last sensation before the blackness swallowed her was a horrid warmth as her body convulsed and her bowel contents spurted into her knickers.

Satisfied that she was unconscious, Tangalenna carried the girl a little deeper into the forest then laid her down. He struggled with the laces of her trainers but once her feet were bare he stripped her easily as if he were skinning a wallaby, bundled the clothes together and stuffed them beneath a rotting log. His nostrils wrinkled and he grabbed a handful of moss and scrubbed her clean.

Although he worked quickly, Ellie began to stir before he was finished. She spluttered and retched, became aware of an overpowering stench, heard the piping of wrens and someone's breathing. Hands wiped the lower half of her body with hard, impersonal strokes that jerked her mind to a time she had unwittingly soiled her bed in hospital: now, as then, she was overwhelmed by a sense of utter humiliation. Confusedly she wondered if she were ill and this was all some kind of dream but before she could summon strength to open her eyes, the hand clamped her mouth and she was lifted again.

This time Ellie did not struggle. She was exhausted by her previous efforts but she had also remembered advice from school to comply with an abductor's demands, however difficult or painful this might be. And it seemed to work because while she could feel the man's thumb and forefinger against the sides of her nose, he did not close them.

Guessing that the child's people would search for her before nightfall, Tangalenna ran. His limbs were thin and wiry but his loping stride was smooth and seemingly effortless. Gradually the steady rhythm of that pace lulled Ellie into a state of calm, the quietude of a trapped animal which understands the futility of struggling.

Ellie had not yet seen her abductor yet the effects of shock, the gagging hand across her mouth and the man's smell made her head reel. His body odour was rank as that of an old dog, acrid as woodsmoke, rancid as stale butter. At first the gorge rose in her throat then she discerned other layers: the sharpness of sweat and an earthy, metallic tang which made her think of rust. His breathing was steady and even, as of one accustomed to running long distances.

As her panic ebbed, Ellie's mind worked furiously. She guessed that if he meant to kill her, the man would have done so already. To have kidnapped her for ransom made no sense: the farm's mounting debts and the lack of ready cash were the primary cause of her parent's rows. The only other motives she could imagine were sexual. Then she realised she was naked: he must have stripped her when she was unconscious. Where their bodies were in contact she could feel his skin, cool and slick with sweat. He was bare as she.

Revolted and full of dread, she renewed her struggle with a vigour that took Tangalenna by surprise. As she kicked and jerked wildly in his arms, his foot caught on a tree root and he stumbled, dropping Ellie as he flung out his arms to save himself. She landed hard and lay gasping, the breath knocked from her lungs.

Tangalenna leant against a tree and waited until she sat up. Then he stepped forward, intending to pick her up again but her expression stayed him. Her eyes were wide and staring, fixed upon him. He had never seen such terror on a child's face.

'Please!' She crouched and stretched out a trembling hand in entreaty. 'Don't hurt me.'

Had he been on familiar ground, Tangalenna might have tried to comfort her: though he did not understand the words, her attitude and tone required no interpretation. But while the lands he had crossed were empty, he was uneasy because another band's territory could only be entered by agreement with their elders. The people had disappeared but their dreaming lingered and at times, passing an ancient myrtle or lichen-encrusted boulder, he felt a latent hostility as if his presence had awoken the guardian spirits. It was this, more than fear of pursuit, which made him rush suddenly to sweep the cringing child into his arms. She was so rigid he feared her limbs might snap like sticks if she fell again therefore he clamped his right hand firmly over her mouth and nose, ready to cut off her breath if she struggled.

Ellie was slender and of average height but Tangalenna was tiring and her weight dragged upon him. He no longer ran but walked with a long, swift stride. Where low branches crossed the animal trails he was using, he stooped without any noticeable slackening of pace.

Absolute fear cannot, by its very nature, be long sustained and the child gradually relaxed though her jaw was still held as if in a vice. Most of the time she kept her eyes shut because the swaying motion and the twisting nature of the trails her abductor was following made her feel sick. But the easier pace made her feel less frightened because the man himself seemed calmer. At times she seemed to see the two of them from above, as if her mind had somehow detached itself from her body, and this illusion heightened the sense of unreality that settled upon her as she was borne deeper into the forest. She knew that the man could not exist therefore none of it was really happening. Yet those strange disembodied visions where her consciousness glided up through the canopy confirmed that he was bearing her away from habitation, into the wilderness.

The shadows lengthened and still they journeyed on. Tangalenna had halted only once, to drink at a creek in the bottom of a narrow valley crowded with tree-ferns. He did not scoop the water up in his palms but sucked it straight from the surface of the stream like a horse. So exhausted was the child that she did not stir when he laid her down, nor did she respond when he motioned her to come and drink. She lay staring listlessly into space as if uncaring of where she was or what might happen to her.

He picked her up again and she was limp and heavy in his arms. This time he cradled her against him, one arm under her knees, the other locked around her body. When he crossed the stream he made no attempt to conceal his tracks in the wet mud: this deep in the forest he was not afraid of being followed. Having no experience of dogs, he believed he could elude any hunter.

(In fact, they were already further from the picnic place than any search would ever reach. The discovery of the child's soiled clothing proved she had been attacked but there were no definite footprints in the vicinity and it was assumed that if she had been killed, her body would have been dumped close by. A helicopter with infra-red camera was brought in but its search pattern was confined to a narrow area around the farm: when no corpse was found, it was concluded that she had been taken elsewhere. After that, the emergency services concentrated on the roads and logging tracks in the area while a watch was set on every flight and ferry leaving the island. That she might have been carried deeper into the forest did not occur to anyone, even as a remote possibility. And if it had, the State's resources did not extend to searching so vast a wilderness.)

Without the restraining grip around her face, Ellie began to recover. The forest had changed in character, becoming more open than the dense re-growth she was used to, dominated by myrtle with tall growth of lancewood and, here and there, a massive Swamp Gum, the white bark gleaming eerily as the light began to fade. Ferns grew luxuriantly upon decaying stumps and logs and mosses blanketed much of the forest floor. The stillness made this seem a distinct, self-contained world: the very air was moist and heavy with the smells of vegetative growth and decay, yet the place teemed with life: there was a constant background hum of insects; bird calls echoed through the canopy and wallabies paused to watch them pass, ears pricked, eyes bright in the thickening green gloom.

The girl was aware only that she was being carried further from home and the physical appearance of her abductor had been so unexpected, the shock was slow to dissipate. It was not simply his lack of clothing that affected her (having brothers, the sight of male genitalia was nothing new): indeed, his apparent indifference to his nakedness made it less threatening than if he had deliberately stripped in front of her. But his dark copper-tinted skin, wiry limbs and broad shoulders; the patterns of scars across his chest and upper arms; the mop-like arrangement of his hair which, like his beard, was twisted into cords heavy with grease and ochre, confounded the child. She had been taught that the last full-blood Tasmanian aborigine had died over a hundred and twenty years before but this one was, undeniably, alive.

Torn between fear and curiosity, it was not until nightfall, when the man stopped and laid her carefully on the ground, that Ellie thought of her family. From the deep blue-green of the sky she guessed it must be around seven: dinner would be on the table, news on the television. By now her parents must be frantic with worry.

Here, under the trees, it was already dark and a penetrating chill rose from the damp leaf litter. The man had left her and was busy breaking and dragging branches. Ellie sat up, shivering, and hugged her knees to her chest, hoping he would light a fire. Her belly ached with hunger but she decided that if he offered food, she would not eat it. To do so would be to accept his control. This made her feel even more isolated than before and imagining the scene at home, her parents arguing over whose fault it was, her mother in tears, her father blaming the boys while the dinner (for some reason she pictured baked beans, sausages and mash), congealed on their plates, she began to cry.

Chapter 2.

Tangalenna was not making a fire. Without a fire-stick he had no means of kindling one. Instead he was constructing a rough shelter by propping broken branches against a half-rotten log and laying fern fronds and strips of bark over to make it weather-proof. Inside this lean-to he piled the driest moss and leaves he could find until they made a thick bed. The quiet, desolate sobbing of the child sent a pang through him but he blocked it out by concentrating on the tasks in hand. His back and shoulders ached (bearing loads was usually women's work), and he longed to lie down and sleep but he knew he must find food. They were almost two days' walk from his hearth-group's camp and he did not intend carrying the girl much further: inevitably she would slow him down. He had borne her this far only to ensure that if she escaped, she could not find her own way back.

Except when there was thick fog it was never completely dark under the eaves of the forest and though the sky was clouding over, Tangalenna moved freely between the trees, picking his way over fallen branches and moss-covered logs by using touch and smell as much as sight. Ellie, used to brilliant light at the flick of a switch, found she could barely make out her hand in front of her face once the stars were obscured and this increased her misery. All afternoon she had waited for the chance to escape but he had always been there: now he had left, she could not see.

Nonetheless, Ellie was not without courage. She wiped away the snot and tears as best she could and rose cautiously. Her whole body was stiff and her jaw ached from his grip. She was so cold, she could barely think coherently but it seemed to her that although the man had run part of the way, they could not be far from the farm. All she had to do was find a hollow tree and hide there till morning: as soon as it was light enough, she would start back. By then, she was sure, the State Emergency Service would be out searching and when she met them she would set the hunt on her abductor. This time tomorrow she would be at home. Her parents so glad to see her safe they would never quarrel again; her brothers jealous and proud of a sister who had not only been attacked but managed to escape.

All this passed though the girl's mind in the time it took to move a few tentative steps. Her arms were outstretched to feel her way yet her body was hunched from cold and hunger, giving her a strangely twisted appearance. There was a roaring in her ears, suddenly the darkness whirled and she found herself on her hands and knees: she had almost fainted. Then she realised the impossibility of finding her way home in the dark and her euphoria vanished. She curled up on the bare ground, longing for daylight and rescue.

It had not occurred to Tangalenna that having seen the shelter constructed, the girl would have stayed outside. Age-old custom dictated that the most vulnerable, the very young or sick, took shelter once camp was established so that they were protected from hostile neighbours or prowling animals. Tasmanian devils, which he called *tarrabah*, were mainly scavengers but an unguarded baby or sick toddler was easy meat; the animal called 'child-stealer', *kannenner*, had not been seen since his father's time but fear of it remained. A stealthy footfall, a lurking shadow: the spirit of thylacine lived on in the minds of his people.

It was reasonable therefore that when he saw the pale form curled in the middle of the path, Tangalenna had to fight the impulse to run away. He thought he was looking at the thing they had pulled out of his wife's body: it glimmered in the darkness like a ghost. He stared and an icy sweat bathed him. What he had witnessed was forbidden for any man to look upon - birth was a matter wholly for the women of the group – and the dead baby had not had the form of a human child. Instead it was the shape of the ancestor, Tarner the Kangaroo, after his legs had been broken and his tail severed to make the first man.

Tangalenna shuddered and his right hand went to his neck. If this was part of his dreaming, his talisman, the little bone that was the link to his grandmother's wisdom, would be there. But the amulet was where he had left it in the cave, therefore this was no dream. He must face the consequences of his crime alone.

It was because he could not bear Manalewa's screams that Tangalenna had broken the ancient taboo. Afraid that she was dying, he had crept to their hut and lifted a strip of bark to peer within. When the women yanked a bloody mess from between her legs and he glimpsed the bluish, misshapen body that should have been their child, a guilty horror overwhelmed him and he had run into the forest, careless of where he went so long as it was beyond hearing of Manalewa's wails. And then he had found himself on the way to the sacred caves. It seemed to him that his daemon must have led him there, that instead of returning to camp, he should dream and follow the path Korunah revealed.

With hindsight he recognised the cowardice in that decision: Manalewa had seen and heard nothing of him since, racked with pain, she had stumbled into their hut, supported by the other women. But he had succeeded in finding another child, or so he had thought. Now he wondered if the pale girl with her red hair and strange green eyes was not really human at all but something fashioned by the trickster, Wyerkartenner, to punish him.

The mournful call of a hawk-owl sounded close by and Tangalenna sank to his knees. He tried to summon Korunah to counter the malign spirits he felt crawling up his spine and between his shoulder blades: the force of their presence seemed to press him towards the ground and they whispered as leaves stirred overhead in a breath of wind. But eagles rarely fly at night and while he was able to picture the wheeling bird he had spotted earlier in the day, the image, powerful though it was, could not make the pale form disappear, nor dispel his dread.

The owl called again, then swooped so close he heard the sough of air thorough its feathers. Eyes fixed on the huddled figure on the ground, Tangalenna bent in an attitude of supplication, berating himself for his foolishness. At any moment, he knew, the anger he had aroused against himself might manifest: a spirit in the form of Owl might pluck out his soul and leave his body as a husk incapable of speech or movement; a tree might drop a branch to crush him out of life; an underground stream open and swallow him.

But as time, measured by the pounding of his heart, passed and nothing happened, doubt surfaced in Tangalenna's mind; the sweat grew chill on his skin and his pulse steadied. As the horror receded, he was able to see the figure for what it was, no ghost come to avenge itself but the girl he had captured. Guilt had transformed her into what he most dreaded.

The moment this truth struck him, Tangalenna leapt to his feet, overwhelmed by shame and anger. He dropped the food he had been carrying and swept the girl up. She was limp and heavy in his arms and her flesh was cold against his: appalled that she might be close to death, he almost threw her into the shelter and crawled in after. She moaned as he began to chafe her hands and feet, willing life and warmth into her. His rage, aimed at the child for staying outside and against himself for his mistake, was partly assuaged by the action of massaging her body but his shame was slow to dissipate.

Suspended in a kind of limbo in which her mind and body were numb yet the senses of hearing and smell seemed more acute, Ellie had heard the owl-call and an absurd image filled her mind: enormous yellow eyes, a V-shaped beak and long, cruel talons. When she was touched and lifted, she thought a giant bird had mistaken her for a mouse and expected sharp claws to puncture her flesh. Instead she landed with a jolt on a soft bed, was rubbed with firm, hard strokes until her limbs tingled with returning blood. She opened her eyes, saw her abductor's head and shoulders silhouetted against the night sky and wailed in despair.

That cry, more piercing than the night-hawk's, reminded Tangalenna of Manalewa's agony. He gathered the girl in his arms and cradled her against him, crooning a song as ancient as his people. At first she was stiff as a piece of wood but as he rocked her and sang on, she relaxed: his voice and movement were hypnotic. The warmth of his body comforted her; she was, in any case, exhausted. Soon, she slept.

When he was sure she would not easily awaken, Tangalenna, his belly griped with hunger, laid the child down and pulled the dry leaves of the bed close around to keep her warm. A feeling of protectiveness he had rarely experienced made him pause. He put out his right hand to stroke her face but then withdrew it, fearful of disturbing her, and crawled outside.

It was cold: as he groped for the fungi he had gathered, Tangalenna became keenly aware of his isolation. Looking up he saw stars between the branches, the eyes of the ancestors, glittering and remote. Their gaze seemed to radiate disapproval and he finished eating and returned hurriedly to the shelter. The child did not stir when he crept in beside her though it seemed to him that the rustle of leaves beneath his body was the loudest sound in the world. She was curled up and he fitted his body around hers and sank into dreamless slumber.

Ellie awoke to so complete a sensation of comfort and security that she kept her eyes closed, wanting to prolong the feeling as long as possible. Assuming she was in her parents' bed after a nightmare, she snuggled closer to the source of warmth. But gradually the feeling grew upon her that something was not quite right. For a start, she was naked and could feel someone else's skin against hers; then wrens began to twitter, so close it seemed they were within arm's reach. The air was fresh and cool, laden with the scents of eucalypt and something else, a rancid odour that was somehow both threatening and reassuring.

When she opened her eyes, the events of the previous day returned instantly but the experience had taught her caution. Instead of pulling away and making a wild dash for freedom, she lay exactly as she was, forcing calm upon herself as she tried to think what to do.

The man was deeply asleep. His breathing was quiet and regular; his arm relaxed and heavy across her waist. She waited until her breathing matched his then, with infinite care, slid away. The leaf bed, pressed down by their bodies, made less noise than she had feared as she crawled from the shelter and the man, although he groaned softly, did not wake but pulled his hands in towards his chest and curled up. She watched until he had settled and his breathing was steady again. After carrying her for so long, he must be very tired, she reflected: with luck he would sleep on for hours although it was already full daylight.

The air was still and warm, the sky overcast and the forest seemed drab and unwelcoming. Ellie turned slowly, examining each of the trails that spread out from where she stood. There was nothing to distinguish one path from another: all were narrow, winding mazily between the trees, pocked by the claws of passing wallabies and overhung by spindly branches. She could only guess which way they had come.

From inside the shelter came a rasping snore, the kind her father made just before he woke up, and Ellie fled, choosing the broadest trail simply because she could move along it faster than the others. But she was soon forced to stop, sobbing for breath and dizzy. Had she not bent double, hands pressed to her sides, she would have fainted; as it was she retched and gasped, knowing she must keep quiet but unable to help herself.

When at last she was able to stand upright and look around, Ellie found she was shaking. However hard she willed her hands to keep still they would not obey and this lack of control over her own body was as terrifying as the thought of the man coming after her. She staggered off the path and sank to the ground behind a massive, fern-festooned log. Her long hair trailed in the dirt, bright against the dull browns and greens of rotting leaves, earth, fragments of moss.

In Tangalenna's dream, a brown quoll, the little fierce one which in his tongue was *ngali-kiri*, had escaped the jaws of *kannenner*. Therefore when he woke to find himself alone, he was not surprised. Nor was he worried as to the girl's whereabouts for he knew she must be close. His main concern when he crawled out of the shelter and glanced skywards was that he had slept so long.

It was not in his nature to plan far ahead but he had wanted to reach the safety of his own territory before sunset. Now he would have to travel after dark if they were to reach the caves tomorrow and he would need to find better food: that would take time. And the sense of urgency that gripped him was more discomforting to Tangalenna than the absence of the child. It was as if some innate balance, something he could not name but which was central to his being, had shifted. He wondered uneasily if it had to do with the ghost of the dead infant, then pushed the thought quickly aside. There was a living child to care for: by concentrating on her, he could block the other's way into his mind.

In the night, he had missed some of the fungi he had dropped. It had been nibbled by mice in the meantime but he squatted to pick up what remained and gnawed at it while listening for the girl. Such meagre fare could not satisfy his hunger but it blunted its edge. Blue wrens fluttered all around and he watched them with a simple delight until his ears caught the sound of stifled sobbing, the heart-rending distress of a lost child.

Tangalenna was a skilled stalker, renowned even among a people who relied upon hunting. So smoothly did he move that the wrens were not disturbed, nor did a cockatoo, perched in the canopy high above, move save to tilt its head slightly. His bare feet were soundless on the beaten path and he kept his breathing slow and regular as if on the trail of the shyest wallaby. When he reached the girl, he stood watching in silence, unsure what to do. So obvious was her misery that he almost regretted taking her but then he remembered the eagles' flight: there was no doubt this was the child of his dreaming.

Ellie was completely unaware of the man's presence. Though it was a mild day, she could not stop shivering: every-so-often a convulsive tremor shook her whole body. She wondered which, out of the aborigine, the rescue services or maybe by some miracle her parents or brothers, would find her first, or whether she was so deep in the forest that she would never be discovered and would simply die. The numbing effects of shock, exhaustion and hunger detached her mind from reality so that nothing seemed to matter very much. And the dank smells of earth and decay were so strong, it seemed to her that she might lie there undiscovered, her bones slowly mouldering into the soft humus of the forest floor until no trace remained.

When Tangalenna stepped out and spoke, naming her Ngali-kiri like the creature in his dream, Ellie was jerked out of her reverie. She looked up without fear: though his words were incomprehensible to her, there was no threat in his tone. He crouched, bringing his head level with hers. She sat back on her heels and stared at him with a kind of wonder. Beneath the ochre and grease-laden cords of hair which hung low over his brow, his eyes, which were a deep, unfathomable brown, seemed to swallow her gaze. There was a stillness in those eyes that imbued the child with sudden confidence: devoid of guile, his was a countenance which, though strange to her, inspired trust. Yet his apparent benevolence only made it seem less possible that he could exist in her world, supported her growing belief that this must be a parallel reality … or the past …. or some kind of afterlife.

'Are we dead?' she asked.

They journeyed all that day, Tangalenna bearing the girl much of the way since she was too weak to walk far. He found this task much easier than before because she was compliant and he had no need to restrain her. Though his people had no such custom, he carried her piggyback. When he bent to lift her in his arms she had shaken her head and indicated by signs what she wanted and he was glad of the intervention because she was light and he could move at his usual pace where the path was clear and the ground relatively flat.

Soon after setting off, Tangalenna became aware of a deep throbbing that resonated through his whole body, a sound that was almost beyond hearing. Though he had no name for it, the noise made him uneasy. He was glad when it ceased and the quiet of the forest returned.

Had she been able to discern it, the sound of the helicopter would have forced Ellie to realise the truth, bringing wild hope at the thought of rescue, then despair when it faded and did not return. But the child's senses were less acute than Tangalenna's. By nightfall, after climbing a steep cleft to reach the top of a high ridge which blocked their way, they were well beyond the range that the SES considered viable for a fit adult to travel in twenty-four hours over such rough terrain, let alone a child.

They found shelter in the hollow trunk of a giant Swamp Gum. The decayed wood carpeting the floor made a dry, soft bed and when the man laid Ellie down, she curled up and fell asleep at once, worn out by the effort of climbing the escarpment. Although he had eaten fungi, grubs and sassafras leaves along the way, Tangalenna hungered for fresh meat. He felt the light-headedness that came with fasting, knew that without proper food he would be unable to maintain the pace he had set himself. And he was keenly aware that the child's need was even greater. After reaching the ridge-top she had hardly been able to stand unaided. Already her eyes seemed sunken in the frame of her narrow, dirt-smeared face.

The region they were crossing had been empty of people for more than a hundred and sixty years and the animals had lost much of their fear of humans. Soon after sunset, Tangalenna caught a ring-tail possum, yanking it by the tail from the tree where it was watching him and dashing it hard against a boulder until it was dead. Then he returned to the hollow tree, buoyed by a sense of triumph that far outweighed the worth of the kill. Close to the border of his own country he felt more at ease: with fresh meat to sustain them, he and the child would reach camp without hardship.

By shimmering starlight Tangalenna butchered the animal using no more than a sharp, flat piece of stone he found at hand, a short stick and his hands and teeth. The possum was a young male, plump and healthy: its entrails steamed as the man disembowelled it and picked out the choice delicacies. He popped one of the kidneys into his mouth and chewed with great satisfaction, savouring the casing of fat and the rich softness of the organ within. He ate half the liver then, with the sharpness of his hunger appeased, took the rest to the child before it chilled so that she should share some of the relict warmth of the animal. His beard and hands glistened with blood and fat.

Inside the hollow tree, Ellie had woken up. She watched with a kind of detached fascination as Tangalenna tore the carcass open and the smell of entrails filled the air. Her initial repugnance vanished when she saw the relish with which he ate and her mouth watered. When at last he offered her something she snatched the morsel from his open palm and devoured it so quickly, her brain had no time to register that she was eating raw liver. Her senses were overwhelmed by the taste and texture of food.

Tangalenna returned to the carcass and peeled the flesh off the haunches, ribs and shoulders, chewing on a long strip of meat as he worked. The tenderest portion he gave the child; when he had eaten his fill, he put the rest into a scrap of skin for later. There was still much meat left on the carcass when he had finished but without better tools he was unwilling to sped time rendering it though he would have chastised a woman for being so wasteful. He piled the remnants into the main part of the hide and dumped it a little way into the trees.

Once her stomach was full, an irresistible heaviness suffused Ellie's limbs. She licked her fingers clean, wiped her mouth with the back of one hand, then lay down and fell asleep. Tangalenna sat outside for a while, heedless of the chill air. He looked at the stars glittering overhead but this time there was no threat in their pattern. A low hum escaped him. A sound requiring no thought or guidance it was at once an affirmation of his being and acknowledgement of the world to which he belonged. He was completely unaware of uttering it yet it caught his attention and he listened with deep concentration, letting it carry him between the interlaced branches of the great tree and high into the still air until the pattern of forest, hills, rivers, lakes was revealed as his ancestors had understood it when they occupied this place forty thousand years before.

Through the depth of her slumber, the child was aware of the sound and it seemed to her that the tree which cradled her was listening, that the very soil and rocks were giving voice. So compelling was it that though it did not wake her, its pattern was imprinted at her very core.

At length Tangalenna fell silent and the stillness of the night settled all around. He sighed then rose and joined the sleeping child inside the hollow tree. So that no other creature could enter, he curled up across the entrance and fell at once into a light slumber, like that of a guard dog.

By dawn, the sky had clouded over and a fine drizzle fell through the canopy, coalescing into larger drops on the drooping leaves and dripping loudly onto the forest floor. Tangalenna took no notice of the rain other than to stand under a stream of droplets with head tipped back and mouth open to drink. The child's thirst was too great to be so easily quenched and she looked for a puddle or water-filled hollow without success until Tangalenna, guessing her need, showed her how to squeeze the moisture from a handful of wet moss. This enabled her, once she had drunk, to wipe herself clean of the dirt accumulated over the past day, an operation her companion viewed with obvious amusement. When she was finished, Ellie felt refreshed and she ate the strip of meat he gave her without hesitation: it was tough and chewy and strands stuck between her teeth but new strength entered her even as she swallowed.

Tangalenna waited patiently until Ellie was ready to set off. He stood leaning against a young wattle tree, right foot hooked behind left knee, his right hand hanging loose while the left pulled absently at his foreskin. The rain beaded his hair and ran in tiny rivulets down his body, marking pale channels in the remnant of the charcoal he had rubbed over himself in preparation for his dreaming. In the grey light the droplets seemed opaque, like quicksilver, and where streaks of ochre leached from his hair over his back and shoulders the effect was startling, red, black and grey striped like red-gum bark.

It was not until they started that Ellie realised how footsore she was. Although Tangalenna had carried her most of the day before, the climb up the rocky escarpment had not been without cost. Exhaustion had prevented her feeling the pain. Her right foot was especially bad and after a few steps she sat down to examine it. The soles of both feet were lacerated and there was a large splinter in the heel of her right foot. Looking up, she saw that the aborigine was already almost out of sight.

'Please wait!' Her call sounded feeble even to her own ears and she felt resentful at being so completely reliant on the man who had attacked and abducted her. Yet she was more afraid of being abandoned.

To her relief, Tangalenna returned at once. He knelt and took her right foot in his hands, frowning deeply. His gentleness and obvious concern did much to reassure her. After pulling out the splinter, he retrieved the piece of possum skin which had wrapped their breakfast and tied it to make a protective shoe. From that moment she regarded him as a friend.

Ellie's lameness slowed their progress for while Tangalenna

carried her where he could, they had come to a region of rugged hills where the gradients were so steep that at times they had no choice but to scramble up using their hands. Halfway up the last ridge, the forest of myrtle and eucalypt gave way to tough, straggly pandanus trees. Wiry heath and cutting-grass formed dense undergrowth which scratched their legs as they climbed. Tangalenna's pace gradually increased for the summit marked the eastern edge of his band's territory and he longed for the security this afforded. Ellie struggled to keep up but even when black specks danced before her eyes and she began to stagger, she did not cry out.

The top of the ridge was marked by a pile of massive dolerite slabs. Tangalenna's band, the Meelayginnee, held that this jumbled formation of weathered rocks comprised the bones of Tarner's tail, the ridges and valleys to either side being formed when the severed member thrashed in its death throes. Seeing the familiar shapes silhouetted against the sky, Tangalenna hurried joyfully towards them, forgetful of the child toiling far behind.

It was when he reached the first of the crystalline blocks and laid his hand flat upon it so that his land would know of his return that Tangalenna felt again a sense of dislocation, as if something intrinsic to his very being had altered. With his hand still pressed against the weathered stone, he turned, searching for Korunah. The forest-clad folds of the hills rolled away into the distance until they were lost in a grey haze; mist roiled in the valleys but the sky was empty.

The quick, darting movement of a small bird, shrike or thrush, drew his eye back along the way he had come. The heath stood over knee-high and there were few gaps but he could just make out a white shape a long way down. As he watched, it moved with the desperate, lunging action of a wounded or exhausted animal and then he remembered the girl.

He found her on her hands and knees, trying to crawl her way up. She was aware of his presence but all she could see was a dark, bleared shape that was vaguely human. For a moment she stared then, in her weakness, began to cry. Harsh, racking sobs shook her whole frame but no tears came because she was dehydrated beyond thirst. In her determination to keep up, she had forgotten to drink along the way.

Tangalenna did not bend to help her at once. He stood transfixed by a mixture of remorse and pity sharp as the prick of a spearpoint. This thin, pale creature, too weak and ignorant to survive more than a few days on her own, had a power that made him feel afraid. Never before had he experienced such compassion for a child, not even for the son that had been bitten by a black snake when he was barely old enough to walk, because the raising of children was women's work. Now his spine crawled and he felt again that sense of wrongness.

As if aware of his mounting confusion, the girl stopped sobbing and groped with both hands to find him. That blind, questing movement so horrified Tangalenna that he stepped away. It occurred to him that if he abandoned her, no-one would ever know. Once *tarrabah* found her, there would be nothing but a few scattered fragments of bone and gut to bear witness.

In another moment he would have turned on his heel and left had not a piercing call sounded from directly above. The rain had passed and clear blue sky spread in an arc from the west: following the buoyant air a soaring eagle had spotted feeble movements in the heath far below and swooped to investigate. But to Tangalenna the bird's flight was a message. His dreaming had shown him what to do: this child was Korunah's gift. To desert her now would be a betrayal of the law by which he and his people lived: the very earth would spurn him. One day a rock would slip under his foot to send him over a cliff or an overhanging branch fall to crush him and Eagle would ignore his spirit, leaving it to cry alone in the wilderness while his ancestors mocked him from the sky.

Tangalenna hesitated no longer. As the child gave up her attempts to find him and huddled close to the ground in a stupor of exhaustion and despair, he stepped forward and swept her into his arms. The warm smell of him enveloped her; his heartbeat thudded in her ear. She felt safe.

Even in late spring, the ridge was so high that rain commonly fell as snow or sleet which lingered for a while in tiny pockets and hollows between boulders and the wiry stems of such plants as were able to survive such harsh conditions. By the time he reached the rocks, Tangalenna was panting for the girl seemed to weigh heaver than before though he did not attribute this to his own weariness but to Tarner's disapproval of the crime he had been so close to committing. He laid her carefully on a near-horizontal slab and scooped a handful of slush from a crevice. This he sucked from the palm of his hand, savouring the cold, pure taste. The sun was warm against his skin and made the wet rock shine while deprived of its prize, the eagle circled high above. Watching it, Tangalenna felt joy surge through his blood as if he, too, were flying.

The contrast between her bearer's warm, living flesh and the hard wet stone on which he had laid her woke Ellie. She shivered violently and rolled onto her side. When she forced her eyes open, the sunlight glancing off the rock blinded her and she moaned. She was conscious only of her misery and the desire that it should end quickly.

Sensing the depth of her distress, Tangalenna wiped his chilled fingers on some heath and picked her up again. Pain jabbed his neck and shoulders as he settled her in his arms but he ignored it in sudden anxiety for his charge. Her skin was like ice against his; her head drooped and her breathing was weak and shallow.

He ran, using resilient cushion plants as stepping stones: they grew so abundantly on the plateau beyond the ridge as to form a kind of broad pathway. Despite his weariness, there was such strength in Tangalenna's wiry limbs that once he had found a rhythm, aided by the trampoline effect of the plants, the child seemed far less of a burden than when he had toiled up the slope. To his left spread the land of his people, long ridges interspersed with jagged peaks, bare plateaux and deep shadowed valleys filled with forest but his eyes were fixed always a little way ahead.

The sun was directly overhead when he stopped to drink at a tiny pool. The water was deep and so pure that tiny shrimps scuttling over the layer of decaying vegetation at the bottom were clearly visible. The girl was still unconscious and did not stir when he laid wet fingers against her lips but her breathing had become deep and steady. This reassured him though her flesh still felt cold when he lifted her again. He continued to run, his long, loping stride seeming effortless though his skin shone with sweat.

There was no obvious landmark to guide him for the terrain undulated, reflecting the underlying strata. But to Tangalenna the way was as clear as if marked upon the ground he trod. Without pausing to look behind, he veered to the left, slowing only when he reached a notch in the slope. This cleft, strewn with boulders, led into a deep gorge; lower down, the sandstone underlying the dolerite had been eroded into caves. His journey had come full circle.

Chapter 3.

From above, the gully where Tangalenna stood was the only way into the sacred gorge though it made for a difficult descent, almost impossible for a man encumbered with a child. Between wind-torn pandanus trees and clumps of cutting-grass even the dry watercourse leading to the cliff-top was scree-strewn and treacherous.

At times during the descent Tangalenna was forced to stop, leaning his shoulder against the bare rock while he lifted the girl more securely against him. Once, he ended sliding on his back when the loose gravel shifted but he managed to jam his foot against a solid outcrop and this saved them though he heard stones clatter as they fell into the defile below. After that, he climbed onto safer ground, sweating and shaking, but he did not rest. Even early in the afternoon the ravine was filling up with shadow.

Not until he reached the ledge which led to the caves did Tangalenna feel safe. The trees at the top of the cliffs were still golden with sunlight: he could take his ease.

He laid the child down and surveyed the landscape. It was his intention to spend the night in his dreaming cave and enter the camp at dawn but he wanted his presence to remain secret. It did not occur to him that Manalewa might have died after his departure or that the group could have moved on.

Before him lay the whole length of the gorge. Far below, water ran in the channel it had carved through the soft sandstone over aeons uncounted. The rush of it made a constant background noise, hypnotic as the sound of the sea. After a distance of maybe a kilometre, the gorge narrowed to a chute. Here the water poured into a deep pool before flowing on through shallow rapids, winding as the slope lessened and the cliffs diminished to patchy outcrops between crowding trees and tree-ferns. So thick was their growth,

Tangalenna could only glimpse the path through gaps in the leaf-cover but there was no movement upon it save a lone pademelon. From here the rivulet emerged onto the floor of a wide valley where it joined a greater river. This was the axis of his world.

Satisfied that they were alone, Tangalenna picked the girl up again and continued on his way. So long had this place been sacred to the Meelayginnee, the ledge he trod was worn into a channel a handsbreadth deep by the passage of countless feet.

There were caves on both sides of the gorge, ranging from holes the size of a wombat's den to huge echoing caverns, awe-inspiring in dimension. But on the opposite, sunset, side to where Tangalenna walked, they were taboo. It was said that the voices of spirits spoke there and people foolish enough to venture inside were lost or else emerged mad, raving of seeing Tarner himself, greater than any living kangaroo, his face skull-like and terrible. Such were the tales passed from generation to generation: within living memory no-one had trodden that side of the valley.

The place where Tangalenna bore the child was his spiritual home, the centre where dream-self and man-self met and melded. By virtue of his eagle-daemon, through which he was regarded as a seer, Tangalenna had sole right to this cave though he was bound to share his dreams with the rest of his band. This status, like a shaman's, could only be held by one person at a time and it had set Tangalenna apart from the day Korunah revealed itself. As a result, he was resented by those envious of his position; half-revered, half-feared by the rest. Had his mother not been leader of their hearth-group (his father was long dead), he might have been driven out, forced to live on the periphery of the band, sought when they needed his predictions of weather or the movement of game but otherwise avoided.

Having settled the unconscious child on a bed of dried leaves and fern in the centre of the cave, Tangalenna made his way to the back. At its highest the shallow dome of the dolerite ceiling was just within his reach if he stretched fully but he was taller than most of his people and though the walls and lower areas of the ceiling were covered with the ochre and charcoal handprints of previous occupants, the middle was sparsely decorated and there was a bare space at the very centre. The effect of this was to make the cave appear larger than it really was. When he wanted to dream, Tangalenna would stare upwards until the pattern of handprints began to spin around the dark central patch, transforming it into the core of a vortex which swept him to join Korunah.

This time though, it was not his intention to bother his daemon lest Eagle be irritated by his persistence. He knelt and scrabbled in a patch of earth where his most precious possessions were concealed: a fist-sized chunk of red ochre and a talisman. The latter comprised a human vertebra. A kangaroo sinew had been threaded through the hole where the spinal cord had once run so that the bone could be worn as a pendant. Tangalenna muttered a few words of propitiation before putting the thong around his neck and setting the amulet at his breast.

The bone belonged to his grandmother, a woman respected for her strength and wisdom. Korunah had been her daemon also and Tangalenna felt closer to her than to his mother who, while an elder of the tribe, shared neither her dam's sagacity nor far-sightedness. After his Nana's cremation, this single vertebra had remained largely untouched by the fire and Tangalenna had taken it in memory of the woman who had been his mentor, believing that through it he could share her wisdom and strength. Had it not been taboo to carry her remains beyond where she had trodden in life, he would have worn it always.

The force of Nana Bone's will had confined Tangalenna's people to the remotest regions of their world. She sensed evil lurking at the edges of their domain and had instilled such dread of what might befall those who went beyond, no-one dared venture there while she was alive. But she had died just before Tangalenna's initiation into manhood.

Soon after, in an effort to come to terms with his uniqueness and the responsibilities forced upon him by his Eagle daemon, Tangalenna had wandered far into the territories traditionally held by other bands. All those lands he had found empty, rank forest grown where fire should have kept the ground clear for kangaroos and wallabies to graze and where legends spoke of deep valleys and broad rivers he had discovered great lakes behind walls of smooth rock which blocked the mouths of gorges. There he had felt a strange vibration through the earth and Korunah had shown him things he had never dreamed of: white-faced men, *num*, with loose-fitting, strangely coloured skins; gleaming objects which moved swiftly along shining black trails with a noise and stench that alarmed him; great blocks of stone which the *num* entered as if, like ants, they possessed the power to tunnel underground.

Having no understanding of these things, Tangalenna instinctively feared them. It seemed to him that they could not be good for him or his people and he had turned and never ventured so far in that direction again.

Yet though he had more experience of the forbidden country than any of his people, it was only as he stroked the talisman that Tangalenna made the connection between what he had seen on that journey and the girl. Until then he had not questioned her origin: she had appeared where he had expected to find her and that was enough. The child in his dream had been of his own kind and naked but such details were of no consequence against the sacred colour of this girl's hair which marked her as the one he sought. Anyway, wherever she came from, by stripping her false skins he had, so far as he was concerned, claimed and made her wholly his. And she had accepted him.

Reassured by this thought, Tangalenna picked up the ochre and moved to a small heap of charcoal piled against the back wall. Even on the coldest night he had never lit a fire inside the cave but charcoal was so intrinsic to the customs of his people, he always kept some here. Red was the colour of heat and life, sunrise, blood, flame; black was what remained when the fire had passed and the sun had set. The very essence of the world was therefore contained in the two substances, ochre and charcoal: the endless round of birth, life, death from which life always sprang again: soil enriched by the passage of flame; a sapling emerging from the decay of its parent tree; memory kindled from the bones of an ancestor.

So deeply embedded was this knowledge, the basis of the law which governed their lives, none of the Meelayginnee ever questioned it.

Having selected the best pieces of charcoal, Tangalenna skirted round the sleeping child and sat cross-legged in the cave entrance. The last rays of the westering sun had long since left the gorge which was now filled with shade. This enhanced the jewel-like brilliance of the cloudless sky against the black outline of the cliffs and trees and as he began to grind the ochre, using a pair of special stones, one flat, one oval save for the grinding surface which was worn by use, he began to sing though it was not a song as Ellie would have recognised it but a kind of guttural utterance that resounded pleasantly in his chest. Absorbed in his work as he ground the ochre then crushed the charcoal between his hands, Tangalenna was content. Although he was hungry, the pangs were not the dull ache of starvation (he had breakfasted well on possum meat), but the familiar emptiness of a beginning fast. Safe in the heart of his world he had no need to fight the light-headedness he knew would follow and if, later, the dreaming came, he could give himself wholly to it.

When Ellie woke at last to a kind of numb semi-consciousness, she thought she was in bed at home. The cave-mouth formed a window onto the night sky and Tangalenna had covered her with a kangaroo-skin which constituted the nearest to clothing he possessed. She lay still for what, to her bemused mind, seemed an age, trying to reconcile the rough semi-circular opening with the square of her bedroom window, aware that the shape was wrong but incapable of working out why. There was a faint, putrid smell close to her face. It came from the poorly scraped skin but she assumed one of the farm cats must have brought in a dead mouse. She shifted restlessly.

Even that slight movement was enough to make her head swim. As waves of nausea surged through her she realised she must be ill. Last time she had felt so bad was when she and her brothers had been laid low with chicken-pox but this was worse because she could remember nothing of how it had started, only a series of confused and frightening dreams in which a naked black man, an aborigine, had abducted her when she wandered into the forest.

As this memory floated into her mind, it occurred to the child that perhaps these hadn't been dreams because they would explain the wrongness of the window; the smells of decay, sweat and an earthy metallic odour that clung to her skin; the sound of breathing that was not hers. Normally any one of these would have alarmed her but she was filled with a strange kind of detachment which enabled her to make observations with almost clinical objectivity. It was as if her thoughts were separated from her body, as if the place in which she found herself had nothing to do with reality. Even when, from the impenetrable darkness at the back of the cave, she heard Tangalenna toss and moan in the throes of his dreaming, she was not disturbed by it. It was simply something else to note, like the inexorable shrinking of the patch of starlight until there was only darkness and silence.

It was long before dawn when Tangalenna woke but he was loth to sleep again. His dreams had been far from the usual ones where trees, birds and animals spoke to him in Meelayginnee-tongue, a world in which he was secure as the one he walked as living man. Instead, he had found himself in a place devoid of meaning. Greyness had surrounded him, blank and silent like thick fog; he had been trapped by walls smooth as ice but hard as rock. He was lost and vulnerable as a mud-stranded fish or a bird dashed into water by a gust of wind and the only proof that earth, trees, fire existed still was the trace of charcoal and ochre on his skin. Here, he was somehow both alive and dead.

So terrifying was this possibility that for the first time in his life Tangalenna tried to escape a dreaming, fighting the tendrils that clung to his consciousness even as he came to full awareness of himself and felt the cool night air against his face. When at last he managed to force open his eyes and saw the lambent night sky through the cave mouth he sighed with relief though the essence of the dream lingered like a foul taste. He sat up, shivering as fear-sweat chilled on his skin, and took hold the talisman hanging at his breast. The bone was hard and knobbly in his palm but even his Nana's wisdom could not counter the terror of a place unconnected to the living world, beyond the bounds of the law which governed all things, and yet where he might one day find himself.

Unable to dispel the dread of this vision, Tangalenna turned to the child. He had rubbed charcoal and ochre all over her body but her exposed limbs and face were pale against the darkness of the cave. She was sleeping so deeply he could barely discern the shallow movement of her ribs yet when he tentatively slid a hand under the kangaroo pelt to touch her shoulder, the skin was hot and dry. In fact she was sunk in a stupor closer to a coma than healthy slumber but Tangalenna had no way of knowing this and took comfort from her warmth. He remained sitting upright, half-drowsing but never allowing himself to drift fully into sleep and the solidity of the child's body against his thigh anchored him.

By dawn Tangalenna had managed to push the bad dream so far from his waking mind it was, effectively, forgotten. His was from necessity a practical people: the present was their main concern and such was the immediacy of their endless search for food, water and shelter, they dwelt neither on the past or the future. This was the day of his triumphant return and picturing the joy and wonder with which he and the child would be received, he grinned to himself and rubbed more charcoal onto his forehead and cheeks. His freshly ochred hair and beard contrasted sharply with the darkened skin.

But Tangalenna's glee was checked when he lifted the kangaroo skin to inspect and rouse the child. Even her limbs were hot and she did not stir at his touch. Her head lolled and he saw then how the flesh had shrunk to the bones, that her lips were pale and cracked, her eyes sunken in bruise-coloured hollows. Her breathing was quick and irregular. He shook her roughly but though her eyeballs moved under their fragile lids, she did not wake.

The death of children was common among his people but that this child, the product of his dreaming, might die was something Tangalenna could not countenance. He wrapped the skin close around her and picked her up. She was inert and heavy in his arms and her head rolled against the hollow of his shoulder as he cradled her against him and bore her out of the cave. He strode swiftly down the worn ledge until he came to where the ravine narrowed and the rivulet fell in a series of cascades to the broad valley that constituted the centre of his group's domain.

At the top of the waterfalls was a bare crag. Here Tangalenna paused to scan the valley below. Vapour rose in eddies, coalescing to form beads of moisture. Even to the aborigine's practised eye, it was impossible to discern the smoke of cooking fires from the mist rising from the trees, especially since all was veiled by spray. But the touch and smell of water roused the child. She shivered and licked her lips, seeking to quench her raging thirst.

A woman would have divined the child's need at once but Tangalenna, frightened by her weakness, was obsessed by the thought of bringing her to Manalewa alive. Thus he ignored her pathetic whimpering and continued to descend, taking a narrow path which left the precipitous watercourse and wound down the steep slope of the valley side between thick growth of leatherwood, blackwood and tree-ferns, the roar of the cascades a constant background.

By the time he reached the bottom, the child had relapsed. She was limp in his arms and her hands were cold and clammy against his chest. The pallor of her skin was revealed in channels where the moisture in the air had coalesced into droplets and run down, washing away the layers of ochre and charcoal. She looked like a corpse, save for her shallow breathing.

The path eventually rejoined the rivulet which had broadened as the slope decreased. Here in the main valley the forest was more open, the ground beneath the trees covered with thin grasses or patches of tussock and fern. Now Tangalenna grew wary, alert to every sound and moving shadow but there was no sign of human activity until, almost in the same moment, the reek of excrement and the tang of woodsmoke betrayed the close proximity of the camp.

Before European colonisation, most Tasmanians lived on the coast where food was plentiful all year round and the climate relatively mild. Even the groups that spent the summers inland tended to over-winter by the sea, exchanging ochre, hides, sometimes women, with the coastal peoples for the privilege. Tangalenna's band had been no different until, in his great-great-grandmother's time, their hosts were attacked by white strangers. After that, the coastal people had grown wary and hostile and Tangalenna's became effectively land-locked, their lives even harder than before. Ironically it was this that had enabled their survival: as the other bands succumbed to the ravages of starvation, disease, and a policy of removal by the new settlers, they lived in ignorance of what was happening elsewhere.

But their numbers were declining. Previously, an elaborate system of skin-groups had determined who could marry whom. At puberty the kinship of a man or woman was marked in their flesh so that they could be identified on sight and when groups from different bands met, marriages were arranged and women exchanged according to their skin. In this way, diversity within the bands was maintained. Now, in their isolation, the Meelayginnee numbered twenty adults of whom only five were women of child-bearing age. Every year fewer children were born and these comprised mainly boys, many of which died after a few months. It was this that made Manalewa's loss so dire.

So harsh was the environment in which they had been forced to live that small though it was, the band only came together for a child's initiation into adulthood or the funeral of an esteemed elder. Apart from these occasions (when marriages were also arranged and often consummated), they roamed the remote valleys, plateaux and mountains in small hearth-groups. Because of its proximity to the sacred caves, the camp which lay before Tangalenna was large enough to accommodate the whole band but of the twelve shelters, only three were occupied.

The camp lay on a broad area of sward at the confluence of the rivulet flowing from the gorge and the river which meandered across the floor of the great valley. Though there was a space of several metres between shelters, there was no particular order to their siting. The two currently being used were the most sophisticated: domed huts made from layers of bark and grass bound onto a frame of lashed branches; the door of one was jammed open, the other shut. Other shelters comprised lean-to's similar to the one Tangalenna had constructed in the forest while a few, mere windbreaks of bark twined between branches stuck into the ground, hardly appeared like deliberate constructions at all: they might have been blown together by the very gales they were meant to protect against.

Usually the camp would have been empty by this time, the men out hunting while the women and children foraged for other food but a good kill had been made the day before and the whole hearth-group was there. Having feasted and danced late into the evening, the adults were still asleep but two children, a boy and a little girl, were playing solemnly in the ashes of one of the fires. Sensing that they were being watched, the boy looked up suddenly and saw Tangalenna. With a wild, joyous cry, he leapt to his feet and ran to meet him, dragging his sister, who was only a toddler, roughly along.

Both children were skinny and pot-bellied but their faces, framed by tangles of woolly hair, were eager and mischievous, their eyes bright, their teeth white against dark, dirt-ingrained skin. Their enthusiasm was so infectious that Tangalenna found himself grinning in response. Despite his anxiety for the girl in his arms, he felt a sudden rush of affection for the children (he was their uncle); the glade; the very grass beneath his feet: a sense of homecoming. Indeed, it was among children that he felt most at ease because they expected nothing of him except his attention. As soon as they were old enough to realise his powers there was a kind of instinctive withdrawal, a barrier of awe and fear which he knew was necessary to maintain his position yet, at the same time, bitterly resented.

When they were close enough to see what he bore, the children stopped dead. Although he told them there was nothing to fear, that he had brought a new friend, the boy's face screwed up in repugnance and he recoiled. Tangalenna shook his head slightly then walked on. The children's eyes seem to bore into his back.

There was movement within the open hut and three adults came out. These were Tangalenna's closest kin: his mother, Touganana; his sister, Ana-Maïda, with her babe asleep in her arms, and her husband, Warady. His half-brother, Noumati, who had been born with a misshapen foot and was thus doomed to an existence little better than a woman's, crawled out from one of the lean-to's and gazed with surprise and wonder at the child in Tangalenna's arms. Warady, a man embittered by having to live with his wife's kin, watched with open scorn as Tangalenna looked searchingly into his mother's face.

'Where is Manalewa?'

Such abruptness amounted to a challenge and Tangalenna

regretted his impatience as soon as the words left his lips. A faint, sardonic smile twisted Warady's lips while Noumati grimaced and glanced away, embarrassed.

'Yah!' Touganana folded strong arms across withered breasts and tilted her head to scrutinise her son. 'How many times has the sun crossed the sky since he ran away? Now he comes demanding: no doubt he wants to fill up her womb again!' She paused to peer closely at the limp figure of the girl, still cradled against Tangalenna's chest. 'And what's this he's brought? Another dead child? Don't we have enough already?'

Unexpectedly, she tipped her head back and let out a long, high-pitched howl. Tangalenna shivered and gripped the bone amulet with his right hand. But the old woman's keening lasted only moments: when she was quiet and looked again at her son, her eyes were bright and he thought that, secretly, she was laughing at him.

'This is Manalewa's child,' he said. 'Her name will be Ngali-kiri because although small, she is fierce.'

'It looks like a skinned quoll, that's true,' Warady sneered. 'But not a real person. Where did you find it: in a dream?'

With an effort, Tangalenna ignored him. Ana-Maïda laid the baby on the ground and lifted the toddler to her breast. The child squirmed until she slipped her nipple into its mouth. As it settled and began to suck contentedly, Tangalenna saw new bruises on his sister's arms and face. What happened between a man and his woman was their concern but still he pitied her. She caught his eye and jerked her head meaningfully towards the furthest of the huts then bent to put the child down. It yelled in protest at having its feed interrupted but when there was no response, crawled to tug at a stone.

It was clear now where Manalewa was but despite the anxiety that whimpered in his chest, Tangalenna was angry that his achievement should be demeaned. He drew himself up to his full height and took a deliberate pace towards his detractor. So unexpected was this move and so menacing his demeanour that Warady gave way and lowered his gaze.

'This child comes from the very edge of the world.' Tangalenna adopted the detached tone and slow mode of speech he used when relating the content of his dreams. 'She will become Meelayginnee and one day she will bear our children. Korunah led me to her: who says she does not belong here?'

Without waiting for a response (though he had time to notice the gleam of pride in his mother's eyes), Tangalenna turned on his heel and strode swiftly towards the far hut. Behind, he heard Touganana's deep chuckle, then a snarl, 'So you'd make eyes at your brother rather than your husband?' This was followed by the dull thud of a fist impacting soft flesh and a cry as Ana-Maïda fell to the ground but Tangalenna had opened the door of the hut and did not look back.

It took a while for his eyes to become accustomed to the darkness inside and his nostrils to bear the stench for in the days following the stillbirth, Manalewa had been too weak to go outside. She lay on her back with raised knees, her face upturned. Her eyes were open, the whites stark against the darkness of her skin but Tangalenna knew she was seeing nothing. Awkward because beneath the reek of urine and excrement he detected the putrid aftermath of the birth, the man forced himself closer until he could smell the woman herself, her sweat and the tang of milk that had leaked from her turgid breasts, leaving sour trails across her ribs.

'Here is our child,' he said.

She closed her eyes but gave no other sign that she was aware of his presence. Uncertain how to proceed, Tangalenna waited, the weight of the girl dragging at his shoulders. At length he crouched beside the leaf bed. 'Manalewa!'

There was such urgency in his voice that the woman rolled her head to look at him yet the movement conveyed weariness rather than interest. Her eyes gleamed but Tangalenna was chilled by the indifference with which she regarded him.

'Dead,' she murmured. 'Dead!' And closed her eyes to shut him out.

In desperation, Tangalenna laid the child down. He pulled Manalewa's arm around in an embrace, settled the girl's head into the hollow of the woman's shoulder. The unexpected movement made the child whimper. It was a weak sound, more like a sick infant's than a ten-year-old's, and it penetrated where the man's voice could not. Deprived of the babe she had carried almost full term, the woman's whole being hungered to succour and nurture: she shifted until the child's head was pushed against her breast then, when there was no immediate response, pulled at her right nipple to extrude milk and pressed it into the soft mouth that opened instinctively to receive it.

Tangalenna was affected by a sense of deep discomfiture as his wife's face, which up till then had been frozen with grief, softened into an expression of complete fulfilment. It was the stirring of envy that he felt though he had no word for it: his discontent centred in his loins and his penis hardened. He thought briefly of pushing the child off and taking Manalewa as was his right but then he remembered his mother's words and Warady's scorn: he was in no mind to provide them with entertainment as they listened to his mating. Instead, he left the hut and went to find Noumati who would be eager to hear the tale of his journey.

Chapter 4.

Ellie came to full consciousness over a period of days during which she would half wake then sink again into a deep, treacherous slumber that annihilated thought and memory. In that time she reverted to infanthood, her needs and desires fulfilled by the slippery wetness of a nipple in her mouth and the warm sweet liquid that flowed at her demand; the security of the comforting, enfolding presence whence that succour came. Even when, in her weakness, she shat herself, she was too deeply lapped in a delicious, visceral, contentment to care.

It was the matriarch of the group, Touganana, who tended mother and child. Both were at the limits of their strength, Manalewa especially, whose body was now struggling to produce milk whilst fighting infection caused by the forced birth.

'The dead one is jealous,' Touganana declared. 'It will suck out her strength unless she has proper meat,' and so Tangalenna went hunting, returning a day later with a fine male kangaroo. Although it was customary that the women ate after the men had feasted, Tangalenna butchered the animal outside the camp and slipped the liver, kidneys and heart to his mother for Manalewa and their fosterling. To the rest he cited his own hunger to explain the absence of these delicacies. Noumati winked and grinned at this but Warady shook his head and stared at the hunter with hard eyes. His hatred of his brother-in-law festered like an abscess but he was lazy and a coward: it would take more than a plundered carcass to release it.

With rich food and rest, Manalewa slowly recovered even with the needs of a child to attend. But Touganana encouraged her to stay inside. Game was growing scarce and the group would move to another camp once it was known she was strong enough to walk. When the journey had begun, it was the law that those unable to keep up were left behind: the sickly did not live long.

During those days of confinement, a deep and lasting bond formed between the woman and the young girl. Gradually Manalewa's first wonderment gave way to a joy that was more circumspect though no less ardent. Beneath the layers of dirt, ochre and charcoal she found that the girl's skin was the hue of weathered bone but the ill-omen of that discovery was countered by the colour of her hair. Red-haired children were rare among the Meelayginnee and considered blessed because Tarner, the first man, had had hair the colour of fire. The smooth texture of this child's hair and its unnatural length were the subject of much discussion between Manalewa and the matriarch but they decided to leave it as it was until she reached the age when women's heads were cropped as part of their initiation into adulthood. In any case, her hair was but one of the oddities that marked this girl as a newcomer to their world: her paleness; the shortness of her limbs relative to the length of her back; her pointed face with its narrow, high-bridged nose; her green eyes that were like stones seen through water, all were remarkable to the women. Whatever she grew into as she matured, it would be strange to behold they concluded, and a man would have to close his eyes when he mated with her else he might believe he was coupling with a spirit or, Touganana added jokingly, if she lay still and kept silent, a corpse.

For Ellie, as she returned to full awareness of herself and her surroundings, her former life seemed a dream. She had regressed so far into infanthood that when she realised that the taste in her mouth and the wetness on her lips was the milk of the woman who rocked and crooned lullabies to her, she naturally accepted Manalewa as her mother. Gradually she realised she had been very ill but it did not occur to her to question where she was or who these people were. Even the fact she could not understand their speech did not seem strange. When her legs folded beneath her at her first attempt to stand, she simply curled up again and let them tend her.

Manalewa, who had lost two children in as many months, the first to snakebite, the second stillborn, was fiercely protective of her fosterling. When Tangalenna came with meat, she ate her share then masticated soft boluses for the girl. At first Ellie was revolted when she was offered a blob of raw, chewed liver but hunger overcame her repugnance. She took and ate it with closed eyes and an expression which made the women roar with laughter but she hungered for more. Afterwards, she wolfed down everything she was given without hesitation: the craving of her tissues for nourishment could not be denied.

Having reverted to the innate selfishness of early childhood, it did not seem strange to Ellie that her mother should stay with her all the time. Manalewa taught her the rudiments of Meelayginnee speech and played simple guessing games with pebbles and sticks when they were not eating or sleeping and the girl accepted this devotion as her due.

The old woman, Touganana, understood and approved of her daughter-in-law's strategy but secretly the strangeness of the pale child made her uneasy. Others in the hearth-group were less accommodating. Warady, having a wife, babe and two children to provide for, was especially impatient to leave: though Tangalenna was willing to share his kills, Warady, from pride, refused. Thus he and his family often went hungry while the rest feasted.

Eight days after Tangalenna's return, even Noumati began to wonder at Manalewa's tardiness though he did not voice his opinion. His status in the group was ambiguous. His lameness prevented him hunting kangaroo but he was an accomplished storyteller and the spears he made were highly prized, being better balanced then most because he took greater care in their manufacture. Warady's dislike of Tangalenna, which deepened daily, worried Noumati who was half-brother to both. When he warned Tangalenna that his rival's anger was dangerous, the seer laughed, saying that if it came to blows Warady, a hot-headed and reckless fighter, would find himself outmatched. This did not comfort Noumati who guessed that defeat would only make Warady more cunning.

It was this anxiety which eventually compelled Noumati to see Manalewa for himself. She was his half-sister on his father's side, full sister to Warady and she loved Tangalenna: it was his hope to persuade her to move before there was trouble.

Women's laughter and a girl's giggling came from inside the hut. Tangalenna and Warady were away hunting; Ana-Maïda and the children on the endless search for food and fuel, yet Noumati felt ill-at-ease. The door to the hut was open but those inside did not notice his approach until his shadow fell on them.

'Noumati!' Manalewa greeted her half-brother warmly for she had not seen him since the day of the stillbirth. Touganana, who had been kneeling, leant back on her heels and regarded him steadily. Though she said nothing, Noumati's skin crawled with the force of her disapproval. It was unusual for any man to call on the women, especially one with no woman of his own.

This was the first time Ellie had met Noumati and she felt an instant empathy. She noted his misshapen foot, which was cased in a wombat-skin to protect it, and sensed that he was acutely conscious of the deformity. And she was attracted by the open friendliness of his demeanour. His was a broad, kindly face lacking the abrupt fierceness of her abductor's and though he regarded her with mingled curiosity and wonder, she did not fear him for his hair was cropped almost as short as a woman's and his body was covered in scars. Some of these made patterns on his chest and upper arms similar to Tangalenna's but there were others, ragged tears and burn marks, which she guessed were the legacy of a hard and accident-ridden childhood, and then she pitied him.

Circumlocution being natural to his people, Noumati first praised the women's care of the child and only gradually turned the conversation to Manalewa herself. To his eyes it was clear that if not restored to her former strength she was well able to travel but he had lived with the women all his life and understood their ways. His half-sister's argument that she could barely walk and was still bleeding from time to time was belied by the brightness of her eyes and her quickness to laugh but Noumati discerned the true cause of her malingering in the tenderness with which she looked upon and touched the pale child. Though he was glad that her grief had turned to joy, he knew he must warn her of Warady's impatience and growing hostility towards her husband.

To his dismay, Manalewa dismissed his fears with even more derision than Tangalenna though the matriarch frowned and began to knead the child's thin calves as if to force strength into them. But rather than arguing, the storyteller, who hated confrontation, resorted to fable to make his point. Realising that the girl did not understand their language he acted out his tale, using gestures to supplement the words. So wholly did he give himself up to the roles of child and animal, he did not notice Ana-Maïda's children come to watch from the doorway. The story was a variant on 'The boy who cried 'Wolf!'' only in this version the liar was a small girl and the predator a beast called *kannenner* with glaring eyes and fearsome, clashing jaws. At first, Ellie assumed this to be some kind of legendary monster but when Noumati, prowling on hands and knees, raked his hand over his lower back to indicate stripes, she realised he meant thylacine, the Tasmanian Tiger. From the way the children huddled together and the women exchanged half-fearful, half-amused glances when the child was eaten at the conclusion of the story, it seemed that here the animal still roamed at large.

The tale, despite its grim message, ended in laughter, so exaggerated was the beast's relish at snapping up its victim: Noumati smacked his lips and rubbed his belly, then gave a loud belch that delighted his whole audience. Ellie began to clap, much to the astonishment of the rest. From the doorway, the toddler joined in and this gave rise to more hilarity because her co-ordination was poor and she kept missing one palm with the other.

'Stop that!' The mood changed abruptly when Ana-Maïda appeared and swept the child into her arms. It gave a shriek of dismay and pummelled her head and shoulders but she did not let go. Her babe was slung in a wallaby-skin at her side: it added its wail to the toddler's screams and the little boy began to snivel in sympathy. Ana-Maïda cast a despairing glance at those inside the hut, then walked away. She looked thin and strained, her left eye half-closed where Warady had struck her and Noumati, feeling ridiculous, clambered awkwardly to his feet and stared after, unsure whether he should follow and explain.

'Leave it,' Touganana said wisely. 'You'll make an enemy of Warady if he thinks you feel sorry for her. She is his woman.'

'It was because of Warady that I came,' Noumati retorted. 'Will you talk to Tangalenna, then? I am only a lame storyteller.'

With that, he limped away, making a point of passing as close to the adjacent hut as he could, to ascertain whether Warady was there. From the low, angry voices and frightened silence that followed he guessed the hunter had returned empty-handed. When he reached his own shelter, he dug in the loose earth at the back and brought out a handful of shrivelled roots from a secret store to give Ana-Maïda if the chance arose. At least then the children would eat.

Tangalenna did not return that night but there was enough left from the previous day to feed his family. Touganana invited Warady to join them but he ignored her. As she chewed half-burnt meat off fragile bones, Ellie felt a pang of anxiety for her abductor but the others seemed unconcerned. Later, settling down with a full belly, secure in Manalewa's embrace, she soon fell into a contented slumber.

Next day the sun reached its zenith and still there was no sign of Tangalenna. That morning Warady hung about the camp, cuffing his wife and children whenever they were foolish enough to stray within his reach, scowling at Noumati who sat quietly making spears. When Manalewa at last emerged, blinking in the daylight, he stared with open contempt as she yawned and stretched, luxuriating in the warmth of the sun on her skin. Noumati watched uneasily from under half-closed eyelids and the strokes of the stone blade against the spear shaft he was working on were slow and deliberate.

'So the dreamer's wanderings finally prised you from bed?' Warady sneered and when Manalewa looked pointedly away, he turned his attention on Touganana and Ellie who were just leaving the hut. Of the two it was the child that shuffled like an old woman and winced at the sunlight. She clung to the matriarch as if unable to stand unaided.

'If that's the best he could find, maybe you're better off without him,' Warady continued spitefully. 'A living abortion to replace the dead one: was that the deal he made with his precious daemon? It looks like something that has died. Let it come here so I can tell if it's flesh and blood like us or a ghost.'

'Lay a finger on her and Tangalenna will give you a beating,' Touganana said stoutly. 'And why are you lazing in camp when your wife and children are hungry? A fine man to threaten a child while its father is away!'

Warady did not reply but his face hardened and his eyes conveyed such malevolence that Manalewa moved to shield the girl from his glance. At that moment Ana-Maïda entered the clearing, ushering her children before her. They were bowed under loads of firewood which, it seemed, they had walked far to find for the girl and boy were stumbling and silent, the woman panting. All were bleeding from the scratches of thorn bushes. They glanced fearfully at Warady then hurried to dump their loads beside his hut. Only the babe, asleep in its sling, seemed happy. Once unburdened, the woman pushed the children inside. Tired and hungry, they began to grizzle, ignoring their mother's desperate attempts to hush them.

It was too late: they had given Warady the excuse he needed to escape a situation that was becoming intolerable. He strode towards the hut with clenched fists, his face terrifying in his fury. Noumati's hand tightened involuntarily on the spear he held but it was not his place to intervene. As Ana-Maïda's cries tore the forest quiet apart, the storyteller hung his head and the strokes of the blade became more forceful until he was in danger of planing too much away and weakening the weapon beyond use.

Ellie cringed as the screaming stopped and the thuds of the beating became audible, interspersed with groans. But it did not occur either to Touganana or Manalewa to protest. Nor would Tangalenna have acted although Ana-Maïda was his sister: it was for her to please Warady and if he was not satisfied, she would have to bear the consequences.

In Ellie's mind the sounds awoke fears that belonged not to this world but her past life. She found it impossible to ignore the noises of violence and distress coming from so close and when Warady strode out, head held high in triumph, and picked up his spears to go hunting, she had to close her eyes to keep herself from staring. But as the others appeared unmoved so she, over time, became inured to Ana-Maïda's suffering.

Soon after Warady's departure, Tangalenna limped in. He was bruised and lacerated down one side and leaned heavily on a stout stave. He glanced round warily then, realising his rival was not there, relaxed and tried to make light of his injuries as Manalewa, seeing the state of him, chided his carelessness.

'Eh, woman, don't you know better than to berate a man on his homecoming?' Touganana scolded. 'That one has more sense.' And she smiled approval as Ellie, whose heart had twisted painfully at the sight of her guardian hurt, went to fetch the last scraps of food from the hut.

'I fell,' was all Tangalenna would say in reply to their questions and then he ate voraciously, cracking bones and sucking out the marrow. While the others squatted to watch, waiting patiently in case he should speak more, Ellie gathered moss from a nearby log with which to clean his wounds. Such treatment was, it seemed unprecedented, for he flinched and squirmed away from her touch, only submitting when his mother asked pointedly which of them was the child? Then he sat silent and still until, when Ellie had finished, he resorted to the traditional remedy, taking a handful of cool ash from the edge of the fire and rubbing it into every wound.

So contrary was this act to everything she knew about first aid, it made Ellie sharply aware of her isolation, her uniqueness in this world. A place where there were plasters and antiseptics seemed impossible here in this camp of rough shelters, among these naked people who had no concept of their nakedness. The difference was irreconcilable and she continued to stare whilst fighting back tears.

Something of this distress must have been written in her expression because Noumati murmured sympathetically, 'Child?' and jerked his head, indicating that he wanted her to sit beside him. But shame at having her innermost feelings so easily read sparked an irrational anger in her and she stalked away into the trees though the effort of doing so made her head swim.

The rest of the afternoon passed swiftly as a new sense of urgency gripped the group. Even Tangalenna admitted it was well past time to move to better hunting grounds: only he knew how close he had come to death the day before, scrabbling his way back from the crumbling brink of a precipice. He rested by the fire while the women gathered scant possessions into finely woven bags made of grass and pandanus leaves. Even Ana-Maïda ventured out of her hut and joined in the chatter, her babe slung at her side as usual.

Her other children were asleep: no sound came from them. Noumati managed to slip her the roots he had saved and she thanked him and stowed them in the wallaby-skin with the infant though catching Tangalenna's gaze after, she hung her head in shame. It was for her to provide such food while her man fetched meat.

Ellie sulked at the edge of the forest until Tangalenna rose awkwardly, yawned and stretched, then went inside to sleep. Feeling rather stupid, she crept back to the fireplace where Manalewa neither welcomed nor chastised her but simply involved her in the preparations, giving her things to hold before placing them carefully in a bag: a flat grinding stone stained with ochre; a short club; a pointed digging stick; a scallop shell which had cracked and been repaired with eucalyptus gum; a couple of rancid-smelling wallaby skins with the fur worn away where they had been tied as rough capes or into carrying slings. Once all was packed, the women sat together and checked each other's close-cropped scalps for ticks and lice though so early in the season this was more for pleasure than necessity. Ellie submitted resignedly to their inspection, yelping when her hair was playfully tweaked. Then they amused themselves by crushing charcoal from the fire between their hands and smearing it over their own and each other's forehead, cheeks and arms.

The shadows lengthened and Tangalenna's snores came gentle and even from his hut while Noumati told tales, the gist of which Ellie understood by means of his acting. But as kookaburras lined up on low-hanging branches, Ana-Maïda became tense, looking around nervously each time a twig cracked or leaves rustled. And her discomfiture spread gradually to the rest for all were apprehensive of Warady's return.

It was close to sunset when he swaggered in, spears balanced on one shoulder, a dead wallaby slung over the other. He had gutted the carcass to make it lighter for carrying and blood-stains patterned his body so that he looked like the triumphant hero of some deadly battle. Ana-Maïda put hand to mouth at the sight of him and their children, who had crept out to hear Noumati's tales, shrank close as if her body could shield them from their father's wrath.

Warady's gaze passed disdainfully over his cringing family: the old woman (who pointedly ignored him); his sister and his crippled half-brother; coming to rest at last on the pale child. Ellie stared back and her eyes were wide and accusing.

'Well?' Uncomfortable under that steady scrutiny (those eyes! hard as stone and with the green-brown lights of deep water in them as if a spirit looked out from the child's flesh), Warady turned his attention on his wife. She scrambled to her feet, the children scrabbling after. He tossed the carcass towards her and flung down his bundle of spears.

'Tonight we feast, woman. Unless any of Tangalenna's kin are hungry, since he returned empty-handed?'

No-one asked how he knew this but Noumati muttered, 'So Black Snake slid through forest like a dark shadow: his teeth dripped poison,' and a shudder ran through all who heard. Even Ellie, who did not understand the words, caught their menace and drew her knees defensively to her chest. Her gaze had not wavered from Warady's face and she was filled with a mixture of fear and defiance, recognising him as a threat not so much to herself but to her guardian. She hated him as instinctively as she revered Tangalenna.

'Eh, we thank Warady for his generosity.' Touganana smiled ingenuously. 'For he speaks truly: my son had no luck hunting and tomorrow we leave. It will be good to start the journey with full bellies.'

In the silence which followed, Warady's face grew taut with rage: his hands clenched into fists and his body seemed to swell as the muscles bunched under the skin. It was customary that those with meat offered to share it but having refused to eat of Tangalenna's kills, it had not occurred to Warady that his rival's kin would prove less proud. Unable to retract the offer, he stood glaring at the old woman who returned his gaze with a look of bland indifference.

'Is Tangalenna not a man then, that his mother rules his hearth?' Warady turned abruptly and went to sit at his own fire. Ana-Maïda, who had already covered the wallaby with hot ashes, sat opposite. Every-so-often her gaze flicked fearfully from the blaze to her husband but he ignored her. The two children were huddled next to her and they watched the cooking meat with wide, solemn eyes. The reek of burning hair filled the glade, followed by the tantalising odour of roasting flesh. A long thread of spittle drooled from the boy's open mouth and the little girl stared at the blackening carcass as if it were a thing of wonder.

When Tangalenna woke, it was already dark. He groaned and stretched, wincing as dried cuts split. His body ached as if from a beating and he was racked by hunger but he lay awhile, trying to work out what was happening outside. From the voices, it was clear that Noumati and the children were re-enacting a fable; that Warady's hunt had been successful was evident from the stench of burnt fat, thick even inside the hut. It made Tangalenna's mouth water yet still he hesitated. Even if the whole group had feasted, he was loth to partake of such meat lest his hunger be mistaken for weakness.

It was a measure of how well Manalewa understood her husband's nature that she sent the pale child to fetch him instead of going herself: he would not wish to appear at any woman's beck and call. Ellie stood uncertainly in the doorway, her body a slender silhouette against the glare of the cooking fire. She peered into the hut, unable to make out any definite shape in the darkness though from the quietness, she guessed her guardian was awake.

'Tangalenna?' It was the first time she had addressed him directly and she trembled as she spoke. She heard him move, then he loomed before her. His hand descended from the darkness, pushed her gently aside and he stepped out into the firelight.

The women and children sat round one side of Ana-Maïda's fire, watching Noumati who squatted nearby, hands outspread as he began another tale. On the opposite side of the blaze Warady sprawled alone, his face set in an expression of sardonic amusement which changed to a look of gloating satisfaction as Tangalenna walked to join him, trying hard not to limp. Ellie followed like a pale shadow and when he sat down, settled beside him. Tangalenna ignored Warady's obvious displeasure and put his arm round her shoulders to draw her close. The women looked at one another at this flouting of custom (traditionally each gender kept to its own side of the fire), while Noumati, head bowed, smiled secretly to himself. The atmosphere had changed abruptly with Tangalenna's arrival, as if a cold wind had suddenly sprung up but though he sensed this, he refused to acknowledge it.

'Did you keep meat for me?' he asked Manalewa and as she scrambled to serve him the choice scraps she had saved after Warady had gorged, he turned towards his rival. 'Thanks for the sharing of your kill. I was too slow yesterday.'

There was hidden significance to these words which only Warady understood. The previous day the two had been chasing the same wallaby until Tangalenna's fall and then, instead of helping his brother-in-law, Warady had continued the hunt and gone straight back to camp when the wounded animal escaped. Thus Warady's face darkened in a deep flush of shame and he looked away in confusion without replying.

The food was only sufficient to blunt the edge of Tangalenna's hunger yet as he ate he was sharply conscious of the child nestling against him. Her head drooped to rest on his thigh and grew heavy. After he had sucked the grease from his fingers he laid one hand gently on the girl's back, feeling the ribs lift as she breathed. When the gathering dispersed soon after, he carried the sleeping child into the hut after Manalewa and this time, instead of going to join Noumati, he stayed.

Chapter 5.

The group was ready to leave soon after dawn. The men bore spear-bundles but were otherwise unencumbered. By contrast, the women were bowed against the weight of their woven bags. These were balanced by means of a strap across their brows to leave their hands free for the endless work of gathering food and tending children. Ana-Maïda's babe, tied at her breast, was unusually quiet, face squashed between milk-swollen flesh and wallaby-skin; her other children clung nervously to her legs because their father was there. They were all waiting for the matriarch and their breath steamed in the dank air while Tangalenna and Warady folded bark strips into wads for fire-sticks.

'Why are you standing here, like wallabies in the snow?' Touganana asked when she walked out from between the trees. 'Did you think me too old to catch up? It'll be a while yet before my bones go to the fire.'

'Maybe Tangalenna is unsure of the way.' Warady muttered. He did not quite dare speak the words aloud but the air was still and all heard them. A soft exhalation came from the old woman but Tangalenna, squatting to light his fire-stick, ignored the insult. When the bark began to flare, he blew out the flame so that the fire-stick smouldered and did not deign to look at Warady as he rose smoothly to his feet.

'If I go astray, no doubt my brother-in-law will point out the way,' he said and set off along the path that followed the river.

From the manner in which the women waited until the men had passed, it was clear to Ellie that these people journeyed according to a strict precedent so she stayed close to Manalewa all morning. Despite his lameness, Noumati tried to keep up with Tangalenna and Warady, fearing what might come of their simmering hostility. But as the morning wore on they left him behind. He watched them anxiously though they never went completely beyond sight of the group.

Although food and rest had done much to restore Ellie's strength, she lacked the stamina of the nomads. While she found the going easy at first, the path being well-trodden and relatively flat, as the sun rose high and the group displayed no inclination to stop, she felt herself flagging. At the same time Ana-Maïda's little girl gave up and the women took turns carrying her and the babe. It astonished Ellie that even Touganana should take on the extra burden of a tired, grizzling child without calling on the men to help but division of labour was clearly defined in their society and the care of children was women's work.

Before the sun reached its zenith, Ellie began to wish that she also was small enough to be carried and in her mind she begged Tangalenna to come back and bear her if only for a little while. But it was law amongst these people that once a child was of an age to walk all day, it should not be helped. The ability to travel was so vital to the survival of the band that those too sick or weak to keep up were abandoned. As the girl began to limp, Manalewa urged her on with frantic words and gestures and when this made no difference, cast agonised glances towards the men. Yet though Tangalenna heard what was going on behind, he only slackened pace a little.

When the sun's rays came vertically though the leaf canopy (the forest was more open here on the floodplain than in the tributary valley), the group paused to rest and drink. The river was broad, shallow and rapid-strewn: the spray shone in the sunlight. While the men, having quenched their thirst, lay at ease, the women unslung their bags and tended the children. Ana-Maïda suckled her babe and Manalewa helped Touganana feed the others but her eyes kept straying back the way they had come.

They had all finished eating when Ellie staggered into view. When she reached them, she sank onto the grass. Manalewa spoke softly to her and pressed a piece of cold meat into her hand but she dropped it, hardly aware of where she was or what was happening. Warady's eyes were cool and calculating as he watched but Tangalenna, whose cuts and strained muscles were stiffening every moment, averted his gaze. That his foster-child should prove so weak hurt him deeply, affronting his pride and putting into doubt the infallibility of his daemon: he did not want to acknowledge failure.

They rested long enough for the shadows to take on a slight eastwards slant, then Warady, who had been observing the others with silent disdain, rose, hefted his spears onto his shoulder, jerked his head at Ana-Maïda and set off with the same, seemingly effortless stride as before. The woman, who had sunk into a kind of tired reverie, the babe latched onto her breast, scrambled hastily to her feet, forced the infant to her side and bent her head to her load-strap. The babe screamed in protest, milk and saliva streaming from its mouth but she ignored it, nudged the weary children with her foot and trudged after her husband, already a distant figure along the path.

'Eh, come on then.' Noumati levered himself up using one of the half-finished spears he bore as a prop. He set off with Tangalenna and though they walked slowly, they soon overtook Ana-Maïda and her struggling children. Then Touganana got to her feet and settled the load-strap across her brow. She laid a hand on Manalewa's shoulder. 'Time to go.'

Ellie was last to leave and it was fear of being abandoned that goaded her into action for even her foster-mother did not wait. When she stood up, she thought she would vomit from the agony of her swollen and lacerated feet but once she started walking again, the pain dulled. She had drunk deeply from the river and the water was cold and heavy in her stomach: it sloshed at every step. This seemed hilarious and she chuckled to herself until she realised even Ana- Maïda had drawn far ahead.

Before long all the others were lost to the girl's sight but a careless mood had overtaken her and she did not worry. She wandered along the path in a happy daze, fascinated by the play of sunlight and shadow on mosses and fern fronds; the flow of the river over rapids where fleeting rainbows were netted in gyres of spray: the sound of running water made a kind of ceaseless, ever-varied music. So hypnotic were its many notes that eventually she sat on a flat rock to listen, enjoying the sun's warmth on her skin and with every minute she lingered, the thought of getting up and going after the rest seemed less important.

By mid-afternoon the men reached a wide lake. From this open space the distant sides of the great valley were visible and, to the west, a series of jagged peaks. Circles of ash marked the camp and Tangalenna and Warady inspected these carefully, trying to gauge whether anyone had been there since their last visit more than a year before. But the ashes were old and grass had taken root in the circles. While they waited for the women, they gathered branches and strips of bark to make wind-breaks, salvaging much from the wreckage of old shelters destroyed by the weather. When, as the sun sank towards the mountains, the women appeared with the children in their arms, the men immediately ceased work.

'Where's Ngali-kiri?' Tangalenna demanded as soon as it was clear she was not with them. Ignoring Warady's scornful glance, he grabbed Manalewa roughly by the shoulder. 'You didn't leave her?'

'What could I do?' She stared, stricken. 'She's too old to carry. She'll be here soon.'

Tangalenna did not answer. His face was grim as he stared down the path. A light breeze swayed the trees and the patterns of light and shade shifted with them. Even to his keen eyes it was impossible to tell whether anyone was moving there.

'Here.' He thrust the fire-stick into Manalewa's hands. 'Make camp and hope my luck has changed.'

Manalewa took the smouldering wad of bark dumbly. Their exchange had been watched with interest by the others but only Warady dared express the outrage they all felt.

'If you bring that pale abortion back, do not expect us to welcome her,' he said forcefully. 'If she is so weak, she should die. What puts her outside the law?'

Tangalenna ignored him. He chose a spear from Noumati's bundle and walked away, heading back along the path. His weariness was evident from the stoop of his shoulders yet by the time Manalewa had gathered fuel to start a fire in one of the old ash circles, he had gone from view.

An atmosphere of ill-feeling hung over the camp after

Tangalenna's departure. When the children complained of being hungry even Noumati was short with them and they soon wandered off, hand in hand, to dabble at the lake's edge while the women finished the shelters

While the rest were busy, Warady stood worrying at his foreskin while he stared after Tangalenna. His face bore an expression of implacable hatred, the furrows of his cheeks hard and immobile as if carved from wood. Every-so-often, Ana-Maïda cast him a frightened glance but she dared not look long or speak lest she attract his attention and so went about her tasks in silence, foraging at the margins of the lake for bulbous roots and freshwater crayfish.

Exhausted and hungry, Ellie had not moved from the riverside. The rock on which she sat was hard but warm and seemed as comfortable as any bed. Freed from care by the lassitude that washed over her body and her mind, she stretched out and relaxed, falling eventually into a deep and dreamless slumber.

The sun sank and shadows crept over the sleeping child. Smelling warm blood yet ever wary, the carrion-eaters of the forest watched and waited. They wanted cover of darkness ere they made their move but their caution robbed them of a meal. Roused by the chillness of the air, Ellie woke, sat up and stretched out her arms and the devils crept silently away.

Sleep had cleared her head but Ellie's eyes were gummed and sticky so she scrambled down to the river's edge to wash her face and drink. The water was slightly bitter and stirred a vague memory. The creek at the picnic spot tasted the same but so effectively had her mind blocked out her former life, she could not recall either the place or its significance.

Refreshed, she looked round brightly, expecting to see the others camped close by. But there was no welcoming spiral of smoke nor any chatter save that of a flock of blue wrens which fluttered through the scrub to investigate her: aware of a forest raven perched high above, they did not venture into the open.

Ellie thought of Tangalenna's efforts to bring her to Manalewa's care and it seemed inconceivable that they had deserted her. She stood on the slab of stone and peered into the shadowed eaves of the forest lest they be hiding there, waiting for the opportunity to spring out and surprise her but she could not imagine the men indulging in so frivolous a joke. Then she wondered if she should call out but she was afraid. If some disaster had befallen the others, she did not want to draw attention to herself.

Without realising it, Elle was already more at ease in the wild than she had been before. Finding herself alone she did not panic and run blindly into the forest. Instead she waited, watching and listening. She did not know if the Meelayginnee had enemies but if they had been attacked, she would not give herself up lightly. Before setting off, she armed herself with a stout stick.

The sun slid over the rim of the valley and the air temperature dropped rapidly. Ellie hugged herself as she walked, both to keep warm and in an effort to quell the hunger pangs griping her stomach. But her strength soon began to fail.

As he retraced the afternoon's journey, Tangalenna kept glancing upwards in the hope of glimpsing Korunah. Forest ravens he saw, their wings glossy in the slanting sunlight, and flocks of parrots and rosellas flew into the forest as he passed but there was no sign of his broad-winged daemon. The noise of the river drowned all other sounds and so great was his unease, he stopped several times to look behind in case he was being followed. The bands of shadow stretched across the path were undisturbed by the movement of any creature and he went on but the disapproval of his ancestors weighed heavily upon him.

When the light began to fade, Tangalenna went more carefully, fearful of overlooking the child. Accomplished hunter though he was, if she was curled up asleep in some hollow or had sought shelter inside a tree, he knew he might never find her. He quested not only with his senses, his wide nostrils snuffing like a hound's whenever there was a slight change in the air, but with his mind, feeling the forest as if it were part of him. Mindful of Warady's parting words, when a fat pademelon crossed his path he speared it and hoisted the carcass over a branch to pick up on his return.

He was not far from their halt by the river when a squeal tore apart the quiet of the night. The child launched herself at him, twining her limbs round in an embrace so fierce and unexpected that Tangalenna staggered.

'Eh, little one . . .' He held her close, stroked her all over to check for any injury, hissed in sympathy when she winced as he touched her feet. She pressed her face against his, careless of the clay-matted texture of his beard, the rancid wallaby-fat, and he tasted the salt of her tears.

'I thought you'd left me.' She repeated the phrase until it became a refrain in his head: though he did not understand the words, her tone of mingled joy and accusation sent a pang through him. He kissed her gently on the lips in an effort to make her stop and in that moment an owl screeched, so loudly that Tangalenna started. The girl went rigid in his arms then realising it was only a bird, began to laugh. High and clear, the laughter wound its way between the trees, rising through the canopy, and many animals paused to listen and wonder what creature could have made such a sound. Tangalenna frowned and pressed a finger against the girl's lips to silence her. To laugh openly was something for camp or corroboree where people were gathered together, not to be released deep in the forest at night. He let the child slip to the ground. It was as if she had no idea of what was right.

Sensing his disquiet, Ellie was desperate to recover the happiness of only a few moments before. She clung to his arm and pressed his hand against her face in an instinctive gesture of appeasement: when this did not move him, she began to cry. All the wretchedness and uncertainties of the day found release at once and she wept unrestrainedly, letting go Tangalenna's hand and huddling on the bare earth.

As he listened to her sobs, Tangalenna's ire dissolved in a rush of love and pity. He picked her up and began to walk swiftly back the way he had come. As soon as she realised she was safe, Ellie stopped crying and relaxed, settling her head in the hollow of his shoulder. The steady beat of his heart and the warm smell of him were all she desired.

Any hope that he could slip into camp unnoticed disappeared the moment the lake came into Tangalenna's view. The brightness of the stars glittering overhead was as nothing compared to the flaring of campfires: a huge blaze burned on the lake shore, the leaping flames reflected in the still water. Dancing figures wended between the blazes and their chant floated skywards as if borne by the smoke of the fires.

Tangalenna groaned inwardly at the sight. He counted the dancers and knew that another hearth-group had arrived. Most likely they had brought food and gifts but in any case the meeting of families was always a cause for celebration.

If he carried the pale child into camp, he would be condemned by everyone, even Manalewa. Before anyone spotted him, he moved behind a screen of tea-tree scrub to decide what to do.

The girl had fallen asleep and he laid her down beside his kill. As he did so, a great shout rose from the gathering and two men began to stamp out the ritual dance performed when hearth-groups met. Usually Tangalenna would have danced for his group but Warady had taken his place. The other was Tupali, Warady and Manalewa's younger brother. They jabbed spears in mock hostility until, when neither gained the upper hand, they fell down as if exhausted to the laughter of the rest. Then the women raised them and joined in the dancing, enacting reconciliation and the exchange of gifts though the real gift-giving had been done earlier.

From his hiding place, Tangalenna watched enviously though he had no choice but to accept this usurping of his role. Roused by the noise, the child sat up and gazed upon the activity with bewilderment. Suddenly apprehensive, Tangalenna pulled her roughly to her feet and pushed her in the direction of the corroboree.

'Go to Manalewa!'

Ellie did not understand why, after carrying her so far, he should insist she walk the last few metres but his tone frightened her. Half-blinded by the glare of the fires, she moved uncertainly into the clearing. Everyone was now dancing save Noumati, Touganana and a grizzled old man with a huge belly who beat out the rhythm on a hollow log. The dancers' eyes, fixed in a wild inward stare, glinted in the leaping flame-light. They were focused wholly on the dance, their minds detached from their surroundings by the beat of the drum, the pounding blood in their ears, their panting breath. A kind of frenzy had hold on them, an ecstasy which they expressed in shouts of wild laughter when they could no longer contain the force that drove them.

To the child, such unrestrained energy and emotion was terrifying. She stopped at the very edge of the circle of light and her dirt-streaked body was visible only when the flames leapt. The effect was eerie. It was as if her form struggled towards definition, like a stream-bed pebble viewed through rippling water or a tree seen through flowing mist. Save for her eyes, which glinted like polished stones, she looked more like something magicked into existence from smoke and flame than a creature of flesh and blood.

Maliciously, Warady had told the newcomers that Tangalenna had captured a spirit-child and given it to Manalewa to nurse. His parents, Tanglémerna and Pounaté, were sceptical for their eldest son was a well known boaster and stirrer, a trouble-maker who delighted in causing strife between the hearth-groups: Black Snake was his totem. But Tupali, his younger brother, believed the lie. He had not given himself wholly to the dance and while his limbs followed the rhythms of drum and stamping feet, his mind remained anchored in the darkness of the night, the bright flames and the fear which lurked within him whenever his brother was near.

When he saw the ghostly figure at the edge of the circle, Tupali let out a scream which broke the momentum of the dance and switched the prevailing mood to panic. The children and women shrieked (though they had no idea what could have struck such terror into the young man), while Warady rushed to pick up a spear.

'Aiee – the ghost!' Tupali pointed a shaking finger. 'Drive it away! It will destroy us!'

The shattering of their trance left the dancers bemused. Even Manalewa stared at the child without recognition. Warady stood poised to throw his spear but hesitated, filled with superstitious dread. The flickering firelight made Ellie's skinny form appear corpse-like, the streaks of dirt, charcoal and ochre giving it a skewbald look as if skin and flesh were half-decayed.

From where he waited, Tangalenna held his breath. If Warady

cast his spear, he would not miss. He willed the girl to turn and run. The women groped for sticks and stones to fling while the children maintained a steady screaming, the sound of mindless terror.

Caught between firelight and darkness, Ellie trembled. She wanted to flee but she was frightened of disobeying Tangalenna. Her eyes darted from face to face but when at last she found Manalewa, her foster-mother's visage was like all the others: a rigid mask of fear and hate. There was no mercy there.

Unable to go back, Ellie stepped into the full glare of the fires. In an instant she was transformed from threatening ghost to frail child. Manalewa pushed forward and swept her into her arms while Touganana began to chuckle.

As soon as they realised their mistake, all but one joined in the mirth: they laughed until tears streamed down their faces. Only Warady was silent. He watched with a faint sardonic smile as Manalewa cuddled the child then sat down, took her onto her lap and leant back to suckle her. Had she been more careful, Manalewa would have done this in private for the newcomers looked on with open disapproval and their laughter ceased. But in her joy at her fosterling's return she was oblivious to all else and did not register the frowns.

The dour mood did not last long. Noumati began to beat a rhythm on the hollow log and the dancing resumed: even Tupali joined in whole-heartedly. But Warady remained aloof. He stood like a sentinel behind the elders, leaning on his spear, and stared unwaveringly into the shifting darkness beyond reach of the firelight, sure that this pale weakling could not have found the way alone. If Tangalenna returned empty-handed from his 'hunt', Warady could justly accuse him of breaking the law. And he smiled in anticipation, fingering his spear.

To his rival's disappointment, Tangalenna entered camp with a fat pademelon slung over his shoulder and, on seeing the pale child, feigned surprise so skilfully that Warady began to doubt his suspicions: it was possible, after all, that the girl had followed them by chance. When Tangalenna had been welcomed and his hunting skill praised, the corroboree continued.

Because of the incestuous relationship between Touganana and

Pounaté (which had resulted in the birth of Noumati), there was a certain awkwardness between these hearth-groups. This was exacerbated by Warady's resentment at being forced to live with his wife's kin and Tanglémerna's jealousy of Touganana who, she believed, had deliberately teased and enticed her husband. However, they had not met for many months and, since the Disappearing, there was only one other hearth-group, comprising Tanglémerna's kin, in the whole band. Whenever they came together there was therefore great rejoicing despite the underlying tensions.

When he had eaten, and drunk from the lake, Tangalenna got up to dance and the others waited for him to choose the theme. His choice was the story of Tarner, the first man.

This met with approval from all save Warady, who had gone to sit with Tupali. When Noumati and Pounaté rose to join in and Touganana began to beat out a slow, measured rhythm, Warady gave a jeering laugh.

'That is a dance for men, not cripples and the woman-hearted,' he called. 'Better make it 'Ducks on the Water'!'

This was a grave insult for he had named the dance children learned for their first corroboree. The mood changed abruptly from joyous celebration to apprehension. The drumming stopped and the women exchanged worried glances, except for Tanglémerna. Her face expressed a kind of smug satisfaction.

Tangalenna, who had already walked into the dancing space, turned and regarded his brother-in-law gravely. He had not expected to be challenged so soon or so publicly. Manalewa was gazing at him with urgent, pleading eyes but he ignored her.

'It is a long time since I danced that dance, Warady,' he answered after a long silence. 'You will have to show me the steps.'

Warady laughed. 'I forgot them when I became a man. Let your pale child remind you, since she has stolen your wits.'

At this, Manalewa put her arms protectively around Ellie who was sleeping across her lap but Ana-Maïda drew away a little as if contact with the girl would bring ill-fortune. The matriarch, Touganana, frowned but though she was an elder, it was not for any woman to intervene in a quarrel between men.

Tangalenna looked at his enemy and his demeanour was one of

forbearance rather than anger.

'The child has been named: she is ours,' he said. 'If she comes of age, she will marry and bear children like any other daughter of Tarner.'

Warady got to his feet, picking up the spear he had used earlier in the dance. He held it loosely but the threat was clear.

'Since when have the children of Tarner had white skin and pale eyes?' he asked. 'Though you tried to hide it with ochre and charcoal, the truth is plain. You have replaced the failed spawn of your own loins with a *num* weakling. No doubt the eagle you followed wanted to feast on her flesh. Or was it a currawong and you only dreamed korunah?'

A moan like the sough of wind through trees arose at this: to deny or insult another's dreaming was taboo. Tangalenna's face and muscles hardened; his lips drew back from clenched teeth in a snarl. He was so tense that he hardly breathed.

'Eagle stared at the sun and was not blinded; Raven ate a shining wet stone thinking it a star fallen from the sky and it dragged upon him so that he could not fly so high.' Dismayed by the latent violence in the air Noumati spoke loudly and so unexpectedly that both antagonists stared at him in astonishment. 'And thus it was that as Eagle soared and, looking down upon the earth, grew proud, so Raven learned the tongues of all the animals and birds and became cunning and clever. And when they met to feast on carrion they bowed their heads to one another. Otherwise both would go hungry.'

These words were spoken with such artlessness that the old woman began to chuckle. As always, Noumati had embellished his tale with extravagant gestures and it seemed to his audience that they saw Raven's subtlety in the tilt of his head; Eagle's arrogance in the glint of his eye. Even Tangalenna relaxed and Pounaté shook his head and smiled but Warady was unmoved.

'So you'll let a cripple protect you?' he sneered. 'The ghost-child has sucked the heart out of you along with my sister's milk. It should have been left behind and you know it. If it stays among us, we will all be poisoned by its spell.'

So fervent was this speech that many shuddered and Manalewa

returned the hostile glances directed at her with proud defiance. Realising that his efforts as peace-maker were in vain, Noumati bowed his head and moved back a little.

'Before accusing others of being woman-hearted, look into your own bone-cage,' Tangalenna replied. 'What kind of man is afraid of a girl-child? One who raises a spear against an unarmed adversary?' He lunged towards Warady with a fierceness that daunted the other, snatched the weapon and broke the slender shaft across his knee. 'I will fight you tomorrow but heed this: I will not hold back. And now I will take my wife and child and go to sleep.'

Such dignity was revealed in Tangalenna as he cast the broken pieces at Warady's feet, bent to lift the sleeping girl and strode towards their shelter that no-one moved or spoke: a kind of awe had fallen upon them. Manalewa walked a few paces behind him, straight-backed, looking neither to left nor right and pride swelled within her because whatever might happen in the future, tonight her man had won the war of words and at that moment she was envied by all the other women in camp.

Their shelter was no more than a low lean-to with a stone-ringed fireplace in front. While Tangalenna settled the child on the fresh leaf and fern bed, Manalewa replenished the fire with logs that would smoulder until dawn. As she worked she could smell her partner's heat, feel his rising tension and relished the tingle of anticipation in her loins. It took great effort to hold back, prolonging the task until at last Tangalenna's patience broke.

'Will you keep me waiting till dawn?' he demanded thickly. Then they fell hungrily upon one another, heedless of the sleeping child; the people listening nervously from the rest of the camp, discomfited by the events of the day and the coming fight that might see one of their strongest maimed or killed. Nor did Tangalenna care that his love-making broke another of the traditional prohibitions: sex before a fight was thought to sap a man's most vital essence, weakening him when he had most need of his strength. If Warady was listening it would seem to him that Tangalenna was not taking the fight seriously, that he, Warady, was not a worthy adversary and, Tangalenna thought, this could only work to his advantage: an angry fighter is often reckless.

Chapter 6.

An atmosphere of barely suppressed excitement pervaded the camp next morning. Wrestling matches had once been a common method of settling disputes, especially in quarrels between individuals but these events had become rare as numbers dwindled. Before the Disappearing, more deadly fighting between bands for women or territory had been one of the main occupations of the men, their prestige being based largely on their reputation as warriors. But at any time, a match between such adversaries as Tangalenna and Warady would have been a great occasion.

It was traditional for fights to begin when the sun was at its highest, to give the protagonists time to prepare and to allow the women to collect food and fuel for the day ahead. And it was also customary for the fighters to keep to their shelters or in special places beyond sight of their hearth-group: this added to the anticipation and prevented the formation of factions within the band.

Having slept through the argument, Ellie had no idea of what was to come but she sensed the latent excitement as soon as she left the shelter, sensing her foster-parents wanted to be alone. Wherever she went, people stared, not only the strangers but those she had come to think of as her own. Only Ana-Maïda's children greeted her as before and when she crouched to play with them, their mother ran forward and pulled them away though Warady was nowhere to be seen. (Having no patience with his wife, he was being tended by Tupali and Tanglémerna). Pounaté, torn between loyalties to his wife and sister, refused to take sides and sat in companionable silence with Noumati though that in itself was sufficient to rouse Tanglémerna's ire. They watched the pale child as she wandered self-consciously about the camp but kept their thoughts to themselves.

Hurt by Ana-Maïda's hostility, Ellie went to drink at the lakeside. Feeling hungry, she pulled a reed-stem to gnaw the bulbous tuber. It tasted like sludge and she flung it away after a mouthful. She seethed with a resentment she did not fully understand. It tugged her mind to a different forest glade and stone-ringed fireplace only they belonged to that other world, the place of her past which was becoming more remote and incredible every day, having no relevance to her current existence.

'Little one, Ngali-kiri, come here.' Assuming the girl was worried about the impending fight, Noumati took pity on her. Next to her foster-parents, he was her favourite and she forced down her ill-humour and went to sit beside him, avoiding the deep gaze of Pounaté who watched her with a kind of reserved curiosity.

Because she was the cause, Noumati did not want to explain the dispute to the child. Instead he tried to distract her from the almost frenzied activity going on as women and children brought in supplies for the corroboree that would follow the wrestling. First he touched her hair (which by now was matted into dirty hanks), then his own and by a mixture of mime and speech, tried to explain that though she looked different, she was still welcome. Then he took her feet onto his lap and inspected them with exaggerated care, extracting the embedded thorns with much hissing though she did not utter a sound. When he had finished, he scooped a handful of ash from the fire and rubbed it gently into the soles. Ellie found this oddly comforting and, not knowing how else to express her gratitude, hugged him, an act which seemed to surprise and please him: he smiled and held her close, like an old friend.

While the two were thus engaged, Pounaté looked on forbearingly. A little younger than Touganana, in his late forties he already seemed an old man, beard grizzled and face furrowed. The front half of his scalp was shaved, enhancing his grim appearance but his usual demeanour was one of sorrowful resignation rather than menace. He and his children had suffered greatly for the madness that had driven him to seduce his sister.

'Where does she come from?' he asked quietly, stretching out a hand gnarled as an old tree root to finger a lock of Ellie's hair. Feeling its texture, he frowned. 'Are you sure Tangalenna has the right in this quarrel? Has he forgotten what befell the others: the Toogee, the Lairmairrener, the Nuenone? What if her own people come to claim her?'

'What happened in the Disappearing no-one knows for certain,' Noumati replied evasively. 'Yet those bands were foolish: when *num* came they trusted them and so were tricked and lost to the world. We who hid and had no dealings with the strangers are still here and *num* have not tried to find us. Theirs is a separate place and our dreamings are so far apart they will never meet. And Ngali-kiri is happy here: did she not return last night instead of running away, back to her own kind?'

Pounaté grunted and shook his head. He rubbed Ellie's hair between his fingers a moment longer then let go and withdrew his hand with a sigh. 'Eh, she's here now. Though why those two have to fight over her is beyond an old man's ken. She's not even a woman yet. Still, better bruises and aching limbs now than blood spilt later. Are we not few enough already, women dying and babes stillborn, without fighting?'

'Listen to him!' Noumati ruffled Ellie's hair affectionately. She had borne the elder's touch patiently, sensing that he was wary of her, but now leaned towards the cripple, enjoying the attention. 'If you're telling me you're not looking forward to this match, I don't believe you, Pounaté. Or are the tales you tell of your own prowess all boasting?'

'Ay, but when we wrestled it wasn't so serious,' the old man replied thoughtfully. 'It was a way of showing off to the women, of proving who was strongest or most skilful: using up the energy of youth I suppose. There was none of this hate. Where does it come from? It eats at Warady like a canker.'

Noumati was too wise to answer but his silence was reply enough: Pounaté knew that the cause of his eldest son's resentment was the root of his own sorrow. Aware of their sudden awkwardness, Ellie shifted uneasily and Noumati laid a hand across her shoulders to keep her beside him, more to distract his own thoughts than for her comfort. Ana-Maïda, who was tending her cooking-fire close by, shot them a bitter glance: her own children, younger by far then this pale usurper, were tired and irritable from carrying wood all morning. He ignored her and looked into the sky.

'The sun is high.'

As if in response to these words, it was at that moment Tangalenna and Manalewa emerged from their shelter.

To the others it seemed there was a kind of sheen upon the two that day, as if they were no ordinary man and woman but had come down from the stars with the blessing of the spirits. They had risen late, neither stirring when Ellie left, though they heard the activity going on all around. Manalewa lay as she had slept, curled against Tangalenna with her hand pressed between her legs so that none of his precious seed should escape, her nipples erect still and sore from the urgency with which he had sucked them: to him it had seemed that he was drawing the very essence of her into his body, a strength and goodness like that of the earth itself. Waking to a kind of languid consciousness of each other and the morning, they knew they had overslept and did not care. A rare sense of peace wrapped them round: they did not move until the rays of sunlight falling through gaps in the woven bark were almost vertical. Then Tangalenna yawned and stretched until the muscles in his shoulders cracked and Manalewa sat up and reached for her bag of woven rushes. From it she took a pouch of wallaby skin and the stones for grinding ochre along with a piece of folded bark containing grease and a few lumps of charcoal. They adorned one another with the tenderness of lovers who know their time together may be short and when they were done, Manalewa continued to twist Tangalenna's hair, trying to prolong the moment. But then they heard Noumati's voice.

Now, as they walked out into the centre of the camp, the bloom of their love was still upon them. Tangalenna held his head proudly and his eyes were bright and fierce under his freshly ochred fringe. His skin was dark with charcoal save for the cicatrices on his arms, breast and shoulders. These had been painted with ochre and they stood out as if freshly cut so that no-one could doubt his lineage. He walked with slow, deliberate strides and the sun's rays, falling from above, made shadowed hollows of his throat and the grooves of his ribs, picked out the smooth muscles of his arms and thighs as he went to greet Pounaté. He looked what he was, a man in the fullness of his strength but there was something more than pride in the way he glanced at Ellie, a kind of intense inward focus for the sight of her had crystallised his purpose.

Walking a few paces behind as was the custom, Manalewa surveyed the camp with no less pride than her husband. Her skin also had been darkened with charcoal and Tangalenna had rubbed ochre onto her nipples, temples, cheeks and cropped scalp. Her full breasts and tight belly gleamed in the sunlight and her eyes were joyful rather than apprehensive. She bent to pull Ellie to her feet and drew the child close. It seemed to her that on such a day no misfortune could befall those she loved.

To Noumati, limping behind, what set the couple apart was their fearlessness.

With the fires stoked and food gathered, the rest of the women had cleared the wrestling ground of stones, fallen bark and branches, even leaves, anything that might give advantage to one man over the other. As Tangalenna and the others approached, they moved aside. A circle roughly ten metres in diameter was formed, the women and children occupying one half, the men the other, sitting widely spaced to define the arena. Everyone sat down except for Tangalenna who remained standing near the centre. An expectant hush fell.

Tupali and Tanglémerna came late to the circle but Warady was not with them. They sat down without speaking and their faces were closed and scornful. A raven croaked far away and a breath of wind rustled the leaves overhead and whispered in the lakeside reeds. The only other sound was the noisy guzzling of the babe at Ana-Maïda's breast. Her other children looked round with worried eyes, daunted by the atmosphere of anticipation but not understanding it.

Tangalenna waited a little longer before stepping back to squint into the sky. So obvious was his meaning he had no need to speak. Then he shrugged and glanced at Pounaté. The old man held his gaze a moment then looked away, embarrassed. Both knew that if Warady failed to meet his own challenge, he would become a figure of ridicule: such shame could never be wiped out. And for that reason Tangalenna waited on. Warady was Manalewa's brother: he did not want her suffering on his behalf.

The sun had slipped past its zenith when Warady arrived, walking out of the forest from where he had been watching and working himself into battle frenzy. Like Tangalenna, he had darkened his skin with charcoal and ochred his hair but he had outlined his ribs, sternum, eye-sockets and mouth with white clay. Pounaté shook his head sadly at this, seeing in his son's war-paint not only an expression of hatred but a rejection of his ancestry.

Warady did not speak but strode straight into the circle, stopping when he was within arm's length of his opponent. His body glistened: he had coated himself with grease to make his adversary's task more difficult. Seeing this, Tangalenna stooped to rub his palms in the dust. There was no doubting his rival's aggression: a rank smell rose from Warady's skin and his penis was erect, the engorged tip flicking upwards a little at every heartbeat while his eyes had taken on a glazed, mad look. They fixed on Tangalenna's face as he straightened and he bared his teeth. 'Woman's heart!' he hissed.

'That will be seen,' answered Tangalenna grimly and he launched himself at the young man without waiting upon further ceremony.

There were no rules in such matches save that punching was not allowed: the fight was deemed to be over when a combatant submitted or was unable to continue. Blindings, dislocations, broken bones, occasional killings were not unknown even in bouts between women which, while uncommon, occurred when a dispute could not be resolved any other way. To bite or scratch was considered a woman's way of fighting but there was nothing subtle in the wrestling: the only aim was to disable your opponent before he hurt you.

It was years since there had been this serious a contest and so strongly did the onlookers identify with the combatants, they swayed, groaned or shouted encouragement as the fight swung first one way, then the other.

Tangalenna's sudden onslaught had taken Warady by surprise and he was borne backwards. But while shorter in stature than his opponent, he was more squarely built and managed to keep his feet, twisting low in an effort to break Tangalenna's grip and butting savagely with his head. As they pushed against each other, arms locked together, each kicked out, trying to hook his adversary's legs. Their breath came in short, harsh gasps; the muscles writhed in their shoulders and backs, drops of sweat rolled down their bodies. So well matched were they in strength and skill that it seemed they would struggle thus until both collapsed from exhaustion.

However, the grease Warady had rubbed over himself made him slippery as an eel: Tangalenna felt himself tiring more quickly than he had expected. He knew he must try a different tactic. As Warady tried to knee him in the groin, Tangalenna broke free of the armlock in which they had striven for so long and dived for his enemy's legs, pulling him down as he crashed to the ground.

The crowd gasped and yelled as the pair grappled together and rolled over, first one gaining ascendancy, then the other. They were even in weight so that when Warady at last managed to pin his opponent down, sitting astride him and grasping handfuls of hair, intending to bash Tangalenna's head against the ground, his advantage lasted only a moment. Tangalenna gave a mighty heave to free his arms then thrust at Warady's face, aiming rigid fingers at his eyes.

Of the two, Tangalenna had the longer reach. Warady flinched and his grip loosened slightly, enough for Tangalenna to throw him off and reverse their positions. But it was not Tangalenna's purpose to kill or cripple his enemy. He managed to catch hold Warady's wrists and pressed them against the earth, ignoring the knees pummelling his back. Warady jerked and writhed and it was like Tangalenna's first hunt as a boy of thirteen when he had speared a wallaby as heavy as himself, then wrapped his arms around its neck and held tight until at last it weakened and died. Now, as then, he hung on grimly, staring remorselessly into his rival's wild eyes, waiting for him to submit, to cease fighting and accept defeat with as much dignity as he possessed. But he had underestimated his brother-in-law's animosity. Warady continued to struggle, his body slick with sweat as well as grease. Tangalenna's arms began to tremble with the effort of holding him; the breath rasped in his throat. He shook the sweat from his eyes and in a low, harsh whisper that only Warady could hear, said, 'Give up now: I don't want to hurt you.'

Warady's eyes narrowed in a look of such loathing that Tangalenna shuddered. Without slackening his grip on his adversary's wrists (the hands were clenched defiantly into fists), he twisted forward and pressed his elbow against Warady's neck, pushing one knee hard into his groin at the same time. 'Submit!'

As his breathing became more and more constricted, the violence of Warady's efforts increased. His face darkened and blood suffused his eyeballs but still he fought on though the thrashing of his body was no longer fully under his control but came from the involuntary spasm of oxygen-starved muscles. And his stubbornness turned Tangalenna's anger to a kind of frenzy, a need to stop the desperate striving for life going on beneath his hands. With a force that seemed to come from beyond the limits of his strength, Tangalenna pressed harder upon his enemy's throat, felt the struggles gradually subside and tightened his grip. It seemed to him that a dark power surged through his blood, roaring like a great wind, unstoppable as a torrent. As Warady's body heaved and his bowels broke, Tangalenna's whole being swelled with the glory of taking a life. This was power: he had become death.

The spectators had fallen silent but none intervened. By refusing to submit, Warady had surrendered himself to the mercy of his enemy. Even Ana-Maïda did not move or speak; her children stared, transfixed, at their father's throes, thinking them part of some savage game.

Ellie watched appalled as the fight changed from what had seemed no more than brutal sport to deadly combat and Tangalenna pressed home his attack. She also had been on the receiving end of his strength and nausea rushed through her: Warady's desperate wheezing and the stench of shit reminded her of the abduction. She leant forward, hands clenched, then got to her feet, drawn by a kind of morbid fascination. So involved were both hearth-groups in the unfolding drama, none heeded her as she edged slowly into the circle. A single thought ran like a refrain through her mind: 'I am watching a man being killed.' Somehow none of it seemed real.

'Stop!' So shrill and unexpected was her cry, it shattered the spell of greedy anticipation that gripped the onlookers: to Tangalenna it was like being doused in icy water. In that instant his blood-lust evaporated and it seemed to him that he awoke from a dream. He rolled away from his adversary and got unsteadily to his feet, staring at his hands as if unable to believe what he had done. Pieces of torn-up grass and earth stuck to his skin and the lacerations from falling down the cliff bled freely: he looked more like the victim of some natural disaster than a triumphant victor. He paced forward and nudged the inert body with his foot.

'He should not have insulted me,' he said.

As if these words had opened a flood-gate, Manalewa and the others rushed forward, shouting and laughing, to share in the honour and joy of his victory. Even Warady's kin were bound to join in. By tradition, wrestling matches were fought to resolve conflicts, not exacerbate them and so clear an outcome could not be challenged.

Left alone, Ellie stood unmoving, astounded by the change from dreadful anticipation to celebration. Her cry had burst incontinently from her lips and afterwards she had been terrified that she would be punished for stopping the fight. But it was as if no-one cared or even remembered it. They crowded round Tangalenna and some stretched out their hands to touch him as if some of his luck and strength would rub off onto them. He walked with them back into camp, proud in the acknowledgement of his victory.

Warady was left as he had fallen, limbs asprawl and motionless. When his anxious children lagged behind to look, they were pulled roughly away. Not even his closest kin wanted to be associated with him. They joined in as the feasting began and their backs were turned towards the wrestling ground.

Horrified yet fascinated by what she had witnessed, Ellie could not tear herself away. She crept closer to what she, like the rest, assumed was a corpse, then froze. With a horrible sucking inhalation, the body suddenly twitched and shuddered. Ellie looked round lest any of the others had witnessed it then turned her attention back to Warady, ready to flee. Dying or waking, she did not want him to know she was there.

To Warady, the return of consciousness was less painful than the realisation of defeat. All his life he had taken pleasure in bullying those weaker than himself: now he tasted the bitterness of humiliation. He listened to the excited voices and laughter from the camp, smelled the freshly cooked meat and knew they had already forgotten him. In an effort to deny this, he kept his eyes shut and lay still, longing for the blackness to return even if it was the oblivion of death. But his senses would not be still. There was the noise of celebration, the dancing and feasting: he was alive and he had been soundly beaten by a man who had stolen a *num* outcast to replace his own failed offspring, a woman-hearted dreamer who preferred the company of a bastard cripple to that of real men.

Warady ground his teeth and as the full magnitude of his shame dawned on him, he bit at the ground to prevent himself crying out. A gritty paste filled his mouth: he spat it out and groaned then, opening his eyes, saw the pale child, his enemy's fosterling, standing alone, watching him with those green eyes that were like stones. Next moment she turned and ran but at the sight of her the thought of a just and fitting revenge sprang to his mind, one that would crush Tangalenna more completely than any defeat in a wrestling match.

A malicious smile twisted Warady's face as the idea took shape. He remembered Noumati's tale of the eagle and the raven: Black Snake also possessed cunning and patience. He was prepared to wait half a lifetime to bring about Tangalenna's downfall and that the cause should be the child for whom his enemy had risked so much was something to savour long after the plan came to fruition. For now he would bide his time, leave Tangalenna thinking he had won a lasting victory, then, when the girl was of age, he would strike. He cast a baleful look towards the camp, levered himself to his feet and shuffled painfully into the forest.

The celebrations lasted well into the night and Warady was not seen by anyone except Ana-Maïda. He watched from just within the trees and sprang on her when she returned surreptitiously to the wrestling ground to tend her husband's corpse. She became almost hysterical at the sight of him but he told her sternly to be quiet and sent her to fetch food. Although she obeyed, it was with less than her usual submissiveness and after he had eaten, he thrust her to the ground and took her with such violence she could hardly walk afterwards. Then he returned to the shelter of the forest, leaving her to stumble back into camp alone

Chapter 7.

It was by chance that the hearth-groups had come together and two days after the fight, they parted. To Ellie's relief, Warady went with his parents and Tupali, taking Ana-Maïda and the children with him. Only Touganana was sorrowful at their leaving.

Noumati looked on with unfriendly eyes as Warady swaggered around the camp prior to departure. Restored to his own kin instead of being forced to provide for his wife's, it was as if his defeat was of no account. Rather than witness his enemy's strutting, Tangalenna went off to hunt though Ellie suspected he had not gone far but was merely waiting for the group to leave: he returned empty-handed as soon as they were out of sight.

Life for Touganana's hearth-group, though never easy, was more relaxed after Warady's departure. That summer was a good one, the weather warm and rain plentiful, making food abundant. The wattle flowers had barely faded when Manalewa's body began to exhibit the bloom of pregnancy and Tangalenna's eyes gleamed with pride whenever he looked at her. With the spiteful influence of his rival removed, he was certain this babe would be born strong and healthy and, respectful of his daemon, he valued the pale child even more for it seemed to him that her coming had brought good fortune. Thus as Manalewa's belly swelled and she became slow and deliberate in all her actions, Tangalenna treated Ellie with a kind of grave and loving tenderness and he was more indulgent towards her than he would have been to a daughter of his blood.

Tangalenna's fondness was, however, not reciprocated. Since witnessing the savagery of his fight with Warady, Ellie's fear of her foster-father had returned: she could never quite forget that he was also her abductor. Although she enjoyed the attention he lavished upon her, she remained wary: it was Noumati, her confidant and friend, upon whom she bestowed her affections. Tangalenna was secretly hurt by this and though he told himself he was a fool to be so affected by a child, the feeling would not go away.

As the weeks passed, Ellie became more assimilated into Meelayginnee culture and alienated from her own. The shock of her abduction and the days of travelling to join the hearth group had acted like a rite of passage to ease her from one existence into another. As an adult is unable to recall infancy save by selective, dislocated memories, so her former life became remote to her, a time and place to which there could be no returning. Thus she did not mourn or yearn for the family and friends left behind. They had simply become irrelevant though sometimes she dreamt of that world and would wake feeling confused and strangely bereft.

Noumati listened gravely when she confided these dreams to him and, conscious of her distress, tried hard to make her laugh and forget but in his heart he was deeply troubled by her description of unknown, impossible things. Tangalenna, who understood at least in part what she was alluding to, grew morose and angry if he overheard her talking of her former life: she soon learned when to keep silent. But as she became fluent in their language and began to comprehend the nature of things as the Meelayginnee perceived them, so she grew to interpret the memories of her former life as her own dreaming, distinct from the dreams of the others as her skin and hair were different.

It was a particular world in which she found herself, one where rock formations, trees, rivers, lakes had mythical significance, many acting as reminders of the past, both in the Pygeewar, before people were created and in the aeons since, up to the present. And though, as a child, she was not privy to some of the lore, Noumati, who had never had such an eager and attentive listener, nor one with so many strange tales to tell in return, spent much of his time with the girl until Touganana reminded him sternly that she was a minor and would leave the group when she came of age and was betrothed. Then the cripple was downcast and though she tried hard, Ellie could not wholly dissipate his sorrow.

Winter came and the group moved further down the valley to a great swamp surrounded by dense growth of tea-tree and blackwood. Here the climate was milder than in the highlands and there were many kinds of waterfowl to supplement the wallaby and possum meat that formed their staples. The catching of the birds was wet and difficult work because they had to be driven down blind inlets in the reeds where it was impossible for them to take off. It was tradition that the women acted as drivers so Ellie, Touganana and Manalewa paddled out on the water in flimsy rafts made of bark, reeds and branches or else waded up to their necks while Tangalenna and Noumati waited in the reeds to club the trapped birds to death.

One day when they caught five black swans, more than they could eat, Ellie begged that one should be brought back alive and kept to eat later. They pinioned it and she broke the long primary feathers as she had seen her father clip the wings of ducks and chickens on the farm. To keep it safe from quolls and devils, she insisted that the bird share their shelter. Tangalenna was outraged by such an idea and after the first night when it hissed and snapped at the slightest movement, he demanded it stay outside. She made it a pen, much to the amusement of the others but when, after a week of poor hunting and wild weather, they feasted on swan meat, even her foster-father was forced to admit the innovation was a good one. After that, whenever they hunted birds, they caught and pinioned as many as they killed. Though the strategy made Noumati uneasy, (for while they were breaking no law, the keeping of the birds seemed to disturb some innate balance), he could not deny its efficiency: where they would have gone hungry they now had food on demand and so he pushed his misgivings aside. In any case, being the weakest hunter in the group he had no right to complain.

On the farm, Ellie had been particularly susceptible to the cold and would don gloves and scarf as soon as the first frosts came. Tangalenna's people made no concession to winter temperatures except to smear themselves thickly with fat. This had the double effect of insulating them and protecting them from rain and Ellie discovered an unexpected sense of freedom in walking about naked on blustery, wet days, uninhibited by the encumbrance of clothes and boots. By now her feet had hardened and she was so accustomed to using her toes to grip bare rocks, slippery logs and the trunks of trees she scaled in search for possums, she scorned the very idea of shoes. To wear the kind of crude moccasins fashioned by the Meelayginnee was, in any case, an indication of weakness: only those lamed by injury or from birth went shod.

Noumati, who wore a piece of tough wombat skin tied around his deformed foot at all times, watched her development with a mixture of pride and sorrow. She had rejected his offer to protect her feet the same way and he had tried to hide his pain, fearful that as she gained in skills and confidence, she would grow to despise him. But his fears proved groundless. His tales and kindness had captured the girl's heart at the very beginning and the bond between them gradually strengthened for as Manalewa's pregnancy developed, she and Tangalenna became more distant towards their foster-child lest the spirit of the unborn one grew jealous and it refused to come into the world.

As the time of the birth approached, the weather worsened. It was long past midwinter but days of sleet made the animals keep to dense scrub and the birds on the lake had grown nervous of people. The burden of hunting fell mainly on Tangalenna and he would often be away for days. Anxiety for Manalewa and the physical hardship he endured wore him and he lost weight more rapidly than the rest who spent much of their time huddled inside their shelters. When he returned, he would fling down his kill, crawl inside and sleep, waking only when the meat was cooked and the feasting began.

Fire was vital for the survival of the group at this time of year and though the nurturing of it was ultimately Touganana's responsibility, the tasks of collecting fuel and keeping a supply of dry kindling at hand fell largely to Ellie. She soon discovered where the best tinder was to be found and that often when a fire appeared dead, eucalypt bark and leaves were so flammable that it could be re-kindled while there was warmth in the ashes. Even so, there were many nights of gales and torrential rain when she lay awake dreading that the deluge had finally extinguished the last precious embers. From Noumati she had learned that the Meelayginnee had no method of making fire: it was the gift of Lightning and therefore sacred. But in the winter, while storms were sometimes so violent that thunder rolled in the valley like the grinding of huge boulders, the forest was often too wet to burn and this made Ellie's task even more important for they had no alternative source if the hearth-fire was extinguished.

The difficulties plaguing the group increased when Ellie's nose began to run. She shrugged off the illness as a simple cold but the rest succumbed swiftly to the virus and Manalewa, weakened by hunger and the demands of the growing foetus on her body, developed a fever and cough which turned to pneumonia, a sickness the Meelayginnee had no name for.

Tangalenna was away hunting, a task which had become ever more dangerous and desperate as his own weakness increased and game grew scarcer. Noumati, his eyes and nose streaming, helped Ellie to keep the fire blazing day and night (though the work of collecting extra fuel exhausted them both), and Touganana roamed marsh and scrub, searching for fungi and roots so that at least they would have something to put into their stomachs. While they worked, Manalewa lay in the hut they all now shared for warmth. She was too weak to move; her swollen belly stuck up grotesquely and when she coughed it seemed her ribs would snap under the strain. After each paroxysm she would sink back and lapse into a stupor until the next fit racked her.

As soon as it was clear that Manalewa was seriously ill, Ellie had expected the others to help care for her. But though they supplied her with food and water (the latter in a piece of hollow bark since they lacked bowls or drinking vessels), they appeared to be more concerned over Tangalenna's reaction if he returned to find his wife and unborn child dead than for the sick woman's welfare. Neither Noumati nor Touganana deigned to clear away the soiled bedding though the stench inside the hut was overpowering and they watched Ellie undertake the task with a mixture of amusement and amazement, dismissing the need for basic hygiene as a whim.

Since none of the others seemed to understand the concept of nursing the sick, it was Ellie who took over her foster-mother's care. When Manalewa was racked by shivering, the girl laid every wallaby skin she could find over to warm her; when her skin burned with fever, Ellie washed her with handfuls of wet moss and during the coughing fits it was she who helped the sick woman into a sitting position and wiped away the blood-stained mucus without flinching.

At school Ellie had learned that diseases brought by Europeans had been partly responsible for the demise of the indigenous Tasmanian population and though those days in the classroom now seemed like a dream, she felt inchoately that Manalewa's illness was her fault. At times she caught Noumati watching her with a hard, suspicious expression though if he thought she had noticed, he glanced away or spoke lightly as if nothing was wrong.

The Disappearing of the other bands was a subject almost taboo among the Meelayginnee, in part from ignorance but mainly due to a superstitious fear that simply to speak of it was to invite a similar calamity upon themselves. Thus neither Noumati nor Ellie discussed the matter yet as Manalewa's sickness worsened and Touganana began to cough, the knowledge remained and acted as a barrier between them so that they became awkward and distant when they had most need of one other's support.

Days dragged past and still there was no sign of Tangalenna. No-one remarked upon his absence and what it might signify yet it overshadowed every waking moment save for the sick whose every breath had become a struggle. Lacking vessels in which to heat water, Ellie could not make steam for them to inhale but she picked tea-tree and pungent gum leaves and mixed these with precious fat to make an ointment which she smeared on their chests and throats. The clean astringent scents purified the foetid air inside the hut and gradually the condition of both women improved. Then, at last, the hunter returned.

He was weary, his skin torn and scratched from forcing his way through dense scrub, but his expedition had been successful and he bore the carcass of a large male wallaby minus the right foreleg and shoulder which, in his hunger, he had eaten raw. When Noumati went to greet him, he smiled and waved but when he was close enough to see his half-brother's expression, Tangalenna dropped the meat and hurried inside.

Manalewa's fever had abated and she was aware of her surroundings but from her wasted limbs and sunken cheeks Tangalenna saw at once how close she had been to death and a cold hand seemed to tighten about his heart and lungs. Then, noting the pile of fresh leaves beside her head and the thick salve on her chest he frowned, fingering the bone talisman that hung at his breast. The healing power of such amulets was the age-old remedy against all kinds of sickness and he was uneasy as he watched Ellie tend the old woman, whose fever was mounting rapidly, lest the spirits of the dead be offended. Almost he was tempted to throw the leaves and the bark curl containing the ointment onto the fire but he did not dare: there was an air of authority about the child which daunted him. Instead he crouched to touch Manalewa's brow to reassure himself that she was truly alive. With an effort, she caught hold his wrist to keep him there and whispered, 'Myrtle-Tree came but it was not the time. Ngali-kiri sent him away.' An ancient myrtle close to the sacred gorge was her daemon.

With fresh meat and Ellie's continuing care, Manalewa recovered quickly but Touganana was slow to regain her health and was left with a persistent dry cough. The weather improved, becoming warm and dry though game remained elusive and Tangalenna was more often away on the hunting trail than in camp. Before the Disappearing, the group would have spent the winter months on the coast where they would have been assured of food: shellfish and seal-meat supplemented by, if they were lucky, a beached whale. Now they stayed within their own bounds, Nana Bone's warnings entrenched in custom. And Tangalenna, having glimpsed the changes wrought by *num* upon the very nature of the land, sensed that this tradition safeguarded the band's very survival: once it was broken they also might disappear. In any case, with Manalewa about to give birth, to move camp was impossible.

Tangalenna was away when Manalewa's labour started. As was the custom among her people, she left the hut when the waters broke and stole away to a crude shelter in the brush she had prepared secretly as soon as she was strong enough to walk. Here she squatted and gritted her teeth as the pains increased in frequency but when they grew stronger she could not restrain her cries.

Having no experience of the agonies of a natural birth, Ellie had to be physically restrained from running to help when she heard the screams and groans coming from the edge of the scrub. Both Touganana and Noumati did their best to comfort the girl but she was almost sick with worry. Yet for Manalewa, for whom this was the third labour, there was no fear. She had felt the babe alive inside her before the pangs began and so crouched, panting, and pushed with all her strength and the child was born alive within a few hours.

It was a boy and the lust for life was strong in him: he wailed and stretched out his arms and when she put him to her breast, slimy with womb-grease and blood as he was, he sucked so hard it hurt. Tears of joy and triumph sprang to Manalewa's eyes; she bit the cord to free him and after the last pangs had expelled the afterbirth she wrapped him in a wallaby skin and made her way back into camp.

The day of the boy's birth (for the first few months he would be known only as Cotruluttyé: 'new one'), was truly auspicious for Tangalenna returned from his hunting with a fat possum and a young, tender wallaby. The group feasted well into the night. At length, his belly tight and full, Tangalenna went into the hut where his wife and child were already asleep and took them carefully in his arms. That day he had seen a pair of pink robins fighting, a sure sign that spring was on the way and he sighed contentedly. His world was complete.

To Ellie the arrival of a healthy babe was like a gift. She had always wanted a younger brother or sister to look after: now, that wish was granted. After the first few days Manalewa was happy to relinquish care of the infant to so eager a helper: it freed her for the tasks of food and fuel gathering and relieved Touganana who was still weak though she tried to hide it. In truth Ellie was appalled by the apparent indifference of the group towards the babe once the first novelty had subsided. Ignorant of the true harshness of the environment in which she found herself, she ascribed their seeming lack of care to callousness when it was, in fact, a stoic acceptance of the reality that many children born in the winter died within a few weeks of birth and boys were more susceptible to sickness and cold than girls. Necessity dictated that there was no place for the weak and little tolerance of the sick in Meelayginnee culture.

Between Ellie and Manalewa however, this child thrived for his mother provided rich and plentiful milk and the girl made sure he was kept warm and dry (the others would have left him lying at the bottom of a tree while they climbed after possums and thought nothing of it). Indeed, even Manalewa considered the amount of time Ellie lavished on Cotruluttyé, dangling twigs or feathers to entertain him or rocking him to sleep when she should have been busy elsewhere, an unprecedented extravagance. And when she tried to fashion a nappy from a piece of hide lined with grass and moss they watched incredulously and laughed and the babe added his screams to the din until Ellie admitted defeat and resigned herself to letting him go naked as the rest.

Touganana, who felt her authority threatened by the girl's strange and innovative customs, was openly disapproving at first but she knew that without Ellie's care, she, Manalewa and the unborn child would most likely have died from the lung sickness. Therefore she kept her grumblings to herself and if Ellie was at first discomfited by the hostile glances the old woman sometimes directed at her, she soon learned to disregard them. Tangalenna's attitude towards his foster-daughter also softened as his son grew stronger; as for Noumati, his doubts had all been assuaged. Sometimes, when he watched Ellie playing with the babe, he imagined it was their child she dandled and a warm flood would suffuse his loins but then he would berate himself bitterly for such idle maundering: as a cripple and the product of incest, he had little right to a woman of his own. What that meant for Ngali-kiri in the future, he refused to contemplate.

Winter at last released its hold, the wattles burst into flower and the warmth made life a little easier for the group. As soon as the old woman was strong enough and Manalewa fully recovered from the birth, they moved back into the highlands though rather than retrace their steps towards the sacred gorge, they went north-west. Here, ridge after ridge of mountains drove their rocky spikes skywards and the forest was dense. The canopy was so thick that for days they saw little of the sky and nothing of the terrain they were crossing save the few metres of wallaby trail twisting before them.

In this manner, an incessant wandering, the group moved in an endless circuit. Their movement was not random but fixed as the migration of stars according to the changing seasons. As time passed, Ellie's body adapted to the rigors of this life until from a distance she was indistinguishable from the others, skin tanned and dirt-ingrained, limbs wiry, belly protruding because of the worm infestation they all suffered from eating poorly-cooked meat. Her hair, which had formerly hung rippling to her waist was harsh and matted and reached barely to her shoulders. Only her narrow features and green eyes marked her out and her gaze was startling, so unexpected the contrast between eye colour and skin. As she approached puberty her flesh took on a healthy sheen and the development of breasts alternately dismayed and pleased her. Sometimes, when she cuddled her foster-brother, she felt a delicious ache in her ripening body, a longing she could not name.

In the years since her son's birth, Manalewa had been pregnant twice. The first baby, another boy, had been born sickly and died after a few days despite Ellie's efforts to save it but the second, a girl, shared the little boy (now called Cuckana)'s vitality. Manalewa became pregnant again soon after the birth of her daughter and provided little milk but Ellie chewed food for both children and they thrived.

During those years, the hearth group had seen nothing of the other members of the band: Pounaté's group and Tanglémerna's kin, the Broad Ridge people. Tangalenna suspected the old man was deliberately avoiding a meeting which might lead to further confrontation. But the time was approaching when Ngali-kiri would come of age. A corroboree must be arranged and her betrothal decided.

Ellie was now fluent in Meelayginnee speech. She rarely thought in English and only spoke it when trying to describe something for which they had no word. But as she had embraced their culture, so had some of hers become assimilated into theirs. The pinioning of wildfowl was one example and she taught the children to count to a hundred (the Meelayginnee simply described any number over three as *mabbola*: 'plenty'), and the letters of the alphabet which they considered a great game. And Noumati, with his insatiable appetite for tales, constantly asked her about the animals and customs of a world alien to all he knew thus 'television', 'car', 'cow', 'footy', 'school' became entrenched in their tongue though they had a poor understanding of what these things were. When Ellie taught them the kind of improvised footy she had played with her brothers, using a stuffed wallaby bladder as a ball, it was a great success, the whole group joining in except the matriarch, Touganana, who looked on forbearingly.

So distant did Ellie's former life now seem, she wondered sometimes if the memories she was sometimes able to dredge from that time were simply imagined. She was often startled when she bent over a pool to drink and saw her reflection, so different from the faces she was used to seeing around her. Some of her former insecurity returned and she was ashamed, a feeling exacerbated by Tangalenna's changing attitude towards her. At times she caught him staring with a fierce intentness that reminded her of the days following her abduction. Now, as then, she sensed an element of fear or dread in his demeanour, as if he were somehow uncertain of himself.

Though he concealed it from the others, most especially Manalewa, it was the girl's future, more specifically the part he would play in it, that tormented Tangalenna. His dreaming had led him to take her but she was no longer a child. As he looked at her slim, lithe figure, met those startling green eyes, noted her budding breasts and the wholesome smoothness of her skin, desire stirred in him, a yearning he found more difficult to quell as she matured. Traditionally, his people were monogamous (though it was not unknown in times of unusual hardship for a man to take two wives so that the women could help each other), but he found himself arguing that since she was his captive and no blood-relation to any of the Meelayginnee, he could lawfully mate with her. Yet he did not voice these thoughts aloud.

Noumati alone guessed the strength of Tangalenna's feelings and it aroused gnawing envy in him and an anger that was rooted in self-pity. One day as he went to shit, he heard a groan and when he crept to investigate, found Tangalenna masturbating while he watched Ngali-kiri from the cover of the trees. After that Noumati treated his half-brother with a kind of polite diffidence though underneath he simmered with resentment. He knew he could never challenge Tangalenna since a fight would simply bring further humiliation, and this increased his bitterness. When Ellie tried to discover the cause of his unhappiness, he spoke to her more roughly than ever before and sent her away though her stricken look smote his heart. As for Tangalenna, he did not realise he had been seen, nor would he have cared. He did not consider the cripple a rival.

Already alarmed by the physical changes to her body, Ellie was deeply disturbed by the sensations that overwhelmed her one night when Tangalenna relieved his lust not upon the object of his desire but his pregnant wife. His people were unselfconscious about bodily functions, including sex and it excited him that the girl, lying just beyond arm's reach on the other side of the shelter, could hear and smell his love-making. Manalewa, braced to protect the foetus inside her, made no sound as her husband thrust violently into her and her silence made his grunts seem all the louder. The strong smell of his sweat filled Elllie's nostrils; she was gripped by a wild, unimagined excitement and her hands explored her body, probing and caressing: she yearned for him to stroke and fill her. When Tangalenna shuddered and groaned in climax, the girl also quivered. For an instant, poised between pain and pleasure, she was frightened then waves of sensation rolled from her very core, engulfing consciousness, sweeping coherent thought away.

A tiny, pathetic sound, Manalewa's whimper as her husband withdrew, ended Ellie's rapture. She was horrified to discover her fingers deep inside her cleft: when she snatched them back a tingling feeling shot from between her legs into the very centre of her body, followed by a grinding pain. Shame, guilty delight and fear merged with the sounds of Manalewa weeping quietly and Tangalenna's snores as he sank into a sated slumber: Ellie stared into the darkness and wondered whether anyone had ever felt like this before.

Next day, when she was halfway up a tree after a possum, Ellie felt a sharp twinge in her groin as if a remorseless hand were wrenching the muscle fibres apart. The Meelayginnee ascended trees using grass ropes and notches cut in the bark as footholds and Ellie, light and strong for her height, was the best climber in the hearth-group though her lack of weight was against her when it came to yanking a full-grown brush-tail down. Usually her task was to frighten the animal onto a branch that would snap under it or to drive it down to where the other women waited with clubs. This time, scared by the severity of the pain and wondering if it had something to do with the experiences of the night, she dropped to the ground. Manalewa and Touganana looked worried so she muttered '*Tia-noile*' by way of explanation and rushed into the nearest bushes (loose bowels were a common ailment among a people whose diet consisted largely of half-raw meat). Once hidden, she crouched and pressed her hand tentatively between her legs. Her fingers came away slick with blood.

At fourteen, Ellie had a more scientific understanding of the facts of life than any of the people she now lived among but no amount of education could lessen the impact of this discovery. She stared at the dark, glossy liquid and, without knowing why, began to weep. In that moment she felt lonelier than at any time since the first days of her abduction, realising intuitively that Tangalenna's intensity and Noumati's unhappiness were to do with the fact that she was no longer a child but a young woman.

She heard Manalewa calling but crouched lower in the thicket. It seemed to her that if she kept her condition secret she would be safe, could pretend to be a child still. The burden of womanhood seemed to press upon her like a heavy hand. As soon as the others knew she was menstruating, she would be forced to undergo the initiation that would mark her forever as one of Touganana's hearth-group and they would choose her a husband. Even Noumati did not know the full history of the rituals accompanying the transition from childhood to adulthood but he was full of tales of the dire fortune of those who chose to defy them.

When at last Manalewa came to find the girl, she understood at once what had happened. She was sympathetic as any mother but secretly she was also relieved. The changed attitude of her husband towards their foster-daughter had not gone unnoticed and she had begun to suspect his motives in bringing the girl to their hearth. Now Ngali-kiri would go to another hearth-group, out of Tangalenna's sight and also, she hoped, his thoughts. Thus although Ellie begged her to keep silent, Manalewa lost no time in telling Touganana and her husband that the girl was *teebra*.

For Ellie, already acutely conscious of her swollen belly and the moss plugging her vagina, the fact that everyone knew was like a nightmare. It was impossible to be alone for the women relied upon her to care for the children. The only comfort was that the bleeding would stop after a few days but even that was no real consolation: every month she would go through the same ordeal unless she was pregnant and that was something she was not ready to contemplate.

Tangalenna spent the next few days hunting, bringing back enough meat to feed the group for a week or more. Then he walked out of camp and did not return. No-one, even Noumati, would tell Ellie where he was though they all seemed anxious. At first Ellie assumed he had had a sign from Korunah and gone to a sacred place but this did not usually cause concern: whilst dreaming, he was under the protection of his daemon. One night Manalewa's screams woke everyone: she had dreamt that her brothers had ambushed Tangalenna, spearing him in the belly and leaving him to die. After that, Ellie knew he had gone to find the rest of the band.

Chapter 8.

Instead of waiting for Tangalenna's return, the group moved on, heading east. Their pace was leisurely yet Ellie sensed a growing anticipation among her companions. From Noumati's silence and the teasing of the two women it was obvious that whatever was being planned she would be its focus. When she asked Touganana what would happen, the matriarch told her the rituals involved in the initiation ceremony were a closely guarded secret but that they amounted to a test of courage and willpower. Only the bravest and most steadfast, the old woman said gravely, merited a husband and the right to bear children.

It was this veiled reference to her future that forced Ellie to full awareness of her situation. Up till then, life with the Meelayginnee had almost seemed like some kind of game despite the hardships she had endured: although memories of her former life had the remoteness of a dream, they were a talisman for the future. Deep within had lurked the belief that someday, somehow, she would leave this place as she had entered it. Now she realised that this was for life. Her flesh would be cut to mark her assumed lineage and then she would be given to a man, a stranger from another group, to tend his every need and bear his children. When she died, she would be burned on a pyre in the forest and no-one from her own culture would ever know what had happened to her.

In the years since her abduction, Ellie had never tried to escape, mainly because she believed there was no possibility of finding her way home without help. From the moment Tangalenna had taken her from the widow-maker, she had seen and heard nothing to indicate what time or place his people occupied. Occasionally she had heard a distant droning like plane or helicopter engines but she never discovered the cause because the Meelayginnee hid whenever they heard it. Noumati explained it was the buzzing of an evil being called Raguwrapper which flew around searching for the unwary: those it found were left as empty husks, incapable of speech or movement, their spirits stolen away. Whilst Ellie did not believe this, she followed their example. In her Tasmania, ancient aboriginal culture had been all but destroyed more than a hundred and fifty years before her birth, therefore the Meelayginnee must occupy a parallel, separate, world. It was simple logic to conclude that the noise could not come from any kind of aircraft she knew.

Now, despite this conviction, Ellie considered running away but she soon dismissed the idea. She did not, in any case, know where to go. Common sense told her that even with the skills she had acquired, she would be lucky to last long. A fall, a twisted ankle, could mean death to those who wandered alone in the forest. However hard life might be with a man possibly brutal as Warady, it was preferable to a lingering death from thirst or starvation. And she knew also that if she fled and they came after, she would be caught. The shame of that, the idea that her foster-parents would think they had raised a child afraid of her own womanhood, made up her mind. Only a coward tries to escape the inevitable: she had been brought up as, and would prove herself, one of them.

In this frame of mind, both resolute and apprehensive, Ellie came to the riverside camp below the sacred gorge. It was not the first time they had returned since her awakening there but this time she had a sense of having come full circle. Her childhood was nearly over and it was a mark of how completely she had integrated with Tangalenna's people that at fourteen years old she did not think this strange but normal and right. And as any aboriginal woman might have done, once resigned to her future she did not brood upon it. There was too much else to occupy her. Thus she helped Manalewa and Touganana patch up the shelters and kindled a fire while Noumati sat under a tree, pointedly ignoring the children who were vying for his attention.

Despite the storyteller's ill-humour (a mood that deepened as the days passed), it was pleasant by the river. It was now late spring and the weather was mild: swallows returned from the north and their wings flashed in the sunlight as they swooped low over the water to drink or catch insects. Once the camp had been established, a feeling of holiday overtook Ellie. She took a joyous delight in the most mundane tasks and when she caught Manalewa looking at her askance, laughed at her foster-mother's grimness and busied herself elsewhere. Often she took the children to the riverside. While they played, she sat idly watching the rush of the water, the plop and swirl whenever a fish rose after a fly, the dance of light on the dark, glassy surface,.

Afterwards she realised that the poignant happiness of those days was because this was a last chance to savour the relatively carefree existence she had experienced as a child. When Tangalenna returned with the rest of the band, all that would change. Every day of his absence was therefore a reprieve, a gift, infinitely precious. But as the season turned towards summer and the weather became more capricious so that it could be sleeting one day, so hot they took to the river to cool themselves the next, even Ellie was affected by the apprehension that affected the others. Though no-one spoke of it, it was long past the time when Tangalenna should have returned.

Manalewa was most obviously worried by her husband's continuing absence. Fretted also by the child growing in her womb she became thin and uncharacteristically nervous: at times she and Noumati argued bitterly. Their strained voices made Ellie inordinately uncomfortable, stirring half-forgotten memories, and she would pick up the baby and lead the toddler to where the noise of the river or the wind in the trees drowned the bickering. Touganana would watch her go, her expression inscrutable as always: if she was concerned about her son, she did not show it.

To the dismay of all, Pounaté's group arrived without Tangalenna. The old man looked concerned to find his son-in-law missing for it was many days since he had invited them to the corroboree. He had stayed one night, then gone to find Tanglémerna's kin. Warady and Tupali, overhearing, grinned at this explanation and afterwards took great delight in taunting Manalewa and Noumati, saying that perhaps the renowned hunter and fighter had fallen over another cliff or else become lost in the western hills, his wits stolen by the spirits he conjured in his dreaming.

Usually Manalewa would have dismissed her brothers' jibes. She did her best to conceal how they hurt her (though it took great effort to simply shrug and walk away), but she could not forget her dream. Had she known the details of her husband's accident she would have been even more worried. Noumati, in whom Tangalenna had confided the truth, suspected the two had indeed exacted their revenge though he doubted they would have dared kill him outright. Yet though tormented by suspicion, he could do nothing. Without evidence, his only recourse was to challenge Warady to a fight which he, lame and unpractised, had no chance of winning. Thus he watched and waited, enduring the mockery of his half-brothers with clenched teeth and a sullen silence that only provoked them to greater cruelty.

Noumati's resentment was exacerbated by the knowledge that if the Broad Ridge group was not found, Ngali-kiri would most likely be given to Tupali whose first wife, Ana-Maïda's sister, had died in childbirth. The dearth of women in Touganana's hearth group meant that since then he had been alone though Warady was sometimes willing to share Ana-Maïda. She bore their assaults with the stoicism of one who knows there is no choice but had suffered repeated miscarriages in the years since leaving Touganana's group.

Pounaté deeply disapproved of the arrangement but he knew his sons would laugh at him if he spoke out for they never let him forget his own crime. It was his hope that with a new wife Tupali, who was lazy and malicious by nature (though a skilled hunter when he could be persuaded to leave his hearth), would face his responsibilities and grow up. In the elder's eyes Warady's influence had kept Tupali a spoilt child: when Ata-Maïda died, he had not mourned her but berated the fact he would have to fend for himself rather than being slavishly waited upon.

'Am I not also a man?' Noumati thought bitterly as Tupali strutted about the camp or lounged by the river (wherever Ellie was to be found), his hair freshly ochred and skin darkened with charcoal. Both brothers had asked the cripple to manufacture weapons for them and though it irked him to do them any favours, he could not refuse. But his generosity did not curb their cruelty. He was unused to hiding his feelings and they were adept at judging how close he was to breaking point: once his face had hardened into a grimace and his hands ceased their steady planing they would walk away to find some other source of amusement. Each day it became harder for Noumati to keep control and sometimes he had to fight the impulse to pick up a newly sharpened spear and fling it in retaliation but, somehow, he restrained himself.

Although she knew how miserable Ana-Maïda's existence was, Ellie could not help being flattered by Tupali's attention. She loved Noumati with the deep and trusting affection she had felt for her brothers and assumed he regarded her as a sister: it never occurred to her that he might think otherwise. At first, she hated Tupali and Warady for their ceaseless taunting of her friend, knowing how the insults hurt him. But as days passed and she saw how Tupali eyed her, she began to blame the cripple for his meekness. One day she joined in the abuse to impress her would-be suitor but her heart was wrenched by Noumati's stricken expression and she ran away ashamed, vowing never to do it again.

However, although she did not like Tupali, he cast a kind of spell over the girl that she was powerless to resist. She would leave her own hearth-group to visit his, leaning provocatively against him as they ate, luxuriating in the thrill the touch of his smooth flesh sent to her very core. The firelight picked out Ana-Maïda's scars and bruises but these, and the woman's fearful demeanour in the presence of the brothers, did not deter Ellie. It was as if reason had been washed away by the tide of new emotions that made her very skin tingle, as if she were only now becoming fully alive. Her dawning sexuality, given a licence that would have been unthinkable in her own society despite its culture of sex and celebrity, was yet grafted onto a nature that lacked the maturity to understand the significance of her actions. And this was due not only to her lack of experience but the influence of the Meelayginnee who lived almost wholly in the present without thought for the future.

Tupali was well aware that his potential bride possessed a child's capriciousness. In his view she had been pampered by Tangalenna and Manalewa and he watched her with gleeful anticipation, thinking of how he would beat her into submission until, like Ata-Maïda, she trembled at his approach. Yet aware that no final decision had been made, he was careful not to antagonise her for it was still possible that Tangalenna might yet return with members of the Broad Ridge group. Thus he wooed the girl with a persistence that sickened Noumati, and ignored the sardonic eyes of his brother and the watchful gaze of the elders, Touganana and Pounaté, who would decree her future.

The wattle flowers faded and still they waited. Tupali, eager to impress, went hunting with Warady and their success put further pressure on Touganana's hearth group who felt their indebtedness increase daily. Then one morning Ellie was woken by the searing pain that heralded her period. She crept away into the forest and made herself a bed of leaves inside a hollow tree for she felt suddenly young and insecure, as if the cruel, flirtatious part of her had sloughed away with the lining of her womb: she did not want Tupali to see her. She lay with her hands pressed into the hollow of her flank and resolved to remain hidden as long as she could.

When the brothers returned that afternoon after a successful hunt, they missed the girl at once and began to harangue Manalewa, accusing her of conspiring with her husband to secret the girl away, thus preventing her marriage. Warady, still eager for revenge, was most vociferous. When their sister protested that Tangalenna had not yet returned and therefore the girl's absence could be nothing to do with him, Warady glanced towards the elders, who were watching the argument with trepidation.

'How much longer must we wait, then?' he asked loudly. 'It is time we considered him lost, sad though that might be. We are here in good faith for Ngali-kiri's coming-of-age and marriage. He is not needed for those ceremonies. Let us do what we came for, then we can go our separate ways.'

There was a short, uneasy silence. At length Pounaté answered heavily, 'If my son-in-law is dead, I will not leave Touganana's group without a man who can provide for them. And I am growing old. If Tangalenna does not return, our hearth-groups will join together. It will be better so.'

'Eh – so you can live with your sister as a wife?' Warady jeered. 'Clever thinking, old man: that way we'll all be happy except the cripple. I suppose he could have Manalewa though he'd have a hard time digging enough roots to feed the dreamer's children.'

Noumati had borne much since his enemies' arrival but at this something snapped inside him and a hot tide surged through his blood. Before he knew what he was doing, he was on his feet, one of the new spears in his hand with the point towards Warady.

'Ngali-kiri should be mine!' he said and his voice shook with barely suppressed anger. 'Have you forgotten who I am? When Tangalenna returns I shall state my claim. I am no less a man than you!'

Sheer astonishment stopped Warady's mouth for a moment but Tupali laughed nervously and Pounaté sighed and shook his head. Then Warady gave a great shout of laughter, ran lightly forward, snatched the weapon and broke it across his knee.

'That's how much of a man you are!' he scoffed. 'Unfit to carry a spear, let alone have a woman. One day Tupali and I'll fuck you, to show you how it's done! You might even enjoy it.'

Usually Noumati could find the answer to any situation in his great store of stories and fables but this time he had no recourse. Humiliated and ashamed, he sat down again as the others walked away. His eyes were fixed on the ground but his hands sought the broken pieces of the spear and fitted them together while his mind seethed with futile thoughts of revenge.

Once the pains had eased, Ellie soon became bored and hungry in her refuge and she wanted to talk to Manalewa. Now that she was able to consider Tupali's advances dispassionately, she was afraid. She wiped herself clean of blood, plugged her vagina with moss and made her way back. In the dappled sunlight of the forest she moved like a shadow, her bare feet almost soundless on the beaten earth: in four years she had acquired the gait and carriage of the aborigines as well as their language.

As soon as she walked into camp, the girl felt the strained atmosphere and knew that something momentous had happened in her absence. Noumati sat alone, toying with a broken spear; Manalewa was with the children by the river; Touganana and Pounaté sat grim-faced beside the fire while Tanglémerna, plaiting a basket from reeds, glanced up from time to time with a smirk of satisfaction.

The brothers, Warady and Tupali, could not be seen but their laughter came from inside their hut. It was followed by the sound of a blow, a woman's stifled cry and more laughter. Ellie shuddered at the thought of what Ana-Maïda might be enduring in there with the two of them. As the sounds were repeated, Noumati looked up and met Ellie's glance with such artless sorrow that her heart was wrung. She went over and sat opposite him, unconsciously taking up the position of a mature woman rather than a child, her right heel blocking the man's view of her pudenda.

'Ngali-kiri.' He spoke quietly but there was an edge to his voice that could have been interpreted as accusation or defensiveness: he was not sure how much she had seen of his humiliation. He turned the pointed end of the ruined weapon over and over and waited

'What's happened?' Such directness was considered rude, especially from a young, uninitiated woman to a man but she was so alarmed by his tone, she did not care. Then inspired by his continuing silence and the way he watched her surreptitiously though his head was bowed, she asked softly, 'Is it because of me?'

'Eh, little one . . .' He reached out to touch her hair then withdrew his hand before making contact, unwilling to betray his feelings not only to the girl but the watching elders. 'My brothers are always eager to prove their strength against me.' He cast aside the broken spear and gave a short, mirthless laugh. 'I did not tell them it was their own weapon they broke: the next one I make may cost them more than they expect.'

Ellie was far from satisfied by this explanation and she was disturbed by his latent threat. Then a shrill clamour arose from the river where the children had started to quarrel. This gave her an excuse to leave without further upsetting Noumati.

'My mother needs me,' she said and rose rather awkwardly to her feet. She did not want Noumati or any of the others to know her period had started, not realising that to these people whose senses were so much keener than her own, a woman's menstrual state was evident from her smell.

As she walked away, Noumati also got to his feet. From the grunts and moans coming from the hut he guessed that the brothers would soon be finished. His face was set in a strange expression that mixed anger and wistfulness, the look of someone about to embark on a course they know will end in failure but which they cannot give up. Eyes downcast, he picked up the broken spear, limped to the fire and tossed the pieces in. The flames licked hungrily around the dry wood and Noumati sat down opposite Touganana and Pounaté and watched in silence until the pieces were consumed.

The old man's relationship with his illegitimate son had, at first been ambivalent: the very existence of the child was a reminder of the crime that had blighted his life. Only a drastic decline in the band's numbers had prevented Pounaté being outcast: he had suffered the punishment of ritual spearing and bore the scars on his legs, arms and back. Touganana had been severely beaten and her affections had turned towards her brother after her husband's death: her wish then was that the hearth-groups would amalgamate because Tangalenna was still young and she had three other children to support. But Pounaté's shrewish wife, Tanglémerna, had refused to countenance such an idea and instilled her envy of Touganana and her kin into their sons, Warady and Tupali.

As the two boys matured, Pounaté saw how their minds had been turned against him and he tried to make amends by sending Warady to live with Touganana's hearth group in the hope that he would learn tolerance instead of hatred. This, he now realised, had been a grave mistake. And recognising in Noumati's pain the fruit of his own machinations, Pounaté longed to help him for it seemed punishment enough to have been born a cripple.

'Father, mother.' Noumati raised his head and looked penetratingly into the faces of the two elders. Their expressions remained impassive but secretly they were shaken: never before had he addressed them so openly, acknowledging not only his status as son of the leaders of two hearth-groups but also the shame of his illegitimacy. 'All these years I have lived almost as a woman, digging roots and tending fires. But although I have never hunted kangaroo I am a man no less than any of the others: my spears are the best and my stories the greatest. Do I not therefore have the rights of other men? I am older than Tupali yet I have never had a woman. Those of our hearth-groups are forbidden me but Ngali-kiri, although she will soon be of our skin, is not of our blood. I want her as my wife.' He paused to lick his lips, then added defiantly, 'And I will fight anyone who disputes my claim.'

These last words were spoken with such passion that Pounaté and Touganana were struck dumb. They were so used to their lame son's mildness, it had never occurred to them that he was subject to the same needs and desires as other men. Now Pounaté began to realise how he must have suffered all those years, indebted to those that bullied and reviled him yet unable to complain or retaliate. And because of this, because he also had suffered the scorn of Warady and Tupali too long, the old man made a bold decision. Without consulting Touganana (who after all, was only a woman for all her age and experience), he leaned forward until the heat of the fire fanned his face and said quietly but firmly, 'Once I cursed your birth, now you are more my son than either of the others. Therefore, I will uphold your claim. But understand this, if Tupali or any other challenges my decision, you will have to fight them.'

This expression of support and approval was so far beyond his wildest hope, Noumati did not know how to answer. As he stammered his thanks he noticed that Touganana was frowning, her eyes hard as pebbles in the loose folds of flesh. But she did not argue and her silence meant that while she might not approve her lover's endorsement, she would not gainsay it. Noumati bent his head in her direction as a gesture of acknowledgement, then got to his feet and went into the forest to be alone with his thoughts. Seeing him Tupali, who had just left the hut, wondered at the pride in the cripple's bearing.

So noticeable was the change in Noumati that even Ana-Maïda, usually too preoccupied with her own troubles to take much notice of the affairs of others, remarked upon it. Warady, already worried as to what it might signify, told her to be quiet, knocked her to the ground and went to confront Pounaté directly.

It was early evening and a chill wind blew from the south-west. The old man was at Touganana's fire as had become his habit, ignoring Tanglémerna who sat sullenly at her own hearth with Tupali. Noumati, Manalewa and Ngali-kiri shared Touganana's fire and it did not escape the brothers how the cripple seemed to fawn upon their father, handing him choice portions from the dismembered possum cooking in the ashes.

'Like a woman,' Warady thought disgustedly as he squatted beside Pounaté. The pale girl, he noted sat a little behind the others, arms pressed against her ripening breasts, hands covering her crotch and his penis hardened at the thought of her tender flesh and the small, unsullied hole between her legs. Her eyes fixed on him and he felt a thrill of anticipation but then Pounaté coughed. The old man's eyes glinted ironically and his thick lips twitched with amusement as Warady, with a visible effort, met his gaze.

'Was there something you wanted?'

Warady tried to quell the excitement surging though his blood – he seemed to feel the girl cringe beneath his touch – but his voice was unsteady when he answered. 'It is not for myself that I am here but Tupali. Will you wait until his bride is an old woman before acknowledging Tangalenna's demise? In two days the moon is full. Will you keep Ngali-kiri a child forever?'

'The mysteries of the women's side are not the concern of any man,' Touganana replied grimly. 'But we understand your impatience to leave before my son returns. Stay a few days longer and all will be resolved – one way or another.'

To Warady this answer was dissatisfactory in every aspect: he sensed danger in her ambiguity and looked to his father.

'We all came here for the same purpose,' he argued. 'But you must see it is time Ngali-kiri was given to a man. She is my brother's by right: do we have to take her by force and go our own way? Or have you someone else in mind for her?'

Pounaté gave a faint, unreadable smile but would not be drawn.

'That will be seen,' he said. 'But in any case I have told you that if Tangalenna does not return, our hearth-groups will become one. It would be a bad thing if you and Tupali were to leave.'

With every word Warady felt his tenuous position within the band threatened and it was pride, not reason that prompted his reply.

'We may be your sons but we are not children!' he retorted, lunging to his feet. 'I shall decide upon my hearth-companions, not you. This woman,' - he jerked his thumb at Touganana who sat impassive as a boulder – 'has had years' worth of my labour. Now

I'll make my own decisions.'

With that he turned and stalked away into the forest. Pounaté watched until he was beyond sight then sighed. 'I spoilt him as a child to ease my own guilt and he has grown to be a thorn in my flesh,' he muttered sadly. 'Perhaps it would be better if he took his ill-will away. But I fear for my grandchildren.'

'You fear too much,' Touganana replied. 'Tangalenna will return, you'll see.'

Chapter 9.

Next evening Touganana, Tanglémerna and Ana-Maïda took Ellie to the women's cave for her initiation. As her mother, Manalewa was prohibited from attending the ceremony. Her wails of grief, ritual mourning for a lost child, seemed to pierce Ellie's heart as she was led up the steep winding path into the gorge and for the first time in months she thought of her other mother who must also have grieved for her though she would have wept in silence where no-one could see or hear. But soon the awe and terror of the ceremony pushed all such introspection from her mind: what happened to her that night she knew she would never forget nor speak of.

She had been made to fast all day and though she had grown accustomed to privation, hunger combined with anticipation of what lay ahead, endowed her with a light-headed, febrile awareness. She felt the harsh stone beneath her feet, the pumping of blood around her body more keenly than ever before and as the path climbed and the gorge deepened, the river diminishing to a white ribbon far below, the immensity of space just a step to her right enticed her. She was certain that if leapt into it, she would not fall but fly, like the eagles Tangalenna watched with such interest.

Something of this mounting ecstasy was revealed in her face. Even as she walked her eyes became wide and dreaming and her feet began to wander so that at times she was perilously close to the cliff-edge. But Touganana, who had seen many girls initiated, gripped her arm and was pleased. That she should begin her spiritual journey before reaching the cave was auspicious indeed.

Further along the path was a point of light. Against the deepening twilight it was painfully bright: once the eye was caught by it, it was almost impossible to look away. Ellie was drawn to it like a moth to a candle-flame and Touganana let her go. When they came close, the light was revealed as no more than the embers of a small fire. Immediately behind it yawned the mouth of the women's cave and the red glow lit up the banded sandstone and threw the labia-like flutes in the rock into sharp relief.

They made Ellie kneel and Ana-Maïda built the fire into a blaze with wood stacked nearby. By this flaring light the older women shaved the girl's head with sharp flakes of chert, precious as ochre. The hanks of matted hair they threw onto the fire and the stench made Ellie retch and choke. But then Ana-Maïda tossed a branch of tea-tree on and the smoke became at once aromatic and soporific.

'Come.' They helped her to her feet and left her free to follow Touganana into the cavern. The light of the fire, falling through the narrow entrance, made a red path into the cave's interior but the girl stumbled and tried to feel her way like a blind person though she found only empty space. When she was near the centre, hands descended on her shoulders and spun her round so that darkness, firelight and the pungent smoke that had begun to finger its way into the cave became a whirling vortex of which she was the centre. It pulled at her mind and though she felt herself falling, her consciousness remained suspended above her body. This enabled her to watch unflinchingly as, using a stone knife, Touganana made the ritual incisions across the tops of her breasts, upper arms and thighs. The pain did not seem to belong to her at all and she made no sound.

When the matriarch was done, the women withdrew into the darkness to either side, leaving Ellie alone in the centre of the cavern. So many years had the place been used for this ritual that the floor where she lay was lacquered with dark stains. Although there was nothing to restrain her, the girl lay motionless and as the light failed (for the women did not replenish the fire), awareness returned to her body. The wounds stung unbearably but her skin felt oddly tight, as if it would split like a chrysalis if she moved and so she remained still. To keep her mind from dwelling on the pain, she concentrated on breathing. The stench of her own blood was heavy and cloying in her nostrils but beneath it was something aromatic and heady, exciting as the smell of sex.

Ellie was lying on her back and as the smoke seeped into her lungs, her eyes closed involuntarily. From where they crouched on guard the three women could see nothing of her save a pale blur and the reflection of the embers in the blood trickling down her sides. The effect was startling and despite her experience even Touganana shivered: this indicated that the magic they meant to entice from the earth was already stirring. They breathed the smoke in through the gaps between their fingers and began to chant.

That sound, like Tangalenna's song on the second night of Ellie's abduction, was so low and resonant it seemed as if the earth itself gave voice: it did not seem possible that human throats could utter it. And it became self-perpetuating as the women fell under its spell and the rock walls threw it back until at last it melded into a harmony that vibrated through the women's very bones and pushed them into trance.

To Ellie, caught between the voices and the returning echoes, it seemed that her body had become a conduit for a force so powerful, the very essence of her self was being swept away. Once, at the beach, she had been knocked down by a wave and sucked far out of her depth before surfacing and now she experienced the same sense of utter helplessness only this time, beyond fear, she felt a kind of joyous anticipation, warm as the flow that gushed suddenly from between her legs; comforting as the velvety blackness that lapped around her; mysterious as the dappled shapes, red and black, which moved before her in a series of pictures she could not quite grasp the form or meaning of. The patterns mesmerised her, becoming at last images that were both beautiful and terrible though she could never remember if she had been asleep when they came to her or awake, transported at last by the chant of earth and blood, life and death to her own dreaming.

The morning after Ellie's initiation, those at the riverside camp woke to find that Tangalenna had returned in the night. Exhausted and starving, he arrived long after the others were asleep and having gnawed at some bones he found by the fire, crept inside, stretched out beside Manalewa and fell at once into a deep slumber, too far gone to wonder why Warady's children should be there instead of his foster-daughter.

When Manalewa woke at dawn to find her husband asleep

beside her, she had to stifle a scream: she had believed in her heart that he would never return. But the warmth and solidity of his body against hers proved he was no ghost. She stroked him tenderly so as not to wake him and her relief gave way to dismay for he was desperately thin, his skin lacerated as if he had spent days forcing his way through thorn thickets and his face was gaunt, the muscles tense even in sleep as if he dared not relax his guard.

Although she tried to restrain them, the children's excitement at their father's return could not be contained. They scrambled to touch him and he was woken by their clamour. With a groan he opened his eyes, looked round blearily as if uncertain of where he was, then as Manalewa urged the children outside, gave a great sigh and let his head fall back as if the effort of holding it up was too much.

'The Broad Ridge people are lost,' he said at last. 'They have joined the Disappeared. I went to the very edge of the world. They are gone.'

Never had Manalewa heard such weariness and defeat in her husband's voice: she did not know how to comfort him. And guilt that she should so readily have believed him dead also stayed her tongue.

'I'll fetch food and water,' was all she could think of and she rose to go outside. But he reached out and caught her ankle with a ferocity that startled her.

'Where is Ngali-kiri? What has happened?' he growled.

'They took her to the cave last night,' Manalewa stammered. 'It was time: she is not a child anymore.'

With that she hurried out, shaken by the bitter look on his face. When she returned with a bark dipper of water, some shrivelled roots and part of a possum's ribcage to which some scraps of meat still clung, he ate and drank in silence and his dark mood seemed to cloak him like a shadow. Frightened by the change she perceived in him, Manalewa muttered that she must tend the children for there was no-one else to look after them and went out again, leaving him to brood alone.

News of Tangalenna's return was received with dismay by Pounaté who now had no excuse to stay with Touganana; scornful dismissiveness by Warady and Tupali and deep trepidation by Noumati. The cripple had seen a figure steal into camp during the night but when there was no outcry from the huts, he assumed he had dreamt it. When Manalewa told him what had happened (it was Noumati she confided in first), he did his best to reassure her that likely enough Tangalenna was simply worn by a long and arduous journey. But after she had gone to relate the tidings to the rest, he was filled with misgivings for he knew that to gain Ngali-kiri he would need Tangalenna's support.

The sun was high when the other women came down from the cave. Manalewa took the children to greet them while the men, with the exception of Tangalenna, waited in silence at the centre of the camp. Warady and Tupali glanced constantly from the approaching group of women to their enemy's hut. They were apprehensive as to what his return might signify but their faces expressed only a kind of faintly sardonic expectancy.

Walking between Ana-Maida and Tanglemerna as the matriarch led the way, Ellie felt more light-headed than could be accounted for by the loss of her hair. Her wounds throbbed and ached for she had been woken at dawn and then Touganana had re-opened the incisions and packed them with ash from the ritual fire. Somehow she had borne this without flinching or uttering a sound and then they had made her stand with her hands splayed on the cave wall while the matriarch blew finely powdered ochre over them, leaving the prints clearly outlined on the rock when at last she was permitted to move. It was as she was standing there that she realised the mottled appearance of the cave's interior which had so confused her during the night was the result of thousands of such marks, the oldest almost obliterated beneath the more recent. This meant, she realised, that countless women had come of age in this place and she shivered to the depths of her being, overwhelmed by the weight of those generations, awed by the continuity of a tradition unbroken through aeons, recorded in the stratigraphy of handprints.

They had led her outside at last, into the sunlight and when she saw blue sky, heard the churning of the torrent far below and smelt spray mingled with the scents of eucalypt and woodsmoke, it was like being re-born. She breathed deeply, felt the lingering thrill of the ecstasy that had possessed her in the night and the women, recognising her euphoria, laughed and led the way down the cliff. Even Tanglémerna seemed to have put aside her dislike of the pale girl in the clear brightness of the morning.

When the children and Manalewa met them just within the trees, Ellie thought that her foster-mother looked strangely troubled but her news made the girl's happiness complete. In the pain and awe of the ritual, she had forgotten that this was to be the day of her marriage. Buoyed by pride that she had come through the ordeal without succumbing to fear, she held her cropped head high and her stride was long and firm as she made her way into camp.

But Ellie's confidence failed when she reached the central fire. The other women and children had fallen back, leaving her the focus of attention. The men stood in a semi-circle on the opposite side, Warady and Tupali slightly apart from Pounaté and Noumati. Of Tangalenna there was no sign. Noumati glanced towards the hut then looked questioningly at Pounaté but the old man's face was imperturbable. The two brothers stared at the girl and Tupali licked his lips, his hand stealing to his penis. Teeth clenched against the smarting of her wounds, Ellie could not restrain a shudder for in that moment she remembered the true significance of the night's ritual. She could be given to any of these men to use as they wished and her powerlessness appalled her.

'She's already trembling for a man to take her!' Warady's comment was spoken in an undertone but it was meant for Noumati's ears. Pounaté sighed, then took a step forward and said with dignity, 'Welcome, Ngali-kiri to this hearth which is now yours.'

Touganana had instructed Ellie how to respond to the traditional greeting: she sat cross-legged where she had stood, keeping her eyes downcast, thus accepting her place as a woman in the band. But she had been marked as belonging to Touganana's hearth group, not Pounaté's and an awkward silence fell, for no woman could arrange a marriage. The men sat down and the brothers snickered together behind their hands while Noumati glanced anxiously at the closed door of Tangalenna's hut. It opened and he walked out.

Since the news of his return there had been much anticipation of what might now happen regarding Ngali-kiri's future but no-one had foreseen how Tangalenna's journey had affected him. They stared in amazement and even Ellie was transfixed though she should have kept her head meekly bent until her husband was chosen. Not only was Tangalenna so emaciated that all his joints stuck out, he seemed to have aged years in the space of a few weeks: his face was haggard and there were streaks of grey in his hair and beard where the grease and ochre had long since weathered away. Walking stiffly, like an old man, he took his place beside Pounaté without a word and his unnatural silence increased the dread of his hearth-group. None could imagine what might have caused so startling a change in one formerly matchless in strength and endurance, unless there had been sorcery.

Pounaté was deeply disturbed by his son-in-law's appearance but Tanglémerna chuckled and Warady and Tupali could hardly contain their glee. Had he stayed away, they would have lived in dread of Tangalenna's return but to see him so diminished was more satisfying than news of his death would have been. Both were sure that in such a state he would not challenge them, whatever the elders decided.

'Welcome, Ngali-kiri.' Tangalenna made an effort to smile at the girl who was staring as if she could not believe her eyes. Yet to him it was she who appeared pitiable: instead of the red hair that had made her unique, her shaven scalp was mottled and ugly; the way she kept lifting a hand to scratch at her angry-looking wounds then lowering it before touching them made her appear younger and more vulnerable than before. His heart seemed to twist painfully as he looked at her. In a voice that did not seem his own, his gaze fixed on the girl's face, pale as bone beneath the charcoal and ochre, he said firmly: 'This woman, Ngali-kiri, who came to us through my dreaming, I claim as mine. She will tend the children at my hearth and bear more. She is Korunah's gift to me.'

There was an instant of stunned silence, then Manalewa gave a little cry, a wordless exclamation of dismay. In the same moment, Ellie, lapsing into English, breathed an incredulous 'What?' and

Pounaté groaned for this exceeded his worst fears of what might happen at this meeting.

'No!' Noumati struggled to his feet and stared round wildly while a murmur of astonishment and disbelief arose. His eyes rested at last on Tangalenna who sat stone-still, allowing the tumult to wash over him like a rainstorm and seemingly taking as little heed of it. His gaze was still intent on the girl but she, embarrassed and ashamed, not for herself but him, had bent her head. She was shivering violently from a combination of fear, shock and the fever arising from the infected cuts.

'She was promised to me!' Noumati's face was twisted into a grimace, the reckless outrage of a child whose toy has been unfairly snatched away.

'You?' Warady strode forward as if to take his half-brother by the shoulders and shake sense into him but at the last moment he thought better of it and stood still. 'Whoever gave you that idea? Or' – a sneer came into his voice and he glanced sidelong at Tangalenna – 'did it happen in a dream?'

'I said it.' Pounaté spoke quietly but grimly and such was the tension between the protagonists, it was as if he had shouted. A new uproar arose as all his hearth-group protested and the children began to wail, frightened by the mounting hostility.

'Has age destroyed your wits, old man?' Tupali pushed his brother aside and thrust his face almost into Pounaté's (by now all were on their feet save Tangalenna and Ellie). 'What makes this cripple,' – he jerked his thumb at Noumati – 'the bastard you sired on your own sister, better than me?'

'You are younger than he and you have already had a wife,' answered Pounaté in the same grim tone. 'A lame foot does not make Noumati less of a man than any of us. It is right that he should have a son to pass on the stories of our people lest, as time passes, they be lost forever.'

Tangalenna shuddered at these words. But he said nothing.

'Moreover,' Pounaté continued, 'Touganana agrees with me. If the other group was here, the girl would have gone with them since she is marked as Touganana's kin. But it seems they have gone the way of the rest. It remains only for Tangalenna to approve our choice, being the eldest man in her hearth-group.'

'You dismiss his claim then?' Spittle flew from Tupali's lips; his right fist was raised and clenched as if he had a spear poised to throw.

'Tangalenna is Ngali-kiri's father: they are of the same skin,' Pounaté replied wearily. 'You know as well as I that the law forbids their union.'

'Spoken like a true elder,' Warady sneered. 'You reject Tangalenna's claim on grounds of skin, though they are not of the same blood, in favour of a son begot on your sister with whom you share both! By law the girl is Tupali's!'

Even Manalewa, who bore her brothers no great love, joined in the murmur of assent that arose from Pounaté's kin; Noumati bit his lip and looked desperately at Tangalenna. The harsh cackle of a kookaburra sounded from close by and Ellie suddenly buried her head in her hands.

'Well?' Tupali stamped his foot and a puff of ash rose from the ground. 'Do I take her now or must I fight the cripple?'

'She is Noumati's.' Tangalenna's voice was harsh, his face mask-like, eyes hard and expressionless as flint. He clambered awkwardly to his feet and without another word turned and walked away, heading for the path to the caves down which the women had come earlier. There was something so terrible in his demeanour that no-one dared intervene. Just before he disappeared in the darkness beneath the trees, Noumati called: 'Why are you leaving?' but either Tangalenna was deaf to the anguish in that cry or he refused to heed it. A moment later he was gone.

An awkward silence followed: such behaviour at a betrothal was unprecedented. But Noumati, taking advantage of his rival's consternation, moved round the fire, caught hold Ellie's wrist and pulled her to her feet. 'Come,' was all he said and he led her deliberately away from where Warady and Tupali were muttering together. Strangely, now that Pounaté's choice had been affirmed, neither considered challenging Noumati: they were unwilling to flout the law so publicly.

'So that's it?' Unable to vent his frustration on any other, Tupali turned on his father. But Pounaté merely stared at him and spread his hands to indicate his powerlessness.

'Then it's finished!' the young man shouted. His face was contorted with rage: he clenched his fists and ground his teeth before continuing hotly, 'I'll go my own way from now on and find my own woman.' He looked round, pointed a shaking finger at Ellie. 'There must be plenty more where she came from!'

'Don't leave us,' Pounaté pleaded. Before the force of Tupali's passion he seemed suddenly old and frail. 'A man without a hearth-group is no better than an outcast. Think again, my son.'

Although quick to anger, Tupali lacked self-confidence: all his life he had been influenced by his brother. He hesitated and glanced uncertainly at Warady for he was lazy and it occurred to him that life without others to provide for him would be hard and comfortless.

'Ay, steady little brother.' Warady shook his head in mock disapproval. 'Do not upset our honoured father who has been such an example to us. If a woman weak and repulsive-looking as Ngali-kiri is what you want then get one but make sure to bring her back so that we can teach her our ways. Ana-Maida'll welcome her: serving us both is wearing her out before her time.'

Tupali grinned thankfully at his brother who had managed to salvage their pride whilst scorning their father and the newly betrothed. In his relief that the situation had reached a peaceful (if not wholly satisfactory), outcome, Pounaté let the insult pass. Yet from that moment his status within the group was diminished. Despite Pounaté's age and experience, it was Warady who dominated and Tanglémerna's smug smile indicated this was something she had long desired.

'Then I'll leave tomorrow,' Tupali said. 'And I'll get a woman who'll give me children straightaway. Tangalenna was stupid: how long has he waited for the pale one to come of age only to lose her to the cripple?'

'Perhaps his reasons were different,' Touganana answered ingenuously. 'And he already has a wife. But he is gone and it is time to celebrate Ngali-kiri's coming-of-age and marriage. Put aside your differences and join the corroboree. Are you not hungry?'

As a special treat, Touganana and Manalewa had tapped some

rare cider gum trees, collecting the sap in tightly woven bags thickly coated with grease so than none of the precious liquid could escape. This they now brought out, for the meat cooking in the embers was ready and so the corroboree began with feasting.

With the alcohol and the release of tension, a kind of wildness verging on frenzy ruled the celebrations. Even Manalewa, who at first hung back, at once ashamed of her husband's behaviour and concerned for his well-being, was persuaded that to spurn the feasting amounted to a rejection of her foster-daughter and soon became drunk. She began to dance and so compelling was her performance that the other women, excepting the bride, joined in. So exact was their imitation of wallaby scratching, kookaburra swooping, quoll pouncing, it seemed that at any moment they might be transformed into the creatures they portrayed.

Panting, their bodies shining with sweat, the women threw themselves on the trampled grass. The children ran to sprinkle them with water then began their own impromptu dance to the beat of Noumati striking a hollow log. Then Touganana called, 'Ngali-kiri - your turn. Dance us your dreaming!'

A peculiar atmosphere of expectancy fell as Ellie walked reluctantly into the dancing space. Noumati's drum had fallen silent and the children scampered back to their mothers and sat down solemnly to watch.

Although the details of a person's dreaming were regarded as sacred to themselves, it was customary for those newly initiated into adulthood to dance the essence of the dream that had come to them during the ritual so that all should know the identity of their daemon and how they should be referred to after death. Whether through suggestion or because Tangalenna had guessed her true nature when he named her, it was the little brown quoll that had appeared to Ellie during the pain and ecstasy of the night but she had also dreamt the farm as she remembered it. So in her dance she included animals her audience had never seen: cows, sheep, dogs and they watched in wonder and no little amusement. Even Noumati, who through the haze of gum sap was trying to maintain a sense of dignity, laughed until the tears ran down his face and he forgot to keep the beat.

He alone did not dance that day but at sunset, when the rest lay about the fire, exhausted by dancing and sated with food and drink, he began to tell the tales for which he was famous. Mime and gesture were so intrinsic to his story-telling that the fables themselves were a kind of dance, one in which the audience became so involved it was their fingers that the first fire-stick burnt; in their rib-cages that Droémadeener hid the ochre he had taken from the ant-people.

Last of all, to honour his bride, Noumati had made a new tale. He told how when Myrtle Tree lost her child and was weakened to the point of death, Eagle decided to find a cure for her grief. Through the forests and mountains he searched in vain and was about to turn back in despair when a dream told him that Brown Quoll, the little fierce one, knew the secret that would restore Myrtle Tree to her former happiness. Eagle flew high over the forest until, spotting the one he sought, he swept her up in his talons and bore her swiftly to where Myrtle Tree languished. By now her tears had turned the shining river to a torrent which threatened to flood the great marsh and drown all the Meelayginnee but when Eagle alighted and she looked upon Brown Quoll, Myrtle Tree felt the darkness of death fall away from her and she laughed and was healed and so Eagle's dream was fulfilled.

Ellie and Manalewa were initially embarrassed by this rendering of their story but when it was finished, they embraced. Night had fallen and the smoke spiralled up towards stars which seemed to blaze with especial brilliance. Most of the children were already asleep, curled together like a litter of puppies; the eyes of the rest shone with over-excitement and tiredness. All the cider gum sap had long since been drunk and nothing remained of the meat but gnawed bones. Expectant glances began to be directed at the young couple and Ellie became acutely self-conscious. She glanced surreptitiously at Noumati, saw that he was watching her with undisguised hunger and suddenly she wanted to be far away, safe at home in her own room, a child again, and tears sprang to her eyes for that life now lost to her.

Touganana got heavily to her feet as the talk died down and the atmosphere of anticipation intensified. She regarded the group with the studied dignity of the inebriated but her words were grave and deliberate. After thanking Pounaté for bringing his group to their foster grand-daughter's coming-of-age (an acknowledgement the old man accepted with a nod while his wife stared back scornfully), the matriarch turned to Ellie.

'You have been known as Ngali-kiri among us: so your father named you and thus you have dreamed. But now you are a grown woman and must bear a proper name. This we have considered and because you are both Meelayginnee and of another people, you will be known henceforth as 'Warrander-naba'. But Ngali-kiri will remain your hearth-name if it pleases you.'

Never before had the fact of Ellie's difference from the rest been so openly stated and it felt as if a gulf had opened to swallow her: she realised suddenly that while she had assimilated with the group to the extent of thinking of herself one of them, they might not have accepted her as completely as she had believed. The words meant 'our stranger' and she tried to take comfort from that but this naming made her wonder whether all the time she had laboured to match them in skill and hardiness, they had been laughing at her behind her back.

They were watching her expectantly: she was required by custom to answer. For a terrible moment all their language seemed to have forsaken her. Then, embarrassed by her silence, Noumati nudged her and whispered harshly, 'These are your people: they have cared for you since Tangalenna found you. Is this all the respect and thanks you have?'

Ellie had never heard him so stern and sudden fear tinged her apprehension of what was to come. It took great effort to keep her voice steady and reply as Touganana had coached her, accepting given and hearth names and binding herself to Noumati and his kin.

'It is done!' The matriarch smiled. 'Go with him then and may the evil spirit who twisted his foot flee your green eyes and pale skin!'

The banter aimed at a young virgin couple in any culture accompanied the two to Noumati's shelter, advice from the elders as lewd as that from Warady and Tupali though less spiteful. But neither took any notice. Ellie's stomach was so knotted with dread she thought she would vomit for there was no mistaking the immediacy of Noumati's need: his palm in hers was slick with sweat and the tip of his erect penis glistened in the firelight. Someone called 'See how eager he is!' and his hand tightened on hers then they were at the shelter and he let go so that she could crawl in first.

Ellie had hoped he would wait until all the others had gone to bed: she knew they would be straining their ears to hear what was happening. But it was almost six years since Noumati's initiation and in all that time he had never had a woman: although he was a gentle man, his lust would not be contained. With a deep groan he pushed Ellie onto her back, then crawled onto her, pinning her arms behind her head, licking and sucking urgently at her breasts.

The girl lay rigid and scared as, with his free hand, he delved between her legs. When, without further preliminaries, he thrust into her she thought she would split, that he was stuffing her to the base of her throat and a cry escaped her, one that made Manalewa wince while Warady, pulling his exhausted wife towards their shelter, sunk his fingernails deep into her flesh in anticipation. At last Noumati gasped and shuddered powerfully: through her pain Ellie was aware of an unutterable relief that it was over. And yet when he had withdrawn from her, the tender and loving side of his nature returned. He lay on his side, spent and panting, and pulled her against him, murmuring words of comfort and she knew then that it would be all right.

Chapter 10.

It was not only the loss of Ngali-kiri to his half-brother that had driven Tangalenna to seek the sanctuary of the caves. During the previous weeks he had made a great journey, covering the territories of three bands. Two of these were known to have disappeared generations ago but when he found the lands traditionally occupied by the Broad Ridge group empty, it occurred to him that they might have moved to the areas where there had been no hunting within living memory.

As it turned out, he found no sign of them until the end of his travels but in the far south he came across a track where logs had been laid to cross boggy ground. He waited for two days concealed in the dense scrub that characterised the area but when people appeared, they were *num*. Their figures were strangely bulky, padded, he guessed by the layers of manufactured skins he knew were called 'clothes'; their feet clumsy in cumbersome boots which were so loud even on bare earth that he heard their approach from more than a spearthrow's distance. He watched them with a mixture of curiosity, contempt for their inept bushcraft and a vague foreboding that lingered for days after the sighting. After that, although they had not seen him (though one had paused and looked round uneasily, as if sensing the presence of a hidden watcher), he left that region, heading north-westwards until he reached the sea.

Here, too, there were changes though he had never been there before: the colonies of seals that legend spoke of were gone and there was no sign of people. Tangalenna did not linger for the sound of the surf, which was like the roar of the wind through a forest, exacerbated the sense of sorrow that had grown upon him as he wandered the deserted shore. His people had once over-wintered here by tacit agreement with the Toogee band until white sealers began raping and stealing their women: now both sealers and Toogee were gone, like sand washed away by the sea, obliterated by time.

Before leaving the beach, he collected mussels off the rocks. Lacking the means to make fire, he smashed the shells with a stone and picked out the shrinking flesh, wolfing it down unchewed in his hunger. But hours later, as he traversed an area of bog and dune beside the mouth of a wide river, he was doubled over with belly cramps and spent the next two days huddled in the tussock-grass, vomiting and shitting helplessly where he lay. This sickness, he was sure, had been sent by the restless spirits of the dispossessed but without his talisman or ochre he had no means to appease them. He begged their forgiveness for trespassing in their domain and, slowly, the symptoms subsided but he was left weak and shaken by the potency of Toogee malevolence.

Days later he had still not fully recovered from that episode because instead of resting until he recovered his strength, he pressed on, impelled by a strange urgency, a sense that if he did not find those he sought and returned to his own group soon, disaster would overtake them all. He worked his way roughly north along a wide and rugged valley in which the roar of the river that had carved it was a constant companion and then, in a kind of dell surrounded by boulders fallen from the cliff above, he found the first of the funeral pyres.

It was customary for most Tasmanian aborigines to burn their dead but the elaborate tent-like shrines erected over the ashes by some of the southern and eastern bands had never been a tradition of Tangalenna's people nor all those in the west. This pyre was simply an elongate heap of charcoal and ash in which a few charred bones were visible. Having no wish to disturb the spirits of those in whose land he was trespassing, Tangalenna studied the remains without touching. At least one adult and two children had been cremated and recently: though the ashes had been wetted more than once, there was no more than a thin scattering of leaves and twigs over the site. He was not overly dismayed by the number of dead: if a woman died in childbirth, her youngest children often perished soon after.

It was close to nightfall and although the discovery had renewed Tangalenna's hopes of finding the Broad Ridge people, he guessed they must still be some distance away. A clear trail ran from the pyre along the valley side and he followed it stealthily, watching for game, for he had not eaten properly since falling sick. As he walked his practised eyes noted more evidence of human activity: branches snapped to widen the path; notches cut where trees had been climbed after possums. He held his spear loosely but his whole being was alert for the slightest movement.

A pademelon sat in the crook of a great tree root beside the path. Its head was low and its whole body shook to its heartbeat but it made no attempt to flee. Tangalenna stuck it though the chest and it grunted and shuddered, then died. He wondered if he should continue along the path in the hope of finding the Broad Ridge people, then decided to stay where he was and eat. If all the animals in this region were so easily caught, a single pademelon would make no great gift.

He gorged on the choice portions, liver, kidneys, heart and haunches, until his belly was tight and he could eat no more then, too weary to make a more elaborate shelter, gathered some leaves and lay down where he was. Sleep came swiftly but was filled with lurid, senseless dreams. He woke at first light, thirsty and with an odd heaviness in his stomach. When he got to his feet, dizziness overtook him and he had to lean on his spear for support. His heart lurched in his chest and his head reeled as if he had drunk too much cider gum: he bent low and threw up most of the evening's meal. After that, he felt a little better and continued along the path, looking for water.

What he found was another cremation.

This one was more disturbing because it had the appearance of haste. Three adults and several children lay haphazardly amid a tangle of charred boughs. The bodies were only half-cremated and the thick smells of burnt meat and hair hung in the air along with the stench of decay. Flies swarmed and buzzed over the putrefying flesh.

There was no way of telling how these people had died but Tangalenna shuddered when he saw what remained of their faces: twisted, mouths agape so that the teeth gleamed white against the fire-blackened skin. It was clear that whatever killed them had not ended with their deaths but threatened their kin so that instead of treating the bodies with respect and making sure they were properly burned, they had fled.

Even as this thought occurred to him, it had seemed to Tangalenna that if he lingered in this place, he would suffer the same fate. He turned and ran blindly along the trail, desperate to rid his mouth and nostrils of the taint of death but instead of dissipating, the smell grew worse. He slowed, spots dancing before his eyes, his limbs trembling so that he had to lean on his spear for support, and then a small glade opened up before him. Seeing what it contained, he bent and retched violently but when the spasm was over, he moved forward, drawn by the need to know what had happened.

They lay as they had died save where the squabbling of carrion birds and devils had disturbed them or the swelling of the bodies had caused them to shift. An old woman and a child were huddled together; others sprawled face down: furrows marked where they had clawed convulsively at the earth. The stench was unbearable. Some of the corpses had been torn open by animals and what remained of their innards poked out of the rents. Even as Tangalenna edged further into the clearing, a raven flapped down, then swerved aside at the last moment and perched on an overhanging branch to wait until it could resume its feast undisturbed.

Tangalenna guessed that there were no survivors because there had been no attempt to burn the corpses or even to arrange them decently and pile rocks to protect them. Every face was pecked and ravaged: the eye-sockets were empty and the tongues had been torn from most of the mouths. Yet though the softest and most vulnerable parts had been violated, the corpses were otherwise complete, bloated, streaked green and purple where the flesh was decaying beneath the skin.

With a wordless sound of distress, half-moan, half-sigh, Tangalenna squatted on his heels. It was clear to him that all the Broad Ridge people were now accounted for. Torn between revulsion and pity, he did not know what to do. Without any means to make fire, he could not burn the corpses, nor were there any stones nearby to pile over them: it was, in any case too late. Flies buzzed around him but his sweat made poor fare compared with the feast that lay all about. They swarmed so thickly upon some of the corpses that it looked as if they were moving. Wherever there was an open lesion or gash, the glistening, putrescent flesh oozed maggots like pus.

The sun was high and though the forest was dense, a single ray fell onto the swollen abdomen of a man lying on his side. The heat caused the trapped gases to expand: the corpse suddenly rolled onto its back with a fart that to Tangalenna's ears sounded like a groan. Terror overcame him and he leapt to his feet and ran. Guilt exacerbated his fear because the Broad Ridge people were also Meelayginnee and their spirits would have a claim on him if he failed to give them the proper rites. Yet still he fled.

When he could run no more, he sank to his knees, dizzy and fighting for breath. As the pounding of his heart gradually slowed, he became aware of an unnatural silence. The air was still, heavy with the stench of decay but even the buzzing of flies seemed muted. Looking ahead along the path, the light was bright, indicating open ground. He got shakily to his feet and made his way cautiously towards it, desperate to feel a clean wind upon his face. The carcasses of wallabies and possums lay scattered on and about the trail but after what he had seen, he gave them no more than a cursory glance though their number disturbed him and the fact that many were untouched by scavengers.

He reached the edge of the forest and immediately shrank back. A scar of raw earth perhaps ten metres wide encircled a huge area of cleared ground. The perimeter was deeply rutted and torn roots and half-burned branches stuck out of the churned mud. Inside, the ground had been ploughed into straight ridges and furrows as far as the eye could see and on each ridge was a row of spindly saplings of a kind Tangalenna had never seen before. Their large bluish-grey leaves hung limp then rustled loudly in a breath of wind. Nothing else moved; no bird sang nor frog croaked though puddles with a polluted, iridescent sheen had collected in the ruts.

Trembling, Tangalenna forced himself to stay a little longer, trying to make sense of what he saw. He knew this must be the work of *num* and was again amazed and appalled by their power to destroy and reshape the world. A foul-smelling liquid oozed from the broken ground near his feet and he shuddered. He had no way of knowing that this was where the bait used to poison the wallabies and other browsing animals had been buried but the whole place revolted him to the very core. Earth, air, water, all seemed accursed and he was sure that the dead creatures he had seen and the Broad Ridge people had been poisoned by its spell. Yet while none of them had escaped, he sensed that the badness lingered, that the hungry spirit awoken by *num* was not satisfied even with all these.

As he thought this, Tangalenna turned on his heel and stumbled back the way he had come. He knew he must return to his own hearth-group before the evil overtook him also but he felt sickness swell within him. He begged Korunah to guide him but when he looked up, the sky and branches whirled and span and he almost fell. He had just enough presence of mind to turn onto another trail before he reached the clearing where the Broad Ridge people lay. He had no wish to disturb their spirits a second time.

At last Tangalenna found himself in a narrow gully lined with tree-ferns. A tiny creek welled from a hollow under an age-blackened myrtle root and ran between mossy banks for a short distance before plunging underground again. The taint of death still clung in his mouth and nostrils so he knelt and drank, then submerged his head completely in an effort to rid himself of the horror. But when he sat up and shook the water from his ears and hair the foul stench still hung in the air and he shuddered violently, thinking that perhaps this was how the Broad Ridge people had avenged themselves for his lack of respect, making him stink like a corpse so that he would be shunned and mocked by the living. However much he tried to push this idea aside, the stench seemed to worsen.

It was only gradually that he realised what he had taken for a rotting log on the opposite side of the creek was the body of a woman. She lay curled in the shadow of a tree-fern and her skin was taut and shiny: it was this odd texture that had made him look again. Her hands were folded beneath her head as if she was asleep but flies blackened the tongue stuck grotesquely between her lips and roiled in her eye-sockets.

Afterwards Tangalenna wondered how it was that he had not noticed the buzzing of those flies but in truth that sound had remained with him since the discovery of the camp, even as the smell and taste of death had lingered. Despite all he had seen earlier, the sight of this corpse jolted him to the very core, partly because of the unexpectedness of it but also because she resembled Manalewa to such a degree that for an instant he wondered if this were not real but a dreadful glimpse of the future.

He rose to his feet, never taking his eyes from the corpse. It seemed to him that she must have been the last to die, that she had abandoned her hearth-group in a desperate attempt to cheat death though it was already too late: she had been too weak to go far. And impelled by a desire to express his grief and pity, he forced down his revulsion, crossed the stream and bent to touch her on the shoulder. Flies rose in seething clouds and her swollen flesh was horribly soft beneath the taut skin: if he pressed harder he felt his whole hand might sink into it.

He had meant to tell the woman's spirit that though she would not be burnt as was proper, she and her kin would be remembered but as he stood there, flies buzzing inside and outside his head, no words would come. Instead nausea heaved through him and all his strength seemed to ebb: he thought he was about to faint or worse, that the evil that had killed the woman was seeping into him, sucking the life from his body like a creeping fungus that devours all it touches. He jerked his hand back and staggered away until at last the stench of decay was replaced by the clean scents of eucalypt and damp earth but though the buzzing of carrion flies lessened, it did not completely disappear.

The next two days were a living nightmare as Tangalenna tried to find his way back to his own hearth-group. Periods of lethargy were interspersed with bouts of frantic activity when, galvanised by the poison in his blood, he ran blindly through the forest, tearing through thorny scrub, blundering into trees, catching his feet on upstanding roots, oblivious to pain until he literally dropped in his tracks from exhaustion. He had left his spear behind but, in any case, lacked the will to hunt. The taint of death still lingered in his mouth and nose and there was a constant buzzing in his ears that he knew could not be real but was sent to torment him by the spirits of the riteless dead. On the third day a heavy lassitude settled upon him: he sat in the shelter of a hollow tree listening to the running of a nearby creek and the piping of wrens. There was a weight in his chest that spread gradually to his limbs and his thoughts were laboured and slow. Had a black snake not slithered from a pile of leaves close to where he sat, he might have sat there until he died.

Tangalenna watched the snake without fear though the sight of it brought back the memory of his young son jerking convulsively on the ground, white foam spewing from his lips, unable to make any sound save a dreadful gasping as his lungs failed. Yet Tangalenna felt no animosity towards the creature gliding sinuously towards the creek but rather admiration for the gleaming symmetry of its scales, the way it blended with the shadows so that when it was still, it became virtually invisible. The snake was perfectly adapted to and at home in its environment and the sight of it made Tangalenna sharply aware of his own unhappiness. He had lost that innate empathy with his world, was no longer complete in himself.

Brow furrowed, Tangalenna tried to recall when he had first felt this dislocation. His thoughts led straight to the pale child. He remembered how weak she had been so that at first he had been forced to pity her, then how she had grown up and her own ways had infiltrated the customs of his people: the foreign words, the games she had taught not only the children but everyone in the hearth-group, the innovation of catching and pinioning birds alive to stave off the threat of starvation in winter. How, as she matured, so his feelings for her had changed from the tender affection of a guardian and foster-father to the passion of a thwarted lover.

He ground his teeth as he thought of his rivals: Tupali, Warady, even Noumati the cripple. The demise of the Broad Ridge people meant that Ngali-kiri would remain in one of their groups but he had not brought her to his hearth with so much trouble so that she should become the wife of his enemy. In that moment he determined that no man should have her but himself. In his desire to possess her, he forgot it was for Manalewa's sake that Korunah had led him to the child.

With an enormous effort, he clambered to his feet and looked skywards to determine his direction. Alarmed by the movement, the snake slid into the shelter of a muddy crevice and remembering that Black Snake was Warady's daemon, he took the creature's timidity as a portent. He had already beaten his enemy once: there was no-one else to stand in his way. Ngali-kiri would be his.

Now, as he lay in his dreaming cave, Tangalenna's heart was bitter. He was weary from his journey for while the poison had been excreted from his system, it had damaged the tissues of his heart and brain: he tired more easily than before. But though there was a dull ache in his chest and his stomach cried out for food, it was his mind that tormented him. The mere fact that Touganana and Pounaté had thought fit to initiate and give away his foster-daughter irked him; the willingness with which his hearth-group, even his wife, had assumed he was dead felt like betrayal; the dismissal of his claim on Ngali-kiri and the manner in which she had been given to Noumati was an insult that seethed in his blood though he knew that decision was backed by tradition.

His thoughts swirled incoherently: he stared at the ceiling and in the dark space at the centre faces appeared and disappeared, merging one into another as the sun sank and the light faded. The pale face of his foster-daughter as he had seen it last, taut and hollow-eyed with pain and anxiety; Manalewa's, loving and full of dread; the faces of the Broad River people, fixed in their death-agonies, disfigured by the talons, beaks, teeth and claws of carrion-eaters: these he saw and as he watched, they alternated so swiftly it seemed to him that they were all the same, set there to mock and drive him mad.

It was dark when he woke to himself. Stars glittered in the pale strip of sky visible from inside the cave and a cool breeze whispered against the bare rock. Tangalenna rolled onto his side and drew his knees to his chest. He was chilled to the very marrow of his bones and the buzzing in his ears had grown so loud he could barely hear the roar of the torrent far below. Then, one by one, the stars were blotted out by a blackness he knew was no ordinary darkness but the very essence of death. He felt it gather around him, silent, suffocating, and cowered deeper into his bed of leaves, struggling to draw breath. His hand went to his chest, seeking his talisman but he had buried it at the back of the cave when he passed on the southward leg of his journey. With the strength born of desperation, he raised himself to his hands and knees, began to crawl.

Pain clawed at his chest and shoulder. It was so unexpected, so excruciating, he thought he had been speared. He collapsed forward and lay gasping, unable to move. Never had he felt so alone. He longed for Manalewa and it was her face he saw as the darkness closed in, only now she was laughing at him.

Chapter 11.

Though weary from the strain and excitement of the day and the lingering effects of cider gum, Manalewa could not sleep. She tossed and turned until the children complained. Then, telling them sternly to be good and stay inside, she slipped out and closed the door behind her. For a while she stood listening to the night sounds of the camp: the old folk snoring, a sharp cry from one of Ana-Maida's children ensnared in a dream but there was no soft footfall, no striding shadow that could be her husband returning. And remembering his grim look as he had turned to walk away from the corroboree, his claim on Ngali-kiri which Manalewa innocently interpreted as an attempt to save their beloved foster-daughter from Tupali and Warady, fear gripped her that he had dreamed his own death, that whatever had happened to so change him on his journey was not yet ended. Without stopping to think what she was doing she hurried through the camp, past the shelter where the sleeping Ngali-kiri twitched feverishly in her husband's arms, and took the narrow path to the caves.

The weight of the child in her womb dragged at Manalewa as she climbed and several times she was forced to stop to regain her breath for the way was steep and, by starlight, treacherous. Yet her sense of urgency increased with every step until at last, when she had passed the cascade and the cliff path lay before her, she was almost running, supporting her swollen abdomen with both hands, sweat trickling down her body though the night air was chill.

On any normal day nothing would have induced Manalewa to enter the sacred gorge alone; to do so in darkness would have been inconceivable. But she was imbued with a strange confidence. She walked steadily along the narrow ledge until she reached the caves and then she held her breath and hurried past the gaping entrances, black voids in the pale light, willing the guardian spirits to let her pass.

When she came at last to Tangalenna's dreaming cave however, her courage faltered. The entrance was shaped like a half-open mouth: it seemed to her that anyone it swallowed would be lost to the world. Trembling, she crouched to one side and whispered fearfully, 'Tangalenna, my husband, are you there?' In the immensity of the night, against the unceasing roar of the torrent far below, her voice sounded pathetically weak and insignificant. To make sure she was not dreaming, she reached out to touch the gritty rock wall: it seemed impossible that she should be here alone.

A deep groan came from within and Manalewa cowered against the cliff. It sounded more like some exhalation of the earth than anything human. The pounding of her heart filled her ears, shook her whole body but no other sound came from the cave and gradually she became calm. 'I am here in the sacred gorge,' she told herself. 'It is night but I am not alone: Tangalenna is in the cave. What, then, keeps me outside?' And these words lent her courage. She lifted her hand from the cliff and entered the cave.

So complete was the darkness of the interior compared with the lambent starlight that at first she could see nothing and had to feel her way to where she could stand upright. But the curved rock walls magnified what the roar of the river had drowned out: the sound of Tangalenna's breathing. It was harsh and quick and it guided Manalewa to where he lay.

She knelt and though he did not stir when she touched him, relief overcame her because he was alive. His skin was cold and clammy, the underlying muscles rigid and she lay down and held him as closely as she could, yearning to warm and comfort him. She guessed he must be trapped in a bad dream but dared not wake him lest his daemon be angry. Gradually his breathing eased and he relaxed against her. Satisfied that she had come when she was truly needed, her fears assuaged, Manalewa sank at last into a deep and contented sleep.

Manalewa's children were afraid of Tanglémerna and her sons so when they woke at dawn and found themselves alone, the little boy pushed open the door, took his sister and went to find Ellie. Discovering her with the storyteller, they waited outside the lean-to and watched in solemn silence as Noumati stirred. The young woman lay curled with her back against his belly and the touch and smell of her rekindled his desire. He pulled her closer and his penis probed the cleft of her buttocks while with one hand he stroked her breasts.

Ellie woke abruptly to a sensation that filled her at once with delight and revulsion. Her flesh yearned for the man to possess her while her mind shrank from the implications of what was happening. But when she opened her eyes and saw the children, embarrassment swamped all else. With a sharp exclamation of dismay, she thrust Noumati's hands away and writhed free. Her upper thighs were smeared with blood, there was a bruised soreness between her legs and yet her face flushed with a kind of pride as she stood up for she felt that she was now truly a woman. The children continued to stare, sensing a change in her that went beyond the blood, the swollen cuts and cropped hair, something they knew was symbolised by these things but had more to do with what they had just been watching.

'Tell them to go away.' Noumati's body ached for release and he was angry. It was as if the demands of his young wife's foster-siblings were more important than his.

'Something's wrong.' Ellie felt suddenly sick and weak with pain. Her wounds itched and throbbed and her head ached as if a band were slowly tightening about her brow. Picking up the little girl, she followed the boy to Tangalenna's hut and her heart sank when she found it empty. She had thought he would return in the night as before.

The children were hungry so she fed them scraps left over from the feasting then went back to Noumati. He looked at her sullenly and seemed unconcerned when she told him the news. Touganana and Pounaté, who came over to greet the newly-weds, shared his belief that Manalewa had sought out her husband for sex.

'After all, he's been away a goodly while,' the old woman cackled. 'No doubt she wanted to remind him he already has a wife, to stop him running after others. Mind, from the look of him she'd need to be gentle!'

'Yah! it wasn't her he lusted after!' Warady stood before his hut and stretched out his arms, flaunting himself. His body shone in the sun, the muscles smooth and taut beneath his freshly greased skin. He jerked his head contemptuously at Noumati but it was Ellie his eyes rested upon. 'So how does a cripple fuck, little one? A proper man would have got more than one squeal out of you. But don't look to Tangalenna to teach you: he's spoken for. Better come to us.'

Ellie returned his stare for a moment then deliberately turned her back. But instead of responding to the insult, Warady snorted with laughter. At that moment Tupali came outside, his eyes on his brother. Warady pointed at Ellie who was walking towards the forest. 'Are you sure you want one like that, little brother? They're not like our women: they like to be on top.'

'You think I'm not up to it?' A strange expression of desire and determination settled on the young man's face and he strode after the girl with such fierce intent that Warady was taken by surprise. Noumati, who had been watching the brief altercation with mild curiosity, jumped up with a cry of protest but before he could do more, Warady ran to grab his brother's arm and hauled him to a standstill.

'Are you mad?' Warady glanced not at Noumati but towards the path leading to the caves. 'Tangalenna's not dead, only sick. If you rape Ngali-kiri it's not the cripple you'll have to face. We'll get you your own woman: you can do what you like with her.'

Tupali looked penetratingly into the other's eyes and saw fear there and pleading. And because he also feared Tangalenna, he accepted the offer implicit in this speech. He relaxed under his brother's hand, turned back towards the camp. 'We leave today?'

'If you like.' Warady tried to sound casual but a calculating look had come into his eyes. He tilted his head towards the elders and Noumati. They were talking quietly but every-so-often one would glance surreptitiously at the brothers to check what they were up to. 'At least the old man'll be happy: they'll have to stay together until we return.'

'Our mother won't be so pleased,' replied Tupali, grinning, and went to tell her.

To all appearances, Ellie had gone into the forest to relieve herself but the real reason was to discover what had become of her foster-parents. She made a wide circle so as to reach the path to the gorge unseen but when she set foot upon it, she hesitated. The way led steeply up between overhanging myrtles and looked dark and forbidding. It occurred to her that after Tangalenna's claim yesterday, Manalewa might not welcome her intrusion yet it was not that which made her turn and walk thoughtfully back to camp but a kind of prescient dread. More then the others, whose life followed a pattern essentially unaltered for millennia, she sensed impending change. She could not have said why she felt this, only that it had to do with Tangalenna and herself.

When, on returning to camp, she saw Noumati sitting with his father, she realised that as a married woman it would be most fitting to ask her husband to go to the caves: there was, after all, unfinished business between him and Tangalenna. Ignoring Warady's snide comments as she passed, she hurried over. Noumati saw her coming but did not break off his conversation with Pounaté.

Although Ellie was regarded as an adult by the Meelayginnee, at fourteen years old she was still very much a child. Instead of waiting until the two had finished talking as a more experienced woman, even a mature teenager, might have done, Ellie marched straight up and asked outright. As soon as she finished she realised her mistake because Noumati looked embarrassed while Pounaté seemed amused. But the words could not be unsaid.

'Have you still to learn respect?' Noumati demanded. 'You are no child to act as the mood takes you, but my wife. We're hungry. Bring us something to eat, then I will consider what to do. Go!'

At first Ellie thought he was joking: she had never known him so masterful except during a storytelling. But his gaze was hard and unforgiving and she hurried to do his bidding. Only later did she understand that he had acted thus because he wanted to demonstrate his authority: Tanglémerna and her sons were sitting nearby. But as she gathered the meagre remains left by the children and went to forage at the forest's edge, her throat was tight with resentment and she had to fight back tears.

By the time she returned, the two were deep in discussion. In truth Noumati was deeply troubled by Tangalenna's absence and the change wrought in him by his journey. But he was apprehensive also of provoking his half-brother's wrath, knowing how much Tangalenna had desired Ngali-kiri for himself.

Now, as she knelt to lay the food before them, Noumati regretted his earlier harshness but he was afraid of losing face by apologising before the others. Instead, he agreed to go up to the caves if the couple had not returned by midday though he was loth to enter the sacred gorge. Like most of the Meelayginnee he felt a deep dread of the place and had not ventured there since his initiation. He hoped with all his heart that Tangalenna and Manalewa would return before he had to fulfil his promise but seeing the relief on the young woman's face, he was glad he had made the offer.

Tangalenna dreamed that his hearth-group and Pounaté's were afflicted by the sickness that had killed the Broad Ridge people. But though he was the carrier, he did not die and was forced to watch as those he loved vomited then became lethargic and finally jerked in horrible convulsions before sinking into death. Last to succumb was his pale foster-daughter who had used up her strength helping him burn the others: she dragged herself to the river to drink but collapsed on the bank and then her skin spit along the line of her spine and he saw that her body cavity was already packed with seething maggots.

When he woke, shuddering, to find Manalewa sleeping peacefully beside him, Tangalenna wept from sheer relief but the essence of the dream lingered. Carefully, so as not to disturb her, he eased himself away and examined his body for the slightest cut or abrasion, looking for flies or their spawn. Manalewa shifted in her sleep, seeking his warmth but he remained sitting upright, hugging his knees and staring sightlessly to the other side of the gorge where the trees and sandstone cliffs were already lit by sunshine.

As the sun rose, the line of shadow retreated down the cliff but Tangalenna did not move. There was a feeling in his chest as if a boulder had lodged there, a mixture of weariness and dull resentment. He was racked by thirst but could summon neither will nor strength to go down the path to the river. He sat numbly, as if stupefied while the carrion flies of his dreaming buzzed and swarmed.

The sun's rays had reached the deepest depths of the gorge by the time Manalewa stirred. For a moment she lay still, trying to recall where she was and how she had got there then, turning over, she saw Tangalenna silhouetted in the cave mouth. She rose and went to him, wondering at her courage in coming here alone and unasked, then fear pushed all such thoughts from her mind.

At first, from his rigidity and the blankness of his gaze, she thought he was dead but his chest moved slightly as he breathed. Trembling, she laid a hand on his shoulder. There was no reaction. He did not seem to know she was there.

'Tangalenna!' His name seemed to rend her throat. She crouched, mouth dry, appalled.

'Go.' His voice was harsh, inhuman; his visage hard and seemingly unfeeling as stone. To Manalewa it was as if an evil spirit occupied her husband's body, that only a living husk remained of the man she had known and loved. Terrified, she scrambled to her feet and ran from the cave. The yawning maws of the other caverns; the towering mass of sandstone and looming dolerite; the drop to the torrent all whirled before her as she hurried down the cliff path. She sobbed and gasped as she went, realising that the happiness of the night had been an illusion, that after all her efforts Tangalenna had not once acknowledged her presence save by demanding that she leave. Then something at her very core seemed to shrivel and curl up wounded and crying. When she reached the place where myrtles and tree-ferns crowded the path, she did not see Noumati but blundered straight into him, blinded by tears.

The storyteller's anxiety had grown all morning, exacerbated by his memory of Tangalenna's face as he had seen it last, grim, haggard, thwarted. Though the elders were still of the opinion there was nothing wrong that Manalewa could not cure, Noumati, who had endured a lifetime of petty humiliations, thought he understood how his half-brother was suffering.

The sun had not reached its full height when at last he laid aside the spear he was working on and rose. The women and children had long since left camp to go foraging (every day they had to go a little further), and Pounaté was dozing in a patch of sunshine while Warady and Tupali made leisurely preparations for their journey. They should have left earlier but were waiting to see if Tangalenna would return ere midday and if he did not, whether Noumati would dare set off for the sacred gorge alone. Their jibes followed the cripple as he made his way to the start of the path but he ignored them, even when Tupali flung a spear to frighten him.

Once beyond their sight, Noumati breathed a sigh of relief and looked for a stick to use as a staff for he knew the way was steep. This took some time yet soon after setting off again he paused to listen. The clatter of stones on the path ahead indicated that someone was descending.

Noumati waited, for the path was narrow and the approaching footsteps were rapid and sliding: the person was in a hurry. Even so, he was unprepared for the force with which Manalewa crashed into him. She cried out with the unexpected impact and beat frantically at him with her hands until he dropped his stick and managed to catch her wrists, talking to her gently and firmly as if to a frightened child. When she realised who it was, she collapsed into his arms, all resilience gone and he held and soothed her until her sobbing ceased. Then, embarrassed, she pulled away and sat on a moss-covered myrtle root, head bowed, breathing ragged as she fought for control.

He waited, listening for Tangalenna's footsteps but there was only the unceasing roar of the waterfall, the sough of branches overhead, the grating call of a raven. As Manalewa told him haltingly that her husband was still alive but his spirit had fled his body, Noumati felt his flesh creep with horror and he had to look away, unable to bear her gaze. She did not ask him to go and see for himself but he knew he had no choice, not only because of his promise to Ngali-kiri but because he still loved and esteemed Tangalenna.

When Manalewa had finished, Noumati bent and picked up his staff. Her eyes, red-rimmed and swollen, were full of gratitude as he told her to wait in camp and tell no-one what had happened until he returned: she clasped his hand, then rose and walked slowly down the path.

As soon as Manalewa was out of sight, Noumati turned and began the long climb into the gorge. His dread increased with every step but there was a core of pride concealed deep within his nature that would not allow him to turn back. Though his steps were uneven on the rough track, they did not falter nor did he look behind but kept his eyes fixed on the way ahead. He had no idea that he was being followed.

Tangalenna's spirit had not fled his body. Tired almost beyond thought yet outraged to the depths of his being that Manalewa should have invaded the sanctity of his dreaming cave, he had simply waited for her to leave, forgetting how glad he had been to find her there on waking. Every moment she remained was an insult to his standing yet he had lacked the willpower to wake her and this weakness deepened his ire. When, at last, she stirred, the buzzing of flies deafened him to the terror in her voice. It had taken all his strength to force out a single word: 'Go!'

After that, he listened to her retreating footsteps with relief. Now Korunah would guide him. If his daemon did not come, he would know himself lost and walk out over the cliff edge. But then he thought again of Manalewa, of how he had tried to assuage her grief in the past, even stealing the pale child to replace the dead one, and his anger vanished beneath a profound sorrow. He bowed his head, imagining how news of his death would affect the rest: Touganana and Pounaté mourning; Noumati wondering; Ngali-kiri stricken while his enemies gloated and sneered beneath an outward show of grief.

The place where Manalewa had touched him began to itch and the flesh crawled as if maggots were hatching beneath the skin. As he scratched, trying to rid himself of the sensation and the images it conjured in his brain, he realised it was not of his death that Manalewa would speak but of some curse or sickness that afflicted him. Now she had violated his sanctuary, he had no doubt others might do the same. He imagined their sympathy and bewilderment when they saw how he weak he had become; their horror when he told them the fate of the Broad Ridge people and what he had dreamed; how they would pity him at first then, as the full implications sank in, would likely shun and revile him as the bringer of ill-fortune. Even if the doom he had foreseen did not overtake them, each time someone fell sick he would be blamed and, in the end, they would cast him out. And he knew then that he could not do it, not only from pride but because it seemed to him that the only way he could prevent his dream becoming reality was by leaving, either through suicide or self-exile, estranging himself so completely from his people that they would believe him lost. That way, the spirits of the riteless dead might spare those he loved.

Having resolved his dilemma into a simple choice, Tangalenna felt calm and he was able to think of Manalewa and Ngali-kiri with detachment: better they should grieve awhile than die in agony, cursing him for bringing the sickness upon them. Noumati and the girl would look after Manalewa and the children; in his absence perhaps even Warady would take his responsibilities seriously, for it was inevitable that the hearth-groups would unite. And Tangalenna smiled wryly to himself: at least Pounaté and Touganana would be content.

Now that there was a viable alternative, the plunge down the cliff no longer seemed so attractive and he looked hopefully into the sky for his eagle-daemon to appear. He was a resolute man but he was not ready to die. And the fierceness of this conviction persuaded him that even if he could not see it, Korunah must still be with him. He rose awkwardly to his feet and made his way back inside the cave. He knew that once he left he must never return, must remain isolated from his people for as long as his life should last but at least he could take his Nana's relic so that he would have some connection with them, keeping the continuity between past and present, the link with his mentor's wisdom. Then he would have something to counter the loneliness that was bound to affect him, a reminder of why he had chosen this path. He was certain that in such circumstances, her spirit would approve.

He dug the talisman from its hiding place, brushed it clean and placed the thong carefully about his neck so that the bone hung at his breast. Then he shoved the earth roughly back into the hole. He would have liked to take the ochre and at least some of the charcoal with him but he did not want to burden himself with anything he could do without or find elsewhere. And, in any case, the next person to use the cave would need them.

A pang went through him at this thought: though he told himself he could obtain more ochre, he knew that was not the reason. Since coming of age, this place had been the pivot of his world, where his living and dream-selves were centred, and as he picked up the wallaby skin lying near the bed and draped it across his shoulders, he felt again the sense of dislocation that had troubled him since the day he found Ngali-kiri. This time it was so strong it seemed to wrench open his rib-cage. He clutched at the amulet, staggered out of the cave, felt himself fall.

When he came to himself, the drop to the river was but a handsbreadth from his face and the sun's heat pressed upon his back: it was late morning. Slowly he sat up, mouth dry and head reeling. When the rock steadied beneath him, he struggled to his feet. The buzzing of carrion flies in his head was now mixed with mocking laughter: the spirits of the Broad Ridge people deriding his choice. But he remembered Manalewa's face as he had dreamed it, the bloody sockets where birds had pecked out her eyes while she lay dying, and began to climb, following the path down which he had borne the pale child long ago.

Initially satisfied with her husband's promise, Ellie had set out foraging with the rest and endured the good-natured probing and jokes about her wedding night with a kind of dignified forbearance that had the older women laughing and wondering how Noumati had turned her into a wiser woman than they. But her introspection was due to guilt and worry over Tangalenna. As soon as the opportunity arose, she left the others, ignoring the protests of the children who were upset and bewildered by her unusual diffidence.

As she listened to the receding voices, Ellie continued to pick sassafras leaves and only when she was sure no-one was coming back, did she turn and set off for the gorge. So deeply instilled was the lesson of subsistence, the fine line between hunger and starvation, she continued to fill her bag as she went, pausing to dig up especially prized roots. Compared with the easy yet methodical pace with which the women usually combed the land, she worked swiftly yet the sun was past its zenith when she came to the place where Noumati and Manalewa had met. She gave the camp a wide berth so there was no chance of being spotted, thus was unaware of her foster-mother's return.

When she saw the path winding steeply between the dark trees and ferns Ellie was filled with a sense of exaltation. She had almost forgotten the bruised soreness between her legs and Touganana had tended her wounds, exuding the pus and plugging the incisions with fresh ash, but she was still feverish. Her mind soared with a glorious sense of certainty. It seemed to her as she began to climb that her feet were guided by some will other than her own and she gave herself wholly to that unknown power, uncaring that with every step she betrayed her husband's trust and the love he bore her.

By the time Noumati came out on the open cliff face, his body glistened with sweat and he was panting. He leant against the weathered sandstone and looked apprehensively along the narrow ledge. The bottom of the gorge was already in shadow but his side of the valley was bathed in sunlight and he welcomed its warmth which countered the chill he felt within sight of the caves. Those on the opposite, taboo side looked like the gaping eye-sockets of skulls. Their blank stare unnerved him and it took all his courage to set off again.

As Manalewa had done before him, Noumati hurried past the openings of the great caverns where boys and girls were initiated and when he reached the smaller mouth of the seer's cave, he hesitated. There was no smoke, nothing to indicate occupation yet since setting out on the exposed cliff path Noumati had felt acutely self-conscious, as if he were being observed. Then, remembering what Manalewa had told him, he shivered and clutched his staff with both hands like a club. No weapon could touch the throngs of spirits he heard whispering in the waiting darkness, a sound akin to the rustling of bat-wings, but the solidity of the weapon gave him confidence, anchored him in the world of the living. Through dry lips he whispered: 'Tangalenna – are you there?'

There was no reply, only the roar of the river far below and the pounding of his heartbeat in his ears: a cold sweat bathed him. But then he recalled his half-brother's anguish as he had been forced to give away his foster-daughter, how he, Noumati, had gained from that pain. Guilt and love prevented him leaving without knowing Tangalenna's fate. Gripping the staff with all his strength, he bent low and entered the cave.

It was empty and that, to Noumati who had prepared himself to find his half-brother dead or witless, was inconceivable. In disbelief he laid down his staff and felt the leaf-bed, floor, even the sloping walls frantically, like a blind man, as if it were possible that Tangalenna was still there but had somehow become invisible. A high-pitched whimpering came from his throat, a sound he was utterly unconscious of making. Magnified by the rock it became a song of grief and loss, wordless, heart-rending. He searched until the frenzy passed, leaving him weak and shaking. As reason returned to him it seemed clear what choice Tangalenna had made.

Suicide was rare among the Meelayginnee but not unknown. If a person's living-self became so estranged from their dreaming that their daemon forsook them, they were, in effect, already dead: it remained only to still the beating heart that kept the shell of their flesh alive. From the moment he heard Manalewa's tale, Noumati had feared this outcome but the idea of Tangalenna taking his own life was something he had refused to consider. Now, all at once, he was being forced to it.

Sunlight fell through the cave mouth, dazzling him as he groped for his stick and turned to leave. Outside he sank down until he was squatting with his back against the cliff. He leant on his staff, bowed with grief, his forehead pressed against the wood and his silence echoed the void that seemed to have opened up inside him. The unceasing roar of the torrent filled his ears but he could not bring himself to look down to where half-brother's body must lie broken on the rocks below.

The sun slipped westwards and still he sat there. Even when he was engulfed by the shadow which crept inexorably up the cliff face, Noumati did not move. Remembering how Tangalenna had watched Ngali-kiri from the trees; how he had returned from an arduous and fruitless journey to find her given not to a rival but to his crippled half-brother; the passion with which he had made his claim at the betrothal, Noumati began to understand how his half-brother might have been driven to so desperate an act and felt himself at least in part responsible. In baffled anger he ground his teeth, found he had lifted one hand from his staff and was clenching it with such force the nails bit into the palm.

But the tales of his people were embedded as deeply in Noumati's being as memory. As his first shock passed, he began to interpret his half-brother's doomed love for the girl he had stolen as a fable: Tangalenna's desire offended custom surely as Pounaté's coupling with his sister. Thus his grief was gradually tempered into a sorrow that sang through his blood and soothed his mind and while he was not comforted, he at least became calm.

When the whole gorge was in shadow, Noumati stirred at last. His limbs were cold and stiff and despite the support of his staff, he staggered as he made his way down. As he went, he began to formulate how he would break the news. It seemed best to him that only Touganana and Manalewa should know the truth as he understood it: to the rest, the story of Tangalenna's destiny would be a tale of epic proportions. When he reached the crag above the cascades, he paused to regain his breath but he dared not look back, telling himself that the shade of the haunted cliffs would have covered the body in a darkness no mortal eye could pierce.

Ellie had followed so swiftly on her husband's heels that though she took care to keep out of sight, she was close enough to hear his keening as he searched the cave. So distressing was that sound, tears sprang to the girl's eyes and a moan rose to her own throat but with an effort she suppressed it and concealed herself just within the entrance of the adjacent cave. This was the great cavern she had left on the previous morning, head still reeling with the pain and ecstasy of her initiation, but by daylight and in the extremity of the moment the place seemed less dreadful. As Noumati's whimpers became louder and more hysterical, like those of a panic-stricken child, Ellie knew she should go and comfort him but something constrained her. She told herself that she could not because she should not have been there but in her heart she recognised this as an empty excuse. The real reason was loyalty to Tangalenna.

When Noumati emerged and sat beside the entrance of the cave, Ellie guessed her foster-father must be dead but because her husband did not once look into the chasm, she assumed the corpse was inside. Noumati seemed utterly stricken but as the hours crept past and the shadow slid up the cliff, Ellie's pity for him turned to resentment. She could not understand why he had not hurried to break the news to the others so that they could give Tangalenna his rites. As to the fact of her foster-father's demise she could not believe it, would not, until she had seen and touched his body. Her mind was suspended in a kind of limbo as she waited impatiently for her husband to leave.

By the time he rose and limped his way down the path, Ellie was shivering. He walked straight past her and she could have come out then for had he turned to look behind, Noumati was in no state to register anything as unexpected as his wife's presence in the gorge. But now that there was nothing to stop her, Ellie was afraid. Once she saw Tangalenna's corpse, the fact of his death would be irrefutable: until that moment, she could deny it.

In the end, it was a combination of cold, hunger and the realisation that the other women would long since have returned that spurred her to that final, irrevocable move. Automatically picking up her bag and slinging it on her shoulder, she crept out onto the ledge. When she came to the cave mouth she knew her resolve might falter if she hesitated so instead of pausing as Noumati had done, she forced herself to enter.

The interior was so dark she was not certain whether Tangalenna lay there although she sensed the cave was empty. Like Noumati, she crawled forward and felt blindly around the whole floor, dreading the moment she might touch cold, unfeeling flesh. But there was no body, nothing but the pressed-down leaves of the bed, loose dirt and bare rock and her relief was so great she found that she was crying and laughing at the same time. She wondered why Tangalenna's absence should have so distressed Noumati, being ignorant of how fragile the link between self and daemon was; how swiftly and completely the Meelayginnee succumbed to despair once that bond was broken.

There remained, however, one possibility to be eliminated: Tangalenna might have fallen. Her elation checked by sudden dread, she let the bag fall from her shoulder and went outside. Filled with shadow, the gorge seemed fathomless, as if the cliff fell into an abyss and she dropped to her knees and leant carefully over the edge. Her hands gripped the sandstone with all her strength because, for an instant, it seemed to her that if she let herself go, she would not fall but fly.

The white line of the river helped to steady and orientate her: she lay on her belly and as her eyes adjusted to the darkness, made out the shapes of tumbled slabs and boulders at the base of the cliff, the dolerite dark and angular against the sandstone. There was nothing that looked like a human body and while she would not be certain until daylight, this reassured her. She could not, in any case, imagine what might have induced Tangalenna to take his own life, still less believe he had fallen by accident. Diminished as he had appeared at the corroboree, to her he was still unrivalled in strength, more than father and mentor: a kind of hero, and suicide seemed to her the ultimate expression of weakness.

The last of the sun's warmth was leaving the rock on which she lay and no matter how she strained her eyes, she could see nothing new, so Ellie rose stiffly and returned to the cave. She was very hungry so she squatted on one side of the mouth and delved in her bag for something to eat. The leaves were limp but there was still moisture in them: as she chewed, she wondered what to do next. And then, as her thoughts wandered, something crystallised in her mind and she groped her way inside.

It was not even a coherent recollection, more the shadow of a memory. There had been the dome of mottled rock above her, the sound of someone digging close by, then the harsh rhythmic strokes of ochre being ground and a deep ululation, half-chanted, half-sung, which had lulled her deeper into her swoon. A profound feeling of loss and loneliness crept over Ellie as she felt her way to the very back of the cave: she did not even know what she sought. Then her hands found a patch of clods, recently disturbed, and she remembered Tangalenna's amulet.

She dug, possessed by urgency she did not understand. Her fingers jabbed painfully against something hard and she worked it free. It was a lump of ochre the size of her fist. She recognised its earthy, metallic smell, laid it aside and continued to dig until she came to solid rock. Nothing else could be buried there and she replaced the ochre with a feeling of elation. She was certain now that Tangalenna was alive and had taken the talisman away with him. It remained only for her to find him.

Chapter 12.

By the time Manalewa reached the river flats, she had recovered some composure. Tangalenna and Noumati were closer to each other than most siblings and she had faith that if anyone could coax her husband's spirit back into his body, it would be the storyteller.

The camp was deserted except for Pounaté, who sat dozing by the fire. The women and children were still out foraging and Warady and Tupali had departed on their quest. The old man looked up inquiringly as Manalewa crossed the clearing but at the sight of her tear-stained face, he scrambled to his feet.

'Eh, my daughter, what is it?' He scanned her body for signs of violence and, finding none, frowned in bewilderment.

'Is Tangalenna sick?'

The restraint she had forced on herself broke at these words: she fell weeping into his arms. He held her and stroked her head but he was deeply unsettled by this outpouring from a woman who was usually self-contained and proud. As she became calm, she sensed his discomfiture and was herself embarrassed and ashamed at her lack of control. She pulled away abruptly. He was a patient man and so, instead of interrogating her, he waited until she was ready to speak.

At length, in stumbling sentences, she told him what had happened. Pounaté's skin crawled with horror: he remembered the look on Tangalenna's face as he had turned to walk away. With hindsight, it seemed to the elder that it might indeed been the face of one forsaken by his daemon, estranged from the living world, who goes seeking death. Unable to comfort his daughter, he stared helplessly at her as she finished her tale, longing for Touganana to return for she, being a woman, might know what to do. And Manalewa, realising his powerlessness to help her, smiled wanly, thanked him for his sympathy and set off to find her children, to reassure herself that they at least were alive and whole.

With every step Ellie took away from the cave, her excitement grew. It was the same kind of elation she had felt climbing the gate into the forest four years earlier but the irony of this escaped her. She walked up the steep cliff path with a light, swift stride which made Tangalenna's earlier progress seem that of an old man. The sky was that clear turquoise that comes between sunset and the appearance of the first stars: as she ascended it seemed to her that she was climbing into it. When she reached the place where the ledge was truncated by the fault-cleft, she paused to look back. The gorge had become a dark gash, a shadow-filled wound in the earth

It had rained recently and her ears quickened to the sound of dripping water. She had not drunk since early morning and the fever in her blood made her more than usually thirsty. But she had learned patience and, instead of rushing, picked her way carefully into the gully, wary of unstable slabs and snakes basking in the warmth still radiating from the sun-heated stone.

The water was no more than a tiny trickle which seeped through fractures in the rock from the plateau high above. The path it took was stained with iron minerals and tannins, coated with green algae. These, combined with acids leached from the heathlands high above, gave the liquid a strong, bitter taste and Ellie drank sparingly then stopped, assailed by a sudden unease.

The child Tangalenna had carried down this very cleft would have been incapable of discerning it but Ellie's faculties had been sharpened by life with the Meelayginnee. She sensed, though an almost telepathic empathy, that she was not alone. Slowly, she straightened, waiting until the other, person or animal, revealed itself through sound or movement. She was perfectly calm yet alert as a hunter, sensitive even to the caress of the cool night air against her skin. Though she hoped it was Tangalenna, she guessed his enemies must have left camp earlier and did not put it past them to have doubled back in order to revenge themselves upon him. Silently, she edged backwards until she felt solid rock behind, and waited.

'Ngali-kiri!' It was little more than a low growl but in that moment Ellie realised her assumption that Tangalenna would welcome, even desire, her presence had been wrong. After four years of living in close proximity to this man, she knew him almost as intimately as a lover: his voice, the nuances of his body language, even the changed smell of him when he was angry or lustful. She shrank against the rock, elation swamped by fear. From his tone she understood the magnitude of what she had done in coming here.

A shadow detached itself from an angular patch of darkness but instead of his usual lithe grace, Tangalenna moved with the clumsiness of a wounded or sick animal. As he came into the open, Ellie saw that he was feeling his way with one hand as if he had been struck blind. His shoulders were oddly hunched and his left hand clutched something at his breast. When he was within reach, he let go the talisman and grasped her shoulder with such force, she had to bite back a cry. His fingernails dug into her skin like talons.

'Where's Noumati?'

'He went back down.' Shaken by the harshness of his voice, his bitterness, Ellie writhed beneath his grip. 'He doesn't know I'm here.'

'Ah.' Tangalenna let go and sat heavily on a boulder. The lambent starlight lent his skin a greasy texture; his face was like something carved from wax. He looked at her indifferently, with eyes that seemed seared by inexpressible grief but his expression conveyed a terrible resignation. Gradually, Ellie's fear turned to a mixture of bewilderment and pity.

'Father, what's wrong?'

'You are no longer a child: your place is with your husband,' he said. 'And you have not found me. Go away!'

So strange was his inflexion on these last words, Ellie was assailed by an instinctive aversion, that of the whole for the maimed, the sane for the mad. A chill struck to her very core as she looked upon him for he did not seem in his right mind. His eyes stared not at but through her, as if he saw a different world. She stood still, watching him in silence, not knowing what to do.

'Go back to Noumati,' he said at last. 'You should not have come here.'

'But you claimed me,' she stammered, frightened by his sternness, the strangeness of his mood. 'I want to stay with you!'

She heard these words as if someone else had spoken them, a

child blurting to stave off punishment or the doing of an onerous task. And as if he realised this, Tangalenna smiled wryly and murmured, 'Little one, go away,' then rose slowly to his feet and turned to face the narrow cleft and the treacherous climb to the top of the cliff.

'No, wait!' Ellie was afraid to lay hands on him but she darted to block his way. 'Are you hungry? I brought some food.'

He stopped then, not from the hunger that racked him to the sinews but because the shadowed way out, difficult enough by day, suddenly seemed impossible. It was taking all his willpower to stay upright. He snatched the bag she held out to him and squatted to delve inside, hoping she would not notice the tremors running through his body. As he crammed handfuls of leaves, roots, fungi into his mouth, slavering like a dog as he chewed, Ellie felt a curious sense of triumph: now he had accepted food, he would not be able to reject her so easily. And to press home her advantage, she said softly, 'Noumati will understand. He will care for Manalewa and the children.'

Tangalenna did not reply. Even in his bemused state, he knew that now was the time he must be firm and send this woman, who was really still a child, away. But all that was weak rose in him even as this thought crystallised: to be estranged from his kin would be a kind of living death but with Ngali-kiri, Korunah's gift, at his side he could perhaps make a new life for himself. He laid aside the bag, pulled the wallaby-skin closer about his shoulders and settled with his back against a smooth slab where, unable to resist the tide of weariness that overwhelmed him, he closed his eyes and fell immediately asleep. Ellie watched him for a while, longing to touch him but frightened lest he wake and be angry. Instead, she picked up the bag and, using it as a pillow, curled up beside him and though he did not reach out or in any way acknowledge her, neither did he push her away.

With Warady and Tupali gone and Tangalenna assumed dead (since no-one saw reason to doubt Noumati's tale), an ominous quiet settled on the camp even before it was realised that Ngali-kiri was also missing. Despite the tension of the day, her absence was not remarked until nightfall when both hearth-groups had gathered round a single fire to eat and reflect.

Even Noumati, who was most eager for her return, (after the pleasures of their wedding night his body craved more), did not voice his concern though the last streaks of sunset had left the sky. It was not unusual, after all, for a woman out foraging to return late or to go off alone if she craved solitude for a while. Though she had not been in camp when he returned from the cave, nor did the women remember when they had last seen her, he guessed she must have been close enough to hear what had happened and had gone somewhere to grieve privately.

But as the twilight deepened, Noumati's fears grew. Though he quelled them as best he could, his anxiety was betrayed by the way his eyes flicked in the direction of any untoward sound, his look of disappointment when the slim, pale form of his wife did not appear. Yet still he did not unburden himself to Pounaté or Touganana or suggest a search be mounted at first light. In part this was because he might be scorned as an over-protective husband but he also feared how deeply his wife esteemed Tangalenna.

Manalewa, who had been stricken by the news of Tangalenna's demise but continued her daily tasks with a kind of numb, mechanical efficiency, watched Noumati carefully, her face set in a frozen expression of grief. Then, when her children finished eating she took them into their hut and shut the door. She had eaten nothing and Touganana shook her head. 'She's taking it hard, poor girl. What was he thinking of, that son of mine, to do such a thing?' And she folded her arms across her withered breasts and began to rock back and forth, keening quietly to herself.

The old man regarded her with compassion but he was too wise to attempt to comfort her. Instead he turned to his son. 'Has Ngali-kiri already forgotten she has a husband?'

Noumati stiffened. 'I have not seen her since she left this morning with the other women,' he said defensively. 'She was closer to her foster-father than if they had shared the same blood: she will be mourning him in her own way.' As was the custom, he avoided naming the dead.

'That may be but do not forget, my son, her first obligations are to you however greatly she feels our loss,' Pounaté said. 'It is already dark. It may be that she has strayed off the path or a black snake has bitten her.'

As soon as these words left his lips, the old man regretted them for a look of horror spread over Noumati's face and he glanced towards Tanglémerna who sat silent and gloating on the opposite side of the fire. Only then did Pounaté remember that Black Snake was Warady's daemon and in an effort to avert the ill-omen he spread his gnarled hands wide, saying urgently: 'Eh – Noumati – I didn't mean –'

'If he's – if either of them has laid a finger on her, I'll kill them!' Noumati's usually calm eyes were wild: he looked round as if he were about to grasp the nearest weapon and set off after the brothers. But Touganana, whose keening had diminished to a barely audible whine, broke off and fixed her son with so daunting a stare that instead of clambering to his feet and stalking off into the night, he felt the anger drain from his blood, leaving him impotent.

'On this night when my proper son's spirit has been stolen away, you talk of killing?' she asked sternly and it seemed that she had been empowered rather than weakened by her grief. 'If the pale one is grieving, is that something to be surprised at? She has been brought up in our ways but it was he brought her here: he was father and more to her. Tupali and Warady, for all their faults, are respectful of the law and the younger wants his own woman, not one a cripple has mated with.'

These words struck Noumati like sharp blows but he could not deny their truth. His mouth flooded with bile; he muttered, 'Better he had never found her,' then struggled to his feet and limped away to his shelter where he lay down with his face to the wall.

Pounaté watched him go with anguished eyes. Of all his children the storyteller was the one he had come to love best and he was torn between the urge to try and comfort him and knowledge that to do so might be interpreted as a further assault on Noumati's manhood.

'Stay.' Touganana laid a hand on the old man's thigh, feeling the bone beneath slack skin and muscle. 'Likely enough she'll be back by dawn: she'll have wandered further than she thought in her grief and settled down for the night. She's no fool to blunder around in the dark.'

'Eh, you're a clever woman.' Relieved, Pounaté laid his hand over hers, ignoring Tanglémerna's dark stare from the opposite side of the fire. 'Maybe Manalewa will be comforted a little if Ngali-kiri is there to help her.'

'I think it'll take more than the presence of the one he claimed in front of all to balance her loss,' Touganana said sardonically, then lowered her voice to a whisper. 'Yet my heart will not accept my son's death until my eyes have seen his corpse. Let that be a secret between us, Pounaté. If they have run away together, I do not think they will ever return. Better for Manalewa and Noumati if they believe them dead.'

So preposterous was this suggestion, Pounaté laughed.

'Surely –' he began but suddenly it seemed to him that beneath the folds of the matriarch's face, lined with age and experience, he saw the young woman whose beauty and vivacity had aroused a kind of frenzy in him until, when she became another man's wife, he had taken her. That first forbidden coupling had kindled a similar fire in her so that they became infamous, shameless in their insatiable passion, sneaking away whenever chance allowed to make the forest ring with their cries. And recalling Tangalenna's face as he had seen it last, doubt seized him.

'But she is Noumati's!' was all he could think of in response.

'And so?' Touganana's eyes creased as she looked meaningfully at the old man who was both her brother and her lover. 'You of all men should understand. I tell you, and I shall not speak of it again: until I see his body and prepare it for burning, I will not believe he is truly dead.'

'Eh, I don't know.' So agitated was Pounaté that he got stiffly to his feet and stood tugging at his foreskin with more than usual vigour, much to Tanglémerna's amusement. 'To go off with his own daughter? No – I won't have it, Korunah called him and he is lost.'

'Lost indeed,' said Touganana. 'And Manalewa heavy with child and with two others to support. More than ever our hearth-groups must stay as one, even when Warady and Tupali return.'

Pounaté turned his face away, afraid of what she might read from his expression.

'That is how it must be.'

Ignorant of their enemy's disappearance, the two brothers were but half a day's walk down the great valley. They had surprised and speared a young pademelon that had strayed too far from its mother's pouch and being in no hurry, made camp early. Away from the hearth-group they were affected by a rare sense of freedom and as they lounged beside their fire, waiting for the meat to cook, they amused themselves by making fun of the others, Noumati and Tangalenna especially.

'Maybe we let him off too lightly,' Tupali said. 'We should've followed him up to the caves, painted our faces and given him a fright to remember. His dreams wouldn't have warned him of that one!'

Warady shrugged. 'Too late now, little brother. And I for one don't fancy going up those cliffs at night. By the look of him, he's already had one bad dream too many. Wait till you see his face when we bring back another woman like his precious Ngali-kiri. He won't seem so special then.'

'Frightened he'll give you another beating?' Tupali leant forward to poke the bubbling skin of the joey with a stick and so missed the look of rage and shame which passed across his brother's face. 'But both of us together could take him, maybe break his legs so he'd never hunt again.'

'Bluetongue speaks louder than his actions,' Warady said, the lizard being Tupali's daemon. 'What for? Our hearth-groups are one: do you want to have to feed and carry the man you've crippled from camp to camp until he dies? Or face being outcast while he and Noumati enjoy our wives? Forget it.'

Tupali grunted discontentedly but he knew better than to argue. In an effort at appeasement Warady added quietly, 'Listen, I hate him more than you: don't forget I've had to live with him and his kin these past years. But there is some sickness grown upon him lately and Ngali-kiri is to blame. We'll witness his demise without having to lift a finger and when we bring another white woman into camp it'll hasten his fall. You'll see.'

'But I want to have a hand in it.' Tupali whined like a sulky child.

'Oh, you will.' Warady dragged the charred carcass from the ashes and began to pull it apart. 'Make your woman squeal every night, set the marks of your teeth and hands on her skin and it'll drive him mad. In the end he'll rape one of them, yours or his precious daughter, and then we'll have him driven out or worse. Isn't that worth waiting for?'

'Don't judge Tangalenna by what you'd do in his place,' Tupali replied with unusual sagacity. 'If that happened, it'd be a fitting revenge. But he may see it beforehand in a dream and then what?'

Warady snorted, swallowed the mouthful of meat he had torn from the joey's haunch, then spat to demonstrate his contempt for his enemy's gift. 'He can think what he likes but he's no different to the rest of us. He didn't dream of losing Ngali-kiri to the cripple, did he? You could see it in his face yesterday: he'd failed and he knew it.'

'Ay.' Tupali twisted some ribs off the animal's spine and contemplated the strips of flesh hanging from the bones. 'It must have been a blow to one so proud. And a woman like Ngali-kiri will scream more than one of ours: their flesh is softer or hadn't you noticed? We'll have some fun, brother: we only have to catch one!'

It was twilight. A tawny frog-mouth called mournfully from close by and Warady shivered and threw more wood on the fire. 'Eat up then and go to sleep. We'll need all our strength and cunning for this hunt.'

In the riverside camp Noumati lay with his face to the back of his lean-to. He was so still, it seemed he was asleep. But in fact he was in a state of extreme anxiety, teeth and fists clenched as he listened to Pounaté and Touganana talk. At first he heard their voices without comprehending the words but gradually their meaning dawned on him and then he ground his teeth and had to stifle a groan.

Long after the old couple's snores sounded through the camp Noumati tormented himself with thoughts of how easily he had been deceived, challenging Tupali's claim on Ngali-kiri when Tangalenna had been his true rival all along. He was still convinced of Tangalenna's death but now he guessed why Ngali-kiri was missing: she had taken her own life to bind herself forever to her secret lover. And this, to Noumati, was far worse than if he had discovered them copulating in the sacred caves. Wrongdoing by the living could be atoned for but the dead were untouchable and there was no redress for the victims of their crimes.

Recalling how he had betrayed his feelings to the young woman long before he dared considered claiming her for his own, Noumati gnawed his knuckles in shame and self-recrimination, cursing himself for his blindness. He had watched Tangalenna's love for his foster-daughter alter as she matured but he had not foreseen that he would want her as a wife, nor that she would follow him into death when their ambition was thwarted.

Yet as storyteller wrestled with these thoughts, he found it hard to believe that any man, especially one so proud, would destroy himself simply because he could not have a woman. Gradually, as the first wave of bitterness passed, he realised that there must have been some other reason for Tangalenna's suicide, something to do with his fruitless journey, and pity stirred in him though he could not forgive the betrayal. He turned over and stared across the camp then wept in silence, bereft.

Having driven himself to exhaustion, Tangalenna slept deeply on the uneven rock platform but Ellie could not get comfortable. Thoughts of Noumati waiting and Manalewa grieving kept her awake and she was excited by the audacity of what she was doing. Flattered by Tangalenna's claim, she imagined the two of them roaming the forests and remote uplands together until, when she became heavy with child, they would make a home, no flimsy lean-to but a proper house with inside hearth and chimney. Then, one day when they had raised their children (three was the highest number she thought she could cope with on her own), they would return to the others as the nucleus of a new hearth-group.

This romantic dream of life with Tangalenna as her lover lasted maybe half the night, then the reality of her situation sank in. Away from the hearth-group, if either of them fell sick they would be wholly reliant on the other; if they succumbed together, they risked starvation. And then she thought of pregnancy without the support of the more experienced women. If there were complications, Tangalenna could not help her: Meelayginnee men were forbidden to witness the ultimate women's mystery. She would be utterly alone.

For a while she was daunted by these possibilities but when she contemplated the alternative, to return to camp next morning and continue living as Noumati's wife, she realised her mind was already made up. Her love for her husband lacked the passion she felt for Tangalenna and she was young, possessed by an adolescent's yearning for novelty. And Tangalenna had openly declared his feelings at her betrothal, accepted her presence when she found him in the sacred gorge. Though she suspected this last was due more to a kind of profound resignation, a bowing to fatality, than desire, she knew he would not now send her away.

There was a faint translucence in the eastern sky and the squawks of lorakeets and currawongs sounded from the forest when Ellie at last fell asleep. Her head was pillowed on Tangalenna's arm for he had moved closer to her during the night, seeking warmth. His bone amulet, squashed between them, left deep indentations in their flesh when, on waking, they broke apart and stared at one another. For both it seemed that reality was even stranger than their dreams.

Manalewa rose soon after dawn and sent the children to collect fuel while she coaxed the fire into life. She was desperate to speak to Noumati but when she crept to his shelter she found him lying with half-closed eyes in a state so similar to her husband's trance that she ran away. When she reached the river she stopped. Eventually the current would sweep Tangalenna's body down to lodge among branches already snagged on the rocks. She sat on a flat boulder to wait and allowed the myriad voices of the water to lull her into a kind of unthinking quietude while the children, having returned from the woods, splashed happily in a shallow embayment, ignorant of their father's fate.

After what he had overheard, Noumati dreaded meeting his half-sister. Having promised to restore her husband to her, he did not want to reveal how she had been betrayed. He had seen her approach and deliberately feigned trance but when she fled, he was ashamed. After a while he scrambled out of his shelter and followed her, limping heavily because his legs were stiff and sore after the climb to the caves.

Manalewa was sitting still and erect beside the river and had the children not spotted him, Noumati would have crept away rather than disturb her. But the little boy, Puennena, gave a cry of delight and dragged his sister over and the storyteller had no choice but to stay. He crouched to hug them and let them lead him to their mother. Her eyes were fixed on the swirling water which appeared opaque as black glass.

'Myrtle Tree will mourn until Eagle lodges in her boughs,' Manalewa said sadly after Noumati had greeted her. When the hungry children tugged at her hands, she pulled free. 'Let Ngali-kiri look after them until my beloved has been burned. I cannot live again until he is free.'

Grief had lent her dignity and as he looked at her, Noumati was gripped by a sudden wild hatred of the man responsible for her suffering. There were no tear-marks on her skin but sorrow was stamped into her features; her face had grown haggard and fine lines that had not been there before were etched around her mouth.

'And what if he does not come?' Noumati's voice was harsh: he had to force out the words but he knew they must be said. 'There are many places a body might stick between the caves and here: he may not even have fallen into the river. Your children need you for Ngali-kiri is also missing. Nor should you forget the one you carry in your womb.'

He had added the last sentence hurriedly because he was unable to bear the look that passed across Manalewa's face at this news. It was as if a mask had slipped to reveal the turmoil beneath yet she recovered her composure swiftly. Her gaze was no longer fixed on the swirling water but upon her hands which were folded demurely in her lap.

'A day and a night I will give him and if he does not return, I shall burn our hut, our bed, the ochre I have ground for him, in his stead,' she said and her voice took on the rhythm and detachment of a chant. 'All who witness the smoke of that burning will know he is dead: I bereft of husband; our children fatherless. And when Ngali-kiri sees it, she will come back to us. She is a good daughter: why should she have stolen him from me, whose milk gave her life, who made her what she is? She is as much ours as if she shared our blood.'

Something seemed to twist at his very core at these words but Noumati lacked the courage to tell her his suspicions

'I will make sure your children are cared for and I shall bring you food,' he said at last, with an effort. She looked up to meet his eyes and her gaze was now hard and fierce.

'He was our provider, my sustenance and comfort,' she replied. 'Nothing will pass my lips save the water with which his last breath is mingled until what remains of him has gone to the flames. Nor will I speak with any man or woman save him alone and Ngali-kiri until that time is passed. That is the only gift I can give him and if Korunah is not satisfied, he does not have far to seek me.'

Before such control Noumati was humbled and his anger seemed petty and futile, the spat of a frustrated child. Lost for words, he touched her shoulder in acknowledgement and sympathy before clambering awkwardly to where the children had begun pulling up reeds and sedges to bite or suck hopefully at the bulbous roots.

'Eh, come with me and we'll find better food and, if we're lucky, a new tale.' So skilful was Noumati's dissimulation that the children followed him without a backward glance. Manalewa sat on, still and silent as the tree she leant against and her eyes were fixed again on the river.

The rest of the hearth-group were much dismayed when they heard of the vigil but in time the story of how Myrtle Tree waited for Eagle's return after Brown Quoll stole his spirit became one of their favourites. For a woman to deliberately seclude herself was unprecedented: a boy undergoing his trial before initiation was expected to wander away for a time but such freedom was never granted to females. Yet so shaken were the elders by recent events, they respected Manalewa's decision when ordinarily she would have been severely chastised for neglecting her responsibilities to the group.

Only Tanglémerna and Ana-Maïda dared voice their feelings, the older from frustration, the younger from envy though with the two brothers away, her life was much improved. When Pounaté told them to gather food for a funeral feast, they grumbled that it was for the widow to provide for all: only when the old man picked up a club and advanced threateningly towards them did they scurry away into the forest with their food bags. The youngest children stayed with Noumati to learn a new dance in the dead man's honour while Pounaté and Touganana set off into the forest. They carried club and digging stick but the path they took led to the sacred gorge.

The old couple walked in companionable silence to the place where Manalewa had blundered into Noumati the day before and there Touganana sat on a tree root while Pounaté climbed down to the water's edge. From here he could see the pool below the waterfall and the start of the rapids which ran down past the camp. Though he had begun to believe Tangalenna might still be alive, he scanned each place diligently. Then he spotted something brown and smooth lodged against the bank on the far side of the river. His heart lurched and he cried out involuntarily, bringing the old woman scrambling to join him. They stared at the object until their vision blurred. One moment they were convinced it was just a log, the next certain that the dappled sunlight gleamed on the wet skin of a man's body, half-submerged.

The river was fast flowing and deep in places and neither were good swimmers: since their band's estrangement from the coast, swimming, a skill in which the women had once excelled, was no longer widely practised. Tentatively, Pounaté lowered himself into the water, gasping at its coldness, and began to wade. Within a couple of steps he was in up to his thighs. Touganana handed him a stick with which to feel his way for the river bed consisted of smooth, weed-slimed boulders, slippery and treacherous. She watched anxiously as he splashed in a wide arc, following the line of the rapids a little downstream; gasped aloud when he slipped and disappeared under the ripples, laughed with relief when he surfaced, flailing wildly until he regained his balance. Then he pushed his way through grim-faced. His eyes were dazzled by reflected sunlight so it was not until he was within reach of the thing that he could see what it was.

'Only a log!' Touganana could hardly hear his voice above the roar of the torrent but Pounaté's expression was enough. His teeth gleamed in a wide smile and he splashed his way back with the exuberance of a child, sweeping his hands through the water to send up showers of sparkling droplets. It was only now he realised how much he had dreaded finding Tangalenna's body after all.

'Eh – have you lost your wits?' Touganana scolded as she hauled him up the bank, panting and dripping. 'Next time you go for a dip have someone downstream to catch you. Haven't we lost enough folk these last days without foolish old men drowning themselves?'

'Be quiet, woman, and do something to warm me!' There was a triumphant gleam in Pounaté's eyes but he was racked by shivering and water streamed down his body. Touganana clucked her tongue as if to admonish a mischievous child, then took his hand and led him a little way up the path to a sunlit patch of soft grass and moss.

'Come then, we can warm each other if River hasn't sapped all your strength!'

Tangalenna's astonishment at seeing Ellie was followed swiftly by anger. It was the blind, unreasoning rage of a cornered animal and it possessed him with such force, he trembled. He could remember little of the previous day but he knew he should be alone, an exile, estranged from his people in order to protect them. Now the girl for whose sake he had been humiliated was staring at him with wide, adoring eyes. He longed to smash the look of hopeful expectancy from her face but even as he raised himself and lifted his hand, he realised that whatever injustice he inflicted upon her, it would not alter the faith that shone from her eyes: she would follow him to the uttermost limits of her strength. And the intensity of her ardour frightened him. Unable to bear her gaze, he clambered to his feet and turned away, seeking a way out of the gully.

It was not until he began the climb proper that Tangalenna realised how weak he was. The cleft he was following was the one he had descended with the pale child so long ago and while an ascent was at least possible, the looseness of the rocks made every step treacherous. The difficulty of the climb was exacerbated by the black specks which kept dancing before his eyes. Thinking they were the flies that buzzed constantly in his ears, he would scrabble his way up a little way then stop and flap his hands to ward them off until Ellie, watching him beat at empty air, grew afraid. When his vision cleared enough to see the next handhold and he had recovered sufficiently to move again, he lunged forward, clawing at the scree until he found enough purchase to haul himself up.

In this way it took half the morning to reach the top of the cliff and the sun's heat seemed to leach the last of Tangalenna's strength as he dragged himself over the edge. So focused was he on the climb, he did not notice a tug at his neck when the thong of his amulet snagged on a jagged rock and snapped. The bone relic, his talisman, slipped into a crevice and dropped into unreachable darkness.

Ellie was appalled by her companion's painful progress which, as his strength failed, became more desperate, but she was too mindful of his pride to offer help. Instead she followed a little behind, moving with a careless agility that made Tangalenna's efforts appear all the more pitiful. When at last they emerged onto relatively flat ground, Tangalenna cast himself down, gasping for breath, his bloodshot eyes half-closed. It was then that she noticed his pendant was missing but being ignorant of its true significance, she did not remark it.

The buzzing in his ears had grown so loud that when Tangalenna recovered enough to sit up, he could not understand where the flies were: though his vision was blurred, the black specks had disappeared. He rubbed his eyes, which were stinging from the sweat which had run into them, and looked around. The slim, pale form of his fosterling stood in the V of the cleft, looking down, and for a moment he thought he must be dreaming because he could not recall seeing her since leaving the corroboree. To steady himself, he felt for the talisman at his chest. It was not there and panic overtook him: he clutched frantically at his breast, his throat, then groped blindly on the ground, digging his fingers into the stony earth with such force that the fingernails split.

'Where is it? Where is it?' A despairing cry broke from him: he lunged forward and would have plunged headlong down the gully had Ellie not caught his arm and dragged him back.

'Get off!' He fought her, growling and clawing like a cat but she hung on, wrapping her arms round his neck and her legs about his thighs to hamper him. Diminished as he was, his wiry strength was almost too much for her but to him her weight seemed insupportable. It was as if his guilt, the disapprobation of his ancestors, the vengeful spirits of the Broad Ridge people had combined forces to drag him down and crush him. Against these he had no recourse and his struggles grew feeble, like those of an animal exhausted at the end of a long chase. Ellie relaxed her hold though she remained alert to the possibility that he might suddenly rally and run over the cliff edge in a blind dash for escape. But he shuddered beneath her hands and then began to weep in great racking sobs that shook his whole frame.

The Meelayginnee were generally uninhibited in exhibiting emotion yet Ellie had never seen any adult lose control as Tangalenna did now. He rolled his head against the earth, alternately groaning and wailing; beat his fists on the ground or clawed spasmodically at it. His face was smeared with a paste of soil, tears and saliva and his hands were torn and bleeding but he did not stop until exhaustion overcame his frenzy. At last he lay quiet, one arm flung to hide his face, sprawled as if he had been struck down from behind. His breathing was so shallow, his ribs barely moved. The shadow of a twisted pandanus tree slid slowly across his back.

Since the day of her abduction, Ellie had grown to regard Tangalenna as her guardian and mentor; lately she had begun to idolise him, to think of him as infallible, matchless in strength and courage, wisdom and endurance. To see him unmanned shook her profoundly. She felt his degradation like a wound, was embarrassed by and for him: nothing she could imagine justified such behaviour.

She felt suddenly adrift and terribly alone. It was as if she did not know him at all.

The shadow of the pandanus lay diagonally across Tangalenna's body and still he did not move. The air was hot and dry and Ellie was thirsty. There was no water in this part of the gully so she walked up the slope to gain a view of the plateau. She had no memory of the place yet as she looked along the ridge and saw the piled boulders of Tarner's Tail in the distance, it was as if a warning finger pressed against the nape of her neck. She stared, then pushed the feeling aside. The need for water was urgent and she scanned the heathland for the tell-tale signs: a change in vegetation, flocking birds, a shimmer in the air. There was a promising-looking dip about half a kilometre away so she glanced behind to fix her bearings and set off. She did not see the eagle circling high above.

Chapter 13.

Slack and sated in the aftermath of their lovemaking (gentleness had long ago replaced the violent passion of their youth), Touganana and Pounaté walked slowly to the smooth outcrop at the top of the cascades. Cliffs rose high and menacing to either side and the gorge ahead was filled with shadow, making it appear deeper than it really was. Neither of them wanted to go further.

'If he fell into the river, he would already have come down the waterfalls,' Touganana said after a long silence. 'And if he hit the rocks, he is beyond our reach. We can do nothing more.'

The old man was grateful for these words which enabled him to give up the search without losing face. He looked into his lover's eyes and found there a depth of understanding and compassion that humbled him.

'Dead or alive, be sure that one day he will come back to us.' Oppressed by the towering walls of rock, the unceasing roar of water, he looked up into the narrow strip of sky, cried out suddenly and pointed. 'Look there, Touganana! Korunah has not deserted your son. I tell you: he is still alive!'

'Aie . . .' Touganana followed his gaze yet once she had glimpsed the circling eagle, she turned away. 'But maybe he would be better dead.'

The old man watched with a puzzled frown as she began to make her way down the rough path: when she neither looked back nor waited, he set off after, keeping a discreet distance between them all the way back to camp.

Despite the rain, the hearth-group spent the remainder of that day and all the next gathering food and fuel for the funeral. During that time Manalewa maintained her vigil, oblivious to the visits of Noumati and her father who worried lest harm befall her. Puennena and Leena were cared for, grudgingly, by Tanglémerna and Ana-

Maïda. The women offered little sympathy though by now the children had begun to realise that something dreadful had happened to their father and Ngali-kiri. They missed their foster-sister especially because until recently she had always had time to play with them.

Throughout the night, when the water seemed black and glossy as blood, and the long hours of daylight when her eyes grew tired of its swirling, Manalewa watched the river. She left it only when she needed to relieve herself for she would not pollute the flow which bore her husband's body. When she was so tired she could hardly keep her eyes open, she placed a thorny branch behind her back so that if she sagged against the tree, it would prick her awake. But by then she was so bemused by exhaustion that if Tangalenna's corpse had lodged close by, she would not have recognised it.

In the afternoon of the second day, Touganana brought charcoal and ochre to the grieving woman and the blackness of burnt wood seemed to epitomise the bleakness of her spirit while the redness of the ochre was like dried blood. She imagined Tangalenna's body burst open on the sharp rocks at the base of the cliff and shuddered as she ground the powders then made pastes which she smeared on her face, breasts, pudenda, buttocks, those parts most cherished by a husband and lover. But as the rain increased to a deluge, mingling and washing away the pigments, Manalewa was elated by a wholly improper sense of freedom, of liberation. She moved the thorn branch which had made bloody holes in her lower back and leant against the tree, stroking her rounded belly where the child grew, apologising for the privations she had forced upon it during her fast and promising that from now on she would nurture and love it as the last of Tangalenna's blood. When Touganana and Noumati came to escort her into camp, they found her caressing herself and singing softly and they looked at one another askance, fearing an evil spirit had taken advantage of her grief and stolen her wits.

Uncertainty over his true fate and the continuing absence of his foster-daughter made the burning of Tangalenna's hut and possessions an awkward affair. Noumati especially was uneasy. He interpreted the downpour as a sign that his half-brother was still alive, making a mockery of the ceremony that was about to take place: it would become an affront to the man and, more dangerously, his daemon. Although it was already dark, the cripple kept glancing nervously into the streaming sky, half-expecting to see a monstrous eagle circling, ready to stoop and beat out the sacrilegious flames with its wings. Pounaté watched his son with worried eyes, fearing what he might reveal, for it was for him to add Tangalenna's story to the history of the band. The children stood waiting with Ana-Maïda and Tanglémerna. Their toes kneaded the mud and the women's eyes gleamed like polished stones in the leaping firelight for all the fires except the one outside Tangalenna's hut had been built up against the rain.

Inside, branches had been piled over the bed and the couple's possessions: ochre, the grinding stones, his weapons, the scallop shell dipper that had been handed down from generation to generation, Manalewa's collecting bag. Once these had been burned, Tangalenna's name would never be spoken again: he would be referred to obliquely, by kinship or daemon. Even his children were subject to this rule, for fear of disturbing his spirit.

The light from the flaring fire-stick she held was reflected by Manalewa's wet skin as she stooped through the entrance of the home she had shared with husband and foster-daughter. She looked like something from the Pygeewar, a creature of darkness and fire: her face was rapt and still. Even Ana-Maïda and Tanglémerna felt a kind of awe as she thrust the burning brand into the pyre, then stood back. She was instantly lit up from head to foot as the leaves and bark exploded into flame.

The wind roared in the trees, drowning the sound of the blaze but the lashing rain could not extinguish the pillar of fire that consumed the shelter in a matter of minutes. Driven back by the gusting heat, wreathed in smoke, Manalewa stared fixedly into the white centre of the conflagration but her children ran crying to Noumati, not understanding why their mother should have destroyed their home. It seemed to them that the whole world had turned to chaos.

Gradually the flames subsided and the collapsed roof smouldered on a heap of embers, sending up a great plume of smoke and steam that was whipped away by the gale. The pungent odour of burning eucalypt mingled with the reek of charred fur and fat from the other fires where meat was cooking. As the downpour increased, the efforts of Ana-Maïda's children, Touami and Cuckanahu, to keep the cooking fires alight began to fail, not from lack of fuel (they had spent the last two days collecting wood), but because everything was sodden.

From where she crouched in the darkness at the very edge of the forest, Ellie looked on with a mixture of guilt and trepidation. Somehow none of what she was watching seemed real. For the first time in four years she felt like a stranger. When Manalewa suddenly stood rigid, howled and began to claw at her face, breasts and belly until blood streamed down her body, mingling with the rain, Ellie felt neither pity nor sorrow but hot, overwhelming embarrassment. And though the strength of this reaction both shocked and shamed her, the feeling did not go away. Indeed, as the others joined in, the flow of their heart-rending ululation carrying them into a state of trance, she felt something cringe at the very core of her. The beating rain and roaring wind sounded a deep undertone to the wailing; the naked figures shone in the firelight, staggered and whirled in a frenzy of grief. Some fell on the ground and the children added their voices, shrill as the piping of wrens, while she watched unmoved, detached, alone.

At length, spent and panting, the mourners fell quiet and then Noumati began to beat a funereal rhythm on a hollow log while the women, led by Manalewa, began to dance and chant. The world was made long before men, so the Meelayginnee held, but the same law ruled it: life came from the Great Spirit and once made it could not be unmade. Therefore they danced a line that 'moved in a circle around the ruined hut, then went to the river and wound in and out of the trees until the whole camp had been enclosed and fixed. When they returned to the centre, Noumati ceased drumming and gradually fell silent until his voice alone remained and he told the tale of Tarner and his children, expanding and embellishing it to include the story of Eagle and the Brown Quoll who stole his spirit.

After the wild abandon of the wailing, the dignity of the dancing had calmed Ellie. She told herself it was because she knew

Tangalenna was alive and the emotion of this ceremony was all for nothing that she felt so isolated. But as she listened to Noumati's tale, she realised the full significance of what she had done.

As Noumati told it, Brown Quoll, led on by Wyerkartenner, the trickster, had set out to entice Eagle from the start. The Cunning One had smothered Myrtle Tree's unborn babe and sent her husband a dream of another child who would comfort them for their loss. But the new child was pale like one already dead and her eyes were green stones: she was Brown Quoll in disguise and she wanted Eagle for herself. Only Black Snake saw the truth and he wanted to kill the impostor but Eagle fought and defeated him, being blind to his foster-daughter's true intent for she had already beguiled him. And so when the time came for Brown Quoll to take a husband, Eagle went on a long journey so that she could tempt him no longer: he loved Myrtle Tree and their children still. When he returned, weary and tormented by his longing, it was to find Brown Quoll given to his crippled half-brother: he could not challenge him as he might have fought another rival. And so he went to his dreaming place, hoping to rid himself of his base desires because Myrtle Tree looked lovingly upon him and it was not his wish to hurt her. But – (and here Noumati lowered his voice and surveyed his audience with such menace that many shuddered) – Brown Quoll slipped from her husband's arms and sought Eagle out and he was helpless before her. She licked and stroked him until he was overtaken by lust and then she stole his spirit, leaving only the husk of his flesh for Myrtle Tree to find, and she ran away and resumed her true form and the forest rang with her laughter.

Ellie shivered as she listened: there was that in Noumati's voice which struck her to the heart.

'But Brown Quoll's joy did not last,' the storyteller continued darkly. 'For Eagle was not dead: he woke and when he found his spirit gone he wept because he was weak, having expended the strength of his body in their coupling. He looked to the sky for help but his ancestors were angry at the betrayal of Myrtle Tree and turned their eyes away. He tried to dream but his gift had left with his spirit: there was only blackness. And so Eagle, who had been proud and had seen all the world spread beneath his wings, set out to find his lover. He leapt out into the air but without his spirit he could not fly: he fell and his body was broken on the rocks. Brown Quoll wailed and ran in circles when she realised what had happened: she released his spirit but it was too late. The spirit howled and Wind swept it away and she leapt after but always it fled beyond her reach and so she too was lost and was never seen by any of the Meelayginnee again.'

Carried away by the momentum of his story, Noumati had forgotten himself but one look at Manalewa's face shattered the spell. A tense, awkward silence fell where there should have been celebration, for the purpose of the eulogy was to praise the dead and bid farewell: such condemnation as was latent in this speech was unprecedented. And the absence of the bodies added to the disquiet for no-one could be sure that the spirits of the dead man and missing girl were not watching from the darkness. Yet apart from Manalewa, Ellie was most affected. She had not expected Noumati to be so bitter nor so forthright in his accusation and tears of remorse and anger mixed with the rain that streamed down her face.

'It's not true!' Manalewa, who was sitting next to Touganana, leapt unexpectedly to her feet. 'He was her father; I suckled and nurtured her as my own. Are you saying she seduced and drove him to his death? It cannot be! Have you no respect for one who loved you as a brother, even for your own wife?'

Spittle flew from her lips and her bleeding breasts and swollen belly shook when she stamped in rage. Touganana, who had put out a hand intending to offer comfort, withdrew it without touching her.

Daunted by the ferocity of her outburst and astounded by his own daring (he had never intended to betray his suspicions so openly), Noumati stared and could find no words to respond. He longed for the ground to swallow him, for the river to burst its banks and sweep him away but neither of these things happened.

Manalewa stamped her foot again. 'Well?'

All her grief was now transmuted into anger, against the storyteller for insulting her husband's memory and shaming her; against her foster-daughter for leaving when she was most needed;

against Tangalenna himself for losing his spirit and choosing death (she refused to believe Noumati's interpretation). Noumati shrank before her as she stepped forward, hand raised as if to clout a naughty child. His desire was to flee but to struggle to his feet in full glare of the fires would be to expose his deformity, his weakness, before all and so he remained as he was. Tanglémerna could not restrain her laughter: it rang out loud and harsh as a kookaburra's.

'Stricken by her loss, Myrtle Tree wanted everyone to suffer as she was suffering.' From long habit, Noumati resorted to his craft to save himself. 'Though even Sky wept for Eagle, Myrtle Tree did not lift her branches in thanks for the gift of tears but thrashed them as if a mighty storm was blowing. All who loved her begged her to let them comfort her but in her rage and pain she dashed them to the ground, wanting only that they also should hurt, mistaking compassion for envy though her husband's enemies were far away.'

Although, from necessity, he spoke quickly, these words had the desired effect. Manalewa stopped in her tracks and lowered her fist. Her face, which had grown ugly and contorted in rage, relaxed. She glanced at the heap of smouldering embers that had been her home and a look of weary resignation settled upon her features. For a few moments she stood utterly still, then sighed and resumed her place. But to Noumati her silence was worse than any anger. He bowed his head, wishing himself far away but the stench of the burning was strong in his nostrils, the rain beat down and there was no escape.

With peace restored (albeit an uneasy one), the feasting began. Ellie, her stomach griped with hunger, watched in a kind of agony as Tanglémerna and Ana-Maïda dragged the carcasses from the cooking fires and began to divide them, grumbling all the while that if Noumati's tale were true, to feast in memory of the lost couple was a waste: the meat would turn to ash in their mouths and no good would come of it. Clouds of steam rose from the roasted flesh and Ellie's mouth watered uncontrollably but, with an effort, she forced herself to wait: to be spotted now would mean disaster.

Under so strained an atmosphere and in such inclement weather, the feast did not last long. They wolfed down the food as fast as they could, the children squabbling like devils over the choicest scraps. But Noumati hardly touched the wallaby leg he had been given and Manalewa also ate little. After fasting, the taste and smell of meat revolted her at first and her stomach soon felt tight and full.

Usually talk and more dancing would have accompanied the feasting until everyone was too exhausted to do anything but sleep. But this time no-one wanted to speak of the dead. Touganana and Pounaté ate with deliberate concentration, keeping their eyes downcast, and Noumati was silent: he knew he had said too much already.

From the other side of the fire, Ana-Maïda and Tanglémerna watched the rest and their eyes were bright and mocking in the flaring firelight. There was no sympathy for her daughter in Tanglémerna's heart: the rivalry between Tangalenna and her precious son, Warady, had set her against Manalewa's marriage from the start. Now, with her predictions that no good could come of such a match fulfilled, she sat smugly, her bulk and wide, thick-lipped mouth making her appear toad-like. Ana-Maïda, jealous of the love that had existed between her brother and Manalewa, whispered in her mother-in-law's ear and they laughed spitefully together.

Such ill-feeling was unseemly at a funeral and Pounaté longed to vent his anger by dragging his wife to the privacy of his shelter and beating her until she begged for mercy. But he no longer possessed the strength and so he shook his head and pointed the outstretched fingers of his right hand at her, a gesture of disapproval and rejection which prompted her to heave herself to her feet and stare darkly at him before squatting to piss, thus demonstrating her contempt. When she had finished, Ana-Maïda helped her to her feet and the two went into the remaining hut. All the children followed, bewildered, over-full and tired but Manalewa's were pushed outside where they crouched miserably in the rain.

'Yah!' Touganana spat in disgust at such behaviour. 'Has the woman no shame?' She turned her head to look shrewdly at Pounaté. 'Mark my words, there'll be trouble when your sons return.'

'Eh . . .' The old man sighed. 'This is no good. Time to sleep. Who knows, maybe your son and his foster-daughter are still alive after all.'

'Maybe you should keep your mouth shut,' Touganana said firmly. 'Come on, let's get out of this rain before we drown,' and she rose with surprising grace and hauled him to his feet. Neither Manalewa nor Noumati looked up to acknowledge their departure, both being sunk in their own thoughts as the old couple made their way to their secret trysting place in the forest.

It was customary for a dead man's family to wait until after his cremation before building a new shelter, thus no provision had been made for Manalewa and her children. Ashamed of having a water-tight lean-to to himself, Noumati did not move but he could not bring himself to offer shelter to the woman he had humiliated so publicly. The shivering children edged closer to the fire but they feared the change that had come over their mother, turning her from their source of comfort and warmth to a distracted stranger, and so kept away from her. Since no-one bothered to replenish it, the blaze sank to a heap of embers and slowly darkened as a crust formed over the glowing heart.

Crouched in her hiding place, Ellie was growing desperate. If the two stayed where they were till dawn, her expedition would fail. She was so tired, her head kept drooping despite her hunger and she was cold. She thought with longing of the wallaby skin she had rolled as a pillow for Tangalenna's head, though as a young childless woman she would never have dared ask for the loan of it.

The gale had ceased and a cool breeze rustled the branches, sending down a shower of droplets heavier than the rest: so constant was the rain it seemed unremarkable as the fact it was night. But the sudden chill finally prompted Manalewa to move. She got to her feet, casting a strange, unreadable look at Noumati, then led the stumbling children to the least tumble-down of the old, long-abandoned shelters.

With Manalewa gone, there was nothing to keep the storyteller there but he sat as if turned to stone, wondering at the recklessness with which he had spoken. It was as if some malicious spirit had twisted his words, turning what he had planned as fitting tribute to his half-brother and friend to a travesty. Yet nothing he had said was untrue and this paradox troubled Noumati. Despite the sometimes fantastic nature of his stories, he possessed a simple and absolute view of the world and it seemed to him that something had changed, wrenching the very foundations of the law by which the Meelayginnee existed; that while the disappearances of Tangalenna and Ngali-kiri were, in the long history of his people, a small thing, nothing would ever be the same.

Ellie was drowsing and did not see Noumati clamber to his feet and limp heavily to his shelter. When she next looked towards the fire, she was not sure whether he was still there: it was as if the shape of him was somehow imprinted in the pattern of falling rain. Only after she had sat up and rubbed her eyes was she certain he was gone. She forced herself to wait a little longer in case anyone should return but hunger got the better of her. She crept forward, squatted in the ashes of the cooking fire and began to dig for scraps of the three carcasses. So focused was she on the search, she did not realise that with the seal of ash broken, the red glow of the embers made her clearly visible.

When he saw the slender form beside the fire, Noumati first thought it was a ghost. After all that had happened over the past few days he was not surprised but this did not lessen his terror. He lay still, his heartbeat lurching through his whole body. A dreadful chill seeped from the wet earth into his very marrow; the sour smell of old bones filled his nostrils and he shuddered. The density of the rain was such that the figure seemed oddly insubstantial.

Lit from beneath, Ellie's face, the thin muscles of her arms, the curve of her young breasts were sharply outlined while the red light on her wet skin gave her the appearance of something freshly flayed. She crouched, tearing strips of meat from discarded bones and her teeth glinted like those of a small, fierce animal. As he watched, doubt crept into Noumati's mind: there was nothing ethereal in her actions which were quick and jerky as those of any starving creature that has found food. With infinite care, so not to disturb her, he raised himself on one elbow for a better view.

Suddenly she froze and Noumati held his breath. Her eyes

gleamed as she turned her head nervously, probing the darkness beyond reach of the firelight with her gaze. Squatting still, she edged a little way round the fire, digging out scraps of charred flesh, skin, bone, anything with meat or fat attached. These she stuffed into a bag she dragged at her side, looking round all the while, poised to flee at the slightest untoward sound or movement though she, like Noumati, was half-deafened by the drumming rain.

By now the storyteller was convinced this was no spirit, yet still he did not move or speak. He knew that if she ran, he had no hope of catching her: he could not, in any case, force her to stay against her will. And though relieved she was still alive, he was curious, amazed at her audacity in coming here to pilfer from her foster-father's funeral feast. That impiety shocked him even more than the fact of her infidelity though in his innocence he thought that she was acting purely from necessity, that she had fled at first in grief, then stayed away out of guilt and fear. And as he watched and waited, looking on those slender limbs, the delicate bones of her face, he yearned to hold her, to stroke that slim body that looked fragile but was filled with a vibrant strength, to join with her again.

This desire sent a flood of heat through him and his head reeled as if she were indeed in his arms. He rocked and groaned and his hand stole down to work his penis, his eyes closed: for a moment he was lost. A warm, sticky liquid spurted over his fingers; he shuddered and lay still, panting.

When he opened his eyes, she was gone.

Noumati did not sleep for the remainder of that night but instead dozed long into the morning. When the others complained, he said ingenuously that he had dreamt his wife's spirit would come to him in the darkness. Touganana looked at him curiously but the rest were embarrassed and a little afraid: no one spoke of it again but left him to his own devices because they pitied him. And so, every night he lay awake, watching and waiting.

At first, it seemed unremarkable that having been successful the first time, the young woman should return: Noumati knew she had eaten little for days and must be more than usually hungry. It was when she came on the third night that he began to question her true motive. Yet because he believed his half-brother dead, Noumati refused to contemplate the possibility that his wife was taking food for Tangalenna. Instead he told himself she was merely scavenging opportunistically, like her daemon, Brown Quoll.

Hoping that through kindness she would realise no-one meant her harm and, perhaps, be persuaded to stay, Noumati began hoarding food to leave out beside the fires when everyone else was asleep. But though she came every night, slipping from the cover of the forest with the wariness of a young joey away from its mother's pouch, she never lingered, pausing only long enough to stuff the food into her bag before stealing away. After that first time, where hunger had overtaken caution, she did not risk eating in the open and so swiftly did she come and go that Noumati scarcely had time to realise she was there before she vanished into the trees. Yet despite his disappointment, Noumati took some comfort from the way she sometimes glanced towards his lean-to as if she sensed his attention or guessed who her benefactor was. Life as a cripple had taught him to be easily satisfied.

The day came, inevitably, when the elders decided it was time to move on. Game was scarce and without Tangalenna, Warady and Tupali, hunting had become a communal activity, the women and children driving wallabies into a corral of piled branches where Pounaté and Noumati waited to club or spear them. Such hunts ended in failure more often than success and wasted valuable foraging time. They had already stayed near the sacred gorge longer than usual.

In his efforts to persuade Pounaté and Touganana to change their minds, Noumati found himself pleading on his enemies' behalf, arguing that Tupali and Warady would be hard put to find the group once they left the riverside camp. Even as he spoke, he knew the attempt was futile. His father looked at him pityingly and explained, as if to a foolish child, that the camp they had previously occupied dictated the next, for the groups migrated according to a pattern entrenched in tradition, but there was suspicion in Touganana's gaze and when Pounaté had finished, Noumati limped away before she could question him. The missing food had been scarcely noticed and was blamed on scavengers, diseased devils particularly which sometimes wandered into camp in broad daylight.

So horrifying was their appearance, their faces disfigured by monstrous, suppurating tumours, they were regarded as an ill-omen and left alone.

As if to reiterate the need to move, one such animal dragged itself into camp as the group was preparing to depart. It was so weak that when the children, confident that no-one was watching, threw stones and then, emboldened by its apparent apathy, poked it with sticks, it made no attempt to defend itself other than hissing and crouching low to the ground. Revolted by the children's cruelty and the animal's helplessness, Noumati picked up a spear and stuck the devil through the chest. It died with an ear-splitting shriek, the children fled and Noumati broke the spear across his knee and flung the pieces onto the fire. He could not bring himself to touch the carcass: it lay in the middle of the camp and carrion flies soon swarmed so thickly upon it that the glistening sores were covered by a black, heaving mass.

They left soon after, Pounaté leading the way with the laden women and children close on his heels while Noumati limped along in the rear. The appearance of the sick animal had disturbed him deeply: it was as if its diseased flesh epitomised the wrongness of what was happening, a dislocation at the very centre of the world, an irrevocable disintegration of the law. As the day wore on and his tiredness grew, he tried to push these thoughts from his mind but they lingered like a bad dream, something intangible yet inescapable.

When they stopped for the night in a small glade, Noumati forced himself to stay awake though every fibre of his body longed for sleep. Believing that when she found the camp deserted, his wife would simply follow the group, he had not left a cache of food behind. He waited until the others had settled down then took a handful of roots and leaves he had saved from their meal and placed it on a prominent log at the edge of the clearing. Then he lay down to watch.

When dawn came with no sign of the thief, the storyteller was devastated. He had to be shaken awake by Manalewa's children who teased him mercilessly until, in a flash of anger, he yelled at them to go away. The food he had set out was untouched: he reached out as if unable to believe it was still there then, disgusted at such foolishness, stamped it into the ground. The others were already walking away and he followed slowly, raging at his weakness but as his tiredness grew, his resentment subsided, leaving him empty and sad.

When Tangalenna discovered the true source of their food, he was filled with shame but being too weak to hunt, he could not refuse it. He had lain drifting in and out of delirium for two days, sucking water from the dripping reeds pressed to his lips, swallowing whatever was put into his mouth. Fearful that their whereabouts would be discovered if she stole fire from the camp, (even a small blaze would make a bright point in the darkness of the gorge), Elle wrapped the wallaby skin around him when he shivered and trembled and if that failed, she lay beside him, clasping him in a close embrace to warm and comfort him. Sometimes, dreaming that one of the dying Broad Ridge people was clinging to him, he flung her off and lay hugging his knees to his chest, shaking and whimpering in abject fear. On other occasions he would sit up, eyes wild but unseeing, and scratch long furrows where he thought maggots were about to erupt from his skin, before falling back exhausted.

Ignorant of the fate of the Broad Ridge folk, Ellie could make nothing of these frenzies but she learned quickly that to touch him when he was in their grip would provoke a blind attack: he would hit out wildly to keep her away, his face set in a mask-like expression of terror appalling to behold. Unable to help him, she could only watch and wait until he was quiet, then pull the wallaby skin over to keep him warm. Her trips down the cliff to pilfer food were anxious ones for she feared what harm he might do himself while she was away but he never moved from the shelter and gradually, as he recovered, the fits became less frequent.

Dependency on the others was something Ellie had never envisaged when she ran away. The daily descent and climb in twilight or near total darkness, the constant fear of being caught, and anxiety over Tangalenna's health tired her to such a degree that she forgot the camp was, like all those of the Meelayginnee, a temporary one, that the elders had spoken of moving on soon after her marriage. It came as a shock when she crept to her hiding place one evening to find the clearing dark and deserted. Without the glow of cooking fires, the sounds of habitation - a baby crying, children laughing or squabbling, the chatter of women - the place seemed utterly desolate. A mound of ash was all that remained of the hut she had once shared with her foster-parents and the empty shelters seemed oddly forbidding. The door of Warady's hut swung loosely in the breeze: no-one had bothered to fasten it.

The dead devil looked like a log in the deep twilight and Ellie ignored it and went to the places where caches of food had been hidden over the past few days. She suspected Noumati of leaving them and had felt a painful twisting of her heart each night because she guessed he had acted in hope that she would return to him. But now, finding nothing there, she felt a spurt of resentment. Somehow it didn't seem fair that he should have gone with the others.

It was growing late and having fed so well over the previous days, Ellie was hungry and impatient. She squatted by the fireplace and probed the ashes but she found only brittle bones, the remains of meals long past. The breeze brought with it the usual scents of tea-tree and eucalypt but her nostrils quickened to another odour, that of blood. There was no hope of foraging in the dark: her senses were not fine-tuned enough to identify plants and fungi by feel and smell alone but that unmistakeable metallic tang drew her attention to the carcass a few steps away.

Guilt and shame prevented Tangalenna questioning the origin of the tough, rank meat she brought back that night. She gave him the choice pieces: liver, kidneys, heart but there was little fat on them. The liver was unnaturally swollen and foul-tasting: he flung it away after a single bite. When he lay down to sleep, his stomach uncomfortably full, it seemed to him that even in the cool of night he could hear flies buzzing and he put his hands over to shield his head lest they enter his ears, mouth, nostrils and devour him from within.

They both slept fitfully, the meat heavy and sour in their bellies. By dawn Ellie had decided it was time to leave. The departure of the hearth-group had affected her more deeply than she first thought: without the security of knowing they were close at hand she felt isolated and vulnerable. She picked up her collecting bag, still heavy with bones and meat but the thought of eating more of it revolted her and she threw the remainder over the cliff. It already smelled putrid and she wiped the bag out as best she could with a handful of tough grass and waited for Tangalenna to stir.

The sun's rays fell directly upon him as he twitched in the throes of a waking dream. Ellie's eyes filled with tears and became dazzled as she watched him. He looked so diminished, almost frail compared to the man she had first known. Then he had been in his prime, the fullness of his pride and strength, at ease with himself and the world he inhabited. Now it was as if something vital to his very being had broken or was lost. There was a change more significant than could be explained by a simple fever.

He woke at last and for the first time since leaving camp, saw her clearly. He was dismayed at how worn she appeared, hollow-eyed, the narrow frame of her face sharp as if the underlying flesh had melted away. He reached out and traced the bones of her eye-socket, cheek, jaw with a tenderness that took her by surprise. A smothering feeling rose to her throat, dread and desire melded, and she pulled away.

'Ngali-kiri . . .' There was longing in his voice but his face was oddly twisted, as of one in pain. Sensing his passion and frightened by it, she got abruptly to her feet.

'We should move: if you're strong enough.'

When he stood up, Tangalenna was horrified by his weakness. His head swam and his limbs seemed barely under his control. He lurched and staggered like a drunkard from pandanus to pandanus, moving only a few steps before clinging to the trees to rest. Ellie followed a little behind, her fear augmented by pity. She found a stout stick for him but he flung it away and stumbled on, the breath hoarse in his throat, sweat tracing runnels through the dirt and dried blood on his skin.

It was more than an hour before they reached the broad heathland of the plateau, a gentle climb Ellie had achieved in ten minutes on her search for water. Tangalenna's eyes stung with sweat and his vision was blurred but he saw the bareness of the landscape, the broad expanse of sky; smelt the purity of the air which was scented with heath rather than eucalypt, and cast himself down as if at the end of a long journey. He lay still and did not speak.

The sun was high when he stirred again. The heat seemed to press down like a giant, remorseless hand and he thought if he did not move now, he would never have the willpower to try again. And once he was on his feet he found that he was stronger than before: he moved without staggering and the clear air refreshed him. Ellie walked beside him, picking her way between clumps of heath with careful deliberation. As a young woman it was unthinkable that she should tell him where to go but she guided him nonetheless.

When they reached the pool, Tangalenna lay flat on his stomach and sucked the water directly from the surface. The air was still and the pool mirrored the sky perfectly. He drank so long and thirstily, Ellie thought he would never stop: ripples spread from his lips in concentric circles and made his reflection waver. When at last he was sated, he rolled over to stare into the sky and there was a look of such relief on his face that Ellie felt like laughing and crying at the same time.

'We'll stay here,' he said.

Although they were no great distance from the caves and the riverside camp, so different was this wind-scoured upland from the forest where it was a novelty to see more than a hundred metres in any direction, it seemed another world. As days passed and he regained his strength, Tangalenna became noticeably more light-hearted. He helped Ellie construct a shelter, using the natural growth of the heath to make a low, hump-shaped hut, though this was, traditionally, women's work and when they came across a young wallaby, it was Ellie who flung herself upon it and he laughed and let her have the prestige of the kill though it nearly escaped in her efforts to break its neck.

It was summer: while game was scarcer than in the forest, there was enough food on the plateau to sustain the two of them though they spent most of the long days in gathering it. For spears, Tangalenna had to climb down to the tea-tree thickets at the edge of the forest but he avoided the sacred gorge and went east, past Tarner's Tail, though the way was further. Ellie accompanied him on these expeditions. Scrambling over the piled boulders that marked the edge of the group's territory she was aware of a vague unease but she could not remember being there before and did not understand why Tangalenna kept glancing at her with a strange, almost guilty look. He had not forgotten how close he had come to abandoning her there but when he realised she was unaffected, he pushed the memory aside. It could do no good to remind her of that time.

Days passed and neither of them had ever experienced such happiness. They lived contentedly as father and daughter, neither making demands on the other. Freedom from responsibilities Tangalenna had never consciously recognised but which had governed every waking moment of his life (the need to provide for his family; to conduct ceremony and interpret his dreams for the good of the group; even his love for Manalewa), lent him a sense of holiday, a kind of selfishness taken for granted in Ellie's world but experienced only as rare periods of indolence by Meelayginnee men, almost never by their women. He was more relaxed than he had been before, his face lost its habitual fierceness and sometimes he would lie by the tarn oblivious to the biting midges and mosquitoes, and stare into the sky for hours, rapt and tranquil.

Ellie did not disturb him when he was in this mood which often followed restless nights when he reverted to the frenzies of his fever, feeling his body in panic, muttering words she could not follow, the sweat streaming from him though the night air might be chill. She dreaded a relapse into that sickness and when he awoke to himself would greet him with such gladness that any lingering remnants of his nightmares dissipated though he was often exhausted. On such days she would leave him to rest and go foraging alone, bringing back special delicacies which she sometimes walked hours to find: burrowing crayfish, sweet ants, grubs, even the flowers of heath.

One day she returned to find him apparently asleep by the pool, limbs stretched out in careless abandon like a child who knows it has nothing to fear. Ellie stowed her bulging bag in the shade for it was warm though a light breeze ruffled the surface of the pool. The sky was a clear, unsullied blue and as she straightened, she saw a pair of eagles drifting high overhead. They veered and dived, the light glancing from their wings. There was such beauty in their flight that Ellie was entranced: joy surged through her as if she were borne by their effortless grace. She followed the birds as they swooped together then broke apart. They spiralled upwards until they reached their former altitude and drifted away on the wind.

Suddenly she became aware that Tangalenna was propped on one elbow, watching her. There was a look in his eyes she could not mistake. It sent a thrill of anticipation through her whole being. He did not speak: there was no need. They lay together, exploring each other with increasing urgency. Joined under that shining sky, they became the only two people in existence. It was as if, for an instant, time had ceased.

Chapter 14.

The brothers journeyed south at first, following the natural trend of the land. Neither was in any mood to hurry: they felt the same sense of release Tangalenna was experiencing on the plateau. They would walk half the day, then light a fire and go hunting. Here, beyond the boundaries of their band's domain, wallabies were plentiful and so successful were they, hunting as a pair, that they grew wasteful, eating only the choicest parts and discarding the rest in the certainty of killing again the next day. This spared them the effort of carrying food. To Warady's mind the spears, skins, club and fire-stick they bore were burden enough and most of the time he made his brother carry them.

It was after several weeks of easy, meandering progress (which although they were unaware of it, had brought them back towards their own territory), that they found evidence of people. A survey team had been there years before and left a marker: a piece of plastic tape attached to a metal stake. Tupali happened across it by chance when he squatted to shit a few paces from their camp. He looked at it with a curiosity devoid of fear then edged closer to touch and smell it. The tape, faded almost white and torn along the edges held little interest: he simply assumed it to be a scrap of skin weathered almost beyond recognition. But the fact it was tied in a knot intrigued him because it meant some person had been there, and the stake he looked upon in wonder, having never seen a metal object before.

Warady, when called to see, tried to be dismissive. He tore the tape off and after sniffing and putting it to his lips to feel the texture, discarded it. The stake he yanked out and balanced incredulously in his hands, astonished by its unnatural heaviness. The end that had been stuck in the ground was pointed but he could think of no use for it other than as a crude bludgeon. The smell of it was familiar, like ochre, but when he prised away some flakes of rust there was no red powder beneath and he flung it away.

Though neither voiced their discomfiture, not wanting to appear afraid, both were made uneasy by this discovery. It was proof that they were not alone in the world, that the stories Ngali-kiri told of the place she had come from, and the myths of the Disappearing might be true. When Tangalenna brought the pale child from the edge of the world she had been ignorant and the Meelayginnee had assumed *num* culture to be little different from theirs, except in language and ceremony. The girl's descriptions of outlandish animals, and objects beyond their experience, had been dismissed as childish make-believe. Now, those premises were being challenged. It was as if, in Ellie's world, an alien spacecraft had emerged from Antarctic ice.

The brothers walked warily thereafter, alert to every cracking twig, the alarm calls of birds, the slightest untoward movement or sound. So smooth and silent was their gait, they passed between the trees like shadows.

That afternoon they succeeded in catching a half-grown pademelon only after a long and arduous chase. It seemed to them that game was more nervous in this part of the forest and their anxiety increased accordingly. Though they did not know what they feared, the uncertainty increased their sense of isolation. Only pride and the need for each to prove himself against the other compelled them to go on. They decided that their present camp would become their base: travelling burdened as they were, they felt too vulnerable.

They spent a restless night, then made ready for the hunt. Warady, sensing his brother's resolve faltering, crushed some charcoal between his hands and rubbed it over his whole body, indicating that Tupali should do the same. This renewed their kinship with the forest and gave them confidence. After that, they banked up the fire and left, each carrying a single spear. It was just past dawn and the noise of lorikeets, cockatoos and wrens was loud in the stillness between the massive, moss-hung trees.

As the morning passed, the forest became strangely silent. There was a latent tension in the air as if a storm were brewing. Neither of the brothers spoke much but when they did, their voices sounded muffled and toneless. Tupali often paused to look around but Warady kept his eyes on the wallaby trail they were following and refused to give way to his misgivings.

They travelled steadily downhill, following a creek that ran through a narrow valley filled with tree-ferns. By the time the sun's rays fell vertically through the canopy, they had come to the confluence of this tributary with a river wide as the one below the sacred gorge and far deeper. The surface of this river was smooth and black, the water swirled past with a soft rushing sound and only where the sun's rays hit directly did it appear translucent, the colour of diluted blood.

The two knelt to drink where the bank was low and muddy, worn down by the feet of thirsty animals. The number and variety of prints attested to the popularity of this watering place but there was one set that perplexed the brothers. The marks were deep, the size and rough shape of a man's foot but the outline was smooth and rounded, lacking toes, and there were regular indentations forming a pattern across the tread.

'Whoever made these must be lame.' Tupali, recognising the similarity of the prints to those made by Noumati's misshapen and bound foot, had only contempt for a race of men so weak that they had to go shod. 'Remember, Ngali-kiri could barely walk when she first came to us. Tangalenna had to carry her from the edge of the world.'

Warady scowled at the reference to his rival.

'The dreamer is a soft-hearted fool,' he said. 'If he'd forced her to walk at the start, she would have respected him and he could have taken what he wanted instead of running away. He's never raised a hand to his wife or child and look what's come of it!'

Sensing his brother's anger simmering just below the surface, Tupali laughed to please him but he could not help glancing uneasily into the shadows beneath the trees in case their enemy might be lurking there.

'Come on.' Warady concealed his own trepidation behind bravado. 'The pale one we find will have to run all the way back: we have spears to prick her with if she lags!'

Tupali grinned at the deliberate double entendre and such was his anticipation of having a woman of his own, one he could torment and mate with as he pleased, his penis quivered and swelled. Noting this, Warady shook his head sardonically. 'Wait: we have to catch her first!'

Away from the river, the ground was hard and dry. The footprints they were trying to follow were rare and confused by the trails of animals. In the end it was the smell of cooking that alerted the brothers to the presence of others. Odours wholly unknown to them drifted between the trees: re-hydrated spaghetti bolognaise mixed with the reek of methylated spirit.

Warady wrinkled his nose in disgust. 'Faugh! Is that the stink of their armpits? What kind of people are they?'

Tupali did not bother to answer. Gripping his spear so tightly his knuckles whitened, he crept forward.

The track they had chanced upon was a difficult one, used only by a handful of experienced bushwalkers every year. These, five postgraduate students, three men and two women, were weary after ten days' arduous trekking and finding themselves in a pleasant clearing beside a river, had decided to spend the night there instead of pressing on to the next designated camping place. Having pitched their tents, two had remained behind to cook while the rest went for a swim.

Loud shrieks and shouting from the direction of the river made the brothers pause before the camp came fully into view. At first they thought there was a fight going on, then as laughter and the sound of splashing took over, they guessed what was happening though Meelayginnee men only entered water to cross a river. But amidst the cacophony they discerned a woman's voice. Exchanging meaningful glances, they edged closer, for the camp lay between them and the river. They moved with such care even Tangalenna would have been hard-put to spot them.

There was a figure fiddling with a strange flapping shelter. The brothers could not tell whether it was a man or woman because it was swathed in clothes. Another, also dressed but bearded, crouched by a shiny object which hissed and emitted steam. He was stirring something with a long stick. They ignored him.

The first, who was checking the tent-pegs for firmness,

suddenly paused and looked hard into the dappled light and shade. The two froze but a clear view of the face was enough for them to identify a woman. She shook her head impatiently and turned back to her task but she was clearly disquieted because when she moved to the second tent, she paused to look again. The man said something and she replied with a short laugh but continued to glance nervously into the trees.

Everything about the camp and its inhabitants, the tents, the cooking stove, the rucksacks with their contents poking out, all of different colours and textures, offended Warady. Its very existence was an affront, a threat to the balance of his world. The breath hissed between his teeth and he rose, spear poised to throw. Alarmed, Tupali laid a hand on his brother's shoulder. To attack without knowing how many of the strangers they had to deal with might prove disastrous.

With an effort, Warady forced control on himself. Another burst of shouting and laughter from the river-side distracted him. He looked round and Tupali jerked his head. 'Come on!'

The couple in camp were completely unaware of the two aborigines stealing around them but the woman gradually relaxed, as if some unknown threat had passed.

When they came within sight of the bathers, who were frolicking in the water like children, the brothers squatted to decide their strategy.

The three *num* were naked: they were close friends and had not included swimming gear in the equipment they had packed for the trip. One of the men was short but powerfully built: water glistened in his dark hair and beard, the thick growth on his chest and crotch as he stood to splash the others. The other man was slim, almost boyish in physique but tall. Though he had several days' growth of beard, this was not obvious to the watchers because of his fair colouring. It was only when he also stood up that they were certain of his gender.

There was no doubting the sex of the third when she joined in the game. Her blonde hair, sleeked to her head and shoulders, streamed water onto her breasts which were full and pendulous. They joggled as she jumped and dived forward and Tupali could not suppress a groan. She was taller than he and strong-looking but he was sure he and Warady could restrain her though he wished he had had the foresight to bring a length of rope to tie her hands.

'One man each as they come out of the water,' Warady said quietly. 'And then we'll grab the woman.'

He raised himself into the tense, crouching stance of a hunter but Tupali hesitated. Like his brother, he had never killed a man but while Warady did not care, since these were not Meelayginnee, Tupali was more circumspect. Ngali-kiri was of *num* people but she had been initiated and was possessed of a daemon; it seemed to him that these also must have spirits which might return to haunt their killers.

'What's the matter: scared?' Warady's tone was soft and jeering, calculated to rouse both shame and anger. Slowly, Tupali rose into the same ready stance but his eyes were worried as he looked at the three still splashing happily together.

Contrary to their expectations, the woman was first out of the river. They had expected their rules of precedence to apply to all people. Their eyes were drawn to the water-darkened triangle of hair at the fork of her legs, so starkly did it contrast with the paleness of her trunk and breasts. The patterning of her skin, which marked the outline of a swimming costume, intrigued them. It was as if she had stained her limbs, shoulders and face with a mixture of ochre and charcoal but unlike these pigments, it had not washed away.

She clambered onto the bank and turned to face the men, her skin glossed with water. The dark-haired man waved and there was frank admiration in his gaze but the other, embarrassed, looked away and pitched forward into the current. He swam away with brisk strokes, his arms cleaving the ripples with the smooth economical action of an athlete.

The brothers had positioned themselves so that to reach the campsite, the woman would have to pass them. But instead of walking back, she continued to face the river. The dark-haired man, her partner, talked earnestly to her while she began to sweep the moisture from her skin with broad, firm movements of her hands, disregarding the drips running over her shoulders from her hair.

Warady ground his teeth in frustration, sensing their chance slip away. Tupali edged alongside. 'What now?'

'Wait!'

At last the woman turned away from the river but as she began to walk towards the camp, the dark-bearded man waded ashore with vigorous, lurching strides. His sheer vitality dismayed the watchers. Alone, Tupali would have given up for this man was clearly a match for any of the Meelayginnee, even Tangalenna. But he was weaponless. Also, Tupali tried to reassure himself, his frame was padded with slabs of fat: they would be quicker.

All this passed through Tupali's mind in an instant. Then Warady's hand was on his shoulder, thrusting him directly into the woman's path.

Taken by surprise, Tupali dropped his spear and tried to grasp her upper arms. Eyes wide with shock, she struck at him with her hands, trying to push him away then, as he persisted, aiming at his face. Eyes shutting involuntarily at each flailing blow, Tupali groped blindly for her long hair but she was taller than him and all he found was slippery wet flesh. She did not cry out or scream but at each strike gave a soft grunt. Like a fighter, Tupali thought desperately.

A wild shriek came from the dark-haired man. As he rushed from the water like a charging bull, Warady's spear had struck his thigh. He wrenched it out and flung it aside. It fell into the river and was borne swiftly away. Ignoring the blood pouring from the wound, the man plunged to rescue his partner. She had succeeded in punching Tupali in the face but he had managed to wrap his arms round her, as if in an embrace. Locked together, they reeled back and forth like drunkards.

By now, the pair from the tents was running to help and the swimmer was wading ashore. He saw Tupali's discarded spear and snatched it up, then strode forward with a shout of outrage that was like a war cry.

From the cover of the trees (he had not moved since flinging his spear), Warady yelled a warning as the three men and one woman converged on the struggling pair. Something in the clothed man's hand flashed in the sunlight. He wielded it like a weapon.

Tupali looked round frantically. Though half-blinded by blood from a deep cut above his right eye, he realised his danger instantly. He let the woman go and twisted away from the hands that reached for him. The *num* screamed words he could not understand as he blundered to where he thought Warady was, branches lashed his face, he stumbled and than more hands, friendly ones, caught hold and pulled him upright.

The woman had fallen sprawling and the other knelt to comfort her but the men were gripped by a primeval rage. They crashed after their attacker only to come to a perplexed halt a few metres into the forest. To their eyes the aborigines had vanished as completely as if the ground had opened up to swallow them. In the dappled patterns of light and shade which shifted as a light breeze moved the branches, man-shapes formed and dissipated, confusing eye and mind. The fair-haired swimmer looked at the spear he had picked up, a slender, pointed shaft of tea-tree, and snapped it contemptuously across his knee before flinging away the pieces. To him it was crude as a toy weapon fashioned by a child: he was incapable of appreciating the fine balance of the spear, the cunning craftsmanship of the shaft which was not of even thickness but bulged slightly in the centre to give greater accuracy and carrying power. Noumati had spent a whole day in its making.

'Jesus!' As his rage ebbed, the injured man suddenly felt the pain of his wound which was bleeding freely though the spear had missed any major blood vessel. He pressed his hands to the place and limped back to camp. He just made it to the tents before collapsing, nauseous and weak with shock. The women were still at the riverside, trying to wash away the smears of charcoal left by Tupali's skin. His intended victim felt polluted by the black stains and continued to scrub savagely at herself even when the charcoal had gone. The reek of the man, a rank animal odour unlike anything she had smelt before seemed to have cloyed in her nostrils: even after she had scooped up handfuls of water and washed out her mouth and nose, the taint remained. When a foul stench arose from the stove where their untended meal had begun to burn, she almost welcomed it.

Gradually, as outrage gave way to a kind of stunned disbelief, simple practicalities lent some semblance of normality to the camp: the man's wound was disinfected and bandaged, the swimmers dressed, food was eaten. And the doing of these things made the attack seem unreal, impossible. They looked at one another as they ate and drank, seeking verification of their experiences in the faces of the others though the facts of the man's injury, the bruises darkening the woman's arms and face could not be denied. The men were especially quiet, bitterly ashamed at their failure to catch the perpetrators and as their frustration festered, their anger turned in on itself and they began to argue over what they should do next.

The injured man insisted that he would be able to carry on after a few days rest but no-one wanted to linger in the clearing. In the end, after a lengthy and heated debate, they decided to retrace their steps a little then leave the marked trail and climb to more open ground where they could call in help with their emergency beacon. But as they packed up camp and fashioned a crutch to aid the wounded man, they grew increasingly nervous, pausing to look round at the slightest unexpected sound. They felt as if a malign force had been awoken by their presence and their skin crawled to the focus of unseen eyes. To the women particularly it seemed that they had been attacked by no ordinary men but creatures created by the land itself, able to meld back into the shadows and earth of the forest at will. When a kookaburra, made curious by the unprecedented activity, alighted on an overhanging branch as they took a final look round before leaving, it seemed to them that the bird's raucous laugh was the voice of the forest, mocking them.

The two aborigines could have easily outrun their prospective victims but they wanted to see what these clumsy white people would do. Indeed, it amused them when they realised that they were invisible to *num* though Warady was furious at the breaking of his spear. They watched and waited until the party hoisted their rucksacks onto their backs (the wounded man's load had been divided among the others), and began to walk back along the trail. Then, moving with the silent fluidity of shadows, they followed.

Chapter 15.

Without hunters to bring in meat as they travelled, the hearth group made slow progress, held to the pace of the children and Manalewa, who was weak from grief and fasting. At times, the child in her womb seemed to drag upon her like a boulder. Pounaté and Touganana kept a close eye on the others and, if anyone lagged, were quick to spot a delicacy that could not be overlooked or a shape in a tree that might be a possum. The ensuing delay meant that even the slowest could catch up and rest without breaking the law that the weak should be abandoned.

In this manner it took more than a week to achieve a journey that would normally have taken a couple of days. When they reached their destination, a small lake beneath a high dolerite crag, Pounaté and Noumati went hunting, taking Warady's boy, Touami, to act as beater, while the rest made shelters and gathered firewood. With the brothers away, Ana-Maïda's attitude towards Manalewa had softened and the two resumed the friendship that had been interrupted by their husband's fight. Tanglémerna, however, remained scornful and hostile. The elders' shamelessness had reduced her status to that of a second wife and she was filled with resentment.

With success in hunting, Noumati found himself respected as more than a storyteller who made spears but this did not heal the hurt of his wife's betrayal. As days passed and the routine of daily life settled to a new balance, he became sullen and morose, snapping at the children when they pestered him for a tale. Manalewa, who felt Tangalenna's loss most profoundly, was too busy to brood. She never wavered from her belief that her husband was dead: having given him his rites as best she could and mourned him, it was time to live again. But Noumati was tormented by thoughts of Tangalenna and Ngali-kiri living together and the knowledge that the elders shared his suspicions only exacerbated his bitterness.

Since the night of the funeral, Manalewa had avoided the storyteller as much as possible. She sensed he was desperate to talk with her – often she would look up to find his eyes fixed upon her – but once he realised she was aware of him, he would look away as if embarrassed. Guessing the gist of what he would say, she evaded him for she did not want to hear his accusations. And her diffidence, combined with his inability to confront her directly, fuelled Noumati's frustration. He grew restless and Pounaté and Touganana watched him anxiously. They were wise and surmised where his disquietude would lead.

Instead of making spears and gathering roots, Noumati now channelled most of his energy into devising cunning traps, fences of branches and bark which guided the animals chased by Pounaté and the others to where he waited with spear and club. It was considered a crime to kill more than provided for the groups' immediate need but when, as sometimes happened, two wallabies ran into the trap, he would slay both. One day, in a moment of bloodlust, he killed a female with a young joey in her pouch then, overcome with guilt, took the tiny naked creature in his hands. When it died, he buried it as an act of atonement.

That night, lying alone in his shelter, Noumati decided to act. In his heart he had known all along that he must go back but he had delayed, using his lameness as an excuse, because he was afraid of what he might find. Now he could wait no longer: the truth would have to be faced. His endurance was the equal of any man's and his disability had taught him patience but Ngali-kiri was his wife. He would make sure the group was well provided for, then return to the sacred gorge. And having made up his mind, he felt at peace. For the first time since Tangalenna's departure, he slept the night through.

The following day the storyteller was like a man possessed. There was an unusual tension about him. But it was as if the wallabies and pademelons sensed his urgency and instead of heading into the trap prepared for them, they bolted even before Pounaté spotted them. For the first time in days the hunters returned empty-handed, the old man philosophical, Noumati fuming. But the women had better luck and as twilight gathered, the group sat round their single cooking fire to eat a fat possum Ana-Maïda had clubbed out of a tree.

Their success had put the women in an exuberant mood and they teased the failed hunters mercilessly. Pounaté bore their mainly good-natured jibes with studied resignation but Noumati, while he remained silent, stiffened. Manalewa saw his expression and tempered her words but the others were having too much fun to heed the cripple's ill-humour.

'If you're such fine hunters, then you can fetch the meat from now on!' Noumati exploded at last, glaring at the women with wild eyes. 'I, for one, have better things to do!'

They stared at him, astounded, as he lurched to his feet and their scrutiny made him acutely self-conscious. He stood panting, unsure what to do next. He longed to walk away but it seemed to him that his lameness would make him appear ridiculous.

'Eh, Noumati . . .' Touganana at last took pity on him. 'Take no notice.' And as he clenched his fists and stared helplessly at her, she shook her head and clucked her tongue at Tanglémerna and Ana-Maïda who sat smirking. 'Shame on you, pecking for blood like crows. Will you speak thus to Warady when he returns?'

At these words even Manalewa looked abashed while Ana-Maïda pulled her little girl, Cuckanahu, close, pretending to make a great fuss of the child in order to hide her face. And Noumati, under the protection of the matriarch, felt a hot tide swell in him, not anger or lust but a desire beyond these, which enabled him to forget his lameness and ambiguous standing within the group. It was the urge to tell a story in a way it had never been told before, to create something new from the threads of myth and the force that guided every living thing. A great stillness entered him and when he raised his head his eyes had taken on the detached, unseeing, stare of inspiration. A kind of awe fell on the watchers, an expectancy that was hardly to be borne. Children and adults alike barely breathed as they waited for him to begin.

Yet while he was aware of all the characters: ancestral beings, great spirits, the animals that roamed his world, keenly as if they stood beside him, Noumati had not forgotten his sense of purpose. He looked at the eager faces and, for an instant, was tempted to relate one of the great myths and thus revenge himself upon the women for those tales were long and by the end, the listeners would be almost as exhausted as the storyteller, such were the extremes of emotion he could wring from them in the telling. Then he saw how Manalewa sat stroking the curve of her belly where Tangalenna's child lay, how with good food her breasts had swelled until the skin gleamed like that of a ripe fruit about to burst. Pity for her and bitterness at his half-brother's betrayal hardened his resolve. He lifted his head still higher and swept his audience with a gaze of such fierceness that it sent a thrill of fear through them. But instead of embarking on one of the myths they knew and loved, he said harshly, 'Frogmouth sat in the branches of Myrtle Tree, his friend, and her tears fell on him like rain. With words and gifts he tried to comfort her but her grief for her lost mate was deep as River and unceasing. Then Frogmouth's heart grew angry because he knew how Eagle had been enticed away. He vowed to seek out the lovers and break Brown Quoll's spell so that Myrtle Tree would laugh again and the child in her belly would have a father. For though he was lame, Frogmouth could still fly and he was older and wiser than Brown Quoll and her trickery: she would not escape her true husband again.'

The storyteller was at once gratified and disquieted by the silence that followed. The children began to complain, for they had expected a proper tale but Ana-Maïda hushed them sternly. Pounaté opened his mouth to speak but then, seeing his son's expression, shut it again. There was a kind of grim determination in Noumati's face few had seen there before, and it daunted all save Manalewa, on whom his gaze rested. She returned his glance with a look of such sorrow that his heart was wrenched. All at once he was ashamed of his persistence though his resolve was unshaken.

'My husband is dead,' she said, with quiet finality. From where she sat next to Pounaté, Touganana grunted but it was impossible to tell whether in approval or disagreement.

'Brown Quoll came in the night and stole the remains of Eagle's funeral feast,' Noumati said uncomfortably. He had not intended to betray his secret but it was clear that only the truth would change Manalewa's mind. 'Yet when her hearth group moved on, she remained behind to tend her lover. It was for him that she had returned night after night so that he could eat and grow strong again though it was from the mouths of his own kin that the meat came.'

'No!' The cry, piercing, heart-rending came involuntarily from Manalewa's throat. She bent forward and pounded first her temples, then the ground with her fists, rocking back and forth in paroxysms of grief.

'He brought her here to be our child: he would not have done it!' she wailed at last. 'Why can't you let him rest in peace?'

Disconcerted by such passion, Noumati looked towards Touganana but the matriarch's eyes were stone-hard and he turned instead to Pounaté.

'Ngali-kiri is Noumati's wife,' the old man said after a long and uncomfortable silence. 'It is his right to look for her. And if anyone knows my son-in-law's true fate, it is she.'

Exhausted by her outburst, Manalewa lay curled on the ground, arms covering her face. Every-so-often a shudder ran through her but she made no sound other than a stifled whimpering.

'Then I will leave tomorrow.' Noumati turned and made his way to his shelter, keenly aware of the eyes of the group upon him and dreading lest anyone try to dissuade him. But although a low murmur soon arose and he heard his name spoken more than once, they were too dismayed by his revelation and the change in his demeanour to disturb him.

It was not long before dawn and all the others were asleep when Manalewa crept to Noumati's shelter. She put a hand on his shoulder and he woke with a low cry, for his slumber had been filled with uneasy dreams. Her face, striped with the marks of her grief, was stark in the pale starlight and the storyteller shivered. It was thus that he had always imagined ghosts: bones clothed in shadow instead of living flesh. Her voice too seemed barely human, so low and restrained was it.

'Promise me that when you find him, you will burn what remains and set him free,' she said. 'Otherwise I must come with you, to be sure.'

He stared at her, horrified. There was no mistaking her fervour. He understood suddenly that she would sacrifice even the child almost come to full term in her womb for the certainty of seeing Tangalenna's corpse and her steadfastness shook him to the core.

'And if he is alive?' he stammered.

A strange, sad smile curved her lips. 'My man is dead,' she replied. 'Promise, Noumati.'

Realising he had no choice, Noumati agreed. Then the tension which had made her face appear hard as wood dissipated and she hefted a bag hitherto concealed at her side towards him. 'Take this for the journey.'

From the feel of it, the bag contained food for several days and Noumati thanked her. The problem of finding enough to eat as he travelled had bothered him, since he could not hunt alone. But as she rose and walked away, her tread heavy and slow, he regretted his weakness. Now he was bound by a promise he had not wanted to make. The sky was already lightening in the east and the last stars flashed and flickered as the dawn spread but he knew the spirits of his ancestors were witnesses and his skin crawled with a kind of prescient dread.

Ellie's happiness did not last. As days passed into weeks, Tangalenna grew restless and fretful. During the day, this was not so noticeable for they were occupied with finding food, but as the evenings lengthened towards midsummer, he became brooding and silent. Sometimes he would leap to his feet and stalk away as if he could no longer bear to be near her. On occasions he did not return until dawn, leaving her to weep or, as the frequency of these episodes increased, to reflect resentfully on the sacrifices she had made for him. But she never asked where he went. She was afraid that if she offended him he might reject her completely.

One day, sick of eating raw meat and wanting to please him, she managed to make a fire. She used tea-tree left from his spear-making for a block and spinner but it took great patience to make dry kindling smoke by the friction of the two, and then coax the smouldering material into flames. She was inordinately proud of her achievement when at last the twigs and bark caught alight and on seeing Tangalenna returning from his hunt, ran to meet him. He heard her excited chatter without really comprehending it for he was tired and preoccupied but when he saw the thin thread of smoke rising from their camp, he dropped his spears and the echidna he had killed and pushed past her. She watched, aghast, as heedless of his feet, he trampled the little fire out then scooped handfuls of mud from the edge of the pool and flung them on the embers. A hissing steam arose and he crouched to watch as the glowing coals blackened. His face was hard, unreadable; muddy water dripped from his hands; he did not move or speak.

'Why did you do that?' Tears of rage and frustration sprang to the young woman's eyes and she stamped her foot. At this, Tangalenna rose and there was something so menacing in the slow deliberation of his movement and the coldness of his gaze that Ellie was frightened. Yet though she trembled, she stood her ground.

Tangalenna's people cherished and nurtured fire as a gift of Lightning or North Wind. They carried it from camp to camp and, in the past, had often fired the bush as they went: wherever flames passed, undergrowth was burned, grass grew and wallabies flourished. Thus even wild-fire was revered. This was the wisdom of countless generations and it had never failed: children were taught the value of fire early on and the charcoal the people rubbed over their bodies was both acknowledgement and celebration of the gift.

The Meelayginnee therefore had no tradition of fire-making and though it was not forbidden, none of them would have attempted it. But Ngali-kiri, scarcely a woman, her cropped head topping a body still gangly in adolescence, had done so and Tangalenna was profoundly shaken, not so much by the act itself but the difference in mentality it revealed. His people were opportunists, using what the environment provided according to their needs and when food grew scarce in one area, they moved on to the next. But once a man learned to manufacture fire according to his will, it seemed to Tangalenna that he would forget his place in the world, having no cause to be grateful. A long buried memory sprang unbidden to his mind, a great span of smooth stone blocking a valley so that a massive lake spread where once there had been forest and a river; he thought of the *num* he had seen in their loose skins, the shiny objects moving swiftly upon black trails cut across the land, and then he looked at the daughter he had stolen and it was as if he was seeing her for the first time

The difference between them, he saw with a sudden, piercing clarity, was nothing to do with the colour of her skin and eyes, the texture of her hair, the odd proportions of her body: indeed, after so long, to his eyes as to any of her hearth-group, these things were unremarkable. But though Manalewa had brought her up as theirs, teaching her Meelayginnee customs and speech, she did not think as one of them. No-one, not even Noumati, would have conceived the idea of making fire from nothing, much less attempted it: that a woman should have achieved it was anathema. As she stood before him, her green eyes huge as she stared at him in defiance, he understood at last that though frail-seeming and physically small, she possessed a power he could never attain, a kind of knowledge that had no place in his world and the proof of it lay in this steaming pile of mud and ash, the pain of his scorched feet.

And then came another memory, calm as a storm's eye amid the swirling chaos of his thoughts. He recalled how Manalewa had come to the cave on the night of Ngali-kiri's marriage, how he had cut himself off and sent her away, grief-stricken and afraid, and it was as if a mist cleared from his sight and he saw at last how deeply he had betrayed her.

Ellie had no way of knowing what was passing through Tangalenna's mind but she was appalled by the change in his expression from anger to the look of one utterly bereft. His eyes remained fixed on hers but the gradual disarray of his features filled her with dismay. She could not tell whether he was about to collapse in weeping or launch into a violent attack. Then he took a deep, shuddering breath, walked straight past her and cast himself down where the clumps of heath hid him from her view.

From a distance of less than a spearthrow, Tupali and Warady watched the bushwalkers set up another camp. It was almost fully dark and the two had scarcely bothered to conceal themselves for the white strangers blundered about as if purblind and when they glanced into the trees, their fear was almost palpable. Only when they lit a small fire did the brothers withdraw a little and this was more from astonishment at the striking of matches, the unexpected flare of flame in the darkness, than concern that they might be seen. Once beyond the flickering firelight they knew *num* would be easily eluded.

Having touched and smelled the woman he wanted, it was sexual desire that kept Tupali there: he was determined to have her, even if it proved impossible to keep her. But a guileless fascination held Warady. He was filled with wonder at the ineptitude of these people in the most basic bush-craft yet their casual control of fire, the variety of their clothes and tools, were daunting. He was not afraid but he felt an acute self-consciousness that made him oddly dissatisfied. He wished he and Tupali had more spears so that they could kill all the men, enjoy the women at their leisure, then investigate the camp and choose the shiniest object to show the others. But they had left their spear-bundle at their own camp, half a day's walk away, and Warady was too lazy to fetch it or manufacture more.

Exhausted and frightened, the walkers decided to take turns keeping watch while the injured man slept. An argument ensued as to whether they should act in pairs so that the women would not be alone but both protested that they were as capable as the men and need only shout if anything happened. As the girl who had been assaulted was the most vociferous, the men reluctantly agreed.

During the debate, the aborigines had become bored but when all the *num* went inside the tents except for the young fair-haired man, they guessed what had happened and Tupali's excitement became almost ungovernable. Warady could feel and smell the heat rising from his brother's body but while he was stirred by it, he feigned indifference and pretended he wanted to leave. Then, as he had hoped, Tupali promised him a turn on the woman. Beyond their immediate need they did not plan: after the failure of the afternoon, their main purpose had become revenge rather than abduction.

The tedium of the wait almost proved too much. Even Tupali's lust could not be kept at such a high pitch indefinitely and both brothers were hungry. Had the guard relaxed, they might have taken their chance and attacked, relying on the darkness and surprise for success. But the man seemed tireless or else fear kept him alert. Every-so-often he would get to his feet and walk round the perimeter of the tiny camp, flashing his torch randomly into the forest. Once, the beam fell directly across Tupali's torso but in the confusion of shapes and shadows, the man did not recognise it for what it was. To save batteries, he did this only occasionally and kept the little fire blazing brightly. As weariness overtook him, his head began to droop but each time he managed to rouse himself.

The unexpected torchlight had so startled the brothers, their first instinct was to flee. It seemed to them that this was a weapon of terror: the brightness hurt their eyes and for minutes afterwards they could not see properly. Tupali thought the beam came from the man's fingers, that these were not *num* after all but some kind of spirit, and he trembled, poised to run. But Warady, who had seen the shiny cylinder in the man's hand, gripped the nape of his neck as if he were a small child and pressed hard.

'Fool! It's one of their things!'

The fierce certainty in his brother's voice steadied Tupali a little though he was still afraid. Where the beam of light had touched him, he thought he had felt a searing sensation, like flame, but when he put his hand to the place, the skin was cool and moist.

The man on guard yawned and hit the side of the tent where the blonde woman was sleeping. There was a groan and a few moments later she crawled out, dragging a fleece jacket. This she put on while he replenished the fire. He watched, face furrowed with concern, as she pulled a hat over her ears. 'You're sure about this? You'll be okay?'

She nodded and he shrugged and crawled into the tent. The zip of the flap sounded loud and strange in the quiet of the night and the woman frowned and hugged herself before taking his place by the fire. He had given her the torch but she put it on the ground by her feet. She was more afraid of what its beam might reveal than the soft, rustling darkness beyond the circle of firelight.

Warady heard his brother's breathing quicken and put a

restraining hand on his shoulder: he was in no doubt what would happen if they bungled the attack and were caught. They waited for what seemed a lifetime but the stars had barely moved against the black silhouette of the overhanging branches when the sound of a man's snoring arose. The steady rhythm of the snores seemed to soothe the woman because she ceased looking nervously around the camp's perimeter and instead focused on the glowing heart of the fire. Gradually, her head sank towards her chest.

The brothers waited a little longer, to be sure that those in the tents were asleep. Then they rushed forward.

So sudden and unexpected was their appearance, the woman was petrified. Warady's hand choked off her breath: too shocked and terrified to struggle, she was half-dragged, half-carried into the trees. Then she recognised the rank stench of the man who had attacked her that afternoon and fought back with a frantic, convulsive strength until a blow to the side of her head knocked her down. She lay still, stunned, while Warady crouched to sniff at her face and Tupali tore at her clothes. He groaned with frustration as the zips resisted his efforts to rip them open; he was trembling all over. The smells of lust and fear inflamed Warady. 'Hurry up!'

The woman groaned and shuddered powerfully then, feeling hands pull at her trousers, yelled in protest and struggled to rise. Warady knocked her back then crouched and pressed the heel of his hand against her throat, feeling the pulse, strong yet rapid, echo through his own body. At the same time, Tupali yanked her trousers down to her ankles. He was whimpering with anticipation as he spread her knees and clambered between. Warady pulled up her jacket and shirt to expose her breasts: when Tupali thrust into her, he groaned and his fingers tightened convulsively on her throat, making her heave even more violently.

So intent were the brothers on their victim, they were oblivious to all else. But her shout had woken the others. They struggled from their sleeping bags, groped for knives and torches, then ripped open the tent flaps without pausing to consider what kind of threat they faced. It took them only a few seconds to discover what was happening.

Angry yells and glaring beams of light warned the brothers of their danger. With a wild cry, Warady let go the woman's throat and launched himself at the advancing figures but Tupali, bemused by sex, had barely withdrawn when a crushing blow caught him between neck and shoulder. Shouts battered his ears: he felt his victim scramble past; someone kicked him in the ribs as he tried to crawl away. Another blow landed on his back, seeming to drive him into the ground then someone screamed and he was left alone.

Gasping for breath, bewildered, dazed by pain and shock, Tupali dragged himself deeper into the forest. Leaves and dirt clung to his body; the smells of sex, sweat and the hot reek of blood cloyed in his nostrils. At last, when he could see nothing of the camp but a lurid red glow between the trees, he lay still, listening.

None of the bushwalkers would have believed themselves capable of killing another human being before that afternoon. They considered themselves rational and civilised, governed by different laws to those of the natural world they purported to love and understand. But the attack had awoken the most basic instincts of all, to protect mate and home. Even the injured man had slept with his bush-knife close to hand: when Warady threw himself forward to give his brother time to escape, it was a simple matter for them to stab and knock him to the ground. The other woman, grabbing a stout piece of wood from the pile of fuel, had gone after Tupali but once he was down, the raw anguish of Warady's scream brought her to herself. Instead of pressing home her attack, she went to help her friend who was sobbing and pulling distractedly at her clothes.

Warady was on the ground, helpless, surrounded. He had no idea of what had struck him. It was only when he touched his midriff in trying to roll out of the way that he felt a hot gushing wetness and realised he was hurt. With that knowledge came agony beyond anything he had thought it possible to feel and he screamed, wanting to live, but the cry only provoked his assailants. They kicked him with a savagery he could do nothing to counter.

Then the air seemed to solidify. His limbs grew heavy. It was as if he were trying to swim in a liquid that grew more glutinous every moment: he gasped but no air reached his lungs. They stamped on him: broken ribs pierced his organs: blood rushed into his mouth. And although he was already on the ground, Warady felt himself fall into an endless, swooping darkness.

From where he lay hidden, Tupali heard the dull thud of blows, even the sharp crack of bone but there were no more sounds from his brother. He stuffed his fist into his mouth to stifle his sobbing and smelt the secretions from the woman's vagina. The odour which had driven him to a frenzy of lust now made the gorge rise in his throat. He rubbed his palm into the soft dirt of the forest floor but the smell clung to his skin. Nausea swelled within him as shock ebbed and the pain in his shoulder and bruised kidneys grew but he quelled the urge to vomit and bit his knuckles hard instead. If they found him, he was sure they would kill him too.

An unnatural quiet fell. It was as if the forest drew breath. There was only the soft susurration of leaves in a breath of wind, the grunt of a foraging pademelon.

At last, desperate to know his brother's fate, Tupali crawled painfully to where he could view the camp without leaving the protection of the trees. He saw three figures sitting hunched outside the tents, their faces pale in the firelight, like those of ghosts. He saw the body, broken and sprawling with upturned eyes. He saw bloody slits where Warady had been stabbed, a dark blot where his genitals should have been and had to stifle a howl of grief and outrage. Then a woman's squeal rose from inside one of the tents, subsiding swiftly into a rhythmic, drawn-out moaning. That sound, tortured, rapturous, seemed more terrible to Tupali than the fact of his brother's death: it was what they had intended to wring from her. He leapt to his feet and ran with the desperate, blundering action of a wounded animal.

Unexpectedly, the earth seemed to vanish beneath his feet. He fell into a hollow filled with wet leaves and rotten wood. The smell of decay suffused his nostrils and he lay still, lacking the strength or willpower to climb out, too exhausted to care whether he lived or died.

At nightfall Tangalenna returned to the camp. He was hungry and the smell of roasting meat rose tantalisingly into the air (in defiant mood, Ellie had rekindled the fire). He settled himself in his usual place with his back to the shelter and waited to be served. With an effort, the young woman fought down her resentment (there was no trace of contrition in his demeanour), and smiled as she handed him the choicest portion, wanting him to look on her tenderly as before. But he took it and began to eat without acknowledging her.

Tangalenna was no longer angry but he had been overtaken by a kind of profound resignation. It was his secret fear that the disintegration which had begun the moment he set eyes on the pale child would spread until his whole world was destroyed. He had wronged Manalewa and Noumati and in the whisper of the wind he heard the voices of the Broad Ridge people promising to avenge themselves upon him, the man who had betrayed their trust, who had sworn they would be remembered and then kept secret his knowledge of their fate. But it did not occur to him to try and redress what was in the past. It seemed to him that it was already too late.

Though he never spoke of it, the buzzing of carrion flies in his head was growing louder and more persistent every day. He knew their swarming presaged something terrible and irrevocable, something he was powerless to prevent though it would be through him that it would come. There was nothing material to make him think this: the sun's warmth was the same as before, the stars had not deviated from their paths nor the hills and valleys moved. Yet each time he looked upon his lover-daughter, the feeling strengthened.

And yet while it would have been a simple matter for him to send her away, Tangalenna could not bring himself to do so. Noumati had spoken truly when he described Eagle as being beguiled by Brown Quoll, though she had not set out to entrap him. Like an addict who steals to fund his habit but in periods of lucidity despises both crime and addiction, Tangalenna knew that what he was doing was wrong but he did not possess the willpower to stop. In an effort to make sense of what was happening to him, he had returned to his dreaming cave at night, stealing away without telling Ellie where he was going. But his dreams simply reflected his estrangement from all he had once held dear and Korunah did not come to him. His daemon had not yet deserted him, of that he was certain, but he had never felt so alone.

That night they lay next to each other without touching or speaking. Frogs croaked and water lapped against the edge of the tarn while the wind keened against heath and rock. For both, sleep was long in coming.

Noumati, gripped by an urgency he did not understand but dared not question, reached the bottom of the sacred gorge on the second nightfall of his journey. His feet were sore but he was elated at having travelled so swiftly, sure he was close to discovering his half-brother's true fate. He made a bed of leaves close to the place Manalewa had blundered into him, for he did not want to sleep in the deserted camp alone, and ate gratefully from the bag of food she had given him though his promise loomed at the back of his mind like a dark cloud. Then he lay down and tried to sleep while the river roared past and the stars wheeled overhead.

Tangalenna dreamt he was running across the plateau. Behind him came the voices of those he had betrayed, Manalewa, Noumati, Touganana and all the others. Looking back, he saw their faces, twisted in agony, shrunken in death: their empty eye-sockets accused him. In shame and horror he drove himself on until, when he could run no further, he crawled between the heath clumps. Then the wailing was replaced by the buzz of carrion flies, faint at first but growing inexorably louder. He knew that when they found him he would be crushed beneath their weight. They would lay their eggs in his flesh and maggots would devour him from within, leaving his bones to lie on the bare earth, unconsecrated and forgotten. Wind and water would weather them and they would crumble at last to dust but his spirit would wander forever, restless and alone.

At last, when his strength failed, he dragged himself along. The gritty soil scraped his belly; his mouth was full of the taste of earth. The buzzing grew so loud he knew there was no escape. He lay still and covered his head with his hands, hiding his face from the inevitable.

When he woke to darkness, bathed in sweat and trembling; found himself cocooned with his lover in the domed shelter they had made to protect them from the world, Tangalenna almost wept from sheer relief. The young woman, Korunah's gift, turned drowsily and pressed herself against him, seeking warmth. He pulled her close and caressed her with a tenderness poignant as grief. Desire crept over him, dispelling the horror of the dream, and she, in joy at this gentle awakening, began to lick and stroke, savouring the salty moisture on his skin. He entered her and she enfolded him: the same life force surged through them in an unstoppable, overwhelming tide. When at last it ebbed, they sank together into a soft, annihilating slumber, dreamless as death.

As a grey dawn broke, the bushwalker's camp was quiet. The injured man and his partner were asleep inside their tent but the others were still outside. Now, as birdsong echoed through the forest, they sat or lay in a kind of unthinking stupor. They were aware that it was morning but none wanted to be first to stir.

Two forest ravens landed on an overhanging branch. Their grating calls did not rouse the living so they swooped upon the dead. One tore at the staring eyes while the other hopped down the torso to dig in the sunken hole at the crotch.

The dark-haired woman watched in horrified fascination then, as if aware of her scrutiny, the second bird pulled its head out of the body cavity and stared at her, its head reddened with blood. The knowingness of its gaze brought back all the horror of the night and the woman screamed and flapped her arms, unconsciously parodying the bird as it launched itself heavily into the air, followed closely by its mate. They landed on the same overhanging branch to wait until they could resume their feast.

Half-buried in leaves, bemused by grief and pain, Tupali heard the woman's scream and the sound reawakened his terror. He groaned as he dragged himself to his feet and struggled on. The ground sloped at an ever-increasing gradient and soon he was gasping for breath, bleeding from cuts and gashes where thorns had pierced and branches lashed him but he did not stop. The panic of a hunted animal possessed him yet it was not *num* he feared most but his brother's spirit, seeking redress.

At first light, Noumati went to drink at the river. He had slept fitfully, troubled by dreams of blood and violence, of flapping black wings and a nameless, pursuing terror but the cold water brought him back to reality. After eating frugally (he was conserving his food, in order to travel swiftly), he re-bound his misshapen foot. The tough wombat-skin covering had worn through but he managed to re-fashion it, padding it with moss. The foot was swollen and bruised from pushing himself so hard but it was a pain he had become resigned to over the years. Using his spear as a stave, he began to climb slowly up the narrow path that led past the cascades and into the sacred gorge.

Daylight crept over the plateau and the pool reflected it like polished steel. In the semi-darkness of their shelter, Ellie woke to find Tangalenna's arm across her waist. His hand cupped her breast and an echo of their love-making surged though her blood, lapping her in a feeling of profound happiness. She lay still, enjoying the moist warmth of his breath against her scalp, though she knew she should be stirring. And she sensed that he, though relaxed and still, was also awake and reluctant to relinquish their shared warmth, their contentment in one another. She pushed herself gently against him and gave a little sigh of satisfaction as he tightened his embrace.

Tangalenna's body was slack and sated: he wanted to keep her there not so much to prolong the joy they had shared as to stay the onset of day. When at last she tried to pull away (it was long past the time they would usually have set out foraging), he held her back. His heartbeat was loud and rapid in her ear as he pressed her head against his chest.

'Lie still!' he hissed and there was a note of desperation in his tone that made her smile secretly to herself, thinking that she, being the cause, possessed the power to comfort him. She took his hand from her breast and moved it gently to the mound of her belly, soft and yielding beneath the hardness of his palm.

'I am here,' she murmured, 'and maybe a child is also,' and having her back to him she was oblivious to the look of pain that fleeted across his features.

Chapter 16.

Even when he was sure he had escaped, Tupali did not stop until he reached the forest's edge. His skin was streaked with sweat, blood and dirt and at times a cry escaped him, a wordless howl of anguish. Many creatures that heard it paused to listen, uncertain what it signified. The timid recognised fear and crept away to hide while small birds flew away with cries of alarm. Only the bold and hungry, kookaburras, currawongs and ravens were unafraid. Seeing a creature which might, when it fell exhausted, provide an easy meal, they shadowed him for a while and their raucous calls seemed to mock his faltering progress.

At the uttermost limit of his strength, Tupali scrambled to an area of pandanus and tea-tree scrub. He smelt the clean, cold air of the highlands and lay in the shelter of a grass-clump to wait for darkness for he knew he would be exposed and vulnerable on the open slopes. All was quiet: the hum of insects and gentle clash of leaves calmed him. He slept.

Halfway along the sacred gorge, Noumati paused. He thought to hear an intermittent cry above the roar of the torrent far below. It was faint with distance yet so wild and desolate it seemed to pierce his heart. At first he assumed it to be the wail of a wounded or dying animal but as he strained his ears to catch it again, he realised he had never heard such a sound issue from the throat of any bird or beast. More than anything it reminded him of Manalewa's anguish when they had pulled the dead child from her womb and he shivered and hurried on. That such an echo of the past should return now seemed ill-omened. It had, after all, been her cries of grief that had set his half-brother on the path to ruin.

The climb up the gully, difficult enough for Tangalenna and Ellie, was almost impossible for a cripple. Parched with thirst and breathless from fear and exertion, Noumati hauled himself up, freezing when the scree slid beneath him, then climbing doggedly until he reached the first of the pandanus trees and the top of the cleft. Here he rested for a while but there was no water there and so at length he rose wearily and limped on until at last the broad sweep of the heathland lay before him, enclosed by the distant, undulating ridge and, far to the south-east a jumbled pile of rocks which he knew marked the edge of Meelayginnee territory though he had never been there before.

The discovery of the remains of a shelter near the bottom of that precipitous climb had filled Noumati with hope. There had been two sets of footprints close by, one set smaller than the other and narrower than those of the Meelayginnee. These, he was certain, were Ngali-kiri's but as to the rest, he dared not speculate. He did not think she would have gone willingly with Warady and Tupali but the implications of the alternative, that she was with Tangalenna, filled him with trepidation.

Now, as he scanned the plateau, his immediate need was water. There was a faint haze over a dip in the ground not too far away and the vegetation was greener there. He set off towards it as swiftly as his sore foot would allow.

The cloud broke, the sun was high and still Tangalenna and Ellie lay in each other's arms. It seemed to him that while they remained thus, hidden in the womb-like sanctuary of their shelter, he was safe. But he could not hold her there forever, nor did he want to admit his fear.

When, at last, he released her, he was left empty, bereft, though he could hear her moving about outside. He felt a separation more profound than any physical parting. It was how he had imagined it would be if his daemon forsook him.

At the very edge of hearing, there was a dull, persistent throb. It seemed to reverberate through air and earth and it filled Tangalenna with dread. When Ellie returned with a handful of succulent bulbs, he took them from her but could not eat and she was dismayed by his haggard look. She spoke gently and reached out but he flinched from her touch and then she gave up and left him to himself.

Ellie was drinking from the pool when she noticed the

vibration. It was not loud enough for her to identify, more a low resonance through the air than any definable sound, but there was a beat to it, an unnatural regularity that disturbed her. She got to her feet and scanned the horizon, trying to work out its direction. Her eyes rested at last on the boulders of Tarner's Tail but then the noise faded and she dismissed it, having more immediate concerns. The fire was almost out because she had lain so long abed and if, as she feared, Tangalenna's sickness had returned, she would have to find food for both of them. Also, she thought, she must remember to gather tea-tree leaves for the lacerations on his legs and torso which were inflamed from his continual scratching.

With her mind thus occupied, she turned and saw Noumati.

He was still so far away that his figure was no more than finger-nail-high against the background of scraggy pandanus but there was no mistaking his halting gait and rather squat build. She stared, astonished, exclaimed aloud then ran to meet him. She could not have said what thought or desire compelled her save that his arrival marked the end of isolation. In her gladness she had forgotten how she had deserted him.

The storyteller was the last person Tangalenna had expected to see on the plateau. Hearing Ellie's cry, he crawled from the shelter in the hope it was his enemy, Warady, who had come: even a fight ending in defeat would be better than having to face the half-brother he had betrayed. But there was no mistaking the figure making inexorably for the pool. Overwhelmed by shame and remorse he looked skywards, believing that only his daemon had the power to help him. But Korunah was not there.

As Noumati shouted joyfully and waved, Tangalenna cast a last, despairing look into the empty sky. There was a humming in his ears like the distant swarming of bees or flies. As he listened, the resonance increased in volume and intensity, vibrating through his very bones and then the full horror of his dreams crowded his mind. He rose to his feet and a heavy, suffocating feeling centred in his chest; black spots appeared before his eyes: the swarms swirling and closing in.

With a wild cry, he fled.

Ellie and Noumati watched aghast as Tangalenna bounded

from cushion plant to cushion plant, running as if he were being pursued. The storyteller yelled at him to come back but he paid no heed. Once he paused to glance behind, certain the black mass would be following, a great seething cloud that would blot out the sun before smothering him, and they glimpsed his face, stark as something rough-hewn from granite, the eyes wild and staring. Then he swung round and was off again, heading blindly towards the tumbled blocks of Tarner's Tail.

Noumati leaned heavily on his spear and watched the running figure diminish as the distance between them widened. Any anger he felt at how he had been betrayed was lost beneath a surge of pity and wonder. It seemed to him that Tangalenna's madness resulted directly from his flouting of the law: he had mocked the spirits of his ancestors by taking the pale child, his own foster-daughter, as his lover so they had stolen his wits to punish his arrogance. And though no one could summon or converse with another's daemon, Noumati glanced into the sky for a sign his half-brother might be forgiven.

Although she had developed the wiry strength and stamina of the Meelayginnee, Ellie knew she had no chance of catching Tangalenna until he stopped. But he could not run forever so she set off in pursuit. His expression had struck her to the core: even in the worst extremity of his fever he had never looked so anguished. She longed to hold and comfort him, to protect him from whatever had driven him to such a state, not understanding it was she who had altered the balance of his world and estranged him from himself.

As he ran, Tangalenna's mind seemed to fly into three separate entities. One part was occupied with the need to look ahead, to judge the next step, to concentrate on breathing, to drive his body on though his muscles might be tearing from the bone. There was another, more rational portion, unaffected by fear, where he thought of Noumati, of the humiliation he would have to face if he stopped and let them catch up with him. But overwhelming both these was the horror of his dream, the noise of the black swarms which was growing louder every moment. He gasped and sobbed, feeling his strength begin to fail.

The rocks of Tarner's Tail loomed ahead and he veered away, following the slope down towards the edge of the escarpment. The breath seared his lungs and he began to lurch and stumble as he ran. He slowed, trying not to fall, then staggered to a halt.

The noise was now coming from in front, a throbbing vibration that made the very air shudder. It beat upon him like the downdraft of invisible, flailing wings, resonated through his flesh, his bones, the very earth he stood upon. He had tried to run but there was no escape.

Defeated, calm in the certainty of death, he put his hands over his ears and crouched, waiting for the black swarms to appear. There was a strange taint in the air, something he had smelt on his first journey beyond his own world, and in the place where *num* had awoken the evil that had overcome the Broad Ridge people. It seemed to him that the badness must have spread to the boundaries of his own land and he bent lower, whimpering like a child brought to an extremity of pain or fear.

The clumps of heath ahead of him began to toss as if caught in a blustery wind. The noise battered him as a palpable force. Something monstrous, glittering, rose into view. He stared, transfixed, then flung himself upon his face. His hands were clamped over his head, his eyes shut tight. As in his dream, he waited. But the darkness did not come; the crushing swarms held back. Unresisting and helpless, he was grasped and raised then carried through the buffeting wind towards the whirling centre of the cacophony.

Ellie stopped dead and stood rigid, arms held stiff and straight at her sides. Her hands were clenched so tightly that the fingernails dug crescents into her palms.

'No!' Her wail was audible even to the storyteller, left far behind. She sprang forward and ran towards the helicopter which had hovered a moment then landed briefly to pick up Tangalenna. But it was half a kilometre away and the pilot did not see her diminutive, naked figure against the brown heath. As soon as the SES crew gave the signal to go, he took off again, swung the machine around and flew away towards the east.

Noumati knew he was witnessing the manifestation of a

powerful spirit, most likely the evil Raguwrapper, who often appeared in insect-form. Those who had taken Tangalenna into the belly of the monster were lesser spirits, parodying men but with the heads of flies. Knowing himself powerless against the supernatural, the storyteller watched without fear as the thing rose into the air and flew away with a noise more terrible than thunder but his heart grieved for his half-brother. He was certain he would never see Tangalenna again.

As the helicopter diminished to a black speck and disappeared, Ellie sank to her knees. For four years she had believed herself in a world apart from her own, one that was contiguous but completely separate: she had never questioned how Tangalenna managed to cross from one to the other. The Meelayginnee lived at a pace unrelated to her own culture, their existence governed by seasons, not hours and this had enhanced her sense of isolation until memories of her past had become remote and dreamlike. Believing there could be no contact with the places she remembered, no possibility of return, she had learned to forget and be content.

Now that illusion was shattered. Now it was her life with the Meelayginnee that seemed unreal, like some kind of cruel game. Even if the rest had no concept of reality, she was sure Tangalenna must have known the truth and deliberately deceived her to keep her in his power. Now she realised that all the time she had been living a nomadic, stone-age existence, naked, often cold and nearly always hungry, her friends and family were only a few days' walk away. The effect was devastating.

'Ngali-kiri?' Having seen her drop to the ground, Noumati hurried over, assuming she was grieving for Tangalenna. His voice was gentle and full of compassion; he reached out and touched her on the shoulder. Her reaction astonished him: she leapt to her feet and whirled round to face him with a look of revulsion and horror that smote his heart.

'Leave me alone!' Without thinking she reverted to English: seeing his shock and bewilderment she spun round and sprinted away, heading for the landing place. Sobs racked her as she ran because instead of Noumati, her friend, confidant and husband, she had seen a cowed, naked man, his face all disordered by grief, unreachable, a stranger. This transformation, which was a shift in her own perception, was so sudden and unexpected, it frightened her. She touched her head, felt the soft stubble of her shaven scalp, was aware of the darkness of her skin, the ingrained filth, ochre and charcoal and, for the first time, felt ashamed.

A faint stench of fuel lingered where the aircraft had touched down and some of the heath was bent and crushed but there was nothing else to prove that such a thing as a helicopter existed. Ellie wandered distractedly around the landing site while Noumati hurried laboriously towards her. His persistence irritated her and she turned her back deliberately and walked quickly away along the edge of the escarpment, heading roughly in the direction the helicopter had taken. Away to her left, the rocks of Tarner's Tail marked the end of Meelayginnee territory but she did not care.

Every time Noumati drew close, Ellie looked round wildly and set off again. The western sky flamed in sunset and the distant rocks of Tarner's Tail stood out starkly when at last he gave up the chase, mouth parched and lame foot battered and bleeding. He leant on his spear and watched his wife move away with a lithe, even stride: a terrible emptiness filled him. Not until her slender figure was no longer distinguishable against the thin trunks of the pandanus did he turn and trudge back the way he had come.

Such was the confusion of her mind that Ellie walked without any clear purpose. It was simply that the physical act precluded thought to some degree. As the light failed, she had to concentrate more on her footing yet her sense of loss and betrayal was so acute she felt sick.

Only when she was certain Noumati was far behind did she stop. She looked into the sky and the glittering stars seemed to mock her; she looked towards the forest, a dark, apparently impenetrable wall, and shivered. That was the way the helicopter had flown, where she had come from, her world. Tangalenna must have carried her through that forest, a trusting, naïve child. Now, knowing the truth, she could not believe her own credulity.

Overwhelmed by despair, she sank down and bent over until her head rested on her knees. That Tangalenna had been taken she had hardly comprehended. Her whole being was wrenched by a pain that transcended the loss of the man who had been abductor, father, lover and, all the while, her betrayer. She had integrated with the Meelayginnee closely as anyone not born to them could have done, she bore the marks of that identity in her skin and womb yet it was all a sham. She had been tricked into living as a hunter-gatherer in a digital age and the worst part of it was that her own mind had deceived her. She had been taught that ancient aboriginal culture had ceased to exist in Tasmania, therefore when she found herself within it, she had assumed she could not be in the Tasmania she knew. For a child it was simple logic. But wrong.

A moan escaped her, mournful as that of a hawk-owl. Hearing it Tupali, who lay half-insensible no more than a spear-cast away, shuddered, thinking his brother's spirit was abroad and using some night-bird as its mouthpiece. With an effort he raised himself to his hands and knees and began to crawl away, not because he thought he had any chance of escaping Warady's ghost but because to wait helpless in the dark was worse than the physical pain.

The wind and noise lessened abruptly. Tangalenna was forced to sit. The taint of death was overlain by the smells of human sweat, blood, an ochre-like tang that was the smell of metal; a dense, soft web wrapped him round. There were voices like those of men but they spoke nonsense.

Fearful that he might be punished if he looked upon the spirits without leave, Tangalenna kept his eyes shut tight though, unexpectedly, he thought he still possessed a living body. His heart seemed to labour painfully in his chest and the sound of gasping breath was loud in his ears. Then his head was clamped in a grip like the jaws of *kannenner* and something foul-smelling and inflexible pressed against his face. At the same time, bands tightened about his waist and shoulders, pulling him back so that he could hardly move.

Up till then he had been resigned and passive: while tales of what happened to a man's spirit after death were vague, he had expected the ancestors to be angry. But this was a direct assault. He could not sit helpless while he was still able to think and feel.

He opened his eyes.

He was in a tiny space filled with hybrid creatures, half carrion fly, half human. They stood upright and their bodies were like those of men with two legs and two arms but they were clothed in a single loose skin, the hue of ochre only brighter. There were coverings on their hands and feet but when he saw their faces he realised they were white-skinned, like *num*. Where there should have been ears, there were shiny, bulbous protuberances on the sides of their heads while long proboscis-like tubes curved in front. It was as if insect-features had been grafted on the human ones.

The thing they had clamped onto his face was like the mouthpart of a fly: he too had a long proboscis. He was paralysed by this realisation, terrified that once he breathed through that mouthpiece he also would become part insect. All that remained of him revolted against that final submission. He looked desperately for help and saw the bushwalkers.

One lay on a stretcher, with an insect-man bent over him: Tangalenna paid him no more attention. The others sat in a row, staring at him. His figure, his stench, his almost palpable terror epitomised the nightmare they thought to have escaped: a forest where trees oozed sap like blood; a place of shadows, darkness and violence where they had killed and mutilated a man then hidden the evidence and sworn to keep silent. They stared and the hands of each groped blindly for those of the person sitting next to them. Only the fair-haired woman avoided looking at Tangalenna. She was fighting the hysteria that threatened to overwhelm her.

Sensing their fear, Tangalenna decided that whatever the insect-creatures were, these five were true children of Tarner, *num* but human nonetheless. Despite the strangeness of their appearance, their obvious horror at what was happening identified them as fellow captives. Like him, they were strapped down but they ignored the insect-men: their attention was fixed on him. It was as if he was more frightening than the spirits.

His chest was bursting, his eyes bulged: he could hold on no longer. He drew in a huge, gulping breath. His head reeled and he felt the floating sensation that always came after fasting, the gateway to dreaming.

For a moment he was tempted to follow that path. Then the

noise increased to an intolerable clattering roar. He clapped his hands to his ears, moaning, cowed, begging it to stop. After a few moments, it became more bearable and he was able to think again.

The dreaming was a trick, he realised, an attempt to lull him into compliance like the others. He wrenched against the straps but they held him firmly in place. One of the insect-man spoke sternly to him but then clambered past to join the others. They sat down and buckled themselves into their seats. He watched this with amazement: it was as if they wanted to be prisoners.

Then the whole world lurched and swung.

For a moment of sheer, unadulterated terror, Tangalenna thought his bowels were dropping out. A warm flood spread beneath him and the stench of excrement spread overwhelmingly though the cabin, making insect-men and *num* complain in a manner that needed no interpretation. A surge of shame brought him back from the brink of panic. He looked away from the inhuman faces, the cold eyes (which were like Ngali-kiri's, he realised with a jolt), beneath the bulbous insect ones. Through the row of small oval windows he saw the ragged tops of pandanus trees lashed by a mighty wind, glimpsed the forest swing below, then a swaying expanse of sky.

They were flying.

Always when he had dreamed of flight, Korunah had been there to guide him. The world spread beneath their wings and he had shared the vision of his ancestors, soared even to the outer reaches of the sky to honour and acknowledge them. Shining air had borne him, stars had glittered all around: he had known a freedom beyond the experience of earth-bound beings and counted himself among the blessed.

The stinking, crowded space in which he was confined was so alien to this memory of pure, sacred flight, Tangalenna would not, could not tolerate it. He lowered his hands, flinching at the noise and pulled at the oxygen mask. He succeeded in getting it away from his face but thinking he was free of it, let go and it sprang back, hitting his nose with such force, his eyes watered.

The nearest of the insect-men, seeing what he was attempting, leaned forward. Tangalenna froze, expecting some dreadful punishment. The gloved fingers touched his head: there was a terrible pressure on his face followed by unexpected relief as the mask dropped into his lap. The insect-man was talking to him, loudly and slowly as if to a child but Tangalenna cut himself off. Although the words were incomprehensible to him, he knew they were meant to deceive. His hands worked at the buckles of his safety harness but the blanket had fallen down across his shoulder and lap so the creature did not see.

The helicopter tilted and shuddered as the pilot, having gained altitude, set off at full power towards the north-east. In the same moment, Tangalenna released his harness. He flung himself towards the only clear space with a window, the emergency exit. His soiled blanket fell to the floor and he twisted away from the hands that reached to grab him with the supple quickness of a wild animal.

Had he been able to comprehend the instructions pasted on the door, Tangalenna could have opened it easily. But his people had no tradition of pictorial art or writing and so he saw only a meaningless jumble of lines and patches of colour. He wrenched at the handle with both hands, pulling it with all his strength and when that failed, clawed frantically at the edges of the window. All the time a kind of high-pitched keening escaped him, a sound he was unconscious of uttering but which was agonising to hear. It seemed to come from some place of loneliness and pain on the edge of madness and those that heard it felt the hair rise at the nape of their neck.

In a matter of seconds, his hands slippery with sweat, Tangalenna understood that his efforts were futile. He crouched and stared out of the window. Now the mountains, forest, rivers were displayed as Korunah had revealed them. In the last rays of the setting sun the rocks of Tarner's Tail glowed blood-red, growing smaller every moment. They were flying over pale patches where the trees had been cleared: beyond these were bright, twinkling lights. His heart leapt in the hope that they were stars but an instant later he saw his mistake. These lights did not possess the pure, glittering radiance he sought but were dim, tainted with an orange hue, bunched together instead of spreading to fill the sky and some of them, white and red, were attached to small dark objects that moved along narrow strips laid over the land.

Then he realised the truth.

Rage and shame at how easily he had been deceived flowed like fire through Tangalenna's blood. A red mist veiled his sight and he threw himself repeatedly against the door, his face distorted into a rigid mask of hate. Hands grasped him but he swatted them away like flies. There was shouting, the voices hoarse with anger and fear; a woman screamed; the floor tipped, throwing him to one side.

He staggered and fell, clutching at something that slipped from his grip. It was smooth and curved: the handle of the emergency door.

Then came a sharp pain in his right buttock, unexpected as the bite of a bulldog-ant.

He slid into darkness.

Chapter 17.

Noumati was halfway to the pool when he decided to turn back. He was bone-weary, his crippled foot so painful he could hardly put it to the ground, but the sense of isolation that had crept upon him was worse. Having witnessed something beyond his wildest imagining, he felt more alone and vulnerable than ever before. And he guessed that stricken as she was, Ngali-kiri would not have gone far. In his craving for companionship, he forgot how easily she could outpace him.

As he limped along, the events of the day ran endlessly though his mind. Yet what most affected him was the way Tangalenna had fled, as if he, Noumati, was some kind of threat.

'I would have shared Ngali-kiri if you'd asked,' he muttered, hardly aware of what he was saying in his distress. His mind shied away from the appearance of Raguwrapper, the manner in which his half-brother had been taken, but he could not help wondering why Tangalenna merited such direct retribution, something that had not occurred since legendary times. And then he recalled Tangalenna's strange mood when he had returned from his fruitless journey to find his foster-daughter already initiated and betrothed. With hindsight it seemed to the storyteller that he had been like one haunted by some dreadful prescience, who knows he cannot outrun his fate.

'Aie, what did you do to so anger them?' Noumati thought, glancing anxiously into the sky. The stars were high and remote but he felt as if unseen eyes were watching. Then he noticed that away to his left the boulders of Tarner's Tail loomed black against the lambent starlight and he understood. He had already passed that boundary in daylight but at night the spirits were most powerful. Having just seen how terrible their wrath could be, he had no wish to provoke them.

Noumati stood still, irresolute. A light breeze made the pandanus leaves clash to his right and there was a faint rustling in the forest beyond; from far down the sacred gorge came the roar of the torrent, faint with distance. Then a tawny frogmouth called. It was so close, the storyteller started.

Like all his people, Noumati loved and revered his daemon. A warm rush of joy and affection swept away his trepidation as the bul-book! sounded again. This time the call was slightly fainter and he knew then that his guardian spirit was guiding him and there was nothing to fear. Murmuring words of acknowledgement and thanks, he followed. Strength seemed to flow into him with every breath he took because the air had been touched by his daemon's wings. He no longer felt the pain of his bruised and swollen foot as he made his way into unknown territory.

Maybe two hundred paces from where he had first heard it, the frogmouth ceased calling and Noumati stopped. Again he listened, not only with his ears but with his whole being. It was so quiet, even his breathing seemed loud.

There was a sudden rustle deep in the pandanus scrub, the movement of some large animal, wombat or devil. Wallabies generally made less noise unless stampeded. Noumati crouched in a hunter's stance, spear held defensively in both hands. The wind was blowing fitfully from the direction of the sounds and he caught a faint whiff of blood. It was injured then, that accounted for its clumsiness. He hoped it was not a diseased devil: there had been enough misfortune for one day.

More rustling was followed by a gasp, as if the creature had reached the end of its strength. Noumati waited, then came a soft moan, unmistakably human. Heart thumping wildly, the storyteller crept forward, expecting to see the pale form of his wife at any moment. Whatever she had done to herself in her grief, he told himself, he would be patient and care for her. And one day, if he waited long enough, she might join with him again of her own accord.

At last he was close enough to hear quick, ragged breathing. Mixed with the taint of blood was the stink of fear-sweat and an underlying heavy odour, unmistakably a man's. This was not Ngali-kiri.

Noumati hesitated. Although he had been led there by his daemon, he was in another band's territory without permission. It occurred to him that this might be a trap set by survivors of the Disappearing or worse, some manifestation of their guardian spirits. On this day anything seemed possible. He lifted one hand from the spear-shaft and touched the raised scars on his breast for reassurance.

Then a whimpering arose, so weak and pitiful that compassion overcame Noumati's dread. Keeping one hand over the lines of cicatrices on his chest, so that whatever he found he would remember who and what he was, he edged forward. His spear was held loosely in his right hand though he knew that if it turned out to be a trick and he had to fight, he was unlikely to win.

'I am Noumati, storyteller to the Meelayginnee,' he whispered. 'I mean you no harm.'

To Tupali the world had become a dim and distant place. His tongue was swollen, his lips cracked, his eyes glazed with thirst: even pain seemed unreal. But as his other senses failed, his hearing had become more acute and the slight sounds made by Noumati as he approached, the brush of heath and cutting-grass against his legs, the dragging of his lame foot, were enough to rouse his fading consciousness. He guessed *tarrabah* had found his trail; imagined them tearing at his vitals while he lay helpless, too weak to fight them off, and groped blindly for a stick or stone, anything he could use as a weapon.

'This is no way for a man to die,' he thought and then a picture of how he had fled, leaving his brother's mutilated body to the mercy of his killers, filled his mind. Warady's spirit would demand redress for that cowardice. He dug his fingers into the gritty earth and waited, bracing his body against rending teeth and claws. Hearing Noumati's words, he thought he was dreaming.

At first, the storyteller was not sure whether the figure spread-eagled face down on the ground was dead or alive. In the pale light of a rising moon, the body was striped silver and black, as if half-decayed. He crouched, leaning on his spear for support and tentatively moved matted hanks of hair to reveal the face.

'Tupali!' In his relief that this was no stranger or spirit-being, Noumati forgot his half-brother's enmity and his voice was strong and full of joy. With an effort, Tupali rolled onto his back and struggled to focus but the smell of his companion was familiar and the fear that had leapt to his throat subsided.

'Eh . . .' The storyteller shook his head, shocked at the young man's condition. Tupali's body was covered in lacerations and bruises, blood and dirt but it was his expression that most dismayed Noumati. Gaunt with suffering and grief the face was hardly recognisable, wizened like that of an old man, the eyes and nostrils crusted with mucus, the mouth hanging open as if he had lost his wits.

'Is there water?' The words were barely intelligible, uttered in a harsh croak. Noumati was burning to know what could have brought the young man to so desperate a state but he had long learned the wisdom of patience.

'Not here, but close,' he replied.

The helicopter landed at Hobart Airport where police and ambulances were waiting. The bushwalkers were taken to hospital but from his wild appearance and the SES crew's report, Tangalenna was assumed to be an illegal immigrant, probably from Papua or the Solomons, who had been shipwrecked or dumped on the southwest coast. He was sent directly to the high security wing of the state prison.

When Tangalenna awoke, his senses were assaulted by alien smells and sounds. He lay still, trying to assimilate them, while his eyes adjusted to the cold brightness of artificial light. His limbs and throat felt strangely constricted but he dared not move until he was sure he was alone.

There was a constant low hum but it was not the clatter of the flying thing. This sound was quieter, more insidious, unvarying in volume. If it was the buzzing of flies, they were neither coming closer nor going away.

He waited, listening to the sounds of his own breathing, the thud of his heartbeat. He did not wonder why *num* had captured him, knowing little of their world. But he knew he must be careful.

He had seen enough of their power to fear them.

Tentatively, he lifted one hand and felt for his talisman: in his distress he had forgotten it was lost. Instead of touching the bone amulet or the scars which patterned his chest, his fingers encountered a barrier, soft and insensate. He sat up, astonished, found that his body had disappeared in the kind of loose covering *num* wore, what Ngali-kiri called 'clothes'. Only his hands and feet were visible. Outraged and horrified, he tore at the cloth with all his strength. Buttons flew in all directions as he ripped the overalls open but when he discovered his skin smooth and whole underneath, he calmed enough to pull the garment off his legs instead of trying to tear it end to end. Naked, he felt more himself. At least they had not peeled his skin to make him white.

Beyond the humming (which was so constant he had begun to ignore it), there was a disconcerting absence of any sound he recognised, no bird calls, rustling of leaves, no noise of water or wind. And though he realised he was in some kind of hut, there were no comforting smells of hearth-smoke and people, only a bland dryness that stung the back of his throat and the lining of his nostrils when he snuffed the air. He reached out to touch the wall closest to him. It was cold and hard as stone but the surface was smooth and unnaturally flat. It was pale green in colour but its smell contained nothing of earth: having no interest in something so solid yet featureless, he began to explore the rest of his surroundings.

There was a door with a metal grille above it. In the opposite wall another grille was set, too high for him to reach though he sensed the outside lay that way. Other than the platform he had woken upon, the only fittings in the room were a stainless steel washbasin and toilet. These caused Tangalenna much bewilderment: he was thirsty and dipped his hand in the toilet bowl to drink but the liquid, though it looked and sounded like water as it dripped from his palm, smelled and tasted so foul, he spat it out. Beneath the reek of chemical cleaner he detected the taint of someone else's urine and excrement but even these were strange, as if the food they ate was unknown to him.

He avoided the toilet thereafter.

All the time, his whole being was questing for something

familiar but the very air was stale, as if no rain had touched it, nor plant nor any other living creature: it was dead. Discouraged and weary, he returned at last to the sleeping platform.

Cut off from earth and sky he could not contemplate dreaming, so Tangalenna drew his knees to his chest and clasped his arms around them. Head bowed and eyes closed, he breathed in the familiar smells of sweat, ochre, charcoal: himself. The hum of the ventilation merged with the rush of blood in his ears and he began to rock back and forth until the rhythm of movement lulled him into a trance.

Once the first wave of anger and despair had passed, Ellie felt completely drained. She stretched out on the gritty earth and wondered if she possessed the willpower simply to lie there until she succumbed to thirst and starvation. She quickly realised how pathetic that idea was: her stomach was already grumbling with hunger. First she must find food and water. Then she could decide what to do.

The call of a distant frogmouth, Noumati's totem, brought her scrambling to her feet. She looked wearily back in the direction of Tarner's Tail. She doubted her husband would venture so far beyond Meelayginnee land but he had already surprised her twice, firstly by appearing on the plateau at all, then by his persistence in following her. There was no movement along the line of the terrace but this time she headed into the forest.

As she made her way between the trees, descending steadily towards the east, Ellie's resentment smouldered. Now, when she thought of Tangalenna, it was not as the fierce and tender lover but her abductor: she remembered her terror, how he had nearly suffocated her, how gullible she had been to believe him capable of transporting her to a world separate from her own. Although in a way, she realised bitterly, that was exactly what had happened. The two cultures seemed irreconcilable. She could feel the differences between them within herself, threatening to wrench her apart.

Weary and distraught, she began to stumble as she made her way along narrow wallaby trails. Overhanging branches lashed her face and more than once she stubbed her toes against roots which straggled across the path. Then a hollow seemed to open up beneath her feet and she fell headlong, landing with a jolt that emptied her lungs and left her gasping. When she was able to breathe again she did not try to move but lay still. A tide of emotion she was incapable of stopping swept over her: she sobbed helplessly. Even in the first days after her abduction she had never felt so completely alone. Then she had been reduced to a child-like dependency and Manalewa had succoured her. Recalling that soft, sweet warmth, those enfolding arms, Ellie longed for her foster-mother with a deep, visceral yearning that made her curl up and hug her knees to her chest. She moaned softly to herself as the moon rose, sending pale shafts to dapple the forest floor. The night seemed endless.

It was almost dawn when Noumati and Tupali reached the pool. Tired as he was, the storyteller had been forced to support his half-brother most of the way for Tupali was so weak his legs wove into each other and several times the two found themselves entangled on the ground, feet snagged by heath roots. Always Noumati was first to rise on these occasions and each time it became harder to rouse Tupali who wanted only to be left alone to sleep. Realising that once the young man was unconscious, he would be impossible to move, Noumati goaded him into action, calling him coward and weakling and boasting of how Ngali-kiri was his. By the time they reached the camp, both were reduced to crawling for Noumati's foot was now so painful he could not bear to put any weight on it.

When he smelt water, Tupali lunged forward, plunged in up to the elbows and sucked the liquid up. So greedily did he drink, it seemed to Noumati that he would swallow the whole of the rippling, moon-glossed pool. Even the frogs ceased their incessant croaking as if in recognition of this threat and the storyteller raised himself, grasped Tupali's ankles and hauled him back, not from concern for his health but because he felt suddenly that something innate to the whole balance of his world was in jeopardy.

Tupali twisted round, snarling like *tarrabah* disturbed at a carcass, his shrunken face distorted into a mask of rage. There was no trace of gratitude or friendliness in that expression and Noumati felt his new-found confidence falter. Weak as Tupali was, he did not want to fight him. In an effort to avert violence, he asked ingenuously, 'Did you and Warady decide to hunt alone then?'

At this naming of his brother, which although uttered in ignorance would only enrage Warady's spirit further, Tupali gave a dreadful cry that echoed eerily across the heath. With a dragging motion like that of a wounded animal, he crawled into the shelter. Noumati followed reluctantly, drawn by a storyteller's curiosity yet afraid of what might be revealed. That cry had reminded him sharply of Tangalenna's earlier the same day.

'My brother was killed by strangers,' Tupali said after a long silence. 'They were *num*, white-skinned like Ngali-kiri when she first came to us. They wore clothes and had many things but they were ignorant of the law. There were three men and two women. My brother speared one man in the leg and we hunted them until it was dark and they made camp. . .'

As Noumati listened, a kind of horror took hold of him. He thought of how Ngali-kiri had been affected by the sight of the insect-men and wondered uneasily whether the two events, the brothers' attack on the strangers and the appearance of Raguwrapper, were somehow connected.

Had he been speaking to anyone else, Tupali might have left out the details of his brother's death and the mutilation of the corpse, all of which had gone unavenged. But before a cripple who, to his knowledge, had never even killed a wallaby, the shame of his cowardice seemed less acute: Noumati would never have set out on such an expedition even if it meant a lifetime without a woman of his own. Unconsciously perhaps he realised also that the storyteller was the one person in the world who would listen without judgement.

'We must go back and burn his body,' he declared fiercely at the end of his account. Throughout his tale he had kept his head bowed but now he raised it to see Noumati's reaction. It was only then, looking into the storyteller's anguished face, that the strangeness of him being there occurred to him. Sudden anxiety made him reach out to grasp Noumati's shoulder. 'What's happened? What are you doing here? Where is Tangalenna? And Ngali-kiri?'

'She ran away,' Noumati replied, slowly and painfully. 'But I came because of a promise I made Manalewa.'

With that he fell silent and so grim was his expression that Tupali dared not persist. He stretched out on the bed of heath and fell immediately asleep though the eastern sky was already light with dawn.

Ellie's little fire smouldered deep in its bed until a heath root caught alight. A wisp of smoke threaded up through the ash and charcoal into daylight. Kept awake by hunger and the restlessness of his mind which, despite his weariness, would not be still, Noumati smelt it and crawled outside to investigate. Then he saw smoke spiralling up from the stone-rimmed hearth and knew what he must do. Tangalenna was beyond his reach but at least he could help Tupali give Warady his proper rites.

Had he known the origin of the fire he now tended with such care, Noumati would have been horrified. In his ignorance, it seemed to him that the pale flames licking greedily at the dry heath stems he fed them were a sign that order had been restored, that the spirits were satisfied by Tangalenna's punishment. When he was certain the fire would not go out, he went back inside the shelter and stretched beside Tupali. Now his mind was made up, he was able to relax. Neither he nor Tupali were in a fit state to return to tend the corpse: they would forage beside the camp for a day and rest as much as possible before setting out at dawn. He sighed, closed his eyes and gave himself up to sleep.

Hunger roused Ellie from the stupor of exhaustion and despair in which most of the night had passed. When the harsh cackle of kookaburras greeted the pre-dawn twilight, she scrambled to her feet and began to look for food. She moved with a careless confidence the Meelayginnee were born to but which she had had to learn: indifferent to her nakedness she seemed wholly a creature of the forest, apparently oblivious to everything except the appeasement of hunger as she made her way from tree to tree plucking leaves, buds, fungi and cramming them into her mouth as she went.

In truth, it required little thought to recognise what was edible, only the affirmation of the senses. Thus as she picked and ate, Ellie relived the events of the previous afternoon until at last instead of hating Tangalenna she began to wonder what was happening to him. She could not conceive why he had been taken or what the helicopter was doing there but she could imagine his fear and confusion on being transported suddenly into her world. Then nausea overcame her and she bent low and vomited.

When her stomach was empty, she straightened, trembling, and looked around for water to wash away the foulness in her mouth. There was none but the growing light picked out a great tree, the upper bark of its trunk and branches silver against the spreading greyness of the sky. Something stirred deep in the young woman's memory and she walked slowly towards it. At the base of the tree was a wide opening into the hollow centre where she could hide and rest, for she was very tired. But before entering she paused to take stock of her surroundings.

She was close to the edge of a steep escarpment. Forest spread below like a kind of frozen ocean, unbroken as far as the eye could see. To her right was a distant mountain and her heart lurched. The shape of the peak was unmistakeable: it was visible from the farm. This was the tree where she and Tangalenna had sheltered the day after her abduction. Here he had given her meat and she had begun to look upon him as a friend.

From here she could find her way back.

Heart thumping wildly, she crawled inside the tree. In four years she had barely thought of her family: it had been as though they were dead and existed only in her memory. The prospect of returning forced her to consider how she had altered during those years and, for the first time, she realised that her brothers, parents, friends, would also have changed. On the rare occasions she had visualised them it was as she had last seen them, as if they existed only in reference to herself and the world must be as she remembered it. But their lives had not ceased simply because she was not there. She had no idea of what she would find, or of how those she knew would react to her appearance.

Daunted yet excited, she curled up on the dry, soft floor of the tree-cave and lay with her knees hugged to her chest, watching the sky lighten from the colour of ash to the hue of steel . . .

It was mid-morning when Ellie woke. Though she could not remember dreaming, her mind was calm and clear. Her life among the Meelayginnee already seemed remote and unreal: though she had longed for Manalewa in the night, it was the farm that now came to mind when she thought of home. She imagined her parents running to embrace her; her brothers' admiration when she told them how she had adapted and survived. She would have her own room again, hot showers, food that did not have to be laboriously gathered or hunted but came ready to eat from the supermarket. At school she would be a celebrity: newspapers and television companies would clamour for her story, make her famous throughout Australia. Then, when everything had calmed down, she would use the money they gave her to find Tangalenna and teach him to live in the modern world.

Although already a married woman among the Meelayginnee, divorced from her own culture since the age of ten Ellie still possessed the naivety of a child, was unsophisticated, self-centred, trusting. That her plan might have wider implications, affecting the very existence of her hearth-group, simply did not occur to her. She left the hollow tree and began the steep descent, thinking only of the journey ahead which, she estimated, would take at least another day.

At the base of the escarpment, Ellie paused. She remembered little of the previous journey when Tangalenna had carried her, and the forest was so dense there were no clear landmarks. Yet where once she might have panicked, she had learned patience. It was a grey, overcast day but she could tell the position of the sun from the quality of the light filtering through the leaf canopy. And she had learned also to trust what in her culture would have been called 'instinct' but which the Meelayginnee realised in daemon form.

Instead of choosing a broad wallaby trail that seemed to lead in the direction she wanted (but which in fact petered out in a large clearing), she took a twisting path that at first appeared to be little used. This led eventually to the fern-crowded gully where Tangalenna had stopped to drink five years earlier. But until she reached the creek, Ellie had no knowledge of this: she knew only that it felt like the right way.

As she walked, she plucked and ate food along the way though she did not feel hungry. When, in late afternoon, she reached the creek, she lay down and sucked the water up as Tangalenna had done after carrying her there. Afterwards she felt strangely nauseous: she touched her breasts and belly and they were tight and swollen. Although she had spoken to Tangalenna of a child, that had been more in an effort to calm him than from belief she was really pregnant. So she assumed her symptoms heralded her period, which was overdue. Sighing, she turned from the creek and set off again.

The orderlies assigned to look after Tangalenna soon lost patience. At first they had attributed his behaviour to shock but when he persisted in tearing off his overalls and relieving himself anywhere in his cell, they concluded he was mentally deficient or being deliberately provocative. When spoken to, he either assumed a blank indifference (in which he seemed to cut himself off entirely from his situation), or shouted words nonsensical as the jabbering of a child who imitates language but has not learned to speak properly: his lack of response to interrogation (which became ever more aggressive as the frustration of the interviewers increased), was interpreted as a kind of unreasoning stubbornness. Taken to the showers, he flinched at the touch of hot water and tried to claw his way out through the tiled walls; passing a window, he stared at the sky, boxed in by buildings, as if amazed, then, without warning, twisted free of his guards and hurled himself at the glass with such force that had it not been reinforced, it would have shattered. After they shaved off the verminous, greasy hanks of his hair and beard, he scratched open the lesions on his legs and smeared blood over his whole body; left alone, he sat on the bed, rocking incessantly.

News of this behaviour spread quickly through the prison.

It was twilight on the second day after the appearance of the helicopter when Noumati and Tupali reached the glade where Warady had been killed. They were tired and nervous, fearing that the dead man's spirit was watching their every move. Lacking ochre to protect them, they had smeared their bodies with charcoal in an effort to appease the shades of the forest, and built a blazing fire in the middle of the site. There was no sign of the corpse but a large patch of disturbed ground caught their attention. The bushwalkers had strewn leaves and twigs in an attempt to hide the grave but to the eyes of the aborigines this marked the site out rather than concealing it. By the flaring firelight they began to dig, using their bare hands.

Although he had long told tales containing bloodshed and maimings, Noumati was unprepared for the reality of such violence of men against men. The body was not deeply buried and the sight of the gaping wounds and torn eye-sockets, the stench of putrefaction, made him feel faint and sick. He forced himself to help Tupali haul the corpse from the grave but once it was on the surface, he staggered away and vomited. Tupali paid him no attention but knelt and touched his brother's rigid face with a tenderness he had never dared exhibit when Warady was alive.

'Eh my brother, I did not want to desert you,' he murmured and it seemed to him that a whispering throng of spirits, those who had died riteless and forgotten, crowded to listen just beyond reach of the firelight. '*Num* would have slain me too and no-one would know our fate. Tomorrow we will give your flesh back to earth, sky and forest, then we will take news of your death to your kin. You will be free to join our ancestors, Black Snake.'

He sat back on his heels, dazed with grief and weariness. Noumati, who had been watching him surreptitiously, threw a branch on the fire, sending up a shower of sparks. He had mastered his sickness but avoided looking at the corpse as much as possible.

'We'll take turns to keep watch,' he said after a while. 'The fire must be tended and *tarrabah* kept away. Tomorrow he shall have his burning and we must hunt a wallaby for his funeral feast. If we wait until we reach the others, his spirit might be angry.'

'Ay.' Tupali could scarcely keep his eyes open. He left the corpse and moved to the other side of the blaze where he stretched out and fell instantly asleep. He never suspected that behind the storyteller's words lurked a secret hope: that seeing the glow of their fire between the trees, Ngali-kiri would return.

As time passed, Tangalenna grew weaker. Most of the food he was brought was unrecognisable as anything that had once lived while some of the liquids were hot: he did not realise they were meant for drinking. He refused to touch them until his thirst was so great he drank the water they gave him though it smelt as if a corpse had rotted in it. He spent most of the time rocking numbly. His body had become a husk: having nothing to interact with, it was irrelevant. He no longer lived, he simply existed.

On the third day of his incarceration he was sunk so deep in his stupor, he did not hear the door being unbolted, the tramp of booted feet on the bare concrete as four orderlies entered. Only when they coughed and swore at the reek of excrement did he become aware of them and then he was instantly alert. Until that moment he had been incapable of distinguishing between the petty cruelties and small kindnesses he had received since his capture, but he recognised the nature of these men at once. A rank heat rose from them: they stank of virile, male aggression. They were going to hurt him.

The door closed. There was no escape.

As they advanced, Tangalenna at last realised the extent of his isolation, his appalling vulnerability. He fought back with a ferocity that surprised his assailants but his defiance only fuelled their lust to subdue and humiliate. They flung him around the cell: their fists and boots slammed into him. Soon he lay inert, barely conscious, struggling to breathe.

When they were satisfied he would offer no further resistance, they hauled him to the toilet and dunked his head until he spluttered and choked for they wanted him to know what was happening, to understand his powerlessness. Then they dragged him to the bed. His body smeared a red trail through the blood and filth spattered across the floor. After a while, he lost consciousness.

In his weariness, Noumati kept watch all night while Tupali slept. No frogmouth called to comfort him and he worried that Raguwrapper might return. He knew they had no choice than to burn Warady's body but he was fearful that eyes other then Ngalikiri's might see the smoke. Secretly, he hoped for rain after the funeral. Then he would feel safer.

When Tupali woke at dawn he made a show of annoyance at failing to keep his brother's vigil but in his heart he was grateful for the rest. He looked at the corpse, greyish-purple and shrunken in the cold dawn light and though his first act should have been to gather fuel for the burning, he decided to go hunting. They needed a wallaby for the funeral feast and, in any case, he was so hungry the mere thought of it made his mouth water. He was young and his body was recovering quickly from the beating.

Tired but still ill-at-ease, Noumati was content to lend Tupali his spear. When he had left, moving silently between the trees, the storyteller made himself approach the corpse. It was upon him that the dead man's reputation rested, his telling of the tale that would be remembered and perhaps enshrined in myth. And though he had suffered at Warady's hands all his life, Noumati felt no satisfaction at his death. Now that the arrogant bully was reduced to a cold, mutilated carcass he felt only horror and pity.

'Black Snake's poison spilled upon the ground,' he murmured. He turned to look for fuel but then stood still, his mind suddenly as calm and clear as before a storytelling. He knew *num* were responsible for this killing; saw again the beings that had captured Tangalenna, man-like creatures but with the heads of insects, and Ngali-kiri running towards Raguwrapper when any other Meelayginnee woman would have fled or hidden. It had been as if she recognised them. Perhaps they were not spirits but more *num*. That would account for her lack of fear.

To reach this conclusion took a huge leap of intellect but, like all his people, Noumati was essentially pragmatic: he could not deny the logic of his mind. He thought of how Tangalenna had fled and his heart was wrenched by a deep and poignant sorrow: had he not run away, he might still be in the world.

'Aie, did your daemon forsake you after all?' he sighed. 'What am I to tell Manalewa?' and then he set his teeth and limped into the forest to collect wood for the burning.

When Tangalenna woke, there was only pain. He sobbed to Korunah for deliverance but there was no reply, only the buzzing of carrion flies. They were so close, he felt the air tremble. Curled foetus-like on the floor, eyelids swollen shut, he wondered if his body had dissolved and this was the existence to which his spirit had been condemned. But the pain was too immediate. Every part of his flesh throbbed and ached and seemed to take up more space than his skin could hold. He tried to move and such agony shot from the soles of his feet to his skull, he had to bite back a cry. Yet this physical anguish was more bearable than the return of memory.

What they had done to him was so degrading, so shameful, he tried to deny it had really happened. He told himself it was all a dream, a warning to give up Ngali-kiri and return to his hearth-group with the true tale of the Broad Ridge people. He had only to open his eyes and he would wake in the seer's cave, safe and whole.

It took all his willpower to lift a hand to his face. The bones seemed to grate in every joint: even to think was an immense effort. He rubbed his eyes and could only open them to slits. They filled instantly with bloody tears, a red flood that filled him with relief because he thought he was seeing the domed ceiling of his sanctuary. He blinked and the glare of electric light stabbed his brain.

A wordless howl escaped him then, a sound anguished as Manalewa's cry when they pulled the dead thing from her womb. Driven by a desperate need to find some connection with the world inside his head, he tried to raise himself. His legs were numb and would not obey him so he dragged himself to the door. Without proof that earth, sky, forest, water, existed, he was nothing, the broken husk of a creature so abased it could not call itself a man. His daemon would not know him, nor his ancestors. His spirit would cry in the void forever, lost and alone. For him there would be no peace in death.

Mouth and nose pressed to the narrow gap between floor and the bottom of the door, beyond feeling the pain that made his muscles clench spasmodically, he gulped air tainted with some alien, chemical smell that made him retch. Despair rolled over him in a black engulfing wave, irresistible and unstoppable, sucking out the last of his strength. He lay still, defeated, staring sightlessly ahead. His eyelids would not close.

On the flat surface of the door there was a dark, rounded shape. It was the reflection of his head though he did not recognise it. He watched, transfixed and helpless as a face formed inside it: grim, heavy-jowled with deep-set, penetrating eyes. It was his Nana, the matriarch whose relic he had lost. He quailed before the pitilessness of her gaze.

'You squandered Korunah's gift.' Each word lodged like a boulder in his chest. 'Why should we welcome you, worthless one? I should have chosen the cripple: he would have heeded me and avoided *num*. They have destroyed you as they destroyed the others.'

'But Eagle led me!' The protest struggled to the surface of Tangalenna's failing mind; darkness swept in and he fought to hold it back. 'I dreamt a child for Manalewa!'

'And where are they now?' As the old woman spoke, her face grew, the nose narrowing and curving as the bones sank and altered shape. Stabbing pains struck through Tangalenna's chest and shoulder as if talons had pierced deep between the ribs to grasp his heart and lungs. He felt them gripe, once, twice, then contract, squeezing inexorably.

'Korunah take me!' he gasped, and though he could not hear them, it seemed to have taken a lifetime's effort to form those words. The eagle's beak drove like a wedge into his ribcage. There was a moment of excruciating agony, then a soaring release as the darkness closed.

Chapter 18.

Although deeply shaken by the idea that *num* had taken Tangalenna, Noumati did not consider them a general threat. Since they had not gone beyond Tarner's Tail, he assumed that they respected the law and would not venture into alien territory without permission from the rightful guardians. Ignorant of the truth, that the Meelayginnee had remained undiscovered only because of the wildness of the terrain they inhabited and their own deliberate isolation, Noumati believed that once Warady's bones had been burned and he and Tupali were within the bounds of their own lands, *num* could not reach them. And he vowed that if they ever asked leave to enter, he would argue for refusal. Against the power of men that could fly, his people would be helpless.

When he had gathered enough fuel, Noumati kept vigil beside the body. A fine rain drifted between the trees but there was no danger of their cooking fire being extinguished and the pyre was so big, the centre would remain dry. He dug a handful of reddish clay from the empty grave and picked out some lumps of charcoal from the edge of the fire. Although he could not avenge Warady's death (nor, in his heart did he desire to), he could at least ensure his body was properly marked so that earth and sky would know who and what he was when they received him. By mid-afternoon, when Tupali returned with a fine male wallaby slung over his shoulder, all was ready for the burning save that Noumati had not yet adorned himself with clay and charcoal. It seemed to him fitting that he and Tupali should anoint each other as an act of acknowledgement and reconciliation for past wrongs.

The low cloud acted like a lid to keep down the smoke of the funeral pyre and Noumati and Tupali coughed and rubbed smarting eyes as they worked to keep the blaze going. Meanwhile, the wallaby was cooking in the ashes of their little camp-fire. The stench of the cremation was overwhelming and thick greasy smoke befouled everything so that when the time came to eat, both men were reluctant. Yet they found that once they began, they were ravenous.

When they were full, they flung the remains of the meat onto the pyre. By then nothing remained of the corpse but charring bones: by morning these too would be gone. The rain had brought an early nightfall and both Noumati and Tupali were weary almost beyond thought but though neither admitted it, they were loth to sleep. While the dead man's spirit had been freed by the burning, his death was still unavenged and it seemed to them that they could feel his presence watching from the shadows, waiting to see what they would do next.

As they sat silently between the fires, hunched against the rain, Noumati found his mind returning to the tale of Eagle and Brown Quoll. He knew he would have to account for Tangalenna's abduction not only because he and Ngali-kiri had witnessed it but because the truth was necessary to maintain the balance of the world, however strange and disturbing it might be. It was only then he realised how simple that truth was: Tangalenna had invaded *num* territory to steal the pale child and so they had captured him when their chance arose. They had not recognised their missing daughter because she had become Meelayginnee. He shuddered to think what they might do to Tangalenna in return: imagined him being stripped of his skin and identity; forced to wear clothes; coerced into speaking *num* words and eating their food.

As he thought this, Noumati's suspicion that his half-brother was dead grew to a certainty. Even if his body lingered somewhere in *num* world, Tangalenna's dreaming belonged to the forests, the highlands, the running rivers and still pools, the wide sky under which his people had lived since the days of Tarner. And remembering his promise to Manalewa, Noumati was assailed by so piercing a sense of grief and loss that he pressed his hands to his midriff where the ache of sorrow was centred and rocked gently back and forth, keening quietly to himself while Tupali looked on in amazement, thinking he mourned his enemy, now ashes amid a pile of smouldering embers.

Towards evening, Ellie knew she must be drawing close to the forest's edge. She thought she heard the sounds of heavy machinery and chainsaws but they stopped before she could be sure. Instinctively, she veered away from that direction. After so long, she wanted her first contact with her own kind to be with people she knew.

A steady, fine rain had been falling all day and the wind was rising, shaking showers of droplets from the branches. While she travelled, Ellie had been heedless of the rain but she was tired and needed to rest before facing whatever lay ahead. After a careful search she selected a thick log as the basis of a lean-to, scraped the moss off the side and began to gather branches. As she worked, she thought of Tangalenna making a similar shelter after the abduction, how he had tried to comfort her. He had understood how cold and frightened she was and she felt a wave of affection for him. She wondered if anyone was helping him, confused as he must be, but she found it impossible to visualise him wearing clothes, eating and sleeping inside a building, walking along a busy street. It was as if the Tangalenna she knew could not exist in that environment.

When she had stacked the thickest branches against the log and woven bark and twigs between, stuffing the gaps with leaves to make it rain-proof, she scooped the wettest leaf litter from inside. The earth beneath was damp but she knew her body would soon warm it. Now she needed food.

She was lucky: she startled a young possum scratching at the base of a wattle tree. The animal scampered halfway up the trunk but paused to stare at her. Ellie grabbed its tail, yanked it from its hold and swung it hard against the tree until its neck broke. Then she made her way triumphantly back to her shelter. She was no terrified child but a young woman of the Meelayginnee: the forest was not a place to fear.

Having opened up the carcass with her teeth, she ate the warm kidneys and liver with relish, then tore the rest apart with the swift efficiency of her namesake, Brown Quoll. There was a creek close by and when she was full, she wrapped the remains of the possum in its skin, wedged it in the fork of a tree and went to drink. The twilight was deepening and the call of a frogmouth echoed eerily through the hanging mist. She thought of Noumati with sudden longing and wondered if he was angry with her for running away. But he was not the kind of man to harbour bitterness. She knew if he saw her again, he would most likely treat her with kindness and understanding even though she did not deserve it. Tears sprang to her eyes as she thought this and she crawled inside the shelter and lay down, affected by a feeling of profound sorrow. It was as if she had lost something vital and infinitely precious.

With her mind focused on returning, Ellie expected that if she dreamed that night it would be of the farm though it was long before she slept at all. Instead she dreamt of her hearth-group. They were at Little Lake camp and her heart rejoiced to see them again though Manalewa was thinner than before and the furrows scored by her fingernails during Tangalenna's funeral had become long pale scars. There was a tiny baby slung in a wallaby skin at her side. It cried weakly and she lifted and put it to her breast.

A new hut had been built a little apart from the rest. It was small but carefully crafted, the bark tightly woven to make it weatherproof, the door well-fitting on hinges of sinew. This was closed and Ellie wondered who lived there or whether the hut had been made for some special purpose. A ring of stones marked a fireplace and the grass had been cleared around it but no fire burned within.

The women were busy preparing food and apart from Pounaté, who sat beside the main fire, there was no sign of the men. Ellie assumed they were away hunting. She took a deep breath and walked out from the trees.

Any doubts that she belonged among the Meelayginnee were assuaged by the obvious joy with which she was received. Her foster-brother, Puennena, saw her first. A look of wonder and delight transformed his usually brooding features and he ran to embrace her, calling to the others that their sister had returned.

They thronged round, chattering like a flock of rosellas. Amid the excitement, Manalewa sent her little girl, Leena, to the door of the new hut, to rouse whoever was inside. Only Tanglémerna remained aloof.

'Yah! Let's be seeing you!' Next to her foster-mother, it was Touganana's reaction Ellie had feared most but the old woman's face expressed the same gladness as the rest. She winked at Pounaté (who had come to see what all the fuss was about), and touched the young woman's belly. It was so intimate a gesture, Ellie felt a jolt through the very core of her, as if a string had been pulled. 'Looks like I'll be a great-grandmother before my bones go to the fire!'

At that moment, the door of the new hut opened and Noumati came out. He looked at Ellie with a mixture of sorrow and compassion that filled her with guilt. Suspended from a thong around his neck was the bone that had been Tangalenna's talisman.

'*Num* took Eagle from the world,' he said simply. 'And with his passing the madness that had driven Brown Quoll was ended. She returned to her husband and hearth-group and they welcomed her and the child in her womb.'

Overwhelmed by his generosity, Ellie did not know what to say. She glanced towards Manalewa but the older woman avoided her gaze and held her head erect, saying with a kind of proud diffidence: 'At least I was faithful to my husband, even if he abandoned me and his children for a wild dream.' And she turned and walked away, leaving Ellie staring after.

'She'll come round,' Touganana said softly. 'To lose brother and husband in a single moon was hard on her. You are still her daughter.'

'Brother?' Ellie looked round the group, wondering.

'Black Snake bit *num* and so they killed him,' Noumati explained. 'But Tupali returned safely. He is out hunting.' He hesitated and looked deeply into her eyes: he seemed to have grown in confidence and stature since she had seen him last. 'Ana-Maïda is now his wife and he has taken his brother's children as his own.'

There was an unspoken question in his tone but as Ellie struggled to assimilate the complex emotions it aroused in her, the raucous laugh of a kookaburra shattered her sleep. She opened her eyes and saw pale daylight framed by the entrance of her shelter.

Noumati and Tupali did not wait beside the pyre to sift through the ashes: given the manner of his death, no good could come from Warady's bones. In their weariness, both had slept a little during the night but their uneasiness remained. Even in daylight they kept glancing all about as if they might glimpse the murdered man's ghost watching them from the darkness under a clump of leaves, the cleft of a hollow tree.

'Fire ate Black Snake; earth and forest take him,' said Noumati quietly, both to placate the restless spirit and to comfort Tupali who was looking at the mound of red and white ash with a stricken expression as if unable to believe this was all that remained of his brother. 'Come on.'

They walked in silence until they had climbed through the pandanus scrub onto the open heathland and passed the landmark of Tarner's Tail. Once safe inside Meelayginnee territory, Tupali seemed to shrug off his grief and became relaxed and talkative, pestering the storyteller for a tale. But Noumati, brooding on Tangalenna's fate, did not respond and soon Tupali snorted impatiently and strode away. Freed of the constraint of the cripple's slow pace, his figure swiftly diminished and soon he was lost to view as he took the narrow way into the sacred gorge.

Noumati watched him go with a feeling of relief: the young man's cheerfulness had begun to annoy him. He limped slowly after, leaning heavily on his spear, and it seemed to him that he walked in a world subtly altered by the intrusion of *num*, the loss of Tangalenna. Yet the smell of rain-soaked peat and the scents of the eucalypt and tea-tree close by were familiar and welcoming; he looked into the sky, veiled by pale cloud overhead but a clear unsullied blue behind the distant mountains, and though his grief remained, a feeling of peace suffused him, a sense of wholeness, of belonging.

When he reached the top of the gully however, his exultant mood was quelled by the sheer physical difficulty of the descent. He had not really expected Tupali to wait yet he was still disappointed to find the place deserted. The steep, boulder-strewn cleft was wet and looked slippery: a footprint in the mud attested to Tupali's passing. He must be far ahead, hurrying to be first with the news. And a spurt of resentment started Noumati on the way down.

He had barely reached half-way when he was forced to stop. Run-off from the plateau had loosened much of the scree and though he tried to follow Tupali's tracks, he did not possess his half-brother's agility: more than once he found himself slithering helplessly towards the edge. Each time he managed to save himself but his legs shook with the strain of the descent and he was filled with the terror of falling, hearing dislodged stones clatter against the cliff far below, the churning of the torrent. At last he stopped, leaning against a great slab of rock to recover his breath, and looked down. The narrow path, twisting between jagged outcrops and massive boulders was so steep it seemed almost vertical. Only a glimpse of the ledge at the bottom and the impossibility of climbing out and finding another way gave him the courage to leave his resting place.

Sweat ran down his face and stung his eyes but to his relief, the lower part of the descent was easier than the first. He began to move more confidently and the combination of tiredness and complacency almost proved his undoing. A rolling pebble, a moment's lapse of concentration and he was falling.

A scream echoed in the cliff. He did not recognise it as his own. The spear dropped from his grasp: he clutched vainly at rock, grass tussocks, air; banged against the cliff and bounced off, landed with a jolt that knocked the breath from his body. The taste of mud filled his mouth.

Half-stunned, he felt no pain, only amazement that he was still alive.

When he opened his eyes, the roar of the river loud in his ears, he found himself on the ledge that led past the caves. Stones slithered and pattered down on him. The thought that having survived the fall he might be buried alive made him want to laugh but even in such a moment of extremity the awful nature of the gorge daunted him. He levered himself painfully to his hands and knees but something snagged his right hand and panic overtook him. He tugged and managed to jerk it free, crawled a little further along the ledge then paused, intending to throw the object into the chasm.

When he saw what it was, the breath caught in his throat. He stared at it in fear and wonder.

It was Tangalenna's amulet, their Nana's bone. The rain had washed it from the crevice where he had lost it but to Noumati the message was clear. No chance had made him, the storyteller, find the talisman rather than Tupali who had been first down the cliff. It was a gift from their ancestor, to whom it belonged. And it was the final token, if proof had been needed, of Tangalenna's death.

Carefully, with respect, Noumati re-knotted the broken thong, put it over his head and settled the talisman against his breast. As he did so a picture filled his mind: the grim, age-seamed face of the old woman who had doted on Tangalenna and had only blows and harsh words to bestow upon a crippled child whose very existence was an affront. And as when he was a boy, her voice seemed to strike deep into him, wounding with every word: 'It is not for you, fool! Eagle failed: what can Frogmouth do? Our people must be like Brown Quoll, fierce and secretive in their living, invisible to their enemies. Stay deep in the forest and shun *num*. They are not true children of Tarner: they have the spirits of insects and are sundered from the law though one day it will destroy them. Keep to your stories and give Ngali-kiri the bone. For all her strangeness, she will know what to do.'

The storyteller was so shaken by this vision that had it not been for the impossibility of climbing the rockslide he would have retraced his steps from fear that the ghost of the old woman might be lurking nearby. Having no choice, he clambered to his feet and made his way slowly down the path, confused and wondering for he had no idea how far his wife had fled, nor did he dare argue, even to himself, that if she did not return, his Nana's words meant nothing.

When he reached the seer's cave, however, he was overcome by so profound a sense of loss that he paused to peer inside, as if it were possible that Tangalenna had somehow returned to the place where his man-self and his dreaming melded. But the cave was empty and Noumati was loth to enter lest by doing so he anger the restless spirits whose presence made him shiver. He turned and limped on down the narrow path. The moist, cool breeze mingled the scents of the forest with the clear air of the highlands; the noise of the torrent was somehow reassuring in its constancy; he looked into the limpid blue sky and saw an eagle circling far away.

'Eh, my brother, be free,' he murmured. He stood still and

watched until the bird dwindled to a tiny speck and disappeared, and an immense calmness entered him. When he came to the flat rock at the top of the cascades, he knelt and drank. He wondered where Ngali-kiri was, whether she had abandoned the Meelayginnee or was, even now making her way back, and in his heart he called out, begging her to return not because of his Nana's prophecy but because he loved her.

The riverside camp seemed almost welcoming in the bright sunlight and Noumati sighed with relief when he reached it. He was weary with grief and the exertions of the past days: here was shelter, water and food. He decided to rest there for a day or two, before continuing. That way, by the time he reached the others, the tale of Eagle and Brown Quoll would be complete.

After breakfasting on possum meat Ellie set off again but the essence of her dream lingered. She was troubled not only by the idea of being pregnant but a growing sense of regret. When she felt nauseous again she told herself it was because she was upset, and forced herself on. A flock of Fairy Wrens fluttered a little way ahead and she tried to concentrate on them until, inevitably, she could hold back no longer. She knelt and threw up.

Even so early in the day, flies zoomed in to feed on the half-digested mess. Revolted, Ellie clambered to her feet. Through a blur of tears a white shape loomed between the dull greens of dense wattle and dogwood. She rubbed her eyes, moved forward a few paces then stopped and stared. The shape of the tree was unmistakeable: tall, broken-crowned with an opening into the hollow centre. It was the widow-maker that marked the boundary of the farm.

From somewhere close by came the growl of a heavy engine and she had to fight the urge to flee. She thought of Manalewa and Noumati waiting; remembered Tangalenna who had been her father and lover and imagined him dying, lost and unreconciled in her world or else made to conform, changed beyond recognition into a parody of *num*, estranged forever from his true self. Wonderingly, she touched the cicatrices on her chest and then stroked her belly where she was now certain their child was growing. If she returned to her own culture she also would be considered a child: people would stare at the marks of her womanhood and sneer at her pregnancy, blaming it on ignorance and stupidity, not understanding the real nature of the world they inhabited. And Tangalenna, if he was still alive, would be punished for abducting and abusing her.

She turned abruptly and walked back along the wallaby trail. Her bare feet left no trace on the beaten earth and every step deeper into the forest felt like coming home.

The author lived in Tasmania for many years. S. Pitt has published
an anthology of short stories, *Trouwerner,* as well as several novels.

Also by S. Pitt:

The Boy who found Salt

The Cove

Fen-wolf

Cromwell's Promise

Four Wonders

Find out more at:

www.spittbooks.com

www.ingramcontent.com/pod-product-compliance
Lightning Source LLC
Chambersburg PA
CBHW022357110726
47902CB00002BA/319